VAN HORSTMANN

'MEN SEE YOU in their nightmares,' said van Horstmann, knowing the skaven would know the sense behind his words, too. 'But your kind have nightmares too, and when I am done with you, skaven nightmares will be about me.'

The skaven laughed to see this hairless, tailless creature who wanted to match magic with a grey seer. Black lightning flickered around its staff and it drew a chunk of stone from a pouch on the belt of its filthy once-purple robes – the same stone with which it had replaced one of its eyes. It crumbled the stone and inhaled the dust, its eye growing wide.

The lightning flared black and red. With a gesture of its whole body the skaven hurled the black lightning bolt at van Horstmann.

• WARHAMMER HEROES •

WULFRIK
by C.L. Werner

SIGVALD
by Darius Hinks

THE RED DUKE
by C.L. Werner

SWORDS OF THE EMPEROR
(Contains *Sword of Justice* and *Sword of Vengeance*)
by Chris Wraight

LUTHOR HUSS
by Chris Wraight

VALKIA THE BLOODY
by Sarah Cawkwell

• GOTREK & FELIX •

GOTREK & FELIX: THE FIRST OMNIBUS
William King
(Contains the novels: *Trollslayer, Skavenslayer* and *Daemonslayer*)

GOTREK & FELIX: THE SECOND OMNIBUS
William King
(Contains the novels: *Dragonslayer, Beastslayer* and *Vampireslayer*)

GOTREK & FELIX: THE THIRD OMNIBUS
William King & Nathan Long
(Contains the novels: *Giantslayer, Orcslayer* and *Manslayer*)

GOTREK & FELIX: THE FOURTH OMNIBUS
Nathan Long
(Contains the novels: *Elfslayer, Shamanslayer* and *Zombieslayer*)

ROAD OF SKULLS
Josh Reynolds

SLAYER OF THE STORM GOD
An audio drama by Nathan Long

A WARHAMMER NOVEL

VAN HORSTMANN

BEN COUNTER

BLACK LIBRARY

A Black Library Publication

First published in Great Britain in 2013 by
Black Library,
Games Workshop Ltd.,
Willow Road,
Nottingham, NG7 2WS, UK.

10 9 8 7 6 5 4 3 2 1

Cover illustration by Cheoljoo Lee.
Map by Nuala Kinrade.

A CIP record for this book is available from the British Library.

UK ISBN13: 978 1 84970 205 8
US ISBN13: 978 1 84970 206 5

See Black Library on the internet at

www.blacklibrary.com

Find out more about Games Workshop
and the world of Warhammer at

www.games-workshop.com

Printed and bound by CPI Group (UK) Ltd, Croydon, CR0 4YY

This is a dark age, a bloody age, an age of daemons
and of sorcery. It is an age of battle and death, and of the
world's ending. Amidst all of the fire, flame and fury
it is a time, too, of mighty heroes, of bold deeds
and great courage.

At the heart of the Old World sprawls the Empire, the
largest and most powerful of the human realms. Known for
its engineers, sorcerers, traders and soldiers, it is
a land of great mountains, mighty rivers, dark forests
and vast cities. And from his throne in Altdorf reigns
the Emperor Karl Franz, sacred descendant of the
founder of these lands, Sigmar, and wielder
of his magical warhammer.

But these are far from civilised times. Across the length
and breadth of the Old World, from the knightly palaces
of Bretonnia to ice-bound Kislev in the far north, come
rumblings of war. In the towering Worlds Edge Mountains,
the orc tribes are gathering for another assault. Bandits and
renegades harry the wild southern lands of
the Border Princes. There are rumours of rat-things, the
skaven, emerging from the sewers and swamps across the
land. And from the northern wildernesses there is the
ever-present threat of Chaos, of daemons and beastmen
corrupted by the foul powers of the Dark Gods.
As the time of battle draws ever near,
the Empire needs heroes
like never before.

PROLOGUE

THE LIGHT

IT WAS THE cold that woke him. It penetrated right through him, like his flesh was gone and his bones were soaked in it.

His lungs contracted and he could not breathe. Without willing it, he was moving, his limbs thrashing. But he was held fast and could not escape, trapped beneath the ice by hands stronger than him. There was room in his mind for only one thought, which was that he was going to die down there in the merciless cold.

His head was dragged up above the surface. He gulped down air. Every muscle was convulsing with the effort of breathing.

'Lord Teclis,' said a voice. 'Are you there? Do you hear us?'

Even his eyes felt frozen. They would not focus. He could see only a silvery blur in front of him.

Another thought reached him: he was alive.

'I… I am here,' he gasped. 'How long?'

'Three days,' came the reply.

'Thank you,' said Teclis, as his sight swam back and the shapes in front of him became connected to disparate slices of his memory. 'Thank you, Caradryath.'

Caradryath, of the elven Sword Masters of Hoeth, bent over Teclis and pulled him upright. The High Loremaster was immersed in a horse trough of freezing water, the best vessel for their loremaster that the attendant Sword Masters had found at short notice. With something close to fear on their faces, two other Sword Masters knelt behind Caradryath. They did not wear the high plumed helmets of their order, but they wore the rest of their gleaming silver scale armour as if about to march out from the gates of the White Tower.

'Has the fever broken?' said Caradryath.

Teclis leaned against the side of the trough. He could not keep his hands still and his voice wavered. Isha's tears, he was cold. But the fact he could feel anything at all meant he had not died in that pavilion, somewhere in the heart of the half-savage land men called the Empire of Sigmar.

'It is gone,' said Teclis. 'The last thing I remember, its grip was around me. It was a black hand with talons sinking into the back of my skull. I could hear it laughing as it dragged me under. But it is gone now. The cold has broken it. I will live.'

'I had thought this would kill you,' said Caradryath. 'I feared that my loremaster would fall by my hand.'

'The fever would have killed me most surely,' said Teclis. 'You did the right thing. And the magisters?'

'They stand even now at vigil, loremaster.'

'We cannot keep them waiting. Damn the fires of Hoeth! Three days! Our prisoner will be free before the kraken can swim a league! Help me, Bladelord.'

Caradryath had to help Teclis out of the icy water. Caradryath was one of the flower of Ulthuan's youth, strong and proud, fair and tall. Teclis was like a child compared to him, his limbs skinny and his hair lank and black. A few hours before, he had been dying of a disease that the priests of Isha and Shallya could not cure. He looked like he still was.

The Sword Masters tried to dry off their loremaster, but he batted away their attentions. Teclis shrugged on his robe, embroidered with the sigils and marks of rank from the White Tower of Saphery, over wet skin. Caradryath helped him don the Silver Crown, a tall helm of silver and gold with a fat uncut ruby set in its brow, and Teclis tottered under the weight of it. The Bladelord of the Sword Masters let the loremaster lean on his shoulder and helped him out of the pavilion.

There were two Teclises. One was the elf – more properly the boy, for he had the stature and weakness of a boy, skinny and shivering. It was this Teclis who limped and coughed as Caradryath pulled aside the entrance flap of the pavilion and let the sun shine in. This Teclis blinked and screwed up his eyes, like a creature that had lived all its life in a cave.

The second Teclis existed far away, in the endless lands of the aethyr. The winds of magic that suffused the world blew in from the aethyr, a realm not of the senses but of the emotions and the mind, an endlessness of disconnected thoughts, concepts, ideas, wishes, love and hate, and souls lost and drifting. Everyone had another self in that realm, but only a wizard could communicate with that self, could use that self as a lens through which he could focus the winds of magic. Teclis knew his aethyr-self well. The two were close to becoming one. What one felt, the other knew. What one knew, the other perceived as rushes of emotion or plunging depths of fear. That was why Teclis was the High Loremaster. That was why the future of magic itself was in his feeble hands.

The senses of his aethyr-self could see the pulsing magic of Caradryath's heart. That was life, which had its own magic. The celestial power that shone down on him from the sun blinded his aethyr-eyes, for he had been cut off from its prophetic power just as his real self had been cut off from sunlight. Even the arms and armour of his Sword Masters had magic bound in them through the process of their forging, from the concentration and skill of the forgemasters of Saphery, winding through them like filaments of an unseen alloy. Teclis let these senses merge with his own so the same pair of eyes saw both the sun in the sky, and the great well of potential that burned in the heavens, illuminating everything that might yet be.

He could not tell the future. Not here, not now. The paths that diverged led to outcomes too great to be chosen between. Competing futures clamoured at his aethyr-self's mind, and there would be no prophecies made today.

Teclis's pavilion was one of a ring of tents and temporary lodges set up around a great smouldering crater in the ground. It was a clear day and as he blinked away the sun's glare Teclis could see the outskirts of the greatest city of men – Altdorf, the capital of Sigmar's Empire. Already that city was choking the grand River Reik with bridges and quays, and there was no mistaking its future. It would grow, become greater, with all the good and ill that entailed. He could see that future, at least. Altdorf would be at once a jewel and a cesspit, a throne of glory and a swamp of corruption. That was why what had to be done, had to be done here. Only a city with a future that great could cope with the paths of fate that would divide under it. Only Altdorf could survive what Teclis was about to do to it.

Teclis heard the beast before he saw it. The monstrous heave of its breathing was like the sound of rocks grinding deep beneath the earth. The ground shuddered with it. The creature roared, the sound like a winter's gale, and a plume of chill vapour billowed up into the sky.

At the crater's edge stood a forge of heaped-up boulders, glowing as shirtless dwarf attendants worked the bellows. They were all muscular and smeared with soot, looking like they had just come from the depths of the Worlds Edge holds. They hauled great links of iron from the fires, which glowed orange as they were hammered into sections of an enormous chain. Atop the forge stood Marius, one of the first pupils Teclis had ever taken from the lands of men. Marius was close to mastering fire magic, and he called down the winds to fill the forge with an inferno that burned deeper than any mortal flame. Beside the forge worked Auroc, the Gold mage. The magic Teclis had seen in the armour of his Sword Masters was the same that coursed through Auroc then, as with a series of gestures he wove the links of the chain together and struck into them dwarf-taught runes of strength and scorn.

Teclis had tutored both men himself. Without him their

talent at magic would have meandered astray into the petty
corruptions of hedge wizards as they weaved what spells they
could, ignorant of the dangers. Without Teclis the whole of
human magic would have continued in that way, and even the
mightiest of human wizards would have been nothing more
than playthings for the daemons who lurked in the aethyr.
The great incursions of Chaos, halted at the Empire's northern
edges, had found their ways into the lands of men through the
minds of such ignorant wizards. Teclis's task was to make sure
they could never use such an invasion route again.

Teclis saw then two men. Like him, each of his students
had an earthly form, and one that walked in the aethyr. The
two were not on speaking terms as his were, for the human
soul could not accept the understanding of magic as completely as a high elf. But he saw ghosted over his students'
simple trappings the robes and implements of great orders of
magic, traditions of learning that would become great institu-
tions guarding the world from the worst of its corruptions.

'My lord Teclis!' cried Marius as he saw Teclis emerging
from the pavilion. 'You yet live!' The Bright wizard clambered
down from the stones of the forge. He wore the rust-red robes
of his fledgling order and to Teclis's eye they flamed bright,
surrounding Marius in an orange halo. His ruddy beard was
twisted into braids and aethyr-fire lit each one like the wick
of a candle, bathing his face in flickering light. He clasped
Teclis's hand in his own. 'We feared for you, loremaster.'

'The aethyr has plans for me yet, Marius,' said Teclis. He
waved away Caradryath and took his weight on his own feet.
He stayed upright, just. His legs were as weak as a newborn's.

'I cannot die now. Not when we have work to do.'

'It has been difficult,' said Marius. 'I do not believe we could keep it chained for much longer. Though it pains me to admit such weakness, the flames of the aethyr scorch me. They burn my soul. I will burn out before I give in, but burn out I will soon without your help.'

'It will not be you,' said Teclis, 'who burns this day.' He turned to Caradryath. 'My armaments,' he said. The Sword Master bowed and headed back to the pavilion.

Another of Teclis's students came into sight over the lip of the crater. His dark-green robes were smeared with earth and soot from the crater and his straggly dark hair was twined up with twigs and leaves. In the aethyr they flowered, and around the wizard's feet sprang new life with every step. 'Loremaster,' he said. 'The life within it rages unabated. It does not even tire. Never have I felt such strength of the Jade wind contained within a single creature.'

'Krieglan,' said Teclis. 'It is not life nor death that will decide the path of fate here. Let the Jade wind blow strong and look to your fellow pupils. The life within them will not be as durable when the beast flexes its muscles.'

'Death,' came another voice, 'decides everything.' Just behind Krieglan walked the Amethyst mage, Malgos, the hood of his purple robes obscuring a dark, lined face. Hourglasses hung from his waist and the backs of his bare hands were tattooed with skulls and archaic script. He was the aethyric counterpart to Krieglan, his opposite and equal, and the bleak energies of death seethed to Teclis's eye where he walked. 'Death will end this, just as it does all things.'

'Life will conquer death always,' retorted Krieglan. 'Where death has reigned, life always blossoms.'

'And decays again to death,' said Malgos. 'The end of all things.'

'Death is an absence! It is nothing! Life is the force that knits us all together. Death exists not save for the cessation of life. Without life, there is no death!'

'Without life there would be nothing but death.' Malgos's voice did not waver, staying a low monotone. 'Life is an aberration. A detail. A speck on the face of the universe. When nothing else remains, there will always be death. And the beast will be nothing when death has taken its due.'

'No,' said Teclis, and in spite of his weakness there was a sternness in his voice that even gave pause to the Amethyst mage, whose skills were with the magic of death itself. 'Not death. Not here.'

Teclis reached the crest of the crater's ridge. The torn earth formed a deep bowl, and in the centre of that depression was chained the beast that men had come to call Baudros.

Baudros was a dragon, but somehow even the word 'dragon' did not do it justice. Its scaly body had none of the slenderness and grace of the dragons of Ulthuan, the land of the high elves from which Teclis hailed. Nor did it look anything like the spined ice drakes of Norsca or the ferocious fire dragons of the Worlds Edge Mountains. It was bloated and massive, folds of scaled flesh bulging over the tops of its huge legs, its crooked back ridged with plates of bone. Its thick tail lashed back and forth, the clubbing spiky mass hacking plumes of dark earth into the air. Sickly light pulsed through its veins, rippling over it like the mark of some magical sickness, and its talons were permanently crusted with jagged sheaths of dried blood.

But its heads were the worst. Its neck was split in two and supported two enormous heads. One had a brutal undershot jaw full of upwards-jutting fangs, and tiny red eyes buried in ridges of bone. The other was long and slender like a dog's, its asymmetrical eyes rolling and mad, a curtain of silvery drool falling from its lolling mouth. Its long greenish tongue lashed like a caged snake. Its larger left eye, yellowish and veined, rolled around in its socket to focus on Teclis. Something like recognition flickered there and it strained against the chains holding it down. Two tattered wings, broad enough to cast a shadow across the whole crater, unfolded from its back and beat a gale as they fought to lift it off the ground.

Teclis himself had called down the storm that had grounded Baudros. The beast, freed by the bedlam of the recent war, had been on course to crash into Altdorf and turn the young capital into a swathe of ashen ruins. It was the effort of the storm that had allowed the fever to enter Teclis in the first place. The people of Altdorf did not know of the fate they had so narrowly avoided. The storm had been interpreted as a dire portent and the people were huddled up in their homes. Few eyes looked to the fields beyond the city outskirts where Baudros rumbled and growled, and with luck, those that did would think the strange lights and sounds just another set of warnings from the heavens.

The chains held, just. They were driven into the ground by

pillars of enchanted steel, and even the two-headed dragon's strength could not rip them out. Not yet.

The Gold magic in them would fail. The fire magic of their forging would give way and the life magic, the Jade wind that sustained the earth beneath it, would crumble away. Baudros would escape, and it would be more than the predatory monster it had been – it would have revenge on its minds, revenge against the land of men that could ill afford the destruction it would wreak.

'You cannot kill something like that, Malgos,' said Teclis. 'And Krieglan, it is not life that animates this beast. It is something far worse that, thankfully, you will never understand. We must act now. There is no time.'

The mage who stood just within the crater, wrapped in blue robes, was watching the sky through an ornate instrument of lenses and brass gears. Through its largest lens could be seen the stars overhead, even through the blue sky of day. In the future, through the glimpse afforded by Teclis's aethyr-sight, the robes were speckled with embroidered constellations and pages from prophetic volumes fluttered around the mage like falling blossom. The magical tradition that would follow him would scry the stars and tell the future.

'The stars are right!' he called, looking back at Teclis. 'The witch moon turns its eye from us. The Fell Powers are blind, but they will not be for long. Some great providence shines on us.'

'It would not do to waste it, Ceruleos,' said Teclis. 'Prepare the circle! Auroc! Marius! Abandon the forge and take your places! Malgos and Krieglan, if you can spare your bickering for a while, do the same.'

Caradryath had returned with the Moon Staff of Lileath, its slender golden length topped with an ivory image of the elven goddess of the moon. Teclis took it and leaned against it, like a cripple against a crutch. 'Your sword?' asked the Sword Master.

'No sword will help us here,' replied Teclis. 'A thousand blades would not cut deep enough. Retreat from me, Sword Masters. Stay back.'

'Loremaster, we are sworn to–'

'Retreat!' snapped Teclis. 'There is nothing you can do for me here. Whatever happens, you must return to the White Tower and tell of it, whether I am with you or not. I am your loremaster. Obey me.'

Caradryath bowed and led his Sword Masters away from the crater. Teclis looked back at Baudros. All the dragon's eyes were fixed on him now. There was no intelligence in its more bestial head, only a rage that could not be stifled, a raw hatred of everything it beheld. One head knew what Teclis was, the other did not care. Both wanted him dead. No doubt it was a rare thing for them to agree so completely.

From the sky overhead descended a flittering shadow in the shape of a man, coalescing as it landed into the form of a white-bearded mage in grey robes, the head of his wooden staff carved into the shape of a raven. 'I can hide you,' said the mage. 'The shadows will conceal you.'

'Not from this,' replied Teclis. 'I will need the shadow magic that flows through you, Ogmarah. You must take your place. The ritual must be observed. Any break and the winds of magic will turn from us.'

'The Amber wind courses around this beast, not through it,' said a seventh figure, dressed in rough-spun cloth and bear furs. 'It is no beast at all.'

'The circle has but seven places,' said Ogmarah. 'Which one of us will stand apart from it? Which one will stand alongside you? Who, if not a master of the shadow, who can surely confound the senses of this monstrosity?'

'One who is as one with the beast!' replied the seventh mage. 'A monster we face, and a monster I will become!'

'No, Ferok,' said Teclis. 'Nor you, Ogmarah. The Amber and the Shadow winds must flow through the circle. You will not stand apart.' Teclis coughed, bending over as he shuddered with the awful rasping of his wounded lungs. 'The Light,' he sputtered. 'It must be the Light.'

From a pavilion of white silk, on the edge of the crater, emerged a figure in robes the colour of pearl. His head was shaven and his eyes ringed with dark pigment. In one hand was a wooden half-mask and in the other hand was a metal staff wrought into the shape of a hooded desert snake. Where he stood there seemed to exist a pool of tranquility, as if a circle surrounded him into which the troubled world could not reach. In the aethyr, the mask was of gold and the snake-staff had diamonds for eyes, both materials representing the purity that fell around him in a cascade of gemstones.

The Light mage looked down at Baudros. The bestial head reacted to him, turning its beady eyes on him and staring at the newcomer with the same hate it had reserved for the loremaster.

'Malhavar!' called Teclis. His voice was not strong enough

to carry over the grumbling of Baudros's lungs, but the Light mage heard him. 'It is time. It must be done now.'

'Of course, my loremaster.' Malhavar walked across the crater. The hem of his robe picked up no soot or dirt. He passed in front of Baudros's bestial head and it reared back, chest swelling as it sucked in a lungful of air.

Malhavar raised a hand. A circle of white light was emblazoned on the ground around him. A blast of frozen shadow ripped from Baudros's throat, a killing gale billowing up from the Chaos Wastes themselves, dark grey and seething with hatred.

The gale burst against the invisible barrier around Malhavar, parting and swirling around him. The gale passed, drifting up into the sky like a pall of smoke from a pyre. Baudros's brute head saw that Malhavar still stood and roared in anger, shuddering the earth with a peal of terrible thunder.

The other head, the cunning and mad head, cackled as it saw its brother thwarted. The bestial head snapped at it, spitting bile in frustration.

'Are you ready?' asked Teclis as Malhavar came near.

'I am,' said Malhavar. 'The paths end here. I can see that plainly, even if Ceruleos cannot. The Light shines strongest when there are none there to cast a shadow. It shines brightest when we, its servants, are gone.' Up close, he looked less like a man of Sigmar's Empire and more like something ancient, or perhaps ageless, from a land that was now sand and ruins. His skin was coppery and smooth, his profile as proud and angular as if it had been carved.

'That is why it must be you,' said Teclis.

'The way of the Light wind is sacrifice,' said Malhavar.

'It will try to kill me,' said Teclis. 'It must not.'

'I understand.'

Teclis looked up to the sky and planted the Moon Staff in the ground, like a general planting his standard. 'My students! My brothers! Call forth the cage!'

From Auroc's fingers flowed a bubbling torrent of molten gold, forming the spindly shape of a golden cage in the air over Baudros. Baudros's bestial head howled and its mad head shrieked, spitting ropes of hissing drool. The cunning head spewed a jet of acidic bile that sheared through the bars, but the Gold mage twisted his fingers into a defiant gesture and the cage reformed, ornate curling reinforcements spiralling between its bars.

Malhavar stepped forwards and knelt on the scorched ground. 'Shine on us,' he murmured, his words somehow carrying over the bellowing of Baudros. 'Shine through us. Darkness be banished.'

A circle of power shone into existence around Teclis and Malhavar. The bestial head breathed a mass of darkness again, and it swirled around the hemisphere of protective magic cast by Malhavar. The sound was terrible, like an endless roll of thunder.

Teclis raised his hands, and the winds of magic blew through him now. He took the Gold magic coursing through the gilded cage, and brought it down towards Baudros. 'Sons of Ulthuan!' he yelled. 'Hear me! Princes eternal! Stir from your slumber and hear!'

A layer of crackling gold shimmered over Teclis's right

hand. His other hand had a greenish tinge now and flowering roots spiralled around it as the Jade wind blew. Krieglan's head was bowed, his staff of living wood sprouting leaves and flowers. The ground shuddered and began to heave up, as if a great claw of stone was breaking the surface.

'Stones of the Lost Isles, rise!' cried Teclis. The scale of the magic forced him off-balance. The Moon Staff glowed and the War Crown of Saphery burned, flames licking around its jewel.

Standing stones from the Lost Isles of Ulthuan, held immobile there for centuries to channel wild magic away from the Chaos Wastes, rose from the ground. They were smooth with age, cut deeply with words in an archaic form of the elven tongue. Magic burst like lightning between them, forming a fence of stuttering light around the dragon.

The cage descended over Baudros. The dragon's two heads snapped at the bars, fangs bending them out of shape. A shower of burning stone, meteors from a darkening sky, hammered against the dragon's faces, driving it back. Ceruleos, the Celestial mage, called down another volley of them, demanding that the stars themselves send their messengers down. Those stars burned overhead, shining through the black clouds gathering in the sky.

Ogmarah cast beams of darkness across the cage, reinforcing its structure as Marius increased the heat of its joints, forging a strength into them that Gold magic alone could not provide. Ferok wrestled with the bestial magic of the Amber wind, forcing down into the ground so it rose up and fought back against the thrashing of the dragon.

The stones continued to rise, forming buttresses around the cage. They rose until their tips touched over its centre. Slabs of purplish crystal shimmered between them as Malgos forced the winds of Amethyst magic through himself. As lightning flashed overhead it seemed to illuminate a grinning skull where Malgos's face should have been, the chiselled angles of a statue over Auroc's features, talons of gnarled wood in place of Krieglan's hands. The aethyr's connections with them were opening dangerously wide, exposing them to the unpredictable fury of magic's raw source.

Deafening peals of breaking stone boomed around the crater. Baudros was slamming its bulk against the inside of its cage. Even as the cage solidified around it, the stones shuddered and threatened to fall. Bright sigils burst against the ground, symbols of power cast by Teclis to hold the winds of magic in check as they roared through the crater.

'The seal, Malhavar!' yelled Teclis. 'The seal! By Light alone will it hold!'

Malhavar stood, and the circle of protection around him died down. If Baudros broke free now, Teclis and his pupils would die.

Light dripped from Malhavar's hands. His flesh was melting, sloughing off his bones and turning to liquid light.

It pooled on the ground and Malhavar's skeletal fingers beckoned it up into a burning white spike, like a potter forming an object out of clay. It grew higher than Malhavar's head even as his skin turned dull and cracked, flakes of it floating off to reveal the pure light flowing through the veins and muscle underneath.

'You are nothing more than an insect, Baudros!' said Mal-havar through clenched teeth. 'And like an insect, I will pin you down! What burns in you is not flesh, and it cannot be killed, but it can be banished! And so the Light banishes you!'

The lance of light was taller now than the prison. It rose off the ground, dripping undiluted power, and hovered over the prison. Malhavar screamed, light bleeding from his eyes, and drove the spike down through the prison, through Baudros, into the earth.

BAUDROS WAS A dragon in the same way that a knight was a suit of armour. The dragon was just the flesh it wore, the shell into which it had crawled to survive outside the aethyr and the Realms of Chaos. A dragon was terrible enough. A Chaos dragon, mutated by the raw magic of the Chaos Wastes, even more so. But Baudros was far worse.

The spike of power driven through it tore open the caul of power that kept its soul intact. Raw emotion, raw magic, the stuff of the aethyr, poured out in a storm that bathed the two mages standing before it. Much of it was formless insanity. But glimpses of the past played out there in that storm, visions trapped in the decaying brains of the dragon Baudros inhabited and the memories of the entity that had come to possess and meld with it.

A battlefield rolled out amid the chaos. The countryside was dotted with keeps and villages, separated by swathes of forest – a land of men, not the Empire but Bretonnia to the west. Mounted knights, banners streaming from their lances, had brought a dragon to battle. That battle was against Baudros, or at least the creature it had once been. It had but one head and was smaller and more lithe, but it was unmistakeably the same beast, with the same colour scales and spiny crests of bone.

It snatched up a knight in its jaws and threw the body aside. A claw crushed down on a riderless warhorse, talons slicing it into three. The dragon waded into the throng around it, and now the scene became clearer – the heaps of torn bodies, those of peasant bowmen and militia, pulped and shredded in gore-filled ruts in the ground.

Lances hit home. Men died swinging hammers and swords into the dragon's flanks as they surrounded it. The dragon reared up, gulped down a mighty lungful of air and breathed out a torrent of icy vapour over its attackers.

Bodies shattered as they hit the ground. Bolting horses were caught in the roiling fog and cut down as their lungs froze.

The visions showed a chill mountain pass now, blood slicked across the jagged rocks. The dragon was hauling its bulk along. Wounds covered one side. Two legs were all but useless and its head drooped on its serpentine neck. Its torn wings would never let it take flight again. With every moment more blood pumped from the tears in its side, and it was surely dying.

Morrslieb, the witch moon, the harbinger of ill, hung framed by the mountain peaks. It shone with greenish light like a beacon, calling the dragon towards it, and the dragon obeyed as if the moon was a great hypnotising eye.

A dismal hollow among the mountains now, a pit of stone where the sun never shone, bounded by soaring cliffs. The dragon lay there *among the heaps of primitive cairns, adorned with skulls and the well-gnawed bones of hundreds of skeletons. Symbols of forgotten gods were carved into the rocks by generations of fingernails, cries for salvation from those hurled down there to honour the interred. The only movement from the dragon was the tortured heaving of its lungs. It was going to die there, in this foul and miserable place, the burial ground of some forsaken and wicked people who had long ceased to befoul the world.*

From the cairns issued a dark mist, and that mist coalesced into a form something like man, but far bigger, indistinct and ill-proportioned. The dragon's blood gave it form. Three green eyes burned deep inside it, and a voice issued that was barely distinguishable from the cold hiss of the mountain winds.

Its words were obscure, but its meaning was clear. It was without a body, sustained here only by the ancient hate of those people who had worshipped it. The dragon was going to die there if some supernatural force did not intercede. And between them, they were making a pact.

Teclis drove back the storm with a torrent of arcane words. He unhooked a book from his belt and the winds ruffled through its pages, revealing spells he had inscribed there to conjure light and safety amid the darkness.

The pillar of light transfixed the prison. Baudros was screaming as it burned and the light bored through it. Teclis forced open the clearing in the storm and revealed a painful glare of light concealing Malhavar.

Teclis dropped to his knees and reached into the light. He felt Malhavar sink down to the ground and wrapped an arm around the Light mage's waist, dragging him back from the storm. Teclis was barely strong enough to support his own weight and he half-crawled, dragging Malhavar behind him.

The light shining off Malhavar was burning and Teclis could barely see. Baudros was bellowing now, the sound like an earthquake, battering its great body against the inside of his cell. The storm raged.

Then, the light died.

Teclis slumped into the mud, what little strength he had suddenly draining out of him. He lay there, willing his limbs to carry him back to his feet, but they would not.

Marius reached him first. The Bright wizard turned Teclis over and though he was talking, Teclis could not make out his words over the ringing in his ears.

Teclis turned his head. The prison was intact, a great structure of gold, stone and crystal, now wrapped around with intricate scrolling bands of silver.

Krieglan, the Jade wizard, was kneeling over Malhavar. Teclis could see a foot protruding from the Light mage's robes – it was skinless and scorched, like a charred skeleton. Krieglan was turning Malhavar's head and talking to him.

Words were reaching him now. Marius was asking if he was hurt. Teclis ignored him and crawled to Malhavar's side.

Half of Malhavar's face was gone, flaked away revealing scorched bone. His remaining eye turned to Teclis.

'Do you remember,' he whispered, 'what you taught me, loremaster? When I asked you what the Light truly was?'

'I remember,' replied Teclis. 'And so did you, this day.'

'The Light,' said Malhavar, 'is sacrifice.'

Malhavar's head dropped back and his eye rolled upwards. The spark in it went out. Teclis could feel it go.

'I can bring him back,' said Krieglan.

'No,' said Teclis. 'You cannot.'

Krieglan tried anyway. He called forth the few drops of life magic remaining in the tortured earth. Green shoots and flowers burst around Malhavar's corpse. But the damage was too great. The force of the Light magic burning through him had seared away organs and muscles. There was simply not enough man left for the Jade wind to heal.

'Light magic is sacrifice,' said Teclis, putting a hand on Krieglan's shoulder. 'Malhavar gave himself willingly. Not even the Jade wind can counter that.'

The Sword Masters ran down from the pavilion and tended to Teclis, carrying him back to the lip of the crater, dripping medicines brewed by Isha's priestesses onto his tongue. By the time Krieglan walked back out of the crater, Teclis was propped up against the side of his pavilion, Caradryath kneeling beside him and praying to the gods of Ulthuan.

The seven remaining pupils of Teclis stood around him. They were all exhausted. The marks of their magic were on them. Ogmarah's shadow lagged a few seconds behind him, as if he had conjured so many shadows he did not have enough power left to fuel his own. Auroc's hands had solidified into golden gauntlets and flecks of gold were embedded in the skin around his eyes.

'In time,' said Teclis, 'you will take pupils of your own. I must return to Ulthuan with my brother, and see to the defence of my lands. Your colleges will stand in the city you see ahead of you, Altdorf, the crossroads of the Empire's fates. I shall take new pupils and teach them each a fragment of Malhavar's knowledge, and they will found the Light College as you will all found your own. It will be on this site, and it will be the keystone that holds fast the prison of Baudros. Thousands will walk across this place ignorant of what lies beneath them and how their presence helps keep it imprisoned. In the name of Malhavar, first wizard of the Light Order, this will be done.'

'It will,' said Auroc. 'I shall see to it.'

'And I,' said Malgos.

The other mages nodded their assent.

'Without you, there can be no victory,' said Teclis. 'Without men, and magic as they alone understand it. The risks were great. My fellow mages told me it was madness to teach you what we know. But I have seen the threads of fate, and read from them what will happen if men live on in ignorance. You safeguard the knowledge that will keep your race, and all races, alive against the darkness. You are the future. Trust me in this, my pupils, my brothers. Your orders must grow and thrive. Your lives will come to an end, but what you know can never be allowed to die.'

THEY BURIED MALHAVAR near the edge of the crater, a single obelisk raised over his resting place. Already men from Altdorf were filling in the crater, believing it to have been caused by a meteor falling during the strange portents of the previous day. None of them paid much attention to the ceremony happening beside the crater, for without the aethyr-sight the wizards seemed little more than a ragtag band of travellers.

Only Teclis spoke.

'Our brother Malhavar alone understood the nature of sacrifice,' he said, as the sun set. 'That for an evil one to be banished, so must a good one be put beyond our world. That was why it had to be Malhavar. That was why it had to be the Light.'

PART
ONE

CHAPTER ONE
THE GRAVE OF OSTERMARK

WRITERS OF BATTLE-SONGS always missed out the smell.

They did not shy away from the bodies, of course. A battlefield, after the battle, was scattered with knots of corpses marking the sites of the worst struggles. It was that way with Kriegsmutter Field, where the sun was starting to set on a battleground that had been fought over and held by the Grand Army of Ostermark and Nordland. The worse carnage had been on the left flank, where the Imperial cavalry had ripped into the ill-disciplined masses of farmers and labourers who made up the majority of Pretender Count Scharndorff's army.

Bodies in rough sacking and labourers' tabards lay draped over one another, heads split open by the swords of passing riders. A few were still pinned to the ground by broken lengths of lance. They, who had once been men, were becoming something else now, something more like the mud in which they lay. Their skin was turning grey and they were becoming soft and shapeless, merging with the earth. The ground was trampled by hundreds of hooves and into those depressions the rebel dead sank, as if they were trying to return to the earth.

The poets sometimes mentioned the dead horses, too. Soldiers who had seen endless sights of human death could still be moved to tears when they saw the proud bulk of a warhorse split open, red and raw, sinews white to the sky. Discarded helmets, shields and swords were everywhere, as if they had fallen from above. Birds flocked to pick over the dead in the crow's feast those poets loved to write of.

The living were there too. Bands of Ostermark soldiers picked across the churned ground looking for the living. Sometimes they picked up their fallen brother, letting him lean on them as they trudged on. Other times they despatched him on the ground, seeing his wounds were too grave to let him live through the night. The uniforms of Ostermark's soldiers were quartered purple and yellow, a relic of the great ostentatious courts of the province's past counts, and they seemed a mockery now stained with blood and dirt. Those of Nordland were a shabby grey. That province's soldiers, too, turned over bodies to find the wounded, pick up fallen standards and pocket what valuable trinkets they thought they could scavenge without consequence.

Surviving rebels were moving too, trying to hurry into the woodland and barrens northwards. The Pretender Count had promised them a province carved out of the Empire's north, free from the taxes and laws of Altdorf. Quite probably he intended only to build a place he could rule, exploiting the peasants who had fought for him as surely as the worst Imperial count ever did. No one would ever know now because the Pretender Count Scharndorff was dead, his head mounted on a pike near the baggage train of the Count of Nordland. Word was Nordland had killed Scharndorff in person as the cavalry reserves had clashed, and no doubt that was how the artists and history writers would choose to depict it.

Lights speckled the hillsides to the south, where the Imperial forces had camped for the night. A slow trickle of wounded stragglers headed towards the burning campfires, where thousands of their fellow soldiers were warming themselves beside makeshift tents or seeing to the wounds of those who had not come through the battle so fortunately. Banners of Ostermark and Nordland flew as the wind picked up and the evening chill began to set in. An epic poem might mention the strange beauty of the glittering hills as seen from that place of death.

But it would leave out the smell. There was blood, but that was not the worst of it. Voided bowels were far too crude a matter to be brought up in an tale about a glorious Imperial victory, but that was what Kriegsmutter Field stank of. Some had evacuated themselves in fear as they stood huddled behind their shields, or amid the forests of pikes and spears, shuddering to see the field darkening with the advance of the enemy. Others had kept their bowels intact until the first blows were struck and the hours of waiting became short, crunching storms of breaking steel and bones.

When they died, everything inside them seeped out, and

mingled with the mud, and stank like a midsummer cesspit. The scavengers wore cloth wrapped around their noses
and mouths to ward off the stench. A few, the veterans, had
brought pouches of herbs to hold under their noses, knowing
that war was a stinking business even when you won.

At one edge of the battlefield, the Ostermark soldiers had
constructed a tent from the wagon covers of the looted rebel
baggage train. The dead lay around it in great numbers, not
lanced or cut open but burned and broken. Some looked like
they had been crushed beneath a great weight. Some had
been blown apart.

A lone straggler made his way towards the tent. He did not
look like he belonged there. He was not a soldier, for he wore
neither the uniform of an Imperial state soldier nor the rough
clothing of a peasant rebel. It was difficult to tell his age –
old eyes were sunk deep into a long, serious face too young
for them. He wore a travelling cloak down to his ankles and
walked with a staff to help keep his footing across the swamp
of mud and bodies.

The stranger reached the tent and pulled aside the opening. It was dark inside, and only a little of the day's dying
light made its way in.

'Magister?' said the stranger. 'Magister Vek?'

The wounded man lying in the tent looked up feebly. Prior
to that day's battle he had cut a wondrous figure. His robes
were ivory and gold, and though they were now spattered
with gore and mud their gold embroidery still shone. His
shaven head, with a single lock of braided black hair, lolled
against one shoulder. He wore a golden jawpiece which gave

him a stylised single-braided beard. Black symbols were painted on his forehead.

'I am Vek,' he whispered in reply.

'Of the Light Order.'

'Once of that order. Now I belong to nothing. Life itself has discarded me.' Vek held up a hand, which had been clamped to his side. It was thick with blood, and more oozed from the tear between his ribs.

The stranger entered the tent and knelt down beside the dying wizard. 'The Light never leaves you,' he said. 'You will join it.'

'I see only darkness,' said Vek. 'Let me look at you. I cannot see your face.'

A red flame caught in the palm of the stranger's hand. It cast strange shadows across the inside of the tent, glinting off the gold of Vek's jawpiece and the stranger's deep-set eyes. The flame burned without ignition or fuel, a glint of the aethyr's winds as they blew, invisibly, across Kriegsmutter Field.

For a moment Vek studied the man's face, then his eyes lost focus, as if looking beyond him to something only he could see 'Are you sent from Morr?' he asked.

'Yes,' said the stranger. 'I was sent by the god of the dead to see you through to the next world.'

'What… what is there?' asked Vek. 'I always wished to know, but every priest told a different tale, and the winds of magic never offered up the answers. When we are dead, where do we go?'

'To where you deserve to go,' replied the stranger. 'Whatever fate you know you deserve, deep in your heart, that is the fate that will befall you.'

'I think that I have lived a good life. But I have never been sure, not truly, and so I am afraid.'

'Then look back upon your life,' said the stranger. 'For you must be sure, Magister Vek. Look back on how the winds of the aethyr blew through you. Then you will know, and there will be no room for fear.'

'This day,' said Vek, 'I called down the banishment on my enemies. I burned them with the purity of the Light and cast them back with bolts from the heavens. It was my duty, for they raised swords against the Emperor who is my lord. But… they are dead. They were men, like me. Can I have lived a good life, having called down so much death?'

'Good and evil cease to have meaning in battle,' replied the stranger. 'There are only friends and foes. Look further back, magister. Further.'

'The Order of Light!' gasped Vek. 'There, I felt I was… a force for good. Banishing the dark. Holding back the things that lurk beyond. A noble cause. A great cause, with great men. The work of Sigmar, the work of Magnus. I felt like a good man there. A force for truth.'

'Tell me of it.'

Vek smiled. 'You cannot imagine,' he said.

'I have seen much,' said the stranger. 'I have a good imagination.'

'It is the place where the Light wind intersects with the earth. There alone does it flow unhindered into our world, focused like a… like a lance! Like a thunderbolt! So beautiful to behold it. Wondrous to look on of course, but it is more than that. The feel of the Light College, the song it sings in your heart. To have been one of the few to see it, that was good. That made me a better man.'

'You speak of the pyramid,' said the stranger. 'In Altdorf. What brought you there?'

'I was young,' said Vek. 'Decades ago. Longer than most men live. Magnus was upon the throne. The Great War was dying out. I lived through its last years as a child. Dark times. We pleaded for someone to bring us out of the darkness. Magnus and the colleges sent agents to hunt us down, all the witch-children and prodigies. I learned later that in earlier times we would have been put to death. So close we are to the grave. But you know more about that than I do.'

'Indeed,' said the stranger. 'It is a thin veil that had the grandeur to call itself life, one on which we lie though it might tear at any moment. Second by second we live, always the slightest move from falling through into Morr's embrace. But you were speaking of the pyramid. Go on.'

Vek coughed, and blood flecked his lips. 'I am dying,' he said.

'Then there is not much time.'

'They took us to Altdorf. Great men, I remember them. Tall and huge, and we so young. And they tested us. Some were taken early. Of them I never heard again. Some, later, were taken away, and a few of their faces I saw again among the magisters of the other colleges. But not many. And then there was me alone. They brought me to Midday's Mirror, in Altdorf.'

The stranger leaned forward eagerly, as if this was some signal to him. 'The Mirror?' he said.

'Indeed. It was the first time I had seen the sun since they took me. A hand was on my shoulder and a voice spoke. Stand by the Mirror, it said. Give up all you know. The world is not as you perceive it with your eyes. You must perceive it with your mind. There is a world on the other side, and you must inhabit that world, or there is no place for you in that world or this.'

'And?' said the stranger, demand in his voice.

'And there was!' Vek's eyes were light, as if reflecting a fire that only he could see. 'I know not how many others were tried there, and how many failed. But I made it. I told my eyes to be blind and my ears to be deaf! I told my skin to be numb! I told my soul to see! And I did. I fell into that world, and I was there, and the pyramid was before me. Oh, Sigmar's Oath, it was beautiful. The most beautiful thing I have ever seen. It was my greatest sadness that I could see it for the first time but once, and every time after that was bittersweet to remember that wonder.'

'You have lived,' said the stranger, 'well enough.'

The stranger drew a dagger from beneath his travelling cloak. It was stained and rusted. It looked like it had been taken from the ground outside, from the hand of a fallen soldier. The stranger leaned down onto the magister, pinning him to the ground, and drove the dagger into his ribs. He drew it back and stabbed again, angling the blade upwards into heart and lungs.

Vek did not have the strength left to cry out. He gasped, a

dry sound like wind through leaves. The blade went in and out, not frenzied but methodical, making sure that its point went through every organ it could reach.

The stranger let the dagger fall and stood up. Vek was dead. His eyes were turned back in his head and his mouth lolled. Blood ran from his nose, staining the jawpiece. The jawpiece was probably worth a lot of money. Some other scavenger could have it, and live off it for long enough to gamble away what it bought him. The stranger did not care.

As he went to leave the tent, the stranger paused and turned back. He knelt beside the body and picked up the dagger again.

He was not quite done yet.

CHAPTER TWO

THE CITY OF ILLUMINATORS

THE RIVER REIK had not yet been caged by the city that had grown up around it. Even now, with the vastness of Altdorf established as the Empire's most populous city, and perhaps the greatest city of men in all the world, the Reik was not smothered by the towers and heaving tenement masses that crowded on its banks.

As if to remind the inhabitants that their city was fragile, a good quarter of the city – that part which sat in the fork of the Reik's split eastwards of the city's heart – was still a great scar of charred buildings and waist-deep drifts of ash. The Great Fire had torn through the quarter six years before and most of it had still to be rebuilt, the great dark scar now haunted by vagabonds and thieves. Beside that reminder of desolation, the brutal majesty of the Imperial Palace and the banner-hung splendour of Königplatz seemed to lose some of their lustre. The Emperor Wilhelm had reacted to the fire by covering his capital city in bright pennants and parades, but they seemed no more majestic than a handful of colourful trinkets compared to the untamed Reik.

On the left bank of the Reik stood a bustling quarter wreathed in the greasy smoke from a thousand pigment burners and tanneries. The Buchbinder district was one of Altdorf's densest, for it had once been wealthy, and such had been the demand for a home there that upper floors had been piled on top of each other. Every building's upper storeys overhung the streets below, so the narrow, winding alleys were sometimes completely closed off from the sky and a man might lean from his window to light the pipe of a neighbour who lived across the street. The pennants flying from flagpoles and weathervanes hung limp and stained, and even without the haphazard canopy of tenement floors it would have been difficult to see the streets through the permanent fug. The Buchbinder district existed to feed Altdorf's hunger for illuminated prayer books, tomes for the inscribing of rituals and magic, and crude presses for the rags and pamphlets that fed the city's favourite pastime of agitating against a political system no one understood.

Natives of the Buchbinder district knew how the streets worked. They were born in some smoke-stained basement with innate knowledge of the tangled knots of alleyways. Those who came in from outside needed some help.

A courier stood on a street corner. She wore the tabard of a herald in the colours of one of Altdorf's burgher families. She held a leather document satchel under one arm. She looked behind her, the way she had come, and then ahead of her, in the direction she was fairly sure she was supposed to travel.

Then she looked back again, and saw a completely different street that, after a moment of confusion and slight nausea, turned out to be at ninety degrees to the direction it should have lead.

A passing man in a tanner's apron paused and spoke to her. He had a look of condescension on his face, as if he were talking to someone very stupid about something they should nevertheless know. The courier was too exasperated by now to care much about his attitude and listened patiently as he pointed out what she should be doing.

She frowned as, no doubt, she tried to understand how the narrow alley, little more than a shoulder-wide gap between two walls, should lead to a street that was on the other side of the building she stood beside, or how, upon turning left at its exit, she should find herself facing back the way she had come. How her destination should now lie in front of her, she had no idea. But the tanner nodded and smiled, and shook his head and tutted, He seemed to be taking the pleasure a man gets from telling someone – especially a woman – something that he knows and she does not. She thanked him and set off in the direction he had indicated, and he waved as if he was seeing off a tedious child.

Along that same street, ignored by both, was another outsider. He, however, did not wander around in confusion. He was wrapped in a travelling cloak and wore a pack that looked to be full of books. His head was shaven, which was far from uncommon among Altdorfers, but in his case it looked to have been done through choice rather than to keep away the lice. His eye sockets were too large for his eyes and they sank down in the shadow. His nose was long and straight and his pose almost exaggeratedly upright, like a judge walking to the bar in Empire House. A few Buchbinder natives glanced at him, wondering how he could so obviously be an outsider and yet not be perplexed by the district's idiosyncrasies, but he did not return their looks.

He turned right, saw the road behind him now stretching out to the left, and ducked into an alleyway. At the end opened up a square, quite possibly the oldest place in the district. It was still paved with flagstones that had, bafflingly, not been stripped away for building materials or headstones. Equally strange was the shallow rectangular pond in the middle of the square that had gathered none of the trash or grime that caked the rest of the Buchbinder district.

Stallholders had made the square their home. One sold horse and cattle hides. Others hawked cure-alls, trinkets or spices. A pair of old men sat at the foot of a statue of a mounted Reiksguard knight, swapping occasional sentences as they watched the square's comings and goings.

As in the rest of the district, the sky was in short supply. The buildings bounding the square loomed in, looking ready to topple, permitting a square of sky that meant only when it was directly overhead could the sun shine on the unnaturally clear waters of the pond.

The stranger walked up to the nearest stall, the one selling the hides. The stallholder was a woman made greasy and foul-smelling by the work of scraping the hides with a blunt, curved blade.

'Is that Midday's Mirror?' he asked.

The woman looked at him. Smeared, bloody handprints covered her apron. 'What did you expect?' she said, and spat on the ground.

'Do people often come by here?'

'S'pose so.'

The stranger looked back across the square. He wondered how many of the people there knew what this place really was. The stallholder certainly didn't. He doubted the man hawking pomanders and quack medicines did, either. He was crying out that his wares were hand-picked by comely maidens in the hills of Araby and could ward off the plague, rid the face of blemishes, and restore a man's wilting virility.

A gaggle of children ran across the square, playing a game which involved chasing one another and squealing. They might well know. Their parents, of course, would tell them not to entertain childish ideas. The old men had the look of people who had outlived their prejudice against such fantasies. The stranger was certain they must know. Only during the middle of their lives did men refuse to believe what should be obvious to them. The very young and the very old had the liberty to believe.

The stranger walked to the edge of Midday's Mirror. A few copper coins lay on the flagstones at the bottom. He stepped up on the lip of stone running around the pond's edge and spread his arms.

Some of the people in the square, those who believed, could see him. Most could not.

He let himself fall forwards. The cold, clear water rushed up at him.

And he kept falling. The world tipped and twisted around him, tilting at angles that could not exist. He felt a sudden cold dislocation, as if falling through a place that was empty – not even space or time, a void in reality.

He swung up, momentum carrying him up from the surface of the water he should have landed in. His balance kept him from tipping forward and he was standing on the edge of Midday's Mirror again – but this time facing away from the pond.

The square was not the same. It was bigger.

It was immense.

The stranger had to screw up his eyes against the light. He could just about make out the expanse of the square. It could not have fitted into Altdorf normally, for the city would not have permitted such an open space to exist without colonising it with slums, temples, sweatshops, marketplaces, teeming poorhouses or cramped graveyards.

His eyes adjusted. The light did not die down.

In the centre of the square, tall enough to shrink the highest peaks of Altdorf's skyline, was the pyramid. The stranger had heard of it – what he had learned at Kriegsmutter Field had confirmed the sketchy rumours he had collected. But none of that had prepared him for seeing it with his own eyes.

The pyramid was made of white stone, and yet it shone from within. It was all but impossible to look at it directly, just like the sun itself – although the sun now seemed comparatively dim and insignificant in the sky. Smaller structures clustered around the pyramid. From this distance they looked like shrines or mausoleums, cut from white marble. They just made the pyramid itself seem vaster, big enough to fill the senses almost to the exclusion of anything else. Unlike the one around Midday's Mirror, this square was deserted, its white flagstones an empty expanse like a desert of stone.

The stranger held up a hand to shield his eyes as he approached. The shape of a door was just visible in the lowest row of great white stone blocks. The door was enamelled in white and inlaid with gold.

The pyramid contained many light sources, not just one. They separated as he approached. They were not hung on the pyramid but shone from inside it – every light within the pyramid could be seen from outside, and the stranger knew why. Light magic suffused the square, as thick as newly fallen snow. He had tasted it in the Buchbinder district, a constant background sensation like the air just before lightning struck. Here it was unmistakeable. The most blunt-minded peasant, someone without the least sensitivity to the winds of magic, could have felt it.

Beside the door stood a pair of soldiers, the only people aside from the stranger anywhere in sight. Their armour was polished so the segments were like mirrors and they blazed with reflected light. Their faces were hidden behind visors and they each held a halberd, which they lowered to bar the door.

'Your name,' said one of them.

'My name is Egrimm van Horstmann.'

'Are you expected?'

'I am not.'

The guard stepped forwards. 'There is no place for you here.'

'There is always a place,' replied van Horstmann, 'for one such as I.'

The guard made a sound like muffled laugh, and van Horstmann knew he was smirking. He turned around to rejoin his post.

'I know I am older than most you take,' said van Horstmann. 'I was not raised to be sent here. No official of this Empire saw my talent and bade my parents prepare me for the colleges. I have wrestled with this gift and I have not lost my mind, been devoured by daemons or been tied to a witch hunter's stake. That is recommendation enough, is it not?'

The guard turned back to him, and seemed to regard him from head to toe, though it was impossible to be sure from that side of the guard's visor.

'What matters most?' the guard asked.

Van Horstmann looked at the stones of the square for a second, as if gathering up words that had lain inside him for a long time, slumbering, waiting to be spoken.

'Purity,' van Horstmann said. 'And sacrifice.'

The guard took his place alongside his colleague, their halberds once more crossed.

A pause, and the halberds were raised like the bars of a blocked door.

Van Horstmann nodded his thanks, and walked into the Light College.

* * *

'WHAT,' SAID MASTER Chanter Alric, 'is magic?'

His words fell dead against the vast space of the Chanters' Hall. The lower floor of the Light College was a single enormous chamber, pillars of white marble supporting an arched ceiling. Everywhere there was light. Lanterns, impossibly bright, hung from the pillars as close and numerous as clusters of grapes. The raised dais, like a huge altar consecrated to an ancient god of the heavens, had a burning brazier at each corner, yellow-white flames leaping up towards the ceiling.

Three hundred acolytes knelt on the floor. Their heads were shaved, although many had single locks running from the crowns of their heads. They wore simple white robes trimmed with gold. Master Chanter Alric stood on the dais above them, looking down as he spoke. He was a magnificent sight of a man: a great greying beard, eyes the blue-grey of a winter sky, faded circular patterns tattooed on his face and hands. His robes were more gold than white, the golden stitching picking out script in letters of a language that no one outside the Light College was permitted to speak.

'Perhaps,' Alric continued, 'you believe you know. Through you have blown the winds of magic as they have through no one else you have ever encountered. In your home towns, be they villages or fleshpots of the Empire, there were none that you knew who could match your mastery of magic. And so you came to believe you are masters of it. It is my task to teach you that you are masters of nothing!'

Alric passed his eyes across the acolytes. They were the lowest rung of the Light College's pyramid. Both figuratively, for there was no rank lower than that of acolyte, and literally, for they were not permitted to ascend from this lowest floor of the pyramid. They ate and slept here, learned here. Not a few of them would fail here, cast out as the pure wind of Light magic refused to dance to their tunes.

Among the novices was one who, even among the newcomers, was new. He had arrived a few days before, unannounced, one of those relative few who arrived on his own cognisance without having been handed over by witch hunters or recommended by one of the order's magisters. The magisters had taken note of his arrival, though it would not do to have a mere acolyte thinking himself important. They were watching him, as was Alric.

'The least magister of the unworthiest college,' continued Alric, 'is master of forces beyond the understanding of your untrained minds. In you may reside the potential to one day wear the robes of a magister and command the magic of the winds. But before me now kneel not Imperial wizards, but ignorant children, the faint glimmers of powers they possess more dangerous to themselves than useful to anyone else. Some of you have scoured your family homes with unbidden fire! Some have done mystical violence to the bodies of your kin through some act of unconscious brutality! Some have read portents with such accuracy you had to be sent either to the gallows or to Altdorf! Such are the perils of your power. It is my task to compel you to understand your own failures, for only then can you start to build up your strengths.'

Alric hauled a heavy book onto a lectern at the front of the dais. The acolytes snatched glances at him. Instinctively they knew they were supposed to stare down at the floor, as if the riches of the marble and scalding lights were not for their lowly eyes. Those who looked up quickly turned their eyes down as he glared down at them.

Van Horstmann was looking at Alric. Perhaps he had not yet learned the unwritten rules of humility before the Light Order's higher ranks. He would, soon. They all did. A lifetime ago Master Chanter Alric had learned it, before he had been remade as the man who was now lord of the order's acolytes.

'So,' he said. 'What is magic?' He opened the book. 'The soil-stained farmers of the Jade Order will tell you that it is life. The Gold Order's alchemists, hunched in their laboratories, will say that it is the interaction of one substance with another. The morbid masters of the Amethyst College will say, of course, that it is a negative force, the void that is left by death. In some ways, they are all true. But of all of them, what we of the Light Order believe is the truest. For we know what other men are unable to accept, a truth too cruel for them to countenance. We know that magic is sacrifice.'

This time, a stir passed through the acolytes. They did not dare say anything, of course. No one would ever speak out of turn while the Master Chanter was imparting his wisdom. But which of them had not heard the rumours about the Colleges of Magic? Every Altdorfer had. They believed that the Bright College's wizards lusted after fire, some becoming obsessed with it and setting fires at random. They knew, or thought they knew, that the Celestial wizards gazed at the stars for so long they glimpsed the courts of the gods, and sometimes were driven mad when they looked on the faces of the Fell Powers. And, of course, the Light College performed sacrifices. Human sacrifices.

'It is no blade through the heart that gives us power,' said Alric. 'Such sacrifice is crude and hateful to the purity of the Light. No, our sacrifice is of devotion, as demonstrated through ritual and vigil. Thus can an acolyte play his part in the weaving of a spell. He kneels, he fulfils his part in the ritual drawn up by the magisters of his order. He makes his own sacrifice. He chants. *Ula dhaz maaru!*'

The acolytes had been given the passage to memorise, along with dozens of others. It was the lot of the acolyte to learn by rote. Some colleges maintained that magic required imagination, quick-mindedness, that it could be grasped by flights of intuition. The Light Order knew better. Understanding had to be hammered home by repetition and stern admonishment. Only when that framework had been laid down could an acolyte hope to ascend from the First Circle to the Second.

'*Ula dhaz maaru!*' chanted the acolytes in unison. '*Salheh corvun draa!*'

Alric led the chant, turning the pages as the passage was recited. His own voice was deep and sonorous, reverberating around the hall. The pages of the book glowed. The letters inscribed there, written in the alphabet unique to the Light Order, were in silver ink on black-stained parchment and they turned burning white now.

The air turned hazy. The images of the kneeling acolytes distorted and the pillars seemed to bow in, forming impossible angles where they met the ceiling whose frescoes squirmed as if alive.

Magical circles, well-burned into the chamber floor, took light again, white flames licking along the complex designs.

This ritual had two purposes. The first they all knew. It was to reinforce the mystical warping of space around the Light College itself, which kept it hidden in a fold of reality, away from the eyes of the ignorant. Each college was hidden from Altdorf's citizens by some means – this was how the Light Order's pyramid kept itself secret. But the second purpose the acolytes were not supposed to understand, not yet.

The acolytes were not individuals. They were components in the ritual, and they meant nothing on their own. When they were broken down enough they could be rebuilt, gradually given back their sense of individuality. Those whose minds survived strong and intact could find themselves magisters when they reached the Third Circle. Those who failed either remained chanters, assisting the magisters with the sacrifice of their labour, or stayed as mundane servants: the cooks, guards, manservants and librarians of the Half-Circle. It all started here, with the breaking down.

Sometimes they would not break. Alric had no time for them. Misshapen cogs, they were, in a machine that did not need them.

GRAND MAGISTER ELRISSE, the High Illuminator of the Light Order, looked like all the moisture had been drawn out of him leaving a husk as thin as a birch tree and roughly the same colour. His skin clung closely to his skull, sucked in at the cheeks and under the jaw. His eyes and scalp were painted and his face resembled the death mask of an exotic fallen civilisation. Pearls hung from his high collar and his robe was embroidered with gemstones ensorcelled to glow with a steady yellow-white light.

'I am troubled,' said Elrisse.

The Grand Magister sat at the hardwood map table in his chambers. Here, near the pinnacle of the pyramid, the very walls were made of light. The chamber was decked out in the manner of a palace of Araby, with geometric tapestries on the walls, exquisite carpets and the smell of strange spices in the air.

'Then the order is troubled,' said Alric.

'Indeed we are. What news do you bring of our acolytes?'

'They obey,' said Alric. 'Some among them are sharp. I can see them donning the robes of the Second Circle within the year. Others are chaff. They have a crude ability, but nothing that will trouble the fringes of competence. I count Heiden Kant the most intelligent and studious. Gustavus Thielen is the most prominent in terms of raw magical strength.'

'Any that should concern us?'

Alric gave this a moment's thought. Though he lorded over the acolytes as if he was Sigmar reborn, here he was very much of the lower rank. Elrisse had ratified every induction into the First Circle and it was dangerous to suggest the recent intake of acolytes was in any way substandard.

'Not greatly, Grand Magister,' he said. 'Fausten is willful. I think he opposes us, but with childish transgressions.

Misspoken syllables and so forth. I shall grind him down. A few others gather and make plans, but nothing more than stealing luxuries from the kitchens and storerooms.'

The Grand Magister smiled a little. 'Like children,' he said.

'They are children,' replied Alric.

'Of course,' said the Grand Magister. 'How we forget.'

'We were like them once.'

The smile disappeared. 'No, Master Chanter. The man you are is not the same man who knelt as an acolyte. I am not the same man who first walked through the gates of the pyramid. Those men have been erased by the journey from circle to circle. They are as surely gone as any who pass through the hands of Morr.'

'Of course, Grand Magister,' said Alric with an inclination of the head.

'But at least they give us no more trouble,' continued Elrisse. 'You are aware of the nature of the crisis?'

'Crisis? I have heard rumours, but nothing that–'

'A crisis,' said Elrisse. 'As grave as anything since Magnus's passing. It is both dangerous and sensitive. Mere knowledge of it is damaging. The people say the Bright Order did great violence to the city with their recklessness, but that will be as nothing compared to the chaos that will ensue if Altdorfers come to know of our current predicament. I would not have burdened you with it, Alric, but that I fear I shall need your help.'

'Of course, Grand Magister,' said Alric, inclining his head.

'Then gather half a dozen acolytes. It is more important they can keep a secret than have any exceptional skill. Tell none of your purpose and do not be seen leaving the pyramid, if you can.'

'And where are we to go?' asked Alric.

'The Imperial Palace,' said Elrisse. 'And Grand Chanter, pray be quick.'

CHAPTER THREE
THE JESTER

THE IMPERIAL PALACE'S foundations dated to before the birth of Altdorf as a city, when it was a sturdy fortress-settlement on the Reik. In those times the unending war with the greenskins had been waged since before living memory. There were no kings and no heroes, just a desperate banding together to survive. The fortress on the Reik was one of the few places in the lands of men that could stand before the besieging goblin hordes and it had done so many times, its stones stained black with the blood of man and goblin alike.

Then Sigmar had taken up the fight and scoured the green-skins from human lands. He had entered into a pact with the dwarfs of the Worlds Edge Mountains, and they had forged for him Ghal-maraz, Skullsplitter, the Hammer of Sigmar. The battered fortress became the founding stone for the city of Altdorf, first hold of the Empire and sacred city of Sigmar.

The air of those times clung to the stones. It seemed the same air trapped there in the days of Sigmar still circulated through the warren of cellars and dungeons beneath the Imperial Palace. Above was splendour, where ambassadors from across the Old World knelt before the throne of Emperor Wilhelm II. Below, in the forgotten foundations of the palace, the rats and the spiders held court.

One intersection, lit by torchlight, saw the first gathering here for hundreds of years. In one direction were the wine cellars, abandoned and left to decay. In another were the crudely-built oubliettes where enemies of an early emperor had also been left to rot, and where a few well-gnawed bones still poked out from the shadows.

Eight souls were gathered there. One of them was Grand Magister Elrisse, leaning on the snake-headed staff that was his badge of office. Another was Master Chanter Alric. Behind Alric, heads bowed, were the novices he had brought with him. Heiden Kant. Gustavus Thielen. Rudiger Vort. Kryzstof Schwartzgelben. Egrimm van Horstmann. Pieter Diess.

'There have been none here for decades,' said Alric. 'Little of the Light penetrates this place.'

'Faith, Master Chanter,' said Elrisse. 'The Light is everywhere, and we must prepare to call upon it the most when we are in darkness.'

From the shadows emerged another light, in the direction of the cells. It was a lantern held by a small man trussed up in a very expensive suit of breeches, jacket and slashed sleeves, with high hunting boots. He wore a pair of small spectacles and his thinning hair was scraped back. He had picked up a great deal of the dungeons' grime already and did not look happy about it.

'Minister,' said Elrisse. 'These are my brethren on the path of the Light. Master Chanter Alric and the finest of our acolytes.'

'Can they be trusted?' asked the man.

'They are every bit as trustworthy as yourself, Minister Huygens,' said the Grand Magister.

Huygens looked critically at the acolytes. 'Have they been told?'

'They have been told nothing.'

'Then come,' said Huygens, and led the way through into the cells.

The cells went further into the darkness under the palace. Here and there were remnants of other phases of the palace construction: piles of unused building materials and stone blocks, even the outlines of old tombs and burial chambers, all well-stained with age.

'We dare not permit her above,' Huygens was saying. 'We have so far curtailed any wagging tongues, we believe. None but a few servants know and they are sworn to secrecy. His Imperial Majesty is not in attendance, it was thought better for him to journey to Nuln under the guise of a state visit. The more distance he keeps the better, until this matter is resolved.'

'And the rest of the Imperial family?' asked Elrisse as they walked.

'Empress Mathilda would not leave,' replied Huygens.

'Understandable,' said Elrisse.

'She confines herself to the empress's wing, at least,' continued Huygens. 'We could not permit her down here. This is not for her eyes.'

The party rounded a corner. Though the equipment had been taken out of it long ago, its purpose was clear enough. Manacles were still riveted to the walls, and channels were cut into the flagstones to draw off the blood.

'Emperor Gotthold built this,' said Huygens. 'None have used it since, thank Shallya.'

At the far end of the room was a raised stone block forming a table, which still had shackles to restrain hands and feet. Shackled to the table was a woman in a white nightdress, a halo of blonde hair spread across the stone under her head. Over her stood a man in the long leather greatcoat and leather gauntlets of a plague doctor. He had removed the pomander-filled face mask that such doctors wore when tending to the sick, revealing a pocked and angular face. He had laid out several bottles and jars of medicine, along with various implements, on the slab beside the woman.

'Herr Doktor,' said Huygens. 'How is she?'

'She has changed little,' replied the doctor. 'She murmurs in her sleep, but the language I do not know.' He turned to Huygens, his eyes blue with yellowish whites. 'It is not, in my experience, a good sign.'

'Leave us,' said Huygens.

'As you wish.' The doctor bowed and took his leave. As he walked through the archway out of the chamber he cast an unimpressed eye over the wizards.

'I take it,' said Alric, 'that the Light Order is a last resort.'

'The Emperor insisted on science first,' said Huygens. 'He was educated in Nuln. He is a man of reason above all.'

'There is no purer reason than that which can see how the winds of magic blow.' Elrisse walked up to the slab. He shook his head. 'Very young,' he said. 'No wonder she could not fight.'

Alric joined him and the acolytes lined up behind him. Up close the girl's face was clearer – she was indeed young, still a child. She had the delicacy of her mother's features, but with the stern jaw of the Imperial line.

'That's Princess Astrid,' said Rudiger Vort.

Alric glared at the acolyte. Vort turned his eyes to the floor.

'It comes and goes,' said Huygens. 'Now she sleeps.'

'Then we must wake her,' said Elrisse. 'I take it a shower of priests has already been here?'

'Of Shallya first, then Sigmar when it became clear it was no mortal sickness,' replied Huygens. 'We called on a priest of Morr in case of the worst, and he would not commend her soul to Morr's embrace.'

'Why not?' asked Alric.

'Because by then it was clear,' said Huygens, 'that her soul is not alone in there.'

'Form the circle,' said Elrisse. 'I shall be the principal. Alric, lead the chant.'

'And I?' asked Huygens.

Elrisse looked at him much as a parent might look, with forced patience, at a child who asked many questions. 'You will stand back,' he said.

Astrid stirred.

'She knows,' said Heiden Kant.

The princess's lips were tinged with blue and up close, purplish veins were clear beneath her translucent skin. She writhed on the slab, pulling at her restraints. A sudden chill surrounded her and mist coiled from her mouth as she exhaled a long, shuddering breath.

The acolytes formed a circle around the slab, with Alric taking his place among them to form the seventh point. Elrisse stood over Astrid's head, and held a hand just over her face.

'Flow through me, Light,' said Elrisse. 'Accept our sacrifice. Hear our words. Fall upon us the light of banishment!'

'*Ulan tahl she'halla!*' began Alric. '*Tan sechuldar il gaal!*'

'*Ulan tahl she'halla!*' echoed the acolytes, perfectly matching the Master Chanter's cadence as they had been trained. '*Tan sechuldar il gaal!*'

Princess Astrid's eyes snapped open. They were shot through with crimson and the irises were yellow, shining as if a fire burned behind them. The light glittered around the shadowy torture chamber. Her elbows and knees bent almost backwards as she arched off the slab and the restraints were pulled taut.

A cracking and wrenching came from her joints, gristle and bone forced to their limit.

'I see you,' said Elrisse. 'Foul and deceitful thing that wears this innocent flesh. From the Light even your kind cannot hide!'

'*Ulan tahl she'halla! Tan sechuldar il gaal!*'

Silver fire was playing around Elrisse's hands. It flowed out, describing a circle in the air encompassing the chanting acolytes, with Astrid at its centre. Glowing symbols orbited the princess, each a syllable of the secret language they had learned, the tongue with which their voices could reach into the aethyr.

'Down!' yelled Erisse. 'Down! I command you! Burn in the Light, hateful thing. Down!'

The shape of it writhed under Astrid's skin, distorting her youthful features and forming lumpen shapes as it rippled across her torso. With a horrid cracking of bone one hand tore free of its manacle and the princess's body thrashed on the slab. Elrisse was forced back a step by the fury of it, for the princess's nails were suddenly long and tapering, like talons lashing at his face.

The acolytes chanted, but they could not keep their eyes off the princess. Her free arm was bent the wrong way at the elbow, reaching for the Grand Magister as the side of her face bulged horribly. Something inside was trying to get out.

Elrisse grabbed Astrid's wrist with one hand. The other he placed against the slab and flame licked from his eyes as the magic of the Light channelled through him. The slab was bathed in white flame and Astrid's spine bent almost double as the thing inside her tried to escape it.

Waves of cold were coming from the slab. Frost covered the chamber's stones. It was cold enough to hurt, but the acolytes kept up their chant even as pain prickled up their arms and across the exposed skin of their faces.

'What are you?' demanded Elrisse. 'What are you?'

The circle spun faster, the sigils burning brighter. Astrid's breastbone seemed to force its way up towards the ceiling, warping her slender frame until it seemed certain her ribcage would crack open.

'Ulan tahl she'halla! Tan sechuldar il gaal!'

The Light was hearing them. It was accepting the sacrifice of their devotion. The chill enveloped them and the whole chamber seemed to shudder with the force of it.

Kryzstof Schwartzgelben dropped to his knees. He was still gasping the sacred syllables as he pitched onto his front, arms drawn tight around him, blood running from his nose and staining the white robes of the Light Order. Pieter Diess bent to help him up but a glare from Master Chanter Alric stopped him. The ritual was all that mattered. No acolyte was worth more than that.

Astrid's body was distorted beyond all human limits. The writhing shape of the thing inside her was bulging out through her chest, her nightclothes pulled taut. Elrisse moulded the flame around his hand into a sphere, his face lit at unnatural angles in its hard white light. With a shout he cast the fireball up into Astrid's body and she was bathed in the fire, spasming with more violence than a human form could take.

It tore itself free of her. It shed her like a lizard sheds its skin, and she flopped motionless onto the slab. It leapt up onto the ceiling, away from the flame, spreading its inhuman limbs around it to cling on.

It was mostly reptilian. Its skin was a scaly dark green-brown, glistening with secretions. Its eight limbs, neither arms nor legs, but both, splayed around it and its talons anchored it to the ceiling. Its head was located in the centre of its body and it had a wide, lipless mouth lined with teeth, leading to a gullet that disappeared into darkness surely too great to be contained within its pulsating body.

It was asymmetrical. Each limb had a different number of joints and digits. Its mouth was lopsided, fangs spilling out one side with a three-forked tongue flickering between them. It moved in jerking fits, shifting from one posture to another without any visible motion between them.

It stank of ancient decay, like something soured and buried, strong enough to bear down as if the air itself were suddenly heavy. It was accompanied by the sound of twisting gristle and blades through flesh, and a drizzle of transparent gore showered off it as it scuttled across the ceiling.

'Burn, daemon!' yelled Elrisse. 'Burn in the Light!'

Eyes opened up in the daemon's torso and rolled in their oozing sockets as they focused on the Grand Magister. Elrisse shot both hands forward and a ray of silver light leapt from his fingers, scouring along the stone blocks of the ceiling.

The daemon leapt away from the fire, scuttling away faster than anything of its size should have been able to move. An arm lashed down and yanked Pieter Diess from his feet, hauling the acolyte up towards the ceiling. Diess's legs kicked as he struggled. The daemon dashed him against the ceiling and threw him down again, and Diess crumpled against the base of the chamber wall.

The circle was broken. The patterns of light around the acolytes shattered and a shockwave battered through the chamber. The acolytes were thrown to the floor, only Master Chanter Alric keeping his feet.

The daemon leaped down onto Diess. Muscles pumped under its skin as its mouth closed on Diess's head and upper torso, the crunch of bone audible through the crackling of the silver flame still immolating the slab. The daemon shook its head and threw what remained of Pieter Diess across the chamber. The ruined torso, lacking a head and one arm, sprayed blood in a red fountain.

The stones of the chamber warped, a ripple running through them as if they were suddenly turned to liquid. Blocks were dislodged from the floor and ceiling as the ripple hit Grand Magister Elrisse and threw him against the wall. The old man tumbled to the floor, and the high-pitched broken shriek was the sound of the daemon laughing.

EGRIMM VAN HORSTMANN wiped a hand across his face, getting the worst of Diess's blood out of his eyes.

The other four acolytes were struggling to regain their feet. Kryzstof Schwartzgelben was bleeding heavily from his nose and ears. Heiden Kant and Gustavus Thielen were down beside the slab, supporting each other as they got up. Rudiger Vort was curled up in the corner like a child waiting for a nightmare to end.

The room was on fire. The Light magic was uncontrolled now and it was catching on the walls and floor. Van Horstmann placed a palm against the floor in front of him and murmured the rote spell that was the first Light incantation he had learned. The circle of protection shone against the flagstones – a flimsy barrier, but better then nothing.

Princess Astrid lay in a heap on the slab where she had

fallen. She had reverted to her human shape, but there was no sign of life in her pale, skinny form. She might have been unconscious or dead; there would be no way of telling while the daemon was loose.

Pieter Diess's body was a pathetic thing, the torn stump of a torso spilling organs from a ripped-open ribcage. Diess's chewed-up head hit the floor as the daemon regurgitated it.

'Thielen!' shouted van Horstmann. 'Kant!' But he couldn't hear his own voice.

The sound of the unbound magic was so great that it hadn't registered as a sound at all. It was a wall of noise that shut down that sense entirely.

In front of van Horstmann lay the doctor's implements, which had been scattered when Astrid rose off the slab. Among the shattered unguent bottles lay a long, thin knife, very sharp, perhaps used for cutting out growths and tumours. Van Horstmann grabbed the knife's handle and held it up in front of him.

He turned to Rudiger Vort. Vort was shivering like a bullied dog.

The daemon ran across one wall, past Grand Magister Elrisse and off down a side passage. Master Chanter Alric chased it and, though he could not hear Alric's words, van Horstmann knew the Master Chanter was cursing it with all the ferocity the tongue of the Light could muster.

Van Horstmann ran to Vort and grabbed the collar of his robes, dragging him to his feet. He maintained the circle as he did so. Every wizard felt the wind of magic differently. To van Horstmann, the Light was as cold as a winter stream.

It coursed from the core of his body, behind his heart, and swirled around the inside of his chest. The chill ran down his arms and poured from his fingers, it crept up his neck and bathed the back of his brain. It was difficult enough to focus when that power flowed, even sitting alone beside a book of the Light Order's lore. It was more difficult now, but Pieter Diess had not been quick enough to focus and van Horstmann, if he had to die, would not die that way.

No. That was not good enough. He was not going to die here at all. There was no way, because then his work would remain undone, and that could not happen.

Rudiger Vort stumbled after van Horstmann as they followed Alric down the side passage. Cells lined the walls and others were beneath the floor, accessible only by single barred openings. Oubliettes, where past emperors had dumped those they intended to forget about, the prisoners they could not kill but could not permit to live free. Even the Light wind was tinged here with the shudder of despair, the metallic taste of fear.

Ahead was a sinkhole, a circle of darkness that plunged through the floor. Perhaps it had been the site of a foundation since dug up for building stone, or there was a subterranean cavern beneath the dungeons into which a chunk of the structure had collapsed. Its ragged earth sides were illuminated by the bolt of silver fire streaking across it, bursting in a shower of sparks against one wall, a few feet from where the daemon was clinging to the ceiling.

The bolt had come from the hands of Master Chanter Alric, standing on the edge of the hole and shouting magically-charged syllables that van Horstmann could still barely hear.

The daemon glowed with sudden power. A ripple ran out from behind it, deforming the stone as it moved, as if the walls and ceiling were water and a stone had been dropped into it sending ripples in Alric's direction. Alric held up both hands and threw a blue-white sphere of energy about him. The ripples converged on Alric and the floor erupted around him.

Stone burst into flesh. Tendons whipped and tendrils of muscle lashed out, an explosion of living matter growing too fast to see. Blood and torn meat flailed from the impact. Alric was cast off the edge of the pit and into it, followed by a waterfall of pulsing, oozing flesh, thick tentacles and spraying veins, ill-formed false limbs with joints of knobbed and bloodstained bone and spurts of red-black gore.

The daemon turned what passed for its head in van Horstmann's direction.

There was an ocean beyond human sight. The aethyr. It was one thing to speak of it, but to understand it was another. Quite possibly no man, no high elf even, had ever fully understood what it was. It was not a physical place, yet it could only be spoken of as if it were so because no tongue of man could describe the concepts of the aethyr truly. It was spoken of in metaphor. It was an ocean, with each drop enough to power the working of a mage's wonders. It was a city teeming with inhabitants, but they were not people or creatures – they were ideas, concepts, emotions, given a real form in the aethyr. It was a mirror that reflected every mind in the Old World, so that every thought, every fleeting sensation, left its mark on the aethyr like tracks in the snow.

It was a single living being so immense and complex that its consciousness encompassed everything a man knew or ever could know. It was nothing at all and existed only as potential to be tapped, a void to be filled by the act of observing it. It was a puzzle box. It was a map to everywhere. It was a book in which was written every possibility that might ever come to pass. It was a mighty mountain range, down from whose peaks the winds of magic blew. It was the opposite of the physical world, a twin composed of energy and thought. It was every dream ever dreamed. It was an infinite and perfect heaven. It was a hell inimical to sane existence.

No man's concept of the aethyr could be perfect, and so every wizard had his own. It was dangerous to develop such an idea too early, for if the understanding was flawed the interaction with the aethyr might similarly be flawed, and the raw magic could harm or corrupt, or the wizard could find himself prey to the predators that lived there – if the aethyr was an ocean, it had sharks. The training of a wizard therefore involved the laborious study of countless versions of the aethyr, each one laboured at for a mighty wizard's lifetime, each one inevitably flawed. Gradually he was to develop his own, so that by the time he wore the robes of a magister the vision of the aethyr was fully formed in his mind and through that vision he could draw on the winds of magic.

To van Horstmann, the aethyr was a great plain, such as he envisioned might be found in the distant Southlands. This was the image he conjured in his head even as he realised the daemon had seen him and would go for him next.

Upon this plain stood a fortress. It was alone and inviolate. Though the plains were hot and inhospitable, the fortress always stood. It was made of iron, a dull metallic tower rooted deep into the earth. It had enormous doors of studded oak and when van Horstmann willed it – only when he willed it – they would swing open to reveal the cool, dark interior, shielded from the deadly sun.

Inside were a million glowing gemstones in every colour. They had been quarried from beneath the plain, refined instances of the aethyr's power, gusts of the winds of magic frozen and crystallised.

Van Horstmann could walk into this fortress. He did this in his mind's eye as he dragged Rudiger Vort behind a crumbling wall, forcing one half of his mind to focus on the vision as the other commanded his body to do whatever it had to in order to stay alive.

The bolt of change burrowed through the stones of the dungeon and detonated against the wall. Stone shattered and flesh billowed, heavy lengths of bloody tentacle thumping into van Horstmann's back. Vort almost disappeared beneath the mass and van Horstmann pulled so hard on the acolyte's arm he thought he felt it pop from its socket. Vort appeared, slathered in gore, finally shocked out of his stupor and gasping for breath.

'With me, Rudiger,' said van Horstmann.

'What is it?' asked Vort. Van Horstmann did not know him very well – none of the acolytes did, for conversation between them was not encouraged and their waking minutes were dedicated to study and ritual. Perhaps Vort was tough, and would shake off the terror. Perhaps he was not.

In his mind, van Horstmann studied the gemstones arrayed before him. They hung in the air, and above them soared the circular walls of the tower. The upper floors were distant, and the great majority of the fortress was taken up with this chamber in which each sphere of frozen power was held in position like the stars in the sky.

Van Horstmann selected one. This process could not be rushed, no matter how urgent. It was far worse to make the wrong selection than to make a decision too late.

One of the gemstones shone with destruction, but also with hope, a little anger, some fear, and a halo of determination. A dark vein of agony ran through it and normally this would have caused van Horstmann to reject it as flawed. Not now. Now, it was just what he needed.

In the real world, van Horstmann glanced down into the pit. He could just see Alric down in the darkness, lying insensible for the moment. The daemon was gathering itself for another bolt of change. Van Horstmann had seconds, at most.

He drew back a hand. Black fire coalesced around it, thrumming deeply enough to shudder the stones under his feet. Lines of fire crazed up his forearm, and he clenched his fist as the pain hit.

Pain was a part of magic, just as it was a part of everything else. Van Horstmann welcomed it, focused it, forced it into a point and threw it forward.

The bolt of flame arced across the pit like the trail of a

dark comet. It slammed into the daemon and it lost its grip, tumbling into the pit.

Van Horstmann gasped. Hot and cold were flashing through him, the touch of the aethyr.

The edge of the pit crumbled. Blocks of stone shifted beneath van Horstmann and he fell, trying in vain to grab a handhold before he slid into the pit.

Everything was darkness, noise and confusion. Pain battered at van Horstmann from every angle. Beneath him something crunched as he tried to get his bearings.

Bones. The pit was full of bones. Dozens of skulls, hundreds of ribs, gnawed by rats and brown with age. Sigmar knew when this place had been filled, or which emperor had ordered the bodies hidden here. Perhaps they were agitators disappeared from the streets of Altdorf, perhaps prisoners of war no longer valuable as hostages or sources of intelligence. Perhaps they were plague dead from the palace staff.

Van Horstmann clutched dumbly at the bones. His head spun and he had to think to work out which way was up. A short distance away lay Rudiger Vort, his leg pinned beneath a block of fallen stone.

The daemon was on its back, legs curled like a spider. But it was not dead. It shuddered and hawked up a mass of gore and broken teeth. Talons clacked among the bones as it scrabbled to right itself.

Van Horstmann crawled next to Vort.

'What is magic?' said van Horstmann.

Vort looked at him without recognition in his eyes.

'Vort, listen! What is magic? Think! Think!'

Vort could do nothing more than shake his head. The writhing form of the daemon was reflected in his idiot eyes – even the fear had been shocked out of him.

The daemon rolled over. It dug its talons into the dirt and bones beneath it and its mouth yawned open. Van Horstmann could see the churning power in there, a conduit to whatever hellish realm constituted the aethyr for such a monster, a purple-black vortex of decay and destruction.

'Sacrifice,' said van Horstmann.

He forced the point of the doctor's knife up under Rudiger Vort's jaw, feeling the point slide past the jawbone and up under the tongue. Vort finally felt something, eyes widening in shock. His mouth opened and he let out a gurgle as the arteries and veins in his neck were sliced through, blood gushing out. It seemed that it would never end, pouring from the acolyte's mouth even as van Horstmann twisted the blade.

The Light Order preached sacrifice as a concept, not a literal reality. An acolyte learned that the sacrifice written of in the order's most precious tomes was a metaphor for the devotion and labour of the chanting ranks. That was what an acolyte had to believe, because the truth was fit only for one who was ready to ascend to the Second Circle and beyond. But the truth was different.

There was power in sacrifice. There could be great power in the sacrifice of devotion, it was true, if there were both the time and the numbers to make it happen. When they were lacking, the sacrifice had to be immediate and literal.

Van Horstmann jammed the point of the knife further in and it punched through the base of Vort's skull, piercing the lower region of his brain. The acolyte died with a rattling sputter, spraying flecks of blood from his lips.

The life escaped him. Van Horstmann could feel it. The fortress in the aethyr stood now beneath a red sky, battered by a shrieking wind. The power was a flood and van Horstmann fought to contain it – it felt like he would burst, the force building from the centre of his chest and blazing down his limbs.

It could knock him out. It could tear him apart. But it would not.

Van Horstmann was off his feet, lifted above the base of the pit by the force of the magic flowing through him. Pillars of white light fell from above. Skulls crumbled and fallen stone blocks were thrown up towards the ceiling. Van Horstmann was yelling, fists clenched, and the pressure was burning behind his eyes now.

He let the power go, and the circle he projected around him was a blazing cylinder of white light. Pulses of power like bolts of lightning shot across the circle, grounding through everything caught in it. It was banishment and forbiddance, a zone of enforced purity.

The daemon was caught entirely within the circle. Its corrupted flesh was anathema to the purity of the light. Muscle and skin were blasted from its skeleton, leaving green-black bones, twisted and withered. Its cry of despair and abandonment was lost in the sound of a hurricane.

Van Horstmann dropped to the floor of the pit, scattering bones beneath him. He gasped down a superheated breath that scorched his throat. The circle pulsed, once, and van Horstmann's vision greyed out. The world tilted around him as the grey became white and he felt his stomach contracting. He put out a hand to break his fall and felt it plunge into dust and shattered bone.

The white fire flickered out. Where the daemon had been was a scorched crater, the sigils of the Light Order's magic imprinted on the stones. On one side of the charnel pit Master Chanter Alric was stirring, fumbling for his staff in the debris. On the other lay the body of Rudiger Vort, the ground beneath him black with blood.

Every part of van Horstmann ached. Every joint felt wrenched out of place. His eyes were stinging and his throat burned. Breathing hurt in half a dozen places at once.

The noise ringing in his ears was perforated by voices. The face of Grand Magister Elrisse appeared at the lip of the pit. He was pale and blood flecked his face. His eyes passed from Alric to Vort's corpse.

'Attend to the Master Chanter,' said Elrisse. 'Meet me by the slab.'

'SHE LIVES,' SAID the doctor. He carefully turned Princess Astrid's face to one side. It was discoloured from ear to jawline by a livid red mark, as if the skin had been whipped. 'Her breathing and heart rate are steady. I should wish to take account of her humours before I can say anything more.'

Minister Huygens replied with a nod and a grunt. He was pale, sweaty and shaking, and kept mopping his face with a handkerchief. He was leaning against the wall of the chamber, and seemed uncertain if it was acceptable to excuse himself so he could vomit.

'She must be watched,' said Grand Magister Elrisse. He stood be the slab watching intently as the doctor examined Astrid. 'Notes must be taken when she wakes of everything she says. And keep her isolated. None must speak to her save those who can be most trusted.'

'I shall... I shall send word to the Emperor,' said Huygens. 'He will wish to see her.'

'No,' said Elrisse. 'A possession is a disease, minister. It is a contagion. Though the daemon is gone, yet the moral condition in which the victim is left can be as communicable as the plague. Restrict access to her only to those who are essential.'

'I concur,' said the doctor. 'If I may, I suggest I remain in attendance so the princess might be regularly bled.'

'Of course,' said Huygens. 'I should...'

'You may go,' said Elrisse.

Huygens crept out of the chamber, hunched and unsteady as if he had aged thirty years in the last hour.

Elrisse turned to the acolytes who stood, their heads bowed deferentially. Heiden Kant, Egrimm van Horstmann and Gustavus Thielen still lived. Diess had died in the chamber and Vort in the pit, both to the daemon. Kryzstof Schwartzgelben was also dead. When the Light Order's wizards had gathered back at the side of Princess Astrid, they had found Schwartzgelben lying on the floor, eyes locked open and blood still running from his nose. A cursory examination by the doctor suggested that his heart had simply stopped.

All three bodies would be burned.

'Forget what you have seen,' said Elrisse to the acolytes. 'If you cannot, you will be made to. Accompany the Master Chanter to the pyramid. Your work here is done.'

Chapter Four
Dead Man's Robe

EVERY NIGHT, THE fortress changed. Tonight it seemed older, more like the skeleton of a building. The wind that whipped across the plains was shrill through the gaps in the stones, and the battlements were tumbledown and blunted like a mouth full of broken teeth. The banners were tattered.

Often it had a moat and it had one now, filled mostly with mud and choked with weeds. The drawbridge was down, slimy with moss as if no one had bothered to raise it for decades. The plains around it were different, too. A forest was encroaching from one side, turning half the horizon dark and chaotic where the dense growth reached up towards the lower slopes of distant mountains. Once, it seemed, there had been a great civilisation, for it had left the scars of metalled roads and a few crumbling stumps of buildings worn down almost to the foundations. Burial mounds dotted a hillside. Even the sky was old, grey and streaked as if by erosion.

Van Horstmann stood before the doors. They hung on their hinges and would need just a touch to push them open.

He took a long breath. It had taken a long time, longer than usual, to build this place in his mind. It was unusual for the fortress to be in such poor repair. Sometimes it was half-built and shored up by timbers, and on a few very rare occasions it had seemed inhabited, with smoke coiling from chimneys and lights in the windows of the upper floors. Each incarnation meant something, but the pattern was elusive, and perhaps it was something he would never understand.

Van Horstmann approached the gates. The drawbridge sagged under his weight, but even if it gave way there was just mud and tangled undergrowth beneath. The gate swung open.

The darkness inside was familiar. A flapping of wings broke the usual silence – birds had found a way in and roosted. A hundred turned pillars spiralled around each other up into the shadows of the upper levels, studded with dull and scratched gemstones that looked like they had just been dug out of the ground. Van Horstmann ignored them for the time being. He was not here to work magic.

Van Horstmann ascended the stairway that circled the inside of the tower. It shuddered under his weight and threatened to come away from the wall entirely. It was flimsy and wooden. Sometimes it was a flight of grand marble steps, other times a tight, winding stone stairway designed to funnel attackers onto the swords of defenders in ones and twos. Now birds fluttered away from van Horstmann as he reached the planks laid across the rafters, forming a precarious upper floor.

Here, the fortress was unfinished. Perhaps it would never be complete, because van Horstmann's understanding of magic would never be complete either.

Maybe it would one day be a place of reflection and meditation. A library of knowledge that van Horstmann had learned by rote and could recall as clearly as if he were reading it from the page. A sawbones' surgery where he could repair the mental wounds inflicted by the trials of a magister's life. He would not know until it was built.

There was a door in one wall. It had always been here, though it could logically lead to nothing for it was in the fortress's outer wall and beyond it could be only empty space and a fatal drop to the ground. Van Horstmann walked to the door and put a hand against it.

It wasn't locked. It never was. There was a wish, always flickering in the back of his mind, that it wouldn't open. He pushed, and the door swung in.

He walked in. One day it would change. That day might be today. What lay beyond might be different, at last.

But today, it was not.

He sank in up to his waist the instant his foot passed the threshold. The room could not exist except in the geometry of his mind where the rules of reality did not apply. He had tried to excise it from the fortress, spent hours meditating in his acolyte's cell on purging this place of the hidden room, but it was always there.

Scaly bodies coiled around him, thick and smothering. The smell was awful, a mixture of all earthly filth and decay. He tried to draw breath but he couldn't, for his chest was gripped tight and his ribs could not give his lungs room to fill.

He kicked out, but there was no floor beneath him, just the heaving masses of rubbery muscle. He sank in further even as he fought.

He could not help his hands from trying to find purchase. He could not keep the panic from rising. The mass closed over his head and then over the hand that reached up. He could not move at all now, kept tightly swaddled in place, and the darkness was total.

The mass started to crush around him. Though it had felt the same every time he had come here, it felt like he was experiencing it for the first time, as if he had never before felt his lungs burning and his body shivering with what would have been convulsions if he had been free.

He could not even open his mouth, because if he could, he would have begun to scream.

The darkness shattered into a billion fragments.

Air rushed back into his lungs and he was awake. As if falling into place from above, the walls and floor of his cell slotted into his perception. Even in the small room there were no shadows, everything lit by the candles that never went out and which were arranged around the edges of the floor or burned in the candelabra fixed to the walls. Van Horstmann had got used to the constant light – not every acolyte managed the feat quickly enough and were rendered insensible by the inability to sleep.

A bedroll lay at one end of the room. Robes and underclothes were neatly folded and laid out along one side. A shield was fixed to one wall, polished to the sheen of a mirror, upon which was displayed the arms of the Light Order: a candle with a flame in front of a crescent moon. The moon represented the high elf mages, led by Loremaster Teclis, who had taught the first of the Empire's magisters and who oversaw the founding of the colleges, Light College included. The rest of the furniture consisted of bookshelves on which van Horstmann kept his books, most of them volumes of the ceremonies an acolyte had to learn by heart.

These books and clothes comprised everything that van Horstmann owned. They were arranged with geometric neatness, not because the acolytes were required to maintain their cells so, but because that was how van Horstmann preferred to live. Some acolytes were from wealthy families and had suits of fine clothes, jewellery and quantities of money. Others had trinkets given to them by their families, like a painted icon or a father's sword. Van Horstmann did not.

Van Horstmann's meditation had been broken by the shape of a man standing at the doorway to the cell. Though his robes were silver and white he was still fractionally darker than the blazing light of the chanters' cloisters behind him, which in the Light College counted as a shadow. The change had registered in the part of van Horstmann's mind which remained dully sensible, like a sentry dog, while the rest of his perception was turned inwards.

The man was one of the Half-Circle, the stewards, guards, librarians and other staff who served the Light Order. Going by his robe and his great age, he served one of the magisters as a major-domo, valet and secretary.

'Acolyte van Horstmann,' the steward said.

'That is I.'

'Follow me.'

Van Horstmann stood and did as the steward suggested. Outside the cells was the open area where the acolytes learned the patterns and movements of the Light Order's rituals. Several acolytes were doing so at that moment, reciting the ceremonial chants. A couple glanced at van Horstmann as he followed the steward for the rest of the Light Order, even the Half-Circle staff who were no longer permitted to practice magic, rarely associated with the acolytes.

The lowest floor was one huge room, with low internal walls dividing parts of it into cells. In defiance of logic, the higher up one went, the more rooms the pyramid's floors were divided into. The first floor was split into the Light Order's library and the halls where the magisters developed the skills of exorcism for which the Light Order was famed. Van Horstmann followed the steward up the staircase that bisected the two, where the glowing walls were hung with portraits of past Grand Magisters and notable wizards. Each picture was rendered in lacquer and gilt, shining in the light that blazed from lanterns hanging everywhere.

Above that, the floors were divided into dozens of chambers, arranged without any apparent plan or consistency. Some were small study rooms with lecterns and cases groaning with ancient books. Others were armouries with racks of gleaming weapons, or were workshops for illuminating manuscripts or weaving tapestries; some seemed to have no purpose at all. Everything was drenched in light. Some even had pools or fountains filled with glowing liquid. There were, as ever, no shadows.

There, among the labyrinthine interior of the pyramid's upper levels, the magisters themselves lived. The acolytes and the magisters lived separate lives but some acolytes spoke of how the magisters reigned in obscene luxury in the upper levels, commanding hosts of devoted slaves. Van Horstmann saw that the tales were false, but only just. The living quarters he glimpsed were hung with silks or tapestries, some decked out in exotic décor reflecting some far-flung corner of the world – lands like Cathay or the Southlands, which were just words to all but the most learned of the Empire's citizens.

The steward reached a set of polished bronze doors and stopped. He bowed to van Horstmann and left without a word.

This part of the pyramid had trophies on the walls, taken from battles in which the Light Order's battle magisters had fought. Some wizards were academics, spending their lives increasing mankind's understanding of the aethyr and the many winds of magic. Others served as advisors to the Imperial Court or the elector counts, or served as soothsayers, healers and in all manner of capacities to the cities and nobles of the Empire. The battle magisters, however, fought the Empire's enemies in open war. Every wind of magic could be turned to destruction, and Light magic was no exception. The order's magisters had brought back standards and captured weapons from battle – jagged swords, their runes to the Fell Gods obliterated before they were polished and hung on the walls, the bleached skulls of greenskin savages, a tattered banner which had once been a masterpiece of embroidery, perhaps taken from the hands of a dead elf of the Loren forest.

The bronze doors swung inwards. Van Horstmann blinked at the glare from inside, which after a second resolved itself into a chamber dominated by a great globe of silver inlaid with golden land masses and with ocean currents picked out in lapis and agate. The chamber itself was spherical, echoing the contours of the globe. A curved hardwood desk, covered in navigational implements of silver and gold, stood against the wall. Silver crystals hung in bunches from the ceiling, shedding a painfully bright light that blazed off the polished globe.

The light was reflected in every direction, so the figure standing at the desk seemed to shine. He turned and van Horstmann was looking at Grand Magister Elrisse, the old wizard's head surrounded by a halo of silver light.

'Acolyte,' said Elrisse. 'Enter.'

Van Horstmann approached the globe, and his eyes passed across the shorelines picked out across it.

'The world,' said Elrisse. 'As far as our scholars can reckon it. None know what lies beyond the cape of the Southlands, or what might be found far north of Troll Country. And no man, they say, has ventured to the continent of Naggaroth and returned.'

Large areas of the globe, van Horstmann now saw, were featureless. The shape of the Empire was familiar, along with the bordering nations of Kislev, Bretonnia and Tilea, and the gilded caps of the Worlds Edge Mountains and the Mountains of Mourn. He had never before seen a depiction of the Southlands all the way to the dagger-like point at the southernmost tip. But much of the rest was blank.

'I would wish,' he said, 'to see it completed.'

'How so?' asked Elrisse.

'Incompletion is abhorrent to the mind,' replied van Horstmann. 'Like a ritual unfinished or a circle broken.'

'Well, rest assured that men are dying as we speak to map the world's furthest corners.'

'Good,' said van Horstmann.

Elrisse opened a fat ledger with yellowing pages on the desk. 'It has been four years since you walked through our doors,' he said. 'In that time there has been scarce cause for me to hear your name.'

'An acolyte is best known for nothing,' said van Horstmann, 'either good or ill.'

'Quite,' said Elrisse. 'Tell me. What do you imagine Master Chanter Alric has to say about you?'

Van Horstmann did not answer for a moment. 'It is difficult to know how we appear in the eyes of another.'

'It is difficult to call down the Light wind and let it course through us,' said Elrisse smoothly. 'Yet we do it.'

'Studious and deliberate,' said van Horstmann. 'Little trouble. Accurate in his memory of the First Circle rituals.'

'Such are the prerequisites for becoming an acolyte in the first place. Hardly remarkable.'

'I have no ambition to appear remarkable.'

Elrisee smiled, not looking up from the ledger. 'Some would say that we cannot enter into the study of magic at all if we are content to be unremarkable. Is it not rather extraordinary to simply walk through the doors of this pyramid? To enter into the secret coven of Teclis? We work wonders, van Horstmann, do we not?'

'What we do,' said van Horstmann, 'is essential. Without the wizards of the colleges of Altdorf, the Empire is lost. Perhaps the world itself. The agents of the Fell Powers can be met only by the combination of the sword and the spell. Our work is as necessary as the maintenance of soldiers or the rule of the emperors. There can be little room for wonders when we must devote every moment to the survival of our people.'

'Well put, acolyte,' said Elrisse. 'How long have you been working on that for?' He closed the ledger. 'There is one thing for which I and Master Chanter Alric remember you. I know you have not been spoken to about it since it happened. And I know there have been rumours, for Kant and Thielen were unable to hold their tongues completely. But you have said nothing. The exorcism of Princess Astrid is what I speak of, van Horstmann. The deaths of Schwartzgelben, Diess and Vort. Vort, I understand, died in your arms. Is that not so?'

'It is so.'

'Have you revisited that day, acolyte?'

'I have.'

'And what do you see?'

Van Horstmann looked at the chamber's curving floor. 'I see Vort's eyes,' he said. 'I saw when the life went out of him. One moment they were the eyes of a man. The next they were dull. Vort was not a man any more. He was a corpse. I saw that moment come and go. That is what I remember. I see it when I close my eyes.'

'And the daemon? You banished it, van Horstmann. You cast it back into the aethyr. It rages there as we speak, defeated. You have not even spoken of that. There are magisters in this very college who would take every opportunity to crow that they defeated such a creature. But you have said nothing.'

'I called on the Light. I offered it my devotion, and it flowed through me. I remembered the words of Teclis and the founding Grand Magisters. There is not much else to say.'

Elrisse closed the ledger. He pointed up at the globe again. 'Some of us never leave Altdorf. Some of us rarely even leave this pyramid. But there are those among us, of all the orders of magic, who have seen more of this world than most men imagine exists. Do your eyes turn to the horizon, acolyte?'

'Yes,' said van Horstmann. 'I wish to see it. That is where the wonders lie. Not in the works of wizards, but in the places where the winds of magic have carved their secrets into the world.'

'You can,' said Elrisse. 'If you so wish it.'

'My studies monopolise my time and the energies of my mind. It is fruitless to lust for such things now, when I have so far to go before I can even step outside this college as a wizard.'

'Really? I disagree, acolyte. I disagree most firmly. Many of your fellow acolytes will never advance beyond the First Circle. Perhaps they will serve in the Half-Circle, perhaps the Light College will become closed to them. But you are not among them. Whether you are willing to admit it or not, or whether you merely conceal your true thoughts, you are very remark-able. You saw your fellow acolyte die and yet kept your head

enough to match wills with a daemon of the aethyr. You have
shown devotion in your studies and a discipline of mind. On
their own any of these would give us confidence that you can
rise above your current station. Together they leave us little
doubt. Tell me, have you heard the name Obadiah Vek?'

'I have,' said van Horstmann. 'I understand that he was a
magister of this order, and that he was lost.'

'He died here,' said Elrisse. He raised a hand and a glowing
spot appeared on the globe, in the vicinity of the Empire's
northern provinces. 'He served as a battle magister in the
army of Nordland, against the Pretender Count Scharndorff.
A battle was fought at Kriegsmutter Field and in that battle
Magister Vek lost his life. It diminishes us all, acolyte, when
one of us is lost. In times of war we find ourselves much
diminished. This order stood proud alongside Emperor Magnus in the Great War's culmination, and we lost many. Times
are scarcely less perilous now. It is an onerous task to replace
such men as Magister Vek, for they prove themselves bul-
warks against the Empire's enemies and islands of sanity in
the ocean of the aethyr. But replace them we must. Vek died
six years ago and his place has not been taken. There were
none who could take it. I have decided that now, there is.'

Van Horstmann did not reply.

'You may, if you wish, celebrate. Or perhaps thank me.
They are empty emotions but would not be inappropriate.
You cannot deny those petty moments of humanity forever,
van Horstmann. You are permitted them. As of this moment
you are a magister of the Second Circle. A Light wizard. One
of us, van Horstmann, a wizard of the pyramid.'

Van Horstmann bowed his head. 'Thank you, Grand Magister. I shall do everything in my power to prove your decision was the right one.'

'It was not a decision,' replied Elrisse without pause. 'It was fate.'

MAGISTER VEK HAD expected to return to the College of Light. It had not occurred to him that his life might end in the mud and filth of Kriegsmutter Field. His quarters were still fully appointed and stood just as Vek had left them. It was only the withered state of the Lustrian orchids and mandrake root on the alchemy table that suggested Vek had been away at all.

Each magister decorated his quarters in their own way, echoing some far-flung part of the world that a non-wizard might never even hear about. Vek had made use of the arts of the lands beyond the Worlds Edge Mountains, a bleak and hazardous bowl of rocky desert which had once maintained a handsome and far-reaching civilisation. A pair of monumental figures, with the bodies of lions and the heads of men with carved beards hanging in elaborate braids, bracketed the room. The furniture was of carved red-black stone taken from some volcanic quarry: a grand writing desk covered in implements for drawing out the exacting proportions of ritual circles, ceiling-high cabinets and bookshelves, the round alchemy table with its circular slab supported on a tripod, and four polished bronze sculptures of birds and animals that watched from each corner of the main chamber. The bedchamber had a huge four-poster bed with its pillars taken from some long-fallen temple, and cabinets and chests for the vestments of a magister's rank.

Van Horstmann stood in the centre of this room and took note of its contents. The cabinets were piled with books and trinkets, small objects of art or ritual purpose from across the world. It must have taken years, and a near-obsessive eye for the arcane and obscure, to have collected them all. Vek also had a weakness for skulls, especially carved from strange materials: pitted iron, volcanic glass, chunks of jade and marble.

'I trust everything is to your liking, magister,' said the steward who had showed van Horstmann to the chambers. 'Do not hesitate to express your displeasure if it is not.'

Van Horstmann looked back at the steward standing in the doorway. It was impossible to place them – their attitude was permanently locked between haughtiness, servitude, and the feeling they knew something they were not telling. The stewards of the Light College were presumably recruited from acolytes who did not make the grade, but there was no similarity between this inscrutable man and the studious youths of the Chanter's Hall.

'This will do for now,' said van Horstmann.

'Very good,' said the steward. 'Magister Vek's staff is located alongside his robes. All of Magister Vek's belongings were accounted for save for a small hardwood puzzle box he kept on his person. It was not found on his body when it was recovered.'

'I see. Where was Magister Vek buried?'

'He was interred in a field south of Kriegsmutter Field,'

replied the steward, 'alongside the other notable dead of the battle. As a battle magister it was thought fitting to leave him so buried.'

'Of course. Wait a moment.'

The steward stood dutifully by the door as van Horstmann went into the bedchamber. Like the rest of the Light College the chambers were drenched in light, flooding down from a dozen braziers that hung from the ceiling. It would take a great deal of effort to make a hiding place when there were no shadows, but no doubt Magister Vek had possessed sufficient ingenuity. Van Horstmann would have to thoroughly search the chambers to see if Vek had left any secrets behind when he left to join the war in Ostermark.

Van Horstmann opened a chest by the foot of the extravagant bed. It contained several sets of ivory-coloured robes with gold embroidery. One of the robes wrapped something and van Horstmann bent to pick it up.

It was a staff. Vek's staff. It was gilded and sturdy, shoulder-high and very finely made. Its head was that of a hooded snake with emerald eyes. The snake was one of the most persistent symbols of the Light Order. In the earliest mythologies of the world it was a symbol of purity and banishment – its venom could drive out spirits, provided the bitten host survived, and the marks of its winding through the sand were once thought to be the passage of ghosts who followed the snake away from the dwellings of men and back to the netherworld. The snake swallowing its tail was said to be the origin of the ritual circle. A scattering of snake venom over such a circle marked the culmination of many of the Light Order's rituals.

Van Horstmann returned to the main chamber holding the staff. 'Take this from me,' he said.

'Magister?'

'I have a dislike of snakes,' said van Horstmann. 'I shall require a staff made for me. Kruger and Granitebrow of Altdorf shall be commissioned to make it. I understand they are among the finest goldsmiths in the city. It shall be of this height, a staff of gold banded with silver. The top shall take the form of a mask of a young woman, as a death mask but with the eyes open. One eye will be a diamond. I trust this will not be beyond the resources of my order.'

'Of course,' said the steward, taking the offending staff from van Horstmann's hands. 'Masters Kruger and Granitebrow have long been trusted suppliers of the Light Order. You shall have it within the fortnight.'

'That is all.'

The steward nodded and left, closing the door behind him.

Once he was alone, van Horstmann placed the puzzle box on the writing desk.

He had carried this object from Kriegsmutter Field, where he had taken it from a pouch tied to Magister Vek's waist. He had kept it on his person, not trusting the Light Order not to search his acolyte's cell, and its hard wooden corners against his skin were so familiar a set of sensations that when he took it from beneath his robes he felt like a part of himself had been removed.

It had been difficult to keep it hidden at first. It wanted to be revealed, to be admired and toyed with, like a needy pet. But Egrimm van Horstmann had learned to keep secrets and eventually it seemed to have given up, to relinquish its ticklish grasp on the back of his mind.

It was beautiful. He had not ascertained where the box had been made. Elven, perhaps, carved from the living trees of Averlorn in Ulthuan or from the heartroot of some ancient oak of Loren. Magic winked off it, like light off a gemstone.

Van Horstmann had spent a lot of time trying to open the box. There had been enough long nights on the way from Ostermark to Reikland to test out the give in its various panels and carvings. A seashell-shaped panel on one side slid in the width of a fingernail, and another panel could be levered aside to reveal the tightly-wound nests of bark and beaten gold inside, like the innards of a timepiece.

A stud was pressed and a lever pulled halfway. The puzzle box opened up with a series of descending tones.

Van Horstmann paused. He reached into the well of power at the back of his mind, that stemmed from the foundations of the fortress, and imagined a stony depth of silence. He took that idea and let the magic fill it, and it spread out from him in an invisible hemisphere – a magical zone of silence. It was difficult to hide anything for long in the Light College, but it was possible, at least, to keep it silent.

He opened up a pane of polished crystal in the heart of the puzzle box's bloom.

The air above the desk shimmered, as if something beyond a veil of reality was struggling. Then that veil tore and glistening limbs could just be glimpsed, pumping and writhing like organs in a still-living chest. An eye glared out madly, a gnashing maw made wet chomping noises. Its breath could be heard now, a grinding, panting sound that would surely have brought alarmed stewards in from outside if not for the magical silence.

The puzzle box was more than a toy, although it could have been mistaken for one. It was a magical artefact designed to keep objects safe and screened from outside eyes. Van Horstmann had wondered, at first, what use Vek had made of it. Perhaps the magister had not even known what it could do. Van Horstmann had known as soon as he took it from the dead wizard's robe. He had seen its like before, illustrated in the pages of books. Books that according to every law of the land neither he, nor anyone else, should ever read.

The daemon burst from its invisible cage. It looked the same as van Horstmann had seen it last, below the Imperial Palace. It was scorched and battered, some of its eye sockets red and raw where the eyes had been put out, teeth in its lolling maw broken, muscle and ill-formed bone poking through the skin.

It propelled itself onto the ceiling, rattling the braziers hanging there and sending embers fluttering down.

'You,' it hissed, drawing out the syllable into a rattling grind.

Van Horstmann threw out his hands and bands of white fire appeared around the daemon, like the bars of a spherical cage. 'I let you live,' said van Horstmann. 'I could have destroyed you but I did not.'

'Destroy me? Ha! You flatter yourself, you filth-dripper, you walking afterbirth! You less-than-nothing!'

Van Horstmann let the image in his mind contract and the

bars closed in. The daemon writhed and hissed as its limbs touched the flame. 'And I still can,' he said. 'I invoke the pact that binds all your kind.'

'Lick the rump of Sigmar's corpse!' slurred the daemon back. 'Speak your drivel to his holy fundament!'

'I let you live!' continued van Horstmann. 'That means I saved your existence. That means I own you.'

'Leprous ordure-heap! Well of bubbling pus!'

'Tell me it is not so!' demanded van Horstmann. 'I own you. You are mine. Tell me you are not!'

The daemon drew itself against the ceiling and hissed, flicking specks of drool across the desktop.

'I thought as much,' said van Horstmann. 'I shall not be a disagreeable master. No doubt more tolerable than whatever power put you in that girl's body.'

'By the mountains of the aethyr, she stank,' said the daemon. 'Her flesh begged me for corruption. Her mind, too. That voice in the back of her head that lusted to be violated and depraved. She mourned me when I left her. She begged me to return.'

'Now you are rid of her, daemon. Now you are mine. Speak your name.'

The daemon roiled and hissed. A limb touched the cage of white flame and it recoiled, burning.

'Speak it!'

'Hiskernaath!' yelled the daemon. The syllables seemed to burn its mouth as it spat them out. 'I was the Red Stag of Chalons. I was the Beast of Kolnendorf. But in the tongue of the aethyr my true name is Hiskernaath!' The daemon gasped, the effort of speaking the truth, something so alien to it, exhausting. 'Are you pleased, fleshling? Does your heart swell with pride? Do you think you have won?'

'There is no winning or losing,' replied van Horstman. He had not raised his voice, no matter how the daemon railed against him. 'Above us is the same master. Far above, so far that his eye might never fall upon us, but under his mantle we both fall. I know what you are, Hiskernaath. You were torn from his flesh like a seed from the pod. You are a fragment of his will.'

'You speak,' said Hiskernaath, 'of the God of Lies.'

'I walked,' said van Horstmann, 'on the Red Road that leads to the Well of Malice. I drank of its waters. I have stood before the gates of the Eternal City, and heard the song that bade me enter. I tore a tower from its battlements and installed it in my own soul. I looked upon the Isle of Mists and returned with my life. I have travelled, daemon, and I have learned. My mind unshackled, it flew through the coils of the aethyr and returned to my body with these truths intact. My studies are a long way from completion, but I know enough to commune with the Liar Prince. I knew enough to defeat you, and bind you, in the name of he whom we both serve.'

'Tzeentch,' hissed Hiskernaath.

'Tzeentch,' said van Horstmann.

'You are a daemonologist.'

'Not so,' replied the wizard. 'I am a seeker of knowledge. I followed the daemon-binder's path and I walk on the path of Light. Both are my calling. Perhaps I will walk other paths. As it is I have the means to both enslave you, and destroy you if it suits me. Remember that, daemon. I am a magister of the Light Order and we are not known for our mercy to daemonkind.'

'Then,' said Hiskernaath, 'how may this one serve you?'

Van Horstmann regarded the daemon for a moment. It was an inhuman, disgusting thing, a combination of all the worst parts of spiders, vermin, maggots and the ill-formed things that lived beneath the sea – but it was also a sentient thing and its body language could be read after a fashion. It was in submission now, like a slave prostrate before its owner. Gills fanned open and its talons were laid flat against the ceiling, like tools at van Horstmann's disposal.

'I know enough,' said van Horstmann, 'to be certain that as a daemon, you lie. The most mindless of you has within it the capacity for deceit. It is in your nature to lie to me now. You have no intention of serving. You will tie me up in one of the riddles of which Tzeentch is so fond, and at the culmination of my plans you will reveal the loophole you have exploited to turn on me. And I will be destroyed, like so many others before me. Not this time, daemon. Not this master.'

Van Horstmann unfastened his robe, which was still that of an acolyte. Onto his upper chest were tattooed long streams of archaic characters.

'I walked the Valley of Centuries,' he said, 'and found there the pedestal on which rests the Obsidian Codex, carved by madmen into panels of stone. These are the words I read there, the pact which bound Kyrinex the Maw to the Heresiarch Coven. They were written before Sigmar was born, before these lands of men existed, and they have been read by no man since save I.' Van Horstmann pulled his robe open to reveal his whole torso was covered with the words. 'It is a contract, daemon. Unbreakable. And you will sign.'

'Come, master, you insult me!' said Hiskernaath. 'We follow the same dark star, you and I. You are my master. You own me. One such as I can never betray one such as you. No contract is needed, master. Not when Lord Tzeentch himself blesses my servitude!'

The daemon did a good job of forcing genuine hurt and obsequiousness into its voice. Someone who had not walked the roads that van Horstmann had, someone who had not studied the most ancient works of daemonology, might have been convinced.

'Sign, daemon,' said van Horstmann. He indicated the space on his abdomen, left bare for a signature. 'Make your mark.'

One of the flame-cage's bars vanished. Hiskernaath paused then, as if invisible hands were forcing him, and uncoiled a limb towards van Horstmann. Pores opened on the end of its tentacle-like tip and oozed greenish acid that hissed and spat where it dripped on the chamber floor.

For a moment the daemon seemed about to protest one final time. Then it touched the limb to the bare spot on van Horstmann's torso.

Van Horstmann winced. The unsavoury smell of burned skin mixed with the daemon's own stench. When the daemon withdrew its limb, its mark, a letter of that same ancient alphabet, was scorched onto van Horstmann.

He took in a long breath. The contract was signed. Though

every such contract was fallible, for a daemon could weasel its way out of any obligation, it would take centuries for Hiskernaath to find the flaws that would release it from servitude. That was more than enough time for van Horstmann to do what he had come to the Light College to do.

THE LIGHT PYRAMID was one of the great secrets of Altdorf, but there were greater.

True, the general population did not know it was there. The inhabitants of the Buchbinder district ascribed the strange geography of their home to some wild magic resulting from ley lines or a rogue spell in ages past, and the Light Order did nothing to discourage such beliefs. But there were plenty of people who knew of the pyramid, not least the magisters of the other seven orders along with those who had to deal with the Colleges of Magic as political entities: the Imperial Court, the churches of the Empire's major faiths, the orders of witch hunters and others.

A greater secret was that there was more than one pyramid. The second pyramid was a mirror of the first, built underground and inverted, its point as far beneath the ground as the Light College's pinnacle was above it. These were the vaults of the Light Order, a repository for everything they did not want seen by anyone outside the order. It was here, rather than the first pyramid's library, that they kept safe the most valuable and dangerous books, either those penned by the order's earliest and greatest magisters or tomes of blasphemy captured intact and read, under the strictest supervision, to provide an insight into supernatural threats like daemonkind and the undead. In these vaults were kept magical artefacts too valuable and too powerful to entrust to the pyramid above ground – the staves of the great magisters, ritual knives and blood chalices for the most direct of sacrifices, enchanted objects and armaments of every kind.

The magisters of the Fourth Circle, who answered directly to the Grand Magister and who numbered only half a dozen at any one time, were masters of these vaults. They were kept in strict order and perfectly maintained, in keeping with the mindset of the Light Order. The Fourth Circle did not mix with the rest of the order and they guarded their domain with such fervour that all save the Grand Magister were fortunate to even enter the upper vaults with any regularity.

It was therefore Elrisse himself who led the newly-appointed magisters into the vaults to witness what an acolyte could not – some of the greatest secrets that existed in Altdorf, in the whole of the Empire, painstakingly catalogued and studied by the jealous Fourth Circle.

Van Horstmann stood before a pedestal on which sat one such secret. It was one of over two dozen displayed in this vault, one of the uppermost vaults, a long room of cut marble and false pillars. Here were displayed magical swords and talismans created by the Light Order: an amulet of cold-forged iron in the form of two intertwined snakes, a chunk of crystal filled with dancing lights, a golden torc that slowly wept drops of blood. Van Horstmann had ignored most of them, given a few of them a glance, and moved to this pedestal at the far end of the chamber.

'The Skull of Katam,' said Magister Pendorf. Pendorf was

of the Fourth Circle and was the oldest man van Horstmann had ever seen, his face little more than a sheaf of wrinkled skin behind a straggly grey beard. His voice was so dry and strained that it almost hurt to listen to it. He had shadowed van Horstmann the moment he entered, like the owner of a confectioner's following a quick-fingered child.

'From the barrows of the Mourkain,' said van Horstmann.

'You are learned,' said Pendorf.

'We seek knowledge,' replied van Horstmann. 'It is our weapon. We all seek it, you guard it.'

'Quite so.'

The Skull of Katam had, presumably, once been a human skull. Perhaps it had looked like a mundane skull when it was dug up from the burial mound that had once been a part of the prehistoric Mourkain empire. Now it was plated in silver and covered in jewels. Its teeth were diamonds and its eyes two fat rubies. Sigils were cut into the silver, each a variation of a star with eight points.

'Sigmund Haal died a week after he found it,' said van Horstmann. 'They say it spoke to him of his death, and his heart froze solid the next night. And that whoever owns it will eventually be warned of their death, though there is nothing they can do to avoid it. Whenever it speaks, someone dies.'

'Then I give thanks,' said Pendorf, 'that I have never heard it.'

Van Horstmann looked at the old man. His robes were trimmed with black and he wore around his neck a heavy amulet in the shape of a padlock. The image of a key was tat-tooed on his forehead. The magisters of the Fourth Circle were said to have a little madness in them, perhaps a prerequisite for the job of tending the vaults, perhaps the result of isolation from the rest of the their order and exposure to the strange magics of so many artefacts. 'I understand that one magister of the Fourth Circle must die before another can take his place,' said van Horstmann.

'Nowhere is it written, but in practice, yes, that is so.'

'Then maybe it is the Skull of Katam that decides when one of your circle is to be replaced. Perhaps it speaks, one of you hears it and is struck dead, and another takes his place. Could that not be the case?'

Pendorf did not reply. It was impossible to read any emotion from his face. It was barely any more expressive than the jewelled skull.

Van Horstmann reached for the skull.

'No,' said Pendorf. 'The Skull of Katam is ill-starred. It cannot leave these vaults.'

Van Horstmann ignored him and picked up the skull. It was heavy, far heavier than mere bone. He realised it was solid right through.

Power crackled through his fingers where they touched the skull. Sparks of white magic arced from his palms. The rubies glowed brighter, a pink-red light bathing van Horstmann's face. He heard a click as the jaw unlocked.

'Do you know,' said van Horstmann, 'who Katam was?'

'You show no respect to this place!' rattled Pendorf. 'Our secrets are not to be toyed with as your fancy takes it! You... you are not welcome here, magister! You must leave!'

Two more magisters ran in. Both were ancient, though not quite as wizened as Pendorf. One struck the butt of his staff against the ground and flames leaped up around his other hand, boiling in place. The impression given was of a bowman drawing the string, ready to shoot. The other opened the tome he carried and read aloud.

'By the Pact of Teclis,' he said, 'to the sole custody of the Fourth Circle shall be given the vaults of the Light College, and entrusted to them will such artefacts as the Grand Magister deems necessary to be kept secure. No magister save the Grand Magister and those of his choosing may venture there and make use of such artefacts. All are bound to this law and all is forfeit in disobedience!'

'Him,' said a voice from nearby. For a moment, van Horstmann could not place it. 'Him. This one. He will carry me.'

Pendorf looked on dumbfounded. The other Fourth Circle mages were similarly stunned. Van Horstmann realised that it was the skull that had spoken.

He looked down into the ruby eyes of the skull.

'I have not spoken for three centuries,' it said. 'For none have been worthy to hear me. None have been worthy to hear my wisdom. But this one. This one is worthy.'

'I am a seeker of knowledge,' said van Horstmann to the skull.

'And I am a receptacle of knowledge,' replied the Skull of Katam. Its voice had a multi-layered quality, as if it was made up of several voices heard at a distance, or was almost swamped by its own echoes.

'They say that when you speak, people die.'

'They lie. They do so through jealousy, for I will not speak at all to those whose minds cannot contain what I must impart.'

'You… you cannot remove the skull from the vaults!' said Pendorf, his voice shaking.

'Who speaks?' asked the skull.

'One of the Fourth Circle magisters tasked with looking after you.'

'I suffered them with great pain. Now I have found someone to whom I can speak, they will not keep me within these walls if I desire to leave.'

'Then you will leave now,' said van Horstmann. He turned to the three magisters. 'Unless you wish to stop me, magisters.'

The magisters did not reply. They didn't even move. The fire that one had been holding, ready to strike, sputtered and died out.

With the Skull of Katam in one hand, van Horstmann walked past the magisters and out of the chamber. The other chambers of the upper vaults radiated out from the spiral staircase leading up to the above-ground pyramid. They contained a fortune's worth of artefacts – books written in ink distilled from unicorn blood and meteoric iron, swords that could sever a soul from the body, runestones that, when cast, could foretell the outcome of a battle still to be fought. But none of them were the Skull of Katam, and so van Horstmann ignored them as he returned to the pyramid.

CHAPTER FIVE
THE GILDED FORGE

IT WAS ON a bright and clear night that Emperor Wilhelm II died. His physicians ascribed his death to a surfeit of rich foods and wine that lead to a fatal ulceration of his innards.

There was no great grief when the news was called out that dawn from street corners across Altdorf. Wilhelm II had always been a distant man to the people, little interested in the masses of the Empire's citizenry and more concerned with putting down the petty rebellions that had become a national pastime of the aristocracy. And, of course, he could not compare as a man to Magnus the Pious, who had won such a titanic victory in what had, generations later, earned the name of the Great War against Chaos.

Wilhelm was given a state funeral, his body displayed on a carriage that wound in a procession from the Imperial Palace to Altdorf's Temple of Morr, but those who turned out to see it were drawn more by curiosity than by a wish to pay their respects. When Magnus had died, people had seen portents in the sky, a comet rushing from the earth to the stars as if it were the release of a great soul, showers of light like the tears of the heavens. The night sky did not seem overly concerned by Wilhelm II's passing and neither did anyone else. Even his family, including Princess Astrid who had just recovered from a long illness, looked more bored than grief-stricken as they rode in the black-draped carriage behind the Emperor's body.

An Empire without an emperor was a dangerous thing. Sigmar had not founded a hereditary monarchy, and instead had created the tradition that an emperor should be the one man most uniquely suited to the task, as Sigmar himself was. Lacking the presence of any god-kings who might fit the role, the Empire had, after various civil wars and lesser squabbles, instituted the twelve hereditary posts of elector count who would choose the next emperor. In times of great strife their decision would mean nothing but, without any warring claimants to the throne, they decided who should succeed Wilhelm II.

It was without bloodshed or threats that the elector counts decided the least offensive choice was Count Vitek of Stirland, a middle-aged, middle-browed man who had achieved the feat of not making any mortal enemies outside his immediate family. The Church of Sigmar had no objections, and neither was the choice likely to create a major rift with a neighbouring power. Within the week Vitek was Emperor pending his coronation at Altdorf.

* * *

IT WAS THE SECOND time van Horstmann had entered the Imperial Palace and this time he entered through the main gates instead of a hidden entrance to the dungeons. The palace was much more handsome from this angle, with the great frowning gateway proportioned to intimidate anyone crossing the Imperial threshold. For all it might serve as a palace it was still a fortress, the walls still thick and sheer and studded with firing slits behind the banners of the elector counts.

The representatives from the Colleges of Magic included magisters from every college, resplendent in the dress robes that best represented them to the Altdorfers gathered to watch the occasion. Their numbers had been limited by Imperial decree, since at coronations past the colleges had competed to have the most spectacular sight, with Gold wizards firing off alchemical fireworks and the Amber College summoning a menagerie of decorative beasts. Now they were a little more sombre, although the crowds still gasped and murmured at the sight as they were held back by the men of the Reiksguard.

It was the first time van Horstmann had encountered the wizards of the other orders. The Bright wizards smelt of ash and wore red and yellow – even their hair tended towards red, and faint wisps of smoke issued from them as they passed. The Amber wizards, who studied the Lore of Beasts, were perhaps the opposite of the ordered and monastic Light wizards – they wore a patchwork of neutral colours, their staffs were styled like scythes or carved with images of birds and animals, and wildflowers sprung up where they stepped.

Van Horstmann wondered for a moment what the other colleges' magisters must think of the Light Order.

He himself carried his new staff, made to his specifications with the female mask and single diamond eye. He wore the Skull of Katam at his waist, and was sure it got some odd glances from the other magisters as they entered the palace. But even so he was not out of place and many other Light magisters surpassed him in their stern, monastic airs, the richness of their gold-embroidered robes and the diamonds studding their staffs. Among any other company van Horstmann stood out – studious, intense, quiet but with the authority of intelligence. Among fellow magisters, he was one among many.

The audience chamber was already almost full when the wizards filed in. Burghers from Altdorf's mercantile classes, priests from the various faiths, notable members of the aristocracy, ambassadors from distant realms and countless more important people were already standing awaiting the entrance of the new Emperor. Van Horstmann took his place and noticed that among the acolytes the Light magisters had brought with them was Kant, the acolyte who was among the survivors of his last visit. Kant looked nervous – perhaps it was the occasion, perhaps it was the memory of what had happened in a spot right beneath his feet.

The Supreme Patriarch was the last to enter – Maximilian van der Kalibos, Grand Magister of the Amethyst College, the train of his purple-black robes carried by a host of trained ravens, his staff a column of skulls.

Van Horstmann found he was standing alongside Master Chanter Alric. 'It has been some time since last we spoke, van Horstmann,' said Alric.

'Much to my regret,' replied van Horstmann. 'The first lesson I learned is that no magister can be immersed in every aspect of his order, however he might wish it. Sadly, the education of the acolytes is not my calling, and so our paths have not crossed since I left the Chanting Hall.'

'And what path do you walk?' asked Alric.

'Study,' said van Horstmann. 'The words of our past greats require interpretation if our lesser minds are to comprehend them. And there are secrets hidden there awaiting the time we have learned enough to decipher them.'

'A life of dusty introversion, then?' said Alric. 'We all have our strengths and our weaknesses, van Horstmann. Your strength is a certain orderliness of mind, a factor which makes it resistant to the chaotic world beyond the colleges. The way of the wanderer, of the battle wizard even, would suit you best.'

'Perhaps,' said van Horstmann. 'And I desire to see all the world's corners inked on some explorer's parchment. But I see no need to venture there in person when the choicest of knowledge from those places flows instead to us. The secrets just need to be unravelled.'

A babble of conversation near the front of the assembled notables rose up. Perhaps the Emperor was near.

'You spoke,' continued van Horstmann, 'of my strengths. What did you perceive as my weaknesses?'

Alric smiled. 'That same orderly mind,' he said. 'Not everything fits neatly into its nook. I fear for the day when you try to force something into the plan in your head, and it refuses to be so constrained.'

'Perhaps, Master Chanter,' replied van Horstmann, 'you would be surprised.'

The Emperor was ushered onto the throne podium by an honour guard of Reiksguard knights. He was an unspectacular man, with a doughy and indistinct face, and at this distance seemed swamped by his ceremonial golden armour and ermine-trimmed cloak. His guard was led by the Imperial Champion, Reinhardt Blutaugen, a giant who was easily a head taller than any man there and who carried a two-handed blade broad and heavy enough to cut down a tree. His armour, they said, had been ill-made when it was first delivered, because the smiths of Nuln had assumed the measurements they had been given must be wrong. He carried along with his own blade the Runefang of Stirland, the emblem of the new Emperor's rulership over his home province, in a scabbard on his back. It was one of a dozen trappings of power – the Silver Seal that clasped the Emperor's purple cloak, the ceremonial Chain of Justice about his neck that made him the Lord Judge of Altdorf's courts, the griffons and comets on his regalia.

One such emblem of authority was missing. A band of ambassadors from the dwarfn holds stood at the back of the podium, flanked by a regiment of scribes and ministers. The dwarfs were powerful, squat, brutal-looking creatures, their own trappings the pragmatic gear of war. They wore armour of bronze and iron and wore their voluminous beards in elaborate braids hung with talismans. Everything about them spoke of strength, not least the traditional war-axes each one carried. One of them, with a beard that would have dragged along the floor had it not been tied in a dramatic loop of braids, stepped forwards and bowed his head. It was about as submissive a gesture as a dwarf could be expected to make.

'The dwarfs of the Worlds Edge bid you all honour, inheritor of Sigmar,' said the longbeard. 'In the name of the pacts and debts between our peoples, wield this our finest work wherever the Empire of men does war.'

Two more dwarfs joined the longbeard, bearing between them a long-hafted warhammer with a head of glowing bronze. Power radiated off the weapon, and even without the experience and sharpened senses of a wizard, van Horstmann could have identified it as a magical weapon. It was more than that, of course. It was the Hammer of Sigmar, wound about with the most powerful magics of the dwarf runesmiths and presented to Sigmar himself when the two races first went to war against the greenskins. It would have been a magnificent enough badge of Sigmar's authority had it been a mundane weapon, so fine was its workmanship and the balance which allowed the new Emperor to take it easily with one hand. Its magic was such that it had smashed aside daemons and princes of undeath, dragons and champions of the Dark Gods alike.

'May your grudges go unforgotten,' said the longbeard, and retreated with another bow.

Reinhardt Blutaugen stood over the Emperor and placed the Imperial crown on his head. The crown was styled like a hoop of laurels wrought in gold and silver, and sat perfectly on the new monarch's brow.

'All hail,' shouted a cryer from the podium, 'His Imperial Majesty Eckhardt III!'

The dignitaries knelt. Van Horstmann joined them, looking up towards the man styling himself Eckhardt III as he did so. The mind that lurked behind that uninteresting face might decide the fate of the Empire. He might be a religious bigot, a crusading warrior, a poet and aesthete, or a madman. The Imperial crown had been worn by examples of every one in the past. He might be a great man. He might be an incompetent whose rule was marked by catastrophe and whose death was celebrated in the streets. He might leave no mark on history at all, save the record of his name.

It was entirely up to chance. That was how the world worked, if it was permitted. Chance.

'I will not permit it,' whispered van Horstmann to himself. 'Chance will not rule me.'

If Master Chanter Alric heard him, he made no indication of it.

'I swear to obey the Imperial throne,' began the cryer.

'I swear to obey the Imperial throne,' said the assembled dignitaries in unison.

'I will heed its call to arms.'

'I will heed its call to arms.'

'I will adhere to its laws.'

'I will adhere to its laws.'

The words reverberated around the cross-vaulted beams of the ceiling. They seemed as inconsequential as the handful of pigeons roosting up there. Van Horstmann barely heard the words as they escaped his own lips. His mind was twisting them into a vow of his own.

I swear to take what I can from the Throne of Change. I swear to adhere to my own laws.

After the oath of allegiance was made, Emperor Eckhardt III stood and made a speech. His voice was not strong enough so the cryer took up his words. He spoke of a new era of peace and shared prosperity, of an end to petty wars through strong leadership and a greater voice for the Empire's people.

Quite probably the last Emperor had said much the same thing at his coronation. This one was eloquent and diplomatic enough. True to form, he sent no one home overly offended.

Van Horstmann felt neither offence nor admiration. His mind was elsewhere.

THE GOLD COLLEGE was a great steam-powered laboratory, half of it built by dwarfen master smiths, the other half grown from living metal by the wizards of the Gold Order. At their command, beaten iron coiled into springs or curled into the pipes that funnelled alchemical materials around the college's many experimental chambers. It looked like nothing so much as an enormous pipe organ turned inside out, spurting columns of steam and smoke, hissing and gurgling and crowned by galleries of clockwork automata locked in an endless dance.

'Our politics,' said Grand Magister Elrisse as he led the Light Order delegation up the Gold College's main steps, 'are every bit as complicated as those of the Imperial Court.'

'Politics is not what I joined the Light Order to pursue,' said van Horstmann. He had found himself more and more often at Elrisse's side, whether it be researching new rituals from the encoded journals of past magisters or, as now, making the rounds of Altdorf's other colleges to cement relations in the light of the new Imperial reign.

'Nor I,' said Elrisse. 'But we must remember, the life of a magister is not one of leisure. We must sometimes partake in that which we find distasteful, so we might fulfil our calling. This will be an education for you, so pay close attention. In magic you are as learned as a man many decades your senior already, but in politics, you are a newborn.'

'Of course,' said van Horstmann. 'I see already the Gold Order does things very differently.'

While the Light College was a monastery, the Gold College was a workshop. The grand doors swung open revealing an enormous hemispherical hall hung with mobiles and musical automata, playing an endless loop of intermeshing tunes. Gold and brass plated everything, bathing the entire college in an orange-yellow glow. The Gold magisters had sent a delegation to meet the Light magisters, led by their Grand Magister, a man with a ruddy mane of hair, powerful blacksmith's forearms and bronze-coloured skin. Not just tanned but bronze, metallic and reflective, and his eyes had pupils of gold.

Elrisse spread his arms and gave his best beaming smile, which still had a little too much of a cold rictus in it. 'Zhaan!' he exclaimed.

Grand Magister Zhaan embraced Elrisse in his great

muscular arms. 'Brother Elrisse! What an honour! For too many years one of yours has not set foot in our home. There is much to discuss, for times are fast. And we have prepared a feast, of course! Any excuse!'

'Such indeed are the times,' said Elrisse as he emerged from Zhaan's grasp. 'All the colleges have had to turn inwards. Still we have not rebuilt to the strength of Magnus's time, and we only just replaced one of ours who fell in the northern rebellion.'

'I hear your sadness, Grand Magister,' replied Zhaan, his brow furrowing, or rather buckling, the bronze creaking as it folded up. 'A fleet of elven pirates plagued the Sea of Claws and two of our mage-wrights were despatched to assist the Tsar's fleets off Kislev. Alas, they did not return. Will we never see an age untarnished by woe?'

'It is our duty to suffer such woes, and yet fight on regardless,' said Elrisse. 'These magisters who accompany me you will remember, of course, save for van Horstmann. He is the latest to ascend to the Second Circle.'

'A protégé, no doubt,' said Zhaan, and grabbed van Horstmann's hand. He had the strongest handshake van Horstmann had ever felt. 'Elrisse is wise. Too stuffy! Too hidebound! But he is wise, indeed. Listen close to him, van Horstmann!'

'I see already there is more than one way to study the winds of magic,' replied van Horstmann. 'Just being here opens my eyes.'

'Ah, of course. The Gold Order revels in innovation and experimentation. Your order values learning by rote and the slavish repetition of ritual. Is one better than the other? It is not for any of us to say. We create, yes, but your way is safer. We have vaults of mighty magical weapons and artefacts crafted in our smithies, but you have tomes of banishment and exorcism. Without either commodity, many crises would have befallen the Empire that were instead averted.'

As the Gold and Light wizards made their way further into the Gold College, van Horstmann saw rows of furnaces and forges at which Gold wizards worked like blacksmiths. Many of them looked more like skilled labourers than wizards – stripped to the waist and bent over anvils, they hammered at swords or segments of armour, or worked leather and metal with tools of glowing silver. A couple of dwarfs worked among them, probably sent from the Worlds Edge holds as part of some long-standing agreement with the Gold Order to lend their smithing expertise. The air smelled of burning fuel and smoke, and here and there something more exotic from the alchemical labs which bubbled with benches full of tangled glassware.

The feasting hall was something new. The Light Order did not have one. Perhaps the Light wizards placed less value on hospitality than their Gold brothers. Three long tables, heaped high with plates of food, were attended by a small fleet of waist-high automata that scuttled about busying themselves with setting places and filling wine glasses. They were marvels created by Gold wizards past, filled with dwarfen-made clockwork and enchanted with secrets of animation that were already forgotten.

'Sit!' exclaimed Grand Magister Zhaan. 'Eat! Celebrate!'

The Light wizards took their places. The Gold wizards

clinked glasses and looked eager to start. Van Horstmann found himself a place near the head of the table, beside Zhaan.

'A toast!' said Zhaan, standing with a glass in his hand. 'To magic! To us sons of the aethyr! And to the Emperor!'

The magisters echoed the toast and drank. Van Horstmann, who was not one for drink, limited himself to a sip. An automaton was loading slices of meat and piles of roast vegetables onto his plate.

'So,' said Zhaal. 'What manner of studies does the Light Order force on its newest magisters?'

'The lost ceremonies of Egelbert Vries,' replied van Horstmann.

'Not much point,' said another Gold magister sat across from van Horstmann, 'if they are lost.'

'Forgive Daegal here,' said Zhaan. 'He is a practical sort, and does not sympathise with the more academically minded of us.'

'I seek through the work of my own hands,' said Daegal, 'rather than the words of another.' He was probably young for a magister but hid the fact with a beard. His eyes were small and blue and he had a charred, smoky look, no doubt cultivated to give the impression he was always kneeling by a forge.

'They are only lost in so much as we have yet to find them,' replied van Horstmann. 'We know very certainly they are there. Specifically, they are in a long description of the herbs and flora of the Troll Country, hidden in a multi-part cipher. They key is woven into the illustrations, you see. Vries was a wayward soul. He thought that knowledge had to be earned, and so would only pass it on to those who could solve the riddles he used to hide it.'

'Knowledge is a tool,' said Daegal, 'to be used.'

'Interesting,' said van Horstmann. He turned to Zhaal. 'Is that true?'

Zhaal winked. 'Of course!' he said. 'So we believe. That is why the first of us took up the hammer and the tongs, just as we took up the staff and tome. They are all symbols of what magic is to us.'

'And to us,' said van Horstmann, 'it is different. Magic is a force, a realm above us, and only through achieving a higher state of mind can we perceive it. Only through ritual can we connect with it, in a pure form.'

'Pure?' said Daegal. 'So ours is impure? A lower form?'

Van Horstmann smiled his thinnest smile, not letting it reach his eyes. 'Not at all,' he said. 'Our dealings with magic occupy merely a different place on the hierarchy.'

'A place higher or lower than ours?' demanded Daegal.

An automaton, as if sensing tension in the Gold wizard's voice, hastily topped up Daegal's wine glass.

'It is only logic that I employ,' said van Horstmann, in a smooth and supercilious voice that even Zhaan would find objectionable. 'A smith might make an item of great use. Great power, even, as you do in your forges. But he relies on knowledge to do so, knowledge that is collected and written down, and studied and comprehended, by those who need not ever set foot in a smithy to have their own part in such creations. The Light Order occupies a step in that process above that of the mage-wright. This is the simple truth, as all must surely see it.'

'Our ways of magic,' said Zhaan a little too quickly, 'stand upon an equal pedestal to all the other orders, and always have.'

'Teclis never wrote,' replied van Horstmann, 'that all the orders were to be equal.'

Daegal stood suddenly, his chair scraping back. 'How dare you?' he demanded. 'The Grand Magister of our order will be spoken to with respect!'

Van Horstmann held out his hands, a gesture of reconciliation. 'Respect is not an issue between us, Magister Daegal. Does not the good Emperor respect the smiths of his domain, and the peasants in the field? For without them, his authority and the wisdom of his scribes mean nothing.'

'And then we are peasants,' snapped Daegal, 'to your Emperors?'

'Perhaps the analogy was unfortunate,' replied van Horstmann slickly.

'Magister Daegal,' said Zhaal. 'I hear the music of our college is out of tune. Communicate my concerns to the masters of the Chord.'

Daegal shot a look back at van Horstmann, bowed to the Grand Magister, and briskly left the feasting hall.

'The music,' said Zhaal, 'is what keeps us concealed. Its combination of notes confuses the mind of the uninitiated and turns their senses away from our college. Its song is subtle but those who spend enough time here can make it out.'

'Fascinating,' said van Horstmann.

Zhaal pointed a fork at van Horstmann's plate. 'Eat, Magister van Horstmann,' he said. 'You magisters of the Light are all far too skinny.'

Chapter Six

Upon A Throne Of Lies

THE DANCES OF the Old World's moons were such that only the wizards of the Celestial College really understood them. Only they knew when the witch moon Morrslieb would grow fat and sickly green in the night sky, or when the stars would be in alignment to pick out one of the constellations inscribed on the most ancient monoliths, constructed when all known civilisations were yet to be born.

When the Ninth Alignment occurred, when the stars overhead took on the aspect of a serpent winding around the heavens, the Light Order marked the occasion with a series of ceremonies that required the attention of all the acolytes and most of the magisters. The hidden square around the pyramid, concealed in a fold of space around Midday's Mirror, became a parade ground where the acolytes were assembled in seven circles and Master Chanter

Alric led them in the ritual sanctification of implements of sacrifice.

Van Horstmann watched the acolytes taking on the sacred configurations, shifting from place to place in the circles as lines of white fire traced ever more complicated patterns between them.

The square outside was visible through the translucent wall in the Grand Magister's quarters. Van Horstmann saw Alric walk into the centre of the largest circle, a heavy snake, its body as thick as a strong man's thigh, draped around his neck.

'I understand,' said Elrisse, 'that you dislike snakes.'

'This is true,' said van Horstmann.

'And for this reason you seek to be excused from the Ceremonies of the Serpent.'

'Not at all, Grand Magister,' said van Horstmann. 'I would find the ceremonies... trying, certainly, but I would have no quarrel with being assigned to them. But my work on Egelbert Vries's cipher is at a crucial turn. I can feel the answer hovering just beyond me. I must grasp it and the work will be complete. It is maddening, but enticing, and I fear that if my concentration is broken for an hour then I will lose it again. I ask that I be permitted to continue my work.'

'And at what stage is that work?' asked Elrisse. The Grand Magister sat at his hardwood desk, silks from Araby draped behind him and stacks of correspondence before him. He was signing documents with a quill plucked from some exotic bird, and his signature was a long list of honorary titles.

'It's not in the text,' said van Horstmann. 'It's in the illustrations.'

Elrisse sat back in his chair, the throne of a deposed sultan brought back by Imperial explorers. 'The illustrations,' he repeated.

'Vries inserted invented words and strange phrasing to make it seem the text was hiding something,' said van Horstmann. 'There was something of a pattern to it, but not enough to permit deciphering. And some of the supposed cipher fragments were far too obvious for one of Vries's intelligence. It is in the illustrations that they lie. I had a city botanist source a fresh witherbane flower. Vries had drawn the stamens incorrectly. Again, too grave an error for him. That is where the cipher lies. I am so close, Grand Magister. I need just a little while, as mages reckon things, and I will decipher it.'

'I need no magical sense to tell you will shortly ask me for something, magister,' said Elrisse.

'More samples of Vries's work,' said van Horstmann. 'I need the *Codex Aethyrica*.'

Elrisse sucked in his breath sharply. 'The Fourth Circle will scarcely forgive me,' he said. 'Such a tome is guarded more vigorously than the fattest jewel in our vaults.'

'Vries wanted his code broken. Everything needed to do so will be contained in what he has written. If I can study the *Codex Aethyrica* at my leisure then they will soon add *Herbs and Poultices of Troll Country* to the vaults, because it will contain the newly-deciphered lost ceremony of Egelbert Vries.'

'Then it will be done,' said Elrisse. 'Results, van Horstmann. That is what I must demand of you. A mind like yours can be excused the rote learning of our order only if in its place, the total of our order's knowledge grows.'

'It will.'

Elrisse looked at van Horstmann with an expression that he could not read. Many people cultivated inscrutability, but with Elrisse it seemed effortless, as if he had been born with his emotions already hidden. 'It intrigues me what you will come up with, van Horstmann. In the five years you have been here you have greatly refined the rituals for aethyric perception and elemental protection. You learn quickly and you perceive the world not through the cold and dead matter of which it is composed, but in terms of its potential, its capacity for change. My indulgences have their limits, but this one is acceptable. The Fourth Circle will release the *Codex Aethyrica*. I will suffer their complaints. In return I shall preside over the lost rituals of Egelbert Vries.'

'My thanks,' said van Horstmann.

'And if I may say so, magister, you will find yourself much more at home if you can bring yourself to suffer snakes. They have been a symbol of this order since its inception.'

'I will see what I can do in that regard. For now, though, I must to my quarters. The answer to the cipher taps at the front of my skull. I fear it slipping away.'

'Then go,' said Elrisse. 'I shall send word to the vaults. You will have your codex. See to it that the order has its secrets in return.'

WHEN VAN HORSTMANN reached his quarters, a steward of the Half-Circle was already standing at his door, the *Codex Aethyrica* in his hands. Van Horstmann had stopped by the ablution chamber to wash his sweating face, for seeing the snake being used in the ritual had filled his mind with images of fleshy coils and fangs, and it had taken some minutes to banish them again. He took the book from the steward, acknowledged the man's bow, and retreated into his chambers.

Van Horstmann placed the Skull of Katam on the desk beside the book. The skull rolled its emeralds in its sockets and shuddered as the spirit inside it came to the fore.

'It doesn't look like much,' said the skull.

It was right. The *Codex Aethyrica* was old and threadbare. Its cover was of wood covered in thin and tattered fabric, with faded letters stamped on its cover. It had been fitted, some time after being written, with a lock that had fixed bands of steel in place around it to keep it closed. The key to this lock was tied to the book's spine by a short cord.

'There is no more valuable book,' replied van Horstmann, 'in the upper vaults. Certainly, none more valuable that I could get hold of.'

'If it is not enough,' said the skull, 'there will be consequences.'

'And you would know of consequences,' said van Horstmann.

If the skull could have scowled, it would have then. Van Horstmann knew what the Skull of Katam was – *who* it was. That was knowledge no one else in the Light Order had. The Fourth Circle had been ignorant of the skull's true origin for centuries, which begged the question of how many other artefacts in the vaults had power that no one understood.

'I shattered the Nine Blades of Burning Dusk,' said the

skull. 'I crushed them beneath the weight of a thousand corpses. I flung the shards from the pinnacle of Cripple Peak! That was enough.'

Van Horstmann unlocked the cover of the *Codex Aethyrica*. The book was in the hand of Egelbert Vries, making it akin to a sacred relic. Vries was one of the first magisters of the Light Order, tutored by Loremaster Teclis himself.

Flickers of light rose from the pages, as if the syllables were taking flight. Vries's hand was swirling and dense, almost a cipher in itself, and in reddish ink he had filled the margins with annotations and diagrams. Many pages were covered in representations of ritual circles, the first examples of the patterns being created outside the pyramid at that moment.

'Can you feel that?' said van Horstmann.

'I have not felt anything for six hundred years,' said the Skull of Katam.

'Yes, you can.' Van Horstmann took a bronze tray of alchemical instruments from a shelf beside the desk. Magister Vek had loved to collect such things, the trinkets of other, lesser orders of magic. The instruments had been made for a magister of the Gold Order, and van Horstmann recalled his discussion with the wizard Daegal.

They thought that magic was a tool, like a knife or an anvil, to be wielded as the user wished. No imagination. No respect.

Van Horstmann knew what magic really was.

He took two slender silver tubes from the tray and popped off the stoppers that held them closed. He poured the contents of the cylinders onto the open *Codex Aethyrica*. Each tube contained a small quantity of silver-white dust, which burst into orange sparks where they met on the book's page.

The *Codex Aethyrica* caught fire. Grey smoke swirled up towards the ceiling. Van Horstmann waved a hand and cast a circle spell, one he had used many times before to seal off Magister Vek's quarters from outside scrutiny. If anyone passing smelt smoke, they might become suspicious. Light magic made preventing that scrutiny simple enough for van Horstmann.

He could hear Vries's words screaming. It was like the sound of squealing animals, trapped and terrified as their warren burned. They tried to escape, peeling themselves off the parchment, the scraps of ink waving like spiders' legs. But they could not get away.

The *Codex Aethyrica* was as valuable as a substantial Altdorf estate, as the financing for the raising of an army. To the Light Order it was more valuable still, like the bones of a saint or a relic of Sigmar himself. And it burned away to the spine, scraps of paper flittering upwards on the heat of the flames.

Van Horstmann passed a hand over the burning book. Deep cold enveloped it and the flames were instantly snuffed, replaced with a spray of ash and charred fragments that spilled out across the desk. Some spilled across the Skull of Katam.

'And now?' said van Horstmann.

'Hope he hears,' replied the skull.

Van Horstmann looked at the skull. Did its expression ever change? Sometimes he was certain it did. There had been times when that fixed smile had been perhaps a little turned down, as when he wore it among gatherings of other magisters. Maybe it had been offended to be flaunted as a decoration. Perhaps now it looked a little sly, its grin more of a smirk.

'I wait on no one,' said van Horstmann.

He took the puzzle box from his pocket and opened it halfway. Hiskernaath, the caged daemon snickered and cursed inside.

'I need blood,' said van Horstmann.

'Begone,' replied the daemon in the puzzle box. 'I'm busy swyving your ancestors in hell.'

'I command blood from you,' snapped van Horstmann.

One of Hiskernaath's less important limbs unfurled from the box. Van Horstmann grabbed a ritual dagger from a shelf, one of the many such implements that Vek had collected. It had an oddly-shaped blade that curved sharply to one side and became broader at the end, with a hilt of bound horn or ivory. Van Horstmann drove it through the daemon's limb and into the desk.

Thick blood, hissing as if acidic, spread around the knife's point and mixed with the ash from the burned book.

The limb withdrew back into the puzzle box, and the box's intricate panels snickered closed. Van Horstmann forced the point of the dagger into the wood of the desk and scribed a symbol into it. He used all his strength, carving as deep as he could.

The symbol was something like a comet with a pair of tails, and an ignorant man might think it was a debasement of the twin comet of Sigmar. The comet was a portent said to signal Sigmar's arrival and, after his death and passage into godhood, the presence of Sigmar's spirit on the battlefield. But this symbol was a lot older than Sigmar's Empire. Perhaps it was older than the race of men itself.

Van Horstmann put the dagger aside.

'Hear me,' he hissed, teeth gritted. 'Hear me!'

The desk shuddered. The room followed. The braziers swung and dropped burning embers, and Vek's collection of trinkets spilled off the shelves. The two bearded statues swayed and threatened to topple over. Van Horstmann thrust his hands wide and syllables of power flickered across the walls as he held the bubble of silence around the chamber. If he was discovered now, it would be over. In spite of all the precautions, of all the second and third backup plans, there were times like this when a single stroke of bad luck could bring it all down.

The air split open. A purple-black gulf yawned over his head, spilling shadows into the chamber. This place had not seen a shadow since the day the pyramid was built, and now it recoiled from the alien darkness pooling on the floors and in the corners.

Van Horstmann knelt to keep his footing. Alternately scalding and freezing gales battered at him. He forced himself to look up into the chasm, at the boiling mass of energy that seethed there like something that festered.

'I will not be ignored!' he shouted over the wind shrieking in his ears. 'I will be heard!'

The Skull of Katam was laughing. The sound was lost but its expression was clear, eye sockets narrowed in cruel glee.

The black gulf yawned wider and enveloped van Horstmann like a great dark mouth.

* * *

VAN HORSTMANN HAD spent time in his head, navigating places that did not exist as a literal reality. He knew what such a place felt like – which parts of it slid off the senses as if refusing to be perceived, which parts were blown up in impossible clarity. The dirt beneath his fingers felt sharp and prickly, while the sky around him was so indistinct his mind did not register its colour.

Chunks of shattered stone floated like islands. Lengths of spiked and gory chain held them down, criss-crossing between them like the web of an iron spider. Worms as long and wide as the Empire's great rivers looped and plunged through the void, round maws billowing open to scoop down the burning rocks that fell in a bright rain. Trees clung to the islands, bodies twisted and torn up in their gnarled and leafless limbs. Here and there a body fell, marks of torment on its shredded skin, face locked open in an endless scream.

Behind van Horstmann, a staircase rose from the island on which he lay. It was built from blocks of white stone. Fingers and scraps of skin stuck from between the stone blocks, for it had been mortared into place with the bodies of the slaves who had built it.

Van Horstmann drew a breath. The air was infernally hot, almost impossible to inhale. He got to one knee and his mind was aware that he had to ascend. He did not know where the mental command had come from – it made more sense by far to curl up into a mewling ball until this place was gone. But the command was there. He had to climb.

Van Horstmann dragged himself to one knee. He went forwards one step. The sharp rock and dirt scraped the skin from his palms and knees. The pain shot up his limbs, prickling the inside of every limb and organ. Pain, in this place, was magnified, or it was different, a living thing that once released would carouse around the body to take as much as it could until spent.

Another step. Van Horstmann tasted blood in his mouth.

He had gone through worse. He had mentally travelled to some of the most gods-forsaken places of the Old World, the chill corners rightfully forgotten to all but madmen. He had climbed ice-capped mountains and almost died in Araby's northern desert, buried alive by a sandstorm in a robber's cave, all within the confines of a fevered trance. He had survived those. He would survive this.

But even if this place was not real, in the same way that Altdorf and the chambers of the Light Order's pyramid were real, it was still real enough for him to die there. This much, at least, van Horstmann had learned.

His hand touched the lowest step. His fingers left tracks of blood on the stone as he dragged himself onto it. He saw the folds of skin poking from between the stones, and could just make out the loops of crushed eye sockets, tongues and ears. Were these indeed the builders of the staircase, or the remains of those who had tried to climb it?

Van Horstmann pulled himself up step by step, every inch drawing blood from his fingers. The stones seemed to shift and tip, trying to throw him off or send him tumbling to the foot of the staircase, but he forced them in his mind back into shape and he carried on. It was in his head, this place – that did not mean it was not real, but it did give him a presence that he did not have in the physical world. It depended on him to exist. As he changed, so it changed. As he became rigid and unyielding, so it was forced to keep its shape around him.

It was all in his head, but it was also in the aethyr. In the aethyr, these things were real. It was called by some the Realm of Chaos, a domain where all things might become real when sculpted by the right thought. There were parts of the world where the land merged with this realm, where the two worlds touched, and from there marched the armies of the Dark Gods.

If van Horstmann let go of his thoughts, this world would turn into madness beyond description, a boiling pit of impossibility that would scour his mind of everything that made it human. He had read the memoirs of those whose minds had been so touched, and been afraid that the madness would infect him. He had been to this place before in the recollections of the few who had gone there and come out capable of putting quill to parchment.

At the top of the staircase was the throne room. Where below had been an endless but imperceptible sky, here there was an enormous vault with ribs of stone, hung with enough billowing silk and embroidered banners to cover a continent. There, in its gargantuan throne, a heap of burning books the size of a mountain, was the Prince of Lies. The prince was an enormous fleshy mass, somewhat humanoid in shape but lacking a head. Its body was instead covered in faces: a thousand, a million of them, writhing in the pinkish skin in such clarity that van Horstmann could see the exact expression in every one. Every single manner of emotion was contained within it. On that throne sat the sum total of anything a human mind could feel.

Around the Prince of Lies gambolled a legion of a million daemons, all of them glistening knots of flesh and bone that reformed a hundred times a second. All forms of beauty and monstrous horror were there, any given second a dizzying gallery of shapes that did not fit properly into van Horstmann's mind. They were madness incarnate, the Court of Lies that danced a performance of the play in which all things that might come to pass were depicted.

Van Horstmann crushed down the incredulity that rose inside him. It wanted to blind and deafen him, to shut down the feel and smell and taste of the Prince of Lies. He did not let it. He had prepared for a long time for this moment. If ever he were to finish the road he had started to walk, he had to pass through here.

'So,' said the Prince of Lies, 'you kneel before us at last. It has been a long time a-coming, Egrimm van Horstmann.'

The prince's voice was not a voice at all, but van Horstmann's own thoughts, coalescing in his mind like invaders from another realm violating his consciousness. The effect of it made him want to recoil and reel his soul back into the Pyramid of Light, but he had mastered that cowardly part of him a long time ago.

'You are not Tzeentch,' said van Horstmann. 'If you were Tzeentch, I would be struck mad to look at you.'

'And how do you know you are not mad?' said the prince from a thousand mouths.

'You are His servant,' said van Horstmann. 'Perhaps an

aspect of Him. It does not matter. I know that He hears. And I have done as He asked.'

'I asked of you nothing,' replied the prince.

'I have destroyed sacred knowledge on His altar,' continued van Horstmann. 'I have given Him that sacrifice. That is what He asked of a hundred sorcerers who came before me. I have read their words. I know what they did, and what they sought. I seek it too.'

'And you are different from all of them,' said the Prince of Lies. 'You will not fail me. You understand what I ask. You can deliver my demands. You will not break in will or fall in battle. You are different from all the sorcerers who have knelt as you did, and died with their promises to me unfulfilled.'

'Yes,' said van Horstmann. 'I am different.'

'Well, well,' said the prince, and his voice was so heavy with sarcasm that van Horstmann was pushed face down to the floor. 'What a treat. A Light wizard by day, enemy of the daemon. And a daemonologist by night, fawning before the God of Change for His favours. How can this be contained in one man?'

'It was forged in hate,' said van Horstmann through gritted teeth. His blood was spattering from his lips onto the marble floor. Perhaps, back in Magister Vek's chamber, he really was spitting blood. 'Those two can exist together, devote themselves to Lord Tzeentch, if the hatred that binds them is strong enough. And it is. It is as strong as anything a man's mind has ever known.'

'And yet it is a mind too afraid to perceive the god it has chosen,' said the Prince of Lies. It rose from its throne, and whole kingdoms would have been swallowed in the stride it took. Landslides of burning books slid from its throne as it rose to its full height, catching on the silks and sending them smouldering into the air.

'You are… you are as Berthold Wormiaus depicted you,' gasped van Horstmann, even as his senses were assailed by the sight of the god striding towards him, 'in the Norscan Fragments. And as Lady Eiger wrote in her poetry. This is how my mind expected Tzeentch, so that is how this fragment of His will appears.'

'And will you see Tzeentch as He is?'

Van Horstmann, with an effort he felt would break his back, pushed himself up to his knees and looked the Prince of Lies in a pair of eyes on its chest. The expression of that face was smirking, despising, showing pity.

'I will,' said van Horstmann.

Van Horstmann had known it would come to this – that he would have to face the Prince of Lies on the Prince's terms, in a realm where he could control everything van Horstmann's senses perceived. And of course, once given access to everything in van Horstmann's head, there was only one form it could take.

The Court of Lies dissolved into a vast writhing pit. The God of Lies transformed into a mass of snakes, each one fouler than the last around which it knotted itself more obscenely.

Van Horstmann plunged into the pit, and though he had always known this moment would come, it did not keep the horror from overcoming his mind.

* * *

DOWN THERE IN the constricting darkness was a place he had revisited countless times. There had been period of his life when every time he slept, he went back there. Now he would find himself there when he was pushed towards the edges of mental endurance, or when some shock dragged him back there as if, in fleeing whatever trauma was present, he blundered through the door into the last place he ever wanted to be.

It was more real now than the memories had ever been – as real as the time that inspired them. The scales against his skin. The nothing beneath his feet, the awful certainty that below there was nothing but an eternity of snakes running down to the centre of the world.

The sound of them. The smell – they stank. The way he could barely draw breath. It was the same. It was not a memory. He was back there, for real, by every definition of reality that counted.

He reached out like a boy who could not swim groping through the water. His hands found only slabs of scaly muscle sliding past one another, trying to ensnare him in their loops to drag down and crush. Then a finger brushed against something else, something soft and shuddering.

It was another hand. It was slender as he caught it in his own. He felt the ring on its finger and he knew it was her.

The hand was warm. She was still alive.

He fought harder now, pistoning his legs up and down through the mass of snakes to power himself upwards. He thought he felt slightly cooler air on his face, as if he were near the surface. His hand was clamped around hers and he gasped down a foul breath, lungs screaming, as his head broke the surface.

'Lizbeta!' he gasped, the only sound he could make before he was under again.

The coils closed and he could not breath. A new and profound darkness fell.

WHEN VAN HORSTMANN woke he was alone. He could not see anything, and he felt only the sharp ground under his back where he lay. The shallow breaths he took were raw and painful in his throat. It was cold and quiet.

Lizbeta. He had said her name. It rarely got that bad. Usually he tore his mind out of the pit before she was there. But this time, he had not been in control.

A glimmer of light caught his eye overhead, like a single distant star reaching through a cloudy night sky. A faint pool of it gathered nearby, slow as treacle dripping from above. The polished scales that glinted in that light picked out the body of a thick and muscular snake, sidewinding its way towards van Horstmann.

The fear was not there in the same way. Van Horstmann could understand it was not real now, that this was not one of the snakes that had once wrapped its length around him and crushed out all his hope. The fear, this time, stemmed from the fact that the Prince of Lies had delved into his mind and pulled from it that moment, the time van Horstmann had protected so devoutly.

The snake arched up over van Horstmann. It spoke with the voice of the Prince of Lies.

'That,' it said, 'is how I truly am. Not a god that resides beyond, but one that lives inside you, and in the mind of all those who have given themselves to me. Do you understand now what I am?'

'Yes,' said van Horstmann, unable to muster anything more than a whisper.

'And you will still serve?'

'I will.' There was no hesitation. 'I will serve.'

'In return for what?'

'There is only one thing I want,' said van Horstmann. 'You know what it is.'

'I do. And I can give it to you.'

Van Horstmann swallowed, painfully. 'You can have whatever you want from the Light Order. Its vaults, its magisters, anything.'

'I know,' said the snake. 'But I am a god. I can take whatever I want from any ensorcelled vault in the world, and destroy it with a whim. What do I care if you offer up a pyre of books to me?'

'Because the one thing you cannot take is willing obedience,' replied van Horstmann. 'That must be given freely. And so it is the only thing that a god can crave, for it is the only thing that is beyond Him.'

'True,' said the snake, its forked tongue flickering. 'And indeed, I desire it. But you know full well what I really want.'

'You cannot have it,' said van Horstmann. 'I will no more pledge my soul to you than I would pledge it to Sigmar. That is my one rule. Anything else you want, you will have. But not my soul. And it is not much that I ask of you. Just a little information. Most of the path I have to take I have pieced together myself. I just need a few more points on the map and I will never require anything more of you.'

'I will have your soul, Egrimm van Horstmann.'

'No, Lord Tzeentch. You will not. That is the deal I will make. That is the contract I will sign. Everything short of my soul, for the knowledge I need to get what I want.'

The snake seemed to consider this. It was hooded, like a venomous snake from the deserts of Araby or the Southlands, and its eyes were like flecks of amber. Its tail flicked idly from side to side as it thought about the offer.

'That is satisfactory,' said the Prince of Lies, known to some as Tzeentch, the Changer of Ways, or by any one of a thousand names. 'It will be signed.'

Van Horstmann closed his eyes and let out the breath he realised now he had been holding. 'Then tell me,' he said. 'Everything I must know. Tell me.'

'I impart this knowledge only because it suits me that you shall have your revenge,' said the Prince of Lies. 'All that happens will be because I will it. You must never forget that, Egrimm van Horstmann.'

'I know the terms of a deal made with you,' said van Horstmann.

'Then listen.'

Van Horstmann would never be able to say afterwards just how long he lay there, listening to the snake's words. It was quite possible they were imparted in an instant but that the effort needed to process them in his mind meant it felt like hours. Or perhaps it really was hours, in the way that time can stretch and be manipulated inside the mind.

Some of what he learned van Horstmann thought he knew already, but he was now free of doubts that might have turned his hand away from what needed to be done. Some of it was completely unknown. Some helped van Horstmann make the choice between two paths which had previously seemed equally profitable or perilous. And a great deal of it seemed irrelevant, but was filed away by van Horstmann in the fastidious library of his memory, knowing that it would be important one day.

There was always more, the Prince of Lies promised. Everything van Horstmann would ever need to know to destroy his enemies. He could have anything he wanted. He could rule. He could create his own kingdom out of the aethyr, a place founded on magic in which his will would become manifest and he could reign as a god. But the price was too high. It was always the same – van Horstmann's soul, the means by which he could determine his own future. And he would not give that up.

Plenty had, of course. Every other tome that van Horstmann had discovered, hidden in a remote cairn or in the forbidden library of some debauched noble, was the record of some poor fool who had sold his soul to the Dark Gods. They always regretted it. The same parable was written a thousand times, of those who thought there existed in the world something that was worth their freedom over themselves. But there never was. Van Horstmann would not be like them. He might not finish on his path. He might die, be destroyed, be found out and dismembered before a baying crowd on an executioner's platform. But he would take his soul with him when he died.

Finally, the Prince of Lies was finished. The pact had been struck and its parties had agreed the terms. The means for revenge, in return for anything van Horstmann could tear from the heart of the Light Order. The snake vanished, the darkness shattered, and van Horstmann came to lying on the floor of his quarters in the pyramid.

Bitter smoke still hung in the air. Van Horstmann must have thrashed around a little on the floor, because some of Magister Vek's trinkets were scattered around him and he had battered his elbows and knees raw.

The Skull of Katam seemed to look down at him from the desk with an expression of amusement.

'It was like watching a child with nightmares,' said the skull. 'Like a kittling-cat yowling for its mother.'

Van Horstmann stood up, dizzy for a moment as the blood drained from his head. He steadied himself against the desk, which was now inscribed deeply with the symbol of Tzeentch. He would have to find a way to hide it, he thought. He would have to hide a great many things.

He felt a burning pain on the back of his right hand, reaching up over his wrist and forearm. He pulled back the sleeve of his robe to see the words burning into his skin. Unlike the contract on his torso, this one was burned from the inside out, scorched onto the inside of his skin by tendrils of power reaching through from the aethyr.

The words were in one of the tongues of the aethyr, a lyrical language with meanings that shifted with the moods of the reader, and one that van Horstmann had learned early in his pursuit of the daemonology. The last line had the mark of Tzeentch, similar to the one van Horstmann had carved into the desk, while another had the signature of van Horstmann himself. The finished contract covered the back of his hand and wound halfway to his elbow.

Van Horstmann gingerly flexed his fingers. They stung, but the pain was bearable. He went to the bedchamber and found one of Vek's robes which had a black trim, perhaps for wearing at the funeral rites of fellow magister. He tore off the strip of black hem and wound it around his afflicted hand, covering the contract and binding it tight.

'Then it is done,' said the Skull of Katam.

'It is done,' said van Horstmann.

'It is as I said,' continued the skull. 'He will listen, if what you have to offer is valuable enough. The Light Order's treasures, they got His attention, did they not?'

'They did.'

'Then what next?'

'I must think on it,' said van Horstmann. 'You have done for me all I asked.'

'But of course.' The skull's grin seemed to widen. 'We are on the same side.'

Van Horstmann sat on the chair beside the desk. He was aware now of how weary he was. Though the gruelling ascent and the pit had been in his mind, his body had echoed his movements to the extent that his robes were damp with sweat and every joint ached. He ran a hand over his face and felt his scalp beaded with sweat. His throat was raw too, and he wondered if he had shouted while unconscious.

'It seems,' the skull was saying, 'that you should have results from Vries's cipher to dangle before the Grand Magister if he is not to become suspicious.'

'I broke the cipher half a season ago,' said van Horstmann. 'The vocabulary is in the number of petals, the grammar in the number of leaves. Vries didn't even use a sub-cipher, the text is written there plain.'

'Then the path continues?'

'It continues.' Van Horstmann looked at the jewelled skull. Of course he could not trust the thing. If there was one certainty he had learned from his research, that was it. But it had its uses. It had known how to contact the Prince of Lies – an actual audience, not just a dream-message or strange portent but an actual conversation with the god. Or an aspect of the god, or a servant, or a part of his own mind infected by the god's will. An audience, nonetheless, and without the skull that would not have happened. But trust?

Van Horstmann wondered whether he was even capable of trust any more. But then, what was trust? If he had lost it forever, he doubted that he would miss it.

PART TWO

CHAPTER SEVEN
SHALLYA WEPT

WHEN KATAM WAS young, he saw death.

His home town, a place of isolated and fearful people before Sigmar's conquest, was visited by a terrible plague that ripped through everyone Katam loved. That is, the majority of the stories have it so. A plague, perhaps, is useful shorthand for all the many varieties of death that might have afflicted the young Katam. In other variations, goblins attack his home, or roving bandits, or a natural disaster like a flood or a storm. Sometimes, everyone simply dies.

Katam is typically a child during these events. Perhaps he really was. Priests and parablists who told the story certainly saw the impact of that image – a child, alone and afraid, wandering through his home which was now scattered with the corpses of his loved ones.

Katam had seen death. He had escaped it in a physical

sense only. He knew now that everything he had been told was a lie. There were no benevolent spirits or gods who helped determine his future. Being good, avoiding sin and helping the needy did nothing to stave off death. There was no moral currency that could buy extra days of life. There was not even a predetermined date of death, no lot of time which everyone was given at birth to fill as best they could. Death was cold and random, and cruel. In the face of death, everyone was infinitely helpless.

Katam decided that he would not die.

While every story differed, they all came to this point. The young Katam renounced the human vulnerability to death. He refused to obey it, to die when it decided. Most versions simply state that he made this decision. Some have him howl his promise over the bodies of his parents or from a storm-lashed mountaintop or other suitably dramatic location. Many record his exact words, which are of course different in every iteration. But they all agree he made his decision. Katam would not die. He would discover how to foil death, and he would become immortal.

The rest of the story is very short in essence but that did not stop the chroniclers from adding as much as they could about Katam's adventures. In the pursuit of his goal this young nobody bloomed into a practitioner of magic, an explorer, adventurer and warrior. He also became irredeemably tainted by his drive for immortality. He did terrible things. He killed, and tortured. He destroyed. Some chroniclers glossed over this, putting his deeds vaguely so as to avoid sensational-ising the tale which was, after all, a moral parable. Others described every foul thing attributed to Katam and added some of their own, treating the canon of Katam's sins like a cultural repository of broken taboos and gruesome legends looking for a home.

It was these tales that had attracted van Horstmann to the legend of Katam, for at the time he discovered Katam's story he was himself on a similar search. He too had travelled much of the breadth of the Empire and its surrounding lands. Katam was said to have travelled the Dark Lands, to the fringes of Cathay and across the oceans to Naggaroth and the jungles of Lustria, but van Horstmann did not believe that. It was unnecessary. There were plenty of evil little corners to be unearthed in the mundane lands of men. One did not need to circumnavigate the globe to find them.

Van Horstmann had, however, done things that echoed Katam's adventures. He had not been so bloodthirsty or wanton as Katam, mainly because doing so served no purpose and carried the risk of being caught, but it was a man very like van Horstmann who is said to have descended a staircase of six thousand steps into a lightless cavern, where great pale things lived below the surface of a lake and told fortunes in exchange for pairs of lovers thrown into the deep.

Katam's failures were left out but surely he had some. Van Horstmann's own experiences were proof enough of that. He had once bargained for a priceless dragonhide tome in the basement of a gambling den in Couronne, only to find it was gibberish written on horse leather. Surely Katam had swindled his way into possessing some fake prayer tablets, or had his time wasted by a prophecy-spouting charlatan.

Eventually Katam had found what he wanted. He learned how to speak with the Dark Gods. Such gods were not to be spoken of by name and were referred to by euphemism or metaphor: the Throne of Skulls, the Prince of Lies, Grandfather, the Gentle One, the Warlord, the Smiling King. No one knew how many they were or who had first started to worship them. They had no church, just isolated obsessives who sometimes infected others with their fervour to start a cult. The only things anyone could agree on was that they were real, that they were evil, and that they either needed or loved to have mortals do their will in this world.

Katam wanted to live forever. He told the Prince of Lies this. The Prince of Lies replied that he wanted Katam's soul. Katam would exist forever, but the Prince of Lies could call upon him at any time to serve in whatever way the god wished. It was a terrible price, but immortality was a wondrous prize.

Katam was without fear, and cunning beyond measure as a result of his search for eternal life. He agreed to the deal, knowing that the Dark Gods are fickle and capricious, and even slavery to the will of the Prince of Lies would last only as long as it amused the Prince to give him orders. It was far from perfect, but Katam had finally found what he was seeking and the conditions of the pact did not dissuade him.

The words of the contract appeared on the side of a mountain – or a mighty reef below the sea, or written in the stars, or scorched into Katam's skin – and Katam put his name to it beside the symbol of the Prince of Lies.

The Prince of Lies, for once, had not lied. Every detail of the contract was honoured. The contract failed to mention, however, just how much of Katam would be alive. To be alive, one only needed one's mind. The rest of his flesh and bone could perish and crumble, and the conditions of life, as the contract encompassed it, would still be fulfilled.

So Katam went about the world, using his knowledge to seek out greater magical power. He developed the idea that if he learned enough – as he surely would with an infinite lifespan – he could find some loophole or magical spell that would free him from the contract with the Prince of Lies and let him keep eternal life. He gave little attention at first to the fact that he still aged, and even as his skin wrinkled and his hair thinned he reasoned it would take little magical learning to reverse the physical symptoms of age. He could become a young man when it suited him.

Then his heart stopped and he ceased breathing. His body did not respond any more. One of his minions assumed him dead and had him buried in the place he had first sworn never to die. But Katam was alive, and awake.

A flood opened up his grave. His bones were gnawed upon by animals. A child found his skull and sold it for a handful of copper coins to a travelling hawker of fake medicines, who in turn sold it on to a student of anatomy. It was lost and found, purchased and stolen, Katam all the while seeking a way to take control of his fate again. He tried speaking to those into whose hands he fell. Some threw him away in terror, some thought him a symptom of madness. One covered him in gemstones and set him on an altar. He was evidence in witchcraft trials and a collector's item for the idle rich who loved to shock one another with their transgressions.

He told his owners how to speak with the Dark Gods. Some of them did, and were consumed or driven insane. Some did not listen. Katam could not get the attention of the god he had sworn his soul to.

He did not die, at least. Sealed in his skull, spending years in meditation on the pact he had entered, he would have gone mad if he had not abandoned sanity some time before.

Tales spread of a magical skull that knew the secrets of the Dark Gods. People killed one another over its ownership. They bargained away everything they had for a lead on its location. A heretic bought the skull at enormous cost to serve as the centrepiece of the cult he would use to acquire wealth, power and unearthly pleasures. His estate in Altdorf was raided by witch hunters under Imperial orders. The heretic's entrails were scattered across the grounds and the estate burned to the ground. From the ashes the Skull of Katam was found and handed over to the Light College, who could be trusted to keep safe this object that seemed immune to all efforts to destroy it.

The wizards of the Light Order knew only the name of the artefact, and the hazy rumours about how it spoke and knew the future. Everyone who knew what it really was had been quartered or burned alive by the Emperor's witch hunters. But the traces of the truth were left behind in the journals and treatises of madmen, the notes of heretic summoners and the dark philosophies of those who had thought too deeply about the Dark Gods and their realm. In fragments, they told the whole story of the Skull of Katam and the man who still lived inside it.

It took someone like van Horstmann to discover the story of Katam. Zeal, and the willingness to delve into forbidden places to find the fragments of the tale, was not enough on its own. It required an organised mind to extract each piece of the story and assemble it into one, to pare away the lies and guesswork. It took van Horstmann to realise that he needed to speak with the Prince of Lies, and that to do so, he needed the Skull of Katam.

There were so many pieces that had to fall into place. Van Horstmann could only carry on through the certainty that none of them were up to chance. He had control of them all. He had never written it all down, because then he might be discovered – it was arranged in his mind, the building blocks of his fortress, all his plans and certainties spanning between them.

This was his revenge. He had built it in every detail. The greater part of his task was done. His pact with the Prince of Lies had been the final part of the groundwork to be laid, the final strings of theory tied into place. Everything that followed would happen of its own course, with just a tending hand from van Horstmann to see it through.

He already had what he wanted. It would fall into his hands like the Skull of Katam had.

It was just a matter of time.

VAN HORSTMANN COULD usually be found in the pyramid's grand reading room.

That afternoon was a quiet one. Many of the Light Order were at a conclave of magisters from across the Colleges of

Magic, part of the Teclian Pact which demanded each college send representatives every five years. It kept the colleges, if not of united purpose, at least aware of one another and of their diplomatic obligations, and without such clauses in the pact the magisters would, as was their nature, become insular and obsessive without giving magisters of another order a passing thought.

Van Horstmann was insular and obsessive. He sat, as he did on so many days, on a throne brought by some past explorer from the Southlands, carved from black stone in the likeness of antelope horns. With a wave of his hand he took books from the towering bookcases surrounding the circular chamber, and added them to the twenty-high stacks that surrounded him. Most had covers inked in silver and gold, which winked in the light that drenched the reading room as it did every other corner of the pyramid. Here it shone from waterfalls of glowing water that fell from the dome high above, plunging down into the fountain surrounding a statue of Loremaster Teclis himself. Van Horstmann only had to glance up and he would be looking into the face of the high elf who had taught his people's way of magic to men, and founded the Colleges of Magic to help them learn.

Van Horstmann made a gesture and one of the books hovered in front of him, cover opening. The sound of pages flipping by merged with the gurgle from the waterfall of light.

'Light of lore, aethyr's heart, give my eyes the speed of my thoughts.'

The phrase focused his mind, and let him unravel the spell contained there. It was a spell he had researched and created himself, and under its effects van Horstmann could read as quickly as the words could pass his eyes. A minor thing, below the notice of many magister researchers, but van Horstmann had made much of its usefulness.

Then pages flipped past. This book was one of a series of several dozen documenting the legends of the northern Empire. Every other tale was about crazed Norsemen sailing across the Sea of Claws to pillage and despoil. But there were fragments. A name here, a stock phrase there.

Someone else had entered the reading room. Van Horstmann focused one part of his mind on the book, the other on the newcomer, because a faint recognition had fired off in his mind.

'Heiden Kant,' said van Horstmann as the other figure drew close. Framed in the waterfall, Kant looked just as young as van Horstmann remembered. Which was odd, because the last time van Horstmann had seen Kant was at the investiture of Eckhardt III, and that had been twelve years ago. Kant had an unruly mess of dark, curly hair, a long nose and bowed mouth like some fanciful portrait of a well-born boy. As an acolyte he had looked at home. On the battlefield, or in a debate on magical dogma with a dozen magisters, he would look like a lost choirboy.

'My greetings, Comprehender van Horstmann,' replied Kant. 'I trust that I do not disturb your studies too gravely.'

Van Horstmann had only recently been granted the title of comprehender. It was one rarely used, and had first been given to a member of the Fourth Circle who had specific responsibility for written works not in traditional form: tapestries,

inscribed tablets, preserved tattoos and other apocrypha. It
had been given to recognise van Horstmann's completion of
the *Cryptothaumaturgia*, the total of Egelbert Vries's hidden
writings. It was also an unofficial recognition of the fact that
he was of a senior rank to the other magisters, without giving
him a specific role within the order such as Master Chanter or
Lord of Ceremonies.

'Children have studies,' said van Horstmann. 'I have a
calling.'

'Of course, comprehender,' said Kant. Van Horstmann
found himself thinking of Kant as a boy, even though Kant
had joined as an acolyte at around the same time as van Horstmann himself. Kant might even have been the older of the two.

'But no, I am not disturbed.' Van Horstmann let the book
drift back down, like a falling leaf, to the top of its pile. 'I seek
fragments, as ever. There was a story written long ago and
then shattered into a million pieces, and if we are ever to read
it again we must find every piece. They came to rest here, in
these poems and fairy tales. Perhaps it is a compulsion that I
pursue.' He smiled, because he had filed away, along with so
much other information, the necessary expressions and plati-
tudes to be employed when having a conversation.

'We all have our callings,' said Kant. 'I seek the path of
the exorcist. They tell me it is the longest of all. That many
of us, maybe most, never reach the stage where we can trust
ourselves to cast out the daemon. And that it is the most
dangerous. Even the strongest can lose his soul. But I walk it
anyway. I think it must have been compulsion that made us
walk into this pyramid in the first place.'

Van Horstmann indicated the books piled around him. 'Thousands of years ago,' he said, 'something happened in the far north of the Empire, near the shore of the Sea of Claws. Perhaps on the edge of the Kislevite steppe. It left its scars in folk songs and legends, but nowhere is it attested in its entirety. Something fell from the sky, perhaps, or a great magic was wrought. I do not know yet, but I can feel it building up, piece by piece in my mind. Perhaps eventually there will be enough to sponsor an expedition to find what traces of it remain in the earth. Or perhaps it will never be found, and it will always be that maddeningly final step away. It would not be the first. Knowledge degrades such that without diligent custodians it will corrode until it is useless. A sad state. A tragedy. When I think of what has been lost, I feel the need to claw back what I can. Compulsion, as you say, without a doubt.'

'I came here,' said Kant, 'to speak of you about the *Codex*.'

'The *Codex*?'

'The *Codex Aethyrica*,' said Kant. 'I understand it discourses at length about the link between the mind and the aethyr, through which it can be vulnerable. I have spoken with my fellow magisters and they agree that it would be most profitable for me to study it. The last one to do so, I understand, was you, comprehender, and the Fourth Circle would be much more likely to release it for study with your endorsement.'

The *Codex Aethyrica* currently held in the upper vault was just the cover, which had been undamaged by the sacrifice of its pages. That cover held a collection of samples, errors and unclaimed manuscripts purchased from the illuminators of the Buchbinder District and carefully trimmed to give the *Codex* the appearance of being complete. The book had remained locked and undisturbed on its podium in the vault since van Horstmann had returned it to the magisters of the Fourth Circle and it suited him very much for it to stay that way.

'I have studied the *Codex*, it is true,' said van Horstmann, 'and it would have no application to the study of exorcism. Exorcism is a practical art, and the *Codex* is theoretical to the point of wilful obscurity on matters pertaining to the interaction of the aethyric world with ours.'

'Nevertheless...' began Kant.

'Any magister must curry good will with the Fourth Circle,' continued van Horstmann. 'It would earn me no good will to insist on their releasing the *Codex* for such an inappropriate area of study, even if I alone had the power to sway them. I suggest you locate the ninth volume of the *Historiae Prodigium* instead. It lies in this very reading room, though it may take some time to find it.'

'I am familiar with that volume,' said Kant. 'If the *Codex* really is out of my reach for now, perhaps...'

Kant's sentence broke off as the whole pyramid shuddered. Books fell from the shelves, smacking into the floor around the two magisters. The waterfall splashed liquid light across the statue of Teclis and the whole structure groaned as if under a great weight. Both magisters looked around them in shock at the interruption. The pile of books beside van Horstmann toppled and scattered its volumes across the floor.

'Was that an earthquake?' said Kant.

'Sigmar's oath!' swore van Horstmann. 'No, not an earthquake. The fold in space would keep us safe from such. It was something else, heavens know what.'

Magisters were running through the passageway outside the reading room. One leaned in through the doorway.

'An attack!' he said. 'It must be an attack!'

It was rare that the whole body of the Light Order's magisters were moved to act as one. It was easy to forget, with so many of them meditating or studying alone at any one time, the number of them that lived and worked in the pyramid. White-robed figures streamed down the main staircase that lead into the Chanter's Hall, where the acolytes stood in confusion. They joined the general motion out of the pyramid, for whatever had happened its full effects could probably only be appreciated from outside.

Van Horstmann saw Elrisse and Alric among the magisters, fending off questions about what had just happened. The chatter indicated that the magisters engaged in divination magic at the time had felt a great surge of magic, something malevolent and powerful, and had barely had time to wonder what it was when the tremor occurred. A few said the upper floors were damaged, and stewards were heading upwards to prevent what further damage they could.

Outside, on the square surrounding the pyramid, the magisters and acolytes gathered to stare up at the pyramid's pinnacle. Every neck was craned to see it. Even seasoned magisters pointed up in confusion. Van Horstmann joined them, peering up towards the pyramid's upper floors.

'By Manann's bones,' said Kant. 'What is it?'

It was a lightning bolt. Not an actual bolt from the heavens, but a jagged symbol that could only represent lightning. It was gold, and perhaps fifty feet long. It speared the pyramid through its pinnacle, and the smouldering rubble that had spilled down the pyramid's sides showed the force with which it must have hit.

Van Horstmann moved through the crowd to find Elrisse. The Grand Magister was surrounded by the senior wizards of the order, as if they were seeking protection from the aura of his authority.

'Grand Magister,' said van Horstmann. 'What can this mean?'

'I fear to say it,' said Elrisse.

'Can it be anyone else?' said van Horstmann. 'Who else would do this, and in this way? Who else wants the Light Order humiliated?'

'It is too early to say that, comprehender,' said Elrisse.

'Out loud, perhaps. But you are as certain as I. The Gold Order–'

'The Gold Order are no more suspects than anyone else,' said Elrisse. 'I will not have our diplomatic status jeopardised by jumping to conclusions. We are not children. We must investigate.'

'Word will get out.'

'Then it will get out via us, the senior magisters of this order.' said Elrisse.

Burning ash floated down to the square. The crowd was buzzing now, each voice murmuring suspicions about who could have brought the enormous metal lightning bolt down from the heavens in such a spectacular insult. A fire had started in the pinnacle somewhere. There could be found the chambers of the most esteemed magisters, including those of Elrisse himself. Perhaps that, too, had been a deliberate consequence of the attack, another barb to the insult.

'We must move quickly,' continued Elrisse. 'Van Horstmann, Kardiggian, Vranas. When it is safe, examine that… that thing and find out what you can. Assume nothing. Alric and I will answer the questions of our fellow colleges, for they will surely come. They will have felt this happen.'

'It must be an enemy from within the colleges,' said another of the senior magisters. Van Horstmann knew the man, Horst, by reputation, as a fastidious leader of the most complicated Light Order ceremonies. 'It has to be. There are few enough who even know we are here.'

'Then that,' said Elrisse, raising a cautioning hand, 'is what you will find, if it is the truth. If it is not, then you cannot let your prejudices determine your conclusions. Unfounded speculation is ill-fitting for magisters of our order. Let the shadowmages chatter and the Bright wizards fly to anger, we do not.'

Van Horstmann looked up again at the lightning bolt. It could scarcely have been a more carefully calculated insult: striking from above, a position of superiority, penetrating the pyramid in a show of symbolic violation, bringing confusion and chaos to the serenity the Light Order cultivated.

'You have my word,' said van Horstmann. 'You will know the truth.'

* * *

THE QUALITIES OF Elrisse as Grand Magister had been the subject of some debate at his first appointment, almost thirty
years before, and in truth the debate had never died. He was
not a mighty battle magister who could hurl bolts of fiery
death down at the Emperor's enemies, as had at one time
been a prerequisite for heading a college of Altdorf. Few
denied, however, that he was a more than competent diplomat, and at times like these there were few more precious
skills than the ability to speak with those who did not want
to speak with him.

A mission was arranged. Grand Magister Zhaan agreed
that the whole distasteful business should be put aside and
brotherhood between the Light and Gold Orders should
blossom again. Zhaan maintained that the lightning bolt
could not have been sent by a Gold wizard, and was surely
the result of some accident in the experiments and studies of
the Light Order, but it was clear he said this solely to be seen
backing up his own order. Van Horstmann lead the investiga-
tion into the attack itself and concluded that the bolt showed
every sign of having been created in the forges of the Gold
College, animated with the Lore of Metal and cast down in
such a way as to present the maximum injury to the pride of
the Light Order and the maximum glee of the Gold.

The two colleges were isolated from one another. At infor-
mal gatherings of wizards in Altdorf, such as those to present
advice and soothsaying to the Imperial Court, either Light
or Gold, or both, were absent. Groups of newly-appointed
magisters in both colleges spoke of retribution or escalation,
to protect the honour and reputation of their order. The more

experienced wizards spoke darkly of the Great Fire of Altdorf, widely blamed on the Bright Order's fire magic, which might equally have been a ploy by some enemy in another college to blacken the Bright Order's reputation. If it was not stopped, the conflict could grow to just such a scale where Altdorf itself was at peril.

And then there was the Emperor. If the Imperial Court had to step in to quell a dispute between the colleges, which always presented themselves as unified, then Altdorf's wizards would lose all the trust they had so far built up with Eckhardt III. And Eckhardt III was proving a petty and capricious ruler. If he decided the Colleges of Magic could not be trusted, he might cast them out, strip them of their properties and prohibit their studies entirely. Eckhardt III might just be stupid enough to make such a decision. The conflict had to end.

And so Grand Magister Elrisse led a delegation of his most trusted magisters to the Temple of Shallya, nestled near the northern edge of Altdorf. Once it had stood apart from the city, a building of pale marble and slender columns, imparted with a feminine grace to match that of the goddess herself. She was the patron of healers, childbirth, mercy and grief, and always argued for peace and harmony. She had been perhaps the god most worshipped in the lands of men before Sigmar's deification, and even now there were plenty of places in the Empire where her temples and shrines saw more traffic than those of Sigmar.

Van Horstmann had never seen the place before. It was clear the temple had once been beautiful. Even when the cramped streets and haphazard buildings of Altdorf had crowded around the temple, it had stayed beautiful. But it had suffered greatly since then. Columns were toppled and a good third of the roof was still missing, patched up with wood where it had fallen in. Parts of it were scorched, including the pediment sculpture of Shallya herself. She was a matronly figure with long hair, her face turned away, children and the sorrowful kneeling around her.

'I do not believe,' Elrisse was saying as the delegation turned onto the street on which the temple stood, 'that the temple will ever be fully repaired. It is a testament, I think, to intolerance and its dangers. That message would be lost if it were to be pristine again.'

'Grand Theogonist Thoss certainly left his mark,' said van Horstmann.

'Not the one he would have desired,' said Elrisse. 'He wanted all gods but Sigmar obliterated. For some magisters that was in living memory. A terrible time, by what they say of it. But now the temple affects those who see her more than it ever did when it was pristine. Shallya has received many more feet through the doors of her temple now it echoes the sorrows she heals.'

'So when we act in anger, we are as likely to help those we hate as destroy them.'

'Quite so,' said Elrisse.

The delegation was a dozen strong. Elrisse, van Horstmann, Alric and a handful of others had been selected to represent the Light Order. A similar number of Gold wizards would be waiting for them in the temple, which had been chosen as both neutral ground and a holy place where peace was supposed to reign. The Light wizards passed through the grand silver doors, depicting the goddess with her head in her hands, weeping over a host of graves and battlefields.

Altdorf's priestess of Shallya was named Mother Heloise, and van Horstmann knew of her reputation. She ministered to the mad, using the blessings of Shallya to cure their minds, and was thought to be the most successful priestess at such ministrations in all the Empire. She echoed the image of Shallya herself, well-built and stout, with the long hair her priestesses all wore. She wore the white and green of her church, was ritually blindfolded and stood at the altar at one end of the temple.

The Gold wizards were already in place, sitting in the pews along one side of the nave. Grand Magister Zhaan sat at the front, his mane of bronze-coloured hair catching the shafts of light that fell through the temple's damaged roof. Van Horstmann recognised another among their number – Daegal, the young Gold wizard he had held a heated discussion with at the Gold College. That was the moment van Horstmann had learned of the philosophical differences between the colleges, which had led, one way or another, to this meeting.

The Light wizards filed in and took their pews. Van Horstmann sat a couple of rows behind Elrisse, who naturally took the frontmost pew.

'Brothers in sorrow,' began Mother Heloise, 'our hearts have been cleft by the cruelty that is anger. Peace has fled, driven away by hate. It is the wish of Shallya that peace should return, and the wish of her church that I assist you in ending your quarrel. Though there may be differences between you, let them be celebrated, and not used as the foundation of anger. For anger has no foundation, it will crumble and bring us down with it as it falls, and all will be ruin and misery. Only on peace can we build. Grand Magister Elrisse, Shallya bids you speak.'

Elrisse stood before the altar. He looked at home in this place, for both he and the church had a similar air of age and respectability. He steadied himself on his staff and cleared his throat.

'This is not the first time,' he said, 'that two Colleges of Magic have come into conflict. Loremaster Teclis him-self knew that such things would come to pass, and he left instructions that we arbitrate our differences not as men, nor even as high citizens of the Empire, but as beings of learn-ing. We are scholars, and if wealth is our knowledge we are wealthy indeed. Every line of that knowledge teaches us that no good will come of our current conflict, only destruction. We both have much to lose and nothing to gain. The Light Order extends its hand to the Gold. Let hostilities end.'

Zhaal stood now. Compared to Elrisse he was a mighty figure of a man. If anything he looked more powerful and muscular than when van Horstmann had encountered him in the halls of the Gold College. 'The Gold Order, too, desires peace,' he said. 'But it cannot merely be spoken into existence. To take the extended hand, without condition or question, would be to deny that there is any source of quarrel between us. And there is, Grand Magister Elrisse. You and everyone here know well there is legitimate cause.'

'A cause?' said Elrisse. 'That can be put behind us, can it not?'

'No, it cannot,' replied Zhaal. 'Not when accusations fly between all the colleges. We are the subject of foul and unfounded rumours. They say that we orchestrated an attack on the Light Pyramid. That we are petty and scornful enough to place our mark on it through violence! If we simply cease hostilities then that accusation will always hang over us. We must have confirmation in the firmest terms that the Gold Order did no ill, before this can end.'

'And yes,' said Elrisse, 'some ill was done, by someone. And we know not by whom. Nor can we rule anyone out as guilty, including the Gold Order. We are willing to let all of this flow by like the waters of the Reik, into and beyond memory.'

'On your terms,' said Zhaal. 'With the Light Order having painted themselves as forgiving and pure, and the Gold Order as the villains with their crime unpunished. No, Grand Master Elrisse. The Gold Order did not commit the outrage that you say began this feud. Our innocence will be acknowledged. Anything less and we will not leave this place with any agreement.'

His words were underscored with murmurs of agreement from the Gold magisters. Grand Master Elrisse did not show any concern outwardly, but van Horstmann knew he was good at hiding it. This was supposed to be a mere formality, with both sides in agreement.

The Gold Order were insulted too. Because they were accused, and yet they were innocent. They felt themselves as wronged as any of the Light magisters who had witnessed the golden lightning bolt spearing the pyramid.

'We come here with arms open!' said Magister Kardiggian, standing up from his pew. 'We were insulted – no, I say we were attacked! You should be begging us for forgiveness, Zhaal!'

'Forgiveness for what?' demanded Zhaal.

'For the act of shameless aggression of which everyone here knows you are guilty!'

Voices were raised and magisters on both sides stood in anger. Daegal was among them, pointing a finger at Kardiggian. 'You would not say that,' he barked, 'were you not with a dozen of your fellows!'

'Brethren!' called out Mother Heloise. 'Anger corrodes and destroys. This is a place sacred to the goddess of peace. She weeps to hear your sorrow.'

'And Sigmar weeps to hear the men of His Empire acting like whipped curs, when we are innocent!' came the reply from a Gold wizard.

Van Horstmann carried with him, as he usually did outside the pyramid, his mask-topped staff and the Skull of Katam. These were both powerful symbols of a magister's rank, artefacts entrusted to him by his order. But he carried one artefact which he did not display so openly – Magister Vek's puzzle box, nestled safely in the sleeve of his robe. He had practised opening and closing it swiftly and invisibly, earning much vitriol from Hiskernaath in the process.

His fingers danced across its mechanisms now. He felt the box opening up in his hand.

'You have your orders,' said van Horstmann softly, knowing his words would not be heard over the shouting match gaining momentum around him. 'Remember who rules you. Remember who owns you. Do not let me down.'

Hiskernaath slithered out of its prison. Its rippled along the floor, unseen, feeling like a chill draught at shin level.

Van Horstmann knew the path that Hiskernaath would take. He had prepared exhaustively for this moment, formulating his orders to the daemon to ensure there were no loopholes it could exploit. He knew that it would scuttle unseen along the floor of the Temple of Shallya, straight towards Magister Daegal.

Van Horstmann had chosen Daegal for a number of reasons. Possession was most potent when it amplified the natural tendencies of the subject, and Daegal's aggression and quickness to anger would serve van Horstmann well. Given his character, he would be a logical culprit to spark what followed. And then there was the fact that van Horstmann simply did not like Magister Daegal.

Daegal's expression changed when the daemon forced its way into his soul. Hiskernaath craved the wearing of flesh, denied to it for years since he had been driven out of Princess Astrid. It hungrily shredded Daegal's defences, already lowered by anger and frustration. The daemon's pent-up strength blasted a channel through Daegal's soul and opened up the vulnerable heartlands of his mind for invasion.

Daegal raised a hand. Molten gold dripped off it, as if Daegal's hand was melting in one of the Gold Order's forges. It hissed and spat where it hit the stone floor, and only a few of the magisters around him realised what he was about to do. They were too slow to stop him.

Bolts of molten gold spat from Daegal's fingers, as swift and deadly as bullets from a musket. They slammed into one of the Light magisters – van Horstmann knew him as Magister Parsifal, an elderly wizard who had once sought training as a battle magister but ended up a researcher and ritualist.

The bolts punched into his chest and out through his back. Gobbets of molten metal spiralled through him and tore his chest open. Sizzling blood spattered the magisters beside him. Parsifal cried out, a long, rattling wail, and fell backwards over the pew.

'Murder! Murder!' someone yelled.

Daegal swung both hands in an arc. Gobbets of molten metal sprayed in every direction, burning and boring into flesh. Mother Heloise screamed as a bolt burned through her shoulder, and she fell back against Shallya's altar.

Confusion was everywhere. 'Protect Elrisse!' yelled van Horstmann, jumping the pew in front of him.

Already lances of white fire were spitting across the temple nave, met by burning sprays of molten gold. Grand Magister Zhaal conjured a golden shield in front of him and Magister Kardiggian, hands raised, was bathed in a column of white light as pale flames wreathed his arms.

Van Horstmann's words forced the Light magisters into action. Gold magisters rallied around Daegal, assuming he had began casting in response to an aggressive move from the Light wizards. Some yelled for peace, but they were drowned out.

A circle of white fire burst up from the floor. Golden bolts shattered against it. Zhaal turned a white fireball aside with his shield and in response, drew the outline of a golden scimitar in the air with his free hand. The weapon solidified and he grabbed its hilt, blue-hot flame rippling up and down its blade.

Kardiggian hurled balls of fire in every direction. Gold wizards were thrown to the floor or sent stumbling, their robes on fire. A spike of gold shot up from the floor, impaling a Light wizard through the thigh. One of the Gold wizards bundled Mother Heloise to the floor, trying to drag her to safety behind the altar. Another stood screaming, alight from head to toe, his beard coiling up into black ash.

Van Horstmann broke from the safety of the cirlcle. The Gold wizards were splitting up, sending bolts of gold or magical light as they ran. A shower of razor-sharp icy crystals hammered into the pews around him and van Horstmann felt slashes of pain along one arm and leg. He jumped a pew and ran.

In the midst of the chaos stood Daegal. Van Horstmann could see the greenish fire around his eyes that signalled Hiskernaath was inside him. Daegal's own mind would be fighting back, crushed into imprisonment within his own skull, forced to watch through his eyes as he continued the slaughter he had begun. Daegal, being a magister and one whose mind had been well trained, would probably win out eventually. That would make Daegal a witness.

Van Horstmann's hands described a sphere of white light. He had meditated much in the last few days to ensure the fortress in his mind was well stocked. A simple thought plucked a shining gem from its stores and shattered it, sending a torrent straight from the aethyr through his hands. He unleashed the flame and it shot in a jet into Daegal's chest, throwing the Gold wizard clean off his feet and through the screen that separated the nave off from one of the temple's side chapels.

Van Horstmann gasped in a breath. It was ice cold. Channelling too much power had its own dangers. But he could take it. He had to.

He ran after Daegal. Jumping through the wreckage of the screen, he saw the side chapel was dark, a place for contemplation. Prayer cushions were scattered around a statue of an old woman, bent and wrinkled – van Horstmann knew this was Shallya in her role as the Crone, who at the end of every autumn watched over the withering of crops after the harvest to make room for the spring's new growth.

Daegal was sprawled at the base of the statue. Blood ran from his head. Beneath him were the remains of the screen's tapestry. A stray bolt of power sailed over the interior wall that separated the nave from the side chapel and impacted against the rafters of the shored-up ceiling.

Van Horstmann drove the butt end of his staff into the ground. Its length glowed white, except for the single eye of the mask that topped it. The diamond glowed with a purple-black flame. Light magic was perfect for purification, banishment and protection, but only with great force and effort could it be turned to destruction. Van Horstmann had learned that Dark magic was far more efficient at turning the living into the dead, and it was Dark magic that seared from the diamond in his staff.

Van Horstmann held the staff with both hands, like a

sword ready to swing. Black power dripped off it, scorching the floor.

Daegal moaned and rolled over. Van Horstmann made ready to strike. He could take the Gold magister's head clean off if he hit it just right, the dark power hungry to shrivel and tear Daegal's flesh.

'No!' yelled Daegal. With a burst of golden light a form was hurled out through the Gold magister's chest and smacked into the wall. Van Horstmann recognised the shadowy tangle of limbs and talons as Hiskernaath, forced into the real world.

Daegal was stronger than he had expected.

Van Horstmann swung his staff but Daegal was just sensible enough to see it coming and rolled out of the way. He spat a syllable of power and a burning sword shuddered into life in his hands. Van Horstmann struck again but the sword turned the staff away in a shower of black sparks.

'You,' said Daegal. 'You did this. They will see your magic! There are a score of magisters in this chapel who will run here and see you doing evil.'

'They will see nothing,' said van Horstmann. 'I have made pacts. I have worked wonders. The Dark is hidden within me, and not even Elrisse has seen it. No one will know how you died and if there are any traces of Dark magic left in this place, it will be assumed they came from you.'

'Why tell me?' gasped Daegal.

'So that you will know you are defeated and will choose a quick and painless death.'

'Stick a painless death up your fundament,' spat Daegal.

Van Horstmann pointed the staff at Daegal and unleashed

the Dark magic held there. It burst from the staff like a gout of black flame. Daegal was caught full in the flame but the image of golden armour appeared, ghosting over him, and though he stumbled back against the statue of the Crone his magical defences held.

'Daemon-summoner!' spat Daegal. 'Heretic! Murderer!'

'You,' said van Horstmann, 'are the murderer. Blood is on your hands. You saw it through your own eyes.'

'No, van Horstmann. You will not open my mind to your daemon pet again. I will die before I let it in.'

'Then you will die.'

Van Horstmann grabbed a handful of reality with his mind and wrenched at it. The Crone statue toppled forwards and Daegal had to dive out of the way before it crashed onto him and crushed him.

Van Horstmann drove the head of his staff into the ground. The stone slabs of the floor fractured and from the mouth of the mask issued a burning serpent of purple flame. It shot along the floor and arrowed into Daegal.

Daegal cried out and rolled away. The chest of his robes was torn and burned. The skin of his chest was burned away, too, revealing charred muscle clinging to his ribs. He thrashed on the floor to extinguish the dark flames that clung to him.

Van Horstmann stood over the Gold wizard and raised his staff to strike. Daegal coughed out a syllable of power and a shield of golden light appeared above him. Van Horstmann's staff rang off the shield and Daegal dragged himself away.

The shield shimmered and faded. Van Horstmann struck

again, this time swinging the staff down like a miner's pick-axe into a coal seam. The shield appeared again, but weaker, translucent and blurred. It shattered under the blow.

Van Horstmann bent down and grabbed Daegal by the throat. He hauled the Gold wizard to his feet and slammed him against the wall of the side chapel.

Blood was running from Daegal's mouth. One eye was rolled back and bloodshot. He took in a single, gurgling breath, misting blood down the front of his charred robes.

'All this,' he said. 'What for? Why did you do it?'

Van Horstmann dropped his staff. He placed the palm of his hand over Daegal's face.

Learning the ways of Dark magic had not been easy. It was chaotic and insane, and did not fit well into van Horstmann's fastidious mind. The Light was marshalled through order and ritual. Dark magic was an emotional thing, its conduit to the aethyr punched through by force of hatred alone. It had been a tough lesson to learn, allowing his emotions to the fore, channelling them instead of suppressing them.

But in the end, it had almost been pleasurable the first time it had worked. To finally give his feelings free rein had felt forbidden and exhilarating. He felt that savage joy now as his hatred bored through the wall between his mind and the aethyr.

At the pinnacle of the fortress was a hole in the sky, a black chasm from which fell a rain of blasphemous power. Van Horstmann, fortunately, had hatred to spare.

The power rippled through his body and into Daegal. It was uncontained, uncontrolled. The results of this magic could not be predicted, but in that moment van Horstmann did not care.

Instantly, Daegal began to change. His robes billowed as tumorous growths bloomed beneath his skin. The pain on his face was swamped as the structure of his skull warped, one eye bulging wide, one sinking into a growing mass of pulpy muscle. Van Horstmann stood back as Daegal screamed, until even that was lost to him as his throat swelled up and one shoulder burst into dozens of pallid white bulbs like the egg sacs of a giant spider.

It could not be contained. Daegal swelled up to an obscene size, his shape no longer human, skin and flesh mutating at random. Bones cracked. Daegal's ribcage split open and organs spilled out, swelling up and squirming.

The thing that had once been a Gold wizard screamed again, as it gained a moment's control over its lungs. Then it burst, exploding in a shower of blood and shattered bone.

Van Horstmann had ducked behind the statue of the Crone just before Daegal exploded. He felt a warm rain of blood and gore, and though he avoided the worst of the debris shower he could hear the wet smacks as chunks of Daegal thudded against the walls and the statue.

He glanced around the statue. Just a heap of shredded muscle and a pool of gore remained. Daegal's robes had been shredded and soaked in blood, and there was nothing left to suggest he had ever been human, let alone a wizard.

Van Horstmann took a breath. He was shaking with fatigue and adrenaline. He put a hand against the outer wall of the temple and willed raw power through him again, forcing one of the stone blocks out of position. It slid from its place in the wall, crumbling mortar and stone dust showering down as it moved. A fresh draught reached him and he saw he had opened enough of a hole to let himself squeeze out.

Outside, Altdorfers were gathering to see what the commotion was. They shied away when they saw van Horstmann, perhaps because they recalled the Great Fire and other catastrophes blamed on the Colleges of Magic, or perhaps simply because van Horstmann was spattered with blood and probably still smouldering from the barrages of destructive magic.

Overhead, smoke was issuing from the holes in the temple ceiling. The Light wizard delegation were moving as a mass away from the temple into one of the many streets leading away. As van Horstmann ran towards them he saw that they were gathered around Elrisse, and that Kardiggian was carrying the wounded Mother Heloise.

A few were casting bolts of white fire towards the temple doors, answered by sprays of molten gold. But the main battle was done. The Gold wizards remained in the temple while the Light wizards were retreating. Van Horstmann reached the Light delegation and saw he was not the only one who looked fresh from the battlefield. Many were bloodied or scorched. Robes were torn and burned, and some men limped or nursed obvious wounds.

'Van Horstmann!' shouted Elrisse. 'I thought we had lost you, magister!'

'Alas, Morr did not take kindly to my knocking,' said van Horstmann. 'I live yet.'

'Then stay close and see to it that you continue. We must get to the pyramid.'

'The Gold Order struck the first blow,' said Kardiggian. 'We all saw it. There will be consequences, Grand Magister, grave ones for the Gold Order. There must be.'

'There will, magister,' replied Elrisse. 'I swear it. The Gold Order might have started hostilities, but it will be the magisters of the Light who will end them.'

Van Horstmann could just see the faces of the Gold wizards sheltering behind the temple doors. They looked as confused and panicked as the Light magisters did. They were probably making the same promises Elrisse just had – consequences, justice, vengeance. There was no sign among the Light wizards that any of them had glimpsed the use of Dark magic in the chapel. The wards that van Horstmann had cast about him had done their job. Part of the reason for all this, though not the greatest part, was to see if he could cast the magic he needed without its true nature being detected. The test had been a success. As for the rest of it – time would tell.

There were tears in Mother Heloise's eyes, and not just from the pain. Once again the Temple of Shallya, a place sacred to peace, was the site of bloodshed.

IT HAD BEEN relatively simple to send the lightning bolt down.

Procuring the bolt had been the most difficult part. Any smith in Altdorf would have been very curious to know why they had been asked to forge such a thing, and rumours in Altdorf moved quicker than a new breed of plague. If such a smith learned of the golden lightning bolt sent to impale the

Light Order's pyramid, he would be able to tell the authorities about the shaven-headed, sunken-eyed magister who had commissioned it.

Instead, he had used a number of intermediaries to have it made, in sections, by smiths in Nuln, Talabheim and Marienburg, then assembled them himself over several long nights in Altdorf's slaughterhouse district where empty properties were common enough for van Horstmann to appropriate one. It had been tedious and physical labour, but compared to learning the principles of Dark magic between his Light Order studies it had been simple to teach himself the basic smithing needed.

The magic was easier for van Horstmann. Light magic put the bolt in the sky, and Dark magic sent it hurtling down. When Elrisse had commanded van Horstmann be one of the magisters investigating the origin of the attack, van Horstmann had taken the opportunity to stop just short of outright accusing the Gold Order, knowing that most magisters had come to that conclusion of their own accord.

Van Horstmann had never sat down and written out the stages that he hoped would follow, but they were etched into his mind, into the stones of the fortress, and they had all followed one another just as he had imagined. The Gold and Light Orders, already natural adversaries, were pushed into outright conflict. Sooner or later it would explode into open warfare, and the Grand Magisters, of course, would move to head off such an eventuality with a grand diplomatic gesture. A gesture they would both have to partake in, along with a good representative number of their magisters. All those wizards would have to be in the same room at the same time, their guards down, because that was the only way that such a diplomatic solution could be reached.

Add Hiskernaath, and a likely instrument like Daegal, and the bloodshed at the Temple of Shallya had become a logical inevitability.

Hiskernaath had returned after three nights. Van Horstmann had found him in his quarters, as he had known he would. The daemon was squatting against the ceiling, sulking as if van Horstmann had just had the creature whipped. The daemon wanted to gallop back into the warp, away from its servitude, but the contract inked into van Horstmann's skin had held and the daemon had been forced to return to its master. Van Horstmann had put it back in Vek's puzzle box, ignoring the daemon's ever-creative cursing as it was compelled to obey him once again.

The Light Order lost two magisters. One was Parsifal, whose body had remained in the temple and was returned by the priestesses of Shallya the next morning, left beside Midday's Mirror wrapped in funeral vestments. The other had been Magister Olasonn, a young man of Kislevite stock. He had been caught in the scrum for the doors, knocked to the ground and despatched by a conjured blade of gold that fell from the ceiling and impaled him through the throat. Van Horstmann had helped carry Olasonn's body on the way back from the temple to the Buchbinder District.

He had looked into Olasonn's face. The magister was young by the standards of wizards, not long out of the Chanters' Hall. He was handsome and blond, and the rigours of magic had yet to drain him into one of the chill husks who inhabited the Light Order's upper echelons. Everything he could have been, could have done, had been stolen from him in the Temple of Shallya, in a bloodbath that was van Horstmann's responsibility.

Perhaps there had once been a van Horstmann who would have been haunted by that face. Certainly it was a face worthy of haunting a killer. But it troubled van Horstmann no more than the face of Magister Vek, and van Horstmann had not thought of that old magister for years except as the collector of the trinkets that now cluttered up his quarters. He could barely even remember Vek's features. Van Horstmann did spare a few thoughts to wonder just what kind of a person he must be not to care about those he killed. Most people would be unable to sleep at night knowing they had committed just one of van Horstmann's crimes. Vek, Rudiger Vort, the dead at the temple – any one would be enough to drive a man mad with guilt. But any guilt ran off van Horstmann like rain.

Guilt, he concluded, would only get in the way. It would be an obstacle in his path. If he had felt it, he would have to have conquered it before it stopped him from getting what he wanted. Perhaps his subconscious had decided to save him the effort and ignore the guilt entirely. Or perhaps he had never been able to feel it at all. Perhaps he had been born that way.

In the end, van Horstmann concluded it mattered little either way, and returned to his studies while he waited for fate's pendulum to take its next swing.

CHAPTER EIGHT
THE ORDER OF DEATH

MAXIMILIAN VAN DER Kalibos of the Amethyst Order went everywhere accompanied by ravens. Quite probably he could not have gone without them if he had wanted to. Kalibos carried a staff of skulls and wore robes of purple trimmed with black. He did not cast a shadow or a reflection because he was so attuned with death that he existed, some said, partly in the next world. Silence seemed to go with him, and a zone of chill. Plants died when he went near. If he walked on grass he left a blackened trail.

The Pyramid of Light did not like Maximilian van der Kalibos. The pyramid wanted everything drenched in light, lit up from every angle. Maximilian van der Kalibos, and the Amethyst magic that suffused him, wanted him always wrapped in darkness, only his face, bone-white with black hair and goatee, lit as if from a guttering torch held in front of him.

The result was a feeling of unease, a shuddering hint of powers locked in opposition. When he entered the pyramid, divinations all turned towards uncertainty and chaos, and acolytes seemed to lose concentration as ceremonies went awry.

Grand Magister Elrisse met van der Kalibos and accompanied him and the chattering ravens up to one of the conference chambers near the pinnacle. A pair of Amethyst wizards flanked van der Kalibos, shadowing the Grand Magister of the Amethyst as if they were two more ravens.

The chamber chosen for the occasion was circular and ringed with pillars of white marble. A great circular table held a feast of wine and fine dishes from the better markets and cooks of Altdorf, not because anyone had any intention of eating anything, but because that was simply the way one played host to the Supreme Patriarch of the Colleges of Magic.

'The situation,' said van der Kalibos, 'is intolerable.' They were the first words he spoke when he sat down at the table opposite Grand Magister Elrisse.

'We agree,' said Elrisse. He sat surrounded by Light wizards, with Master Chanter Alric at his right hand. 'And we anticipated that the Supreme Patriarch would have to intervene. It is with great regret that we accept the matter cannot be handled solely by the orders concerned, but accept it we do.'

'Then that is the first hurdle overcome,' said van der Kalibos. 'But not the greatest. While the Light and the Gold Orders confine themselves to their colleges, it is I as Supreme Patriarch who have spoken with the priestesses of Shallya. Their temple must be repaired and reconsecrated. Bloodshed pollutes the very stones. It will take months, and great expense.

That comes out of all our coffers. Mother Heloise, though she lives, was so polluted by the violence done against her that she had to abandon her post and take up a hermit's life. On the colleges of Altdorf falls that sin. It will be years before we can make it right in the eyes of Shallya's church. On the Supreme Patriarch weighs the burden of such diplomatic failures. We have all suffered, Grand Magister. Not just the Light. Not just the Gold. All of us.'

'I understand,' said Elrisse.

'Do you?' said van der Kalibos. 'And how do you understand the feud between the Light and Gold Orders will be made right? Because it will be made right. How do you suppose it is to be done?'

'By dialogue,' said Elrisse. 'Small steps, to be sure, for another grand gesture such as the conclave at the Temple of Shallya must be years away. But it will be–'

'No,' said van der Kalibos. No one but a Supreme Patriarch had the right to interrupt a Grand Magister without inflicting a grave breach of etiquette. 'The Imperial Court must never know that wizards can enter into bloody conflict. Eckhardt III is not a brilliant man but even he will learn of it soon enough if it continues.'

'The colleges of Altdorf have clashed with the Imperial Court before,' said Elrisse. 'Surely we can weather that storm if it comes. It is better to ensure the Gold and the Light heal their rift gradually, as prudence demands.'

'Surely?' said van der Kalibos dangerously. 'You sound very certain. And yet it is only to the Celestial Order that I ascribe the ability to divine the future with such accuracy.

Let me tell you what I see for your future, Grand Master Elrisse. The Emperor learns that the colleges of Altdorf were behind the slaughter in the Temple of Shallya. Altdorf at large learns of it. Those to whom the old faiths are dear will demand our expulsion. The priestesses of Shallya will point to the orders of magic as a corruptive and divisive force. The witch hunters of Sigmar will seek to capitalise by seeing heresy and the marks of mutation in every wizard they come across. And every time a Gold or Light wizard sheds the blood of another, every time the aethyr is plumbed to do violence amongst ourselves, we will be proving our enemies right. And we do have enemies, Elrisse. I most know this better than you. The Colleges of Magic will be besieged by those who wish us ill. They might not even survive. Everything will be undone. I know death, and I see it here. Our death. Desolation and ignorance returning to the Empire of Sigmar.'

'It will not go that far.'

'Such was said about the Great War,' said van der Kalibos. 'And all of mankind was almost lost. All of human magic will be lost if the colleges fall.'

'The Empire relies too much on her magisters for such a dire future to come about,' said Elrisse. 'The Light and the Gold can heal our rift. Though the Amethyst Order must see death in everything, we see life and reconciliation.'

'When?' replied the Supreme Patriarch. 'Will the rift be stitched up in a year? In ten years?'

'You know full well that none can say,' retorted Elrisse. 'And there is no other way. For all your doomsaying, there is no solution other than rebuilding the bridges that were torn down, with patience and temperance.'

'There is another way,' said van der Kalibos darkly.

'Then what is it, Supreme Patriarch?' The moment Elrisse spoke, perhaps a little to sharply, a little too challengingly, the tension in the chamber wound tighter. The Supreme Patriarch leaned forwards and the Light magisters present seemed to shrink down in their seats.

'You were there last time it happened,' said van der Kalibos. 'All the Grand Magisters were. You were there when I took on the mantle of the Supreme Patriarch.'

There was silence in response, not because what van der Kalibos had said was shocking, but because they all remembered. Many had seen the event first hand, and those who had not had heard enough about it to build up a vivid picture of their own.

The role of Supreme Patriarch was coveted, but it was one not to be sought lightly. Since the inception of the orders of magic, when at the instruction of Teclis one Grand Magister had to head all the orders, the title had been decided by violence. Only a Grand Magister could challenge for the position, and he had to depose the incumbent Supreme Patriarch by force.

A wizard's combat, to death or incapacitation.

Such was the risk of leaving an order without a Grand Magister, few Grand Magisters challenged for the position unless they were certain of victory or considered the risk less than the potential gain for the orders of magic as a whole. It was a system that kept the Supreme Patriarch's position strong, while at the same time providing for the deposition of tyrants and incompetents. That was why Loremaster Teclis had instituted it.

And that was why Maximilian van der Kalibos was the current Supreme Patriarch. He had appeared one day at the gates of the Jade College and challenged the then Supreme Patriarch, Lord Janeak Ghul of the Jade Order. The two had fought, in the manner decreed by the founding wizards. Kalibos had won. Ghul had died. Though the Empire's citizens were kept ignorant of it, though it was not acknowledged openly even to the Imperial Court, the ultimate conflicts between wizards were settled in violence.

'You speak of a duel,' said Grand Magister Elrisse.

'A wizard's duel,' said van der Kalibos. 'To the death. He who is victorious, his order claims victory in the conflict and the conflict is ended. He who dies, his order pays for its wrongdoing in instigating the rift with the death of its Grand Magister. The conflict will be solved in a single blow. The wizards of both orders will know the place they hold in the rift's conclusion and no further examples of open conflict will occur. The rift will end and Emperor Eckhardt can live on in happy ignorance. The Light and the Gold will be in harmony again, for there will no longer be an argument over who was right and who was wrong.'

'Supreme Patriarch,' said Elrisse. 'I do not believe that–'

'You labour,' said van der Kalibos, interrupting again, 'under the belief that we are engaged in a debate. That you have a say in the matter. You have forgotten, perhaps, that I am your Supreme Patriarch and that I have the power to make this decision. Allow me to disabuse you of such unfortunate notions. I did not come to the Light College today to harvest opinions and seek a solution to which no one would object. I came here to give you your orders. I have already done so to Grand Magister Zhaal. You will fight and one of you will probably die. That is the will of the Supreme Patriarch.'

'And if I challenge that will?' said Elrisse.

'Then you challenge the Supreme Patriarch,' said van der Kalibos. 'And you will fight me for my post. Either way, you fight.'

'Then it is decided,' said Elrisse. He did not let any dismay or fear show through, but it was impossible to imagine they were not there in some form. 'I will fight Grand Magister Zhaal, as you command. The rift between our orders will be healed. For the good of the orders of magic, I do this.'

'I HAVE HEADED this order,' said Grand Magister Elrisse, 'for the majority of my life. And I am not a young man.'

Elrisse was not behind his desk, as he usually was when receiving lower ranked wizards in his quarters. He sat on a couch of velvet and gilt, probably imported from Araby like most of the décor. He did not wear his elaborate robes he had worn to receive the Supreme Patriarch – instead they were plain linen, and wearing them Elrisse had never looked older.

'And in that time,' he continued, 'I have never killed anyone. Does that surprise you, van Horstmann?'

'We are not all warriors,' said van Horstmann. 'If we were, there would not be much of an Empire left.'

'True,' said Elrisse. 'Grand Magister Zhaal is a warrior. He served as a battle magister to Wilhelm II. He conjured the golden spear that killed the greenskin warlord of Splitstone Crag. Under his watch the artillery train of Duke Calimar was routed and his insurrection put down. He was much younger then, of course, and I did not meet him in those days, but I doubt he has forgotten everything he once knew about inflicting his will on an enemy's flesh.'

'The Light has ways,' said van Horstmann.

'Very politically put.' Elrisse unfurled a roll of embroidered cloth that lay at his feet. The roll contained several implements of silver and gold, studded with jewels. 'The Dagger of Lady Erkeneth,' he said, pointing to one. 'Enchanted to seek the heart. Intended for daemons, but it works just as well against a mundane organ. And these,' he said, picking up a pair of silver blades so sharp the light bled through them. 'Created by the priests of Myrmidia to excise the mind and cut out a soldier's cowardice. Struck from silver mined at the lowest depths of the sea and sharpened on a stone that fell from the sky. I have a few others. Gifts, or items I have come to acquire during my research. Marvels, all of them, but nothing that can compare to whatever armoury Zhaal has amassed. What weapon he does not have to hand he can conjure from the air.'

'I must speak bluntly,' said van Horstmann. 'It does your order small honour to have its Grand Magister speak so defeatistly.'

'You are right, of course,' said Elrisse. 'Though a duel is not where my art excels, I must approach it with certainty of purpose and vision of victory. That is why I asked you here. Plenty of Light wizards can talk to me of battle magic and no doubt they will school me as best they can in the next four days. That is how long van der Kalibos has given myself and Zhaal to prepare.'

'I am afraid I can help you little in that regard,' said van Horstmann. It was a lie, of course. Van Horstmann had proven to himself at the Temple òf Shallya that he could kill as effectively as any in the Light Order. But to the rest of that order he was the comprehender, a wizard of bookish wisdom and nothing else.

'You are on good terms with the Fourth Circle,' said Elrisse. 'Especially as we now count you among the Third Circle, the order's most senior minds. That the Skull of Katam spoke with you made no little impact on the guardians of the vaults, though they are not the type to admit it. Your work on Vries confirmed your reputation. I need you to fetch something for me, van Horstmann, from the vaults. The inner vaults.'

'The inner vaults.'

'That is correct. Even I am loathe to enter them. It is… not a privilege that should be given to one who has temporal power. There are dangerous things in there. I need one of them. The Scimitar of the Thirteenth Dynasty.'

Van Horstmann's eyes were drawn to one of the tapestries hung on the walls of the Grand Magister's chambers. It depicted red-skinned, muscular beings fighting with an army in golden armour, on the slopes of a mountain before an ash-blackened sky. It was depicted with the stylisation typical of Araby's arts, and yet told its story with the vividness that only a master could achieve. The mightiest of the red warriors wielded a curved sword with an eye embedded in its hilt.

Light bled off it, and around his feet were heaps of charred corpses.

'Cut from a single diamond,' said Elrisse. 'Forged in the fires of a volcano and quenched in the blood of a dune dragon. It was made for the king of the dynasty's djinns. Would that I could tell you how the Light Order came to acquire it, but no one truly knows. All that is certain is that it lies in the inner vault, and that it might just be the equal of whatever Zhaal brings to our duel. Speak with the Fourth Circle. Convince them to open the inner vault and bring me the Scimitar.'

'I am only glad that I can help,' said van Horstmann.

'My thanks, comprehender,' said Elrisse, leaning forwards and clasping one of van Horstmann's hands. 'I knew it when you first walked the Chanter's Halls. When Alric chose to bring you to that dark time beneath the Imperial Palace. I knew you might just be the best of us.'

THE FOURTH CIRCLE, as was their way, engaged van Horstmann in a lengthy debate on matters of philosophy and arcane theory before he even broached the subject of the inner vaults.

Van Horstmann had never sought to enter the inner vaults before. He had not even seen the entrance, nor knew where it was or what form it took. He had entered the upper vault only twice before, once to retrieve the Skull of Katam and once to return the *Codex Aethyrica* – or at least what remained of it. He was surprised to see that Magister Pendorf was still alive, but not that it was Pendorf who ensnared him in a discussion of the human mind and how it related to the physical material of the body.

Van Horstmann was firm but gracious in maintaining that the mind and body were mixed, or rather that neither could exist without the other, while Pendorf maintained doggedly that the mind was part of the spiritual aspect of the human and that it could exist separately of the body were the means to be discovered to create a vessel to contain and sustain it, and that the body itself was mere gross matter not intrinsic to an individual's existence or identity. The matter took them into the night to discuss, and they did not resolve it because the question was not intended to have an answer.

The conversation turned to history, and to the culpability of rulers for the actions of their people when the means by which they exercised their power was so flawed and fractured, and dependent on others as intermediaries whose collective power far outstripped any single ruler. Pendorf argued on the side of blaming kings, but van Horstmann was more inclined to ascribe the weight of history's responsibilities to the ruling class who interpreted and often ignored the will of their sovereigns. Pendorf was delighted to speak with someone who disagreed with him so completely on everything, and allowed himself a good shot of well-aged brandy to celebrate not being able to reach any kind of compromise.

Van Horstmann asked to be allowed into the inner vault. Grand Magister Elrisse's life depended on it, and on the Grand Magister's life depended the stability of the Light Order. Anyone else might have been sent from the vaults with a lesson on the dangers of even knowing about the inner vault. Pendorf laughed at van Horstmann, and when he realised he was serious, bade him follow.

Van Horstmann had expected to find the entrance to the inner vaults disguised as something mundane, a place no one would look to find it. Of course, that was exactly what someone trying to enter the inner vault would expect, and so the door was a magnificent set of platinum-plated double doors set into a wall of the outer vault's largest chamber, which van Horstmann had always assumed to be a set of temple doors taken from a distant shrine to a deity of wealth and excess. Pendorf opened it with a set of tiny keys apparently carved from human teeth.

The first thing van Horstmann saw were the shadows. They clung to the floor, revealed as the doors swung open. They slithered along the ceiling. They seemed to slink towards the door, not shy away, though the ever-present light of the pyramid should have banished them.

It was the only place in the pyramid where a shadow could take form. The inner vault seemed to hide all the shadows that would have been cast were it not for the fierce light of the pyramid.

'Stay close,' said Pendorf. 'Do not stray.'

He led the way in. The air was chill. Van Horstmann could just make out the shape of the inner vault – a warren of niches and side rooms, criss-crossed by staircases at haphazard angles, a jumble of rooms and architecture that might ensue if the pyramid was shaken up and its parts rearranged like a child's building blocks. Here was a cornice like one from a corridor in the upper chambers, there a pillar like those in the Chanter's Hall, but none of it married up or made sense.

'This was built to echo the pyramid above,' said Pendorf.

'But it changes. We cannot map it. Takes this old man's intuition to know the way. What is it you seek?'

'The Scimitar of the Thirteenth Dynasty.'

Pendorf sucked at his teeth like a craftsman sizing up a fee. 'That will not be easy. Some of the artefacts are better at hiding than others. The Scimitar thinks itself a noble among commoners, and it disdains their company. As I said, stay close.'

Van Horstmann did as he was bid, but his eyes strayed. The door boomed shut behind the two magisters and only a light that Pendorf cast into the air in front of them cut through the darkness. Van Horstmann added light of his own, shining a beam of it from his outstretched palm, peering into the deepest corners as they passed them.

A standard of red silk stitched with the image of a headless skeleton, holding its skull in its hands. A gigantic hunting horn cut from the tusk of some gigantic monster. The shell of a similarly huge sea creature, carved into an intricate throne. Books. Swords and shields, suits of armour. Cases holding amulets, necklaces, crystals in settings of silver. Flies and spiders clustered against the glass of one case containing a wand of twisted white wood. A ceiling-high mirror showed fragmented reflections of people who were not there.

A key. Van Horstmann looked as closely as he could as he passed, not wanting to raise the suspicions of Pendorf. It was cut from red gold and hung on a golden chain. It was carved into the shape of a dragon's head, the key's teeth the dragon's fangs, an emerald for an eye. It hung around the neck of a marble torso without a head.

'Here,' said Pendorf. He was pointing at a steel arch across which was stretched a web of golden threads. 'Lady Malbelagia's Web. The Scimitar seems to desire its company.'

'Not many dreams down here for it to catch,' said van Horstmann.

'Ah, you know of the Web?'

'I have read of it, in passing.'

'So few appreciate such an artefact. When it was stored in the vault above we would find dreams caught up in it from time to time, wrapped in gold and silver. Quivering little things that turned to dust when looked upon. And every time an acolyte from the floor above would wake with his hair turned grey. No such trouble, as you say, since we moved it down here.'

The Web had an odd beauty to it, the way the light caught it and the shadows spiralled around its threads when the light was withdrawn. But it was not what van Horstmann was looking for.

'There!' hissed Pendorf. He indicated a staircase leading down into a room that looked like it should have had windows and balconies on three sides, but instead looked out on only panes of blank stone. A dark-red cushion lay on the floor, and on that was the Scimitar.

Van Horstmann knelt beside the sword and went to pick it up.

'Careful,' said Pendorf. 'That blade saw the fall of the Thirteenth Dynasty and the three that followed it. The djinns of Araby used it on their banners and sacrificed in its name.'

Van Horstmann picked the Scimitar up. It hummed in his

hands and the grip seemed to change to fit his hand. Its balance changed, too. It felt suddenly so light that he could have been holding nothing. On the curved blade was momentarily reflected a host of spears, the silhouette of an army, rising and falling with the tide of battle. Then the light shifted and the image was gone.

'How many lives must this have taken?' asked van Horstmann, more to himself than to Pendorf.

'More than anything else in these vaults,' said Pendorf. 'But I would wager the Gold Order have in their hands a weapon that has taken more. Such artefacts are their speciality. What any mage of the Fourth Circle would give for an hour in their armouries! Surely there is none like it in all the world.'

'Perhaps,' said van Horstmann. 'But no blade of theirs will have a Light wizard behind it.'

'True. Very true.' Pendorf looked around him. 'The shadows sound hungry,' he said, though there was no sound except the two men's voices.

'There is one thing,' said van Horstmann, 'that I have long wished to ask of you.'

'We should leave, comprehender. We take great care not to disturb the inner vaults unduly.'

'In a moment,' replied van Horstmann. 'I have wished to know what lies beneath the inner vault.'

Pendorf did not answer.

'You know,' said van Horstmann, 'that I have the authority and the confidence of Grand Magister Elrisse, and that it would be a grave breach of duty to lie to me or to withhold what I seek to know? I understand your desire to maintain secrecy, Magister Pendorf, but the wizards of the Fourth Circle have no cause to keep such secrets from the senior members of their own order.'

'Why would you wish to know?' asked Pendorf.

'Because there is a very good chance, whether we wish to speak it aloud or not, that Grand Magister Elrisse will die in four days,' said van Horstmann. 'The Light Order will have to be restructured should such a thing come to pass. A complete understanding of all its workings will be essential.'

Magister Pendorf bowed his head. 'Out of deference to the comprehender,' he said, 'I shall not make any quarrel with you. The Pinnacle Vault lies in direct opposition to the upper-most chambers of the pyramid above. We do not visit it, save to induct a new inhabitant.'

'Because it is dangerous?'

'Out of respect. The artefacts kept there are not interred so because they are dangerous, or because they are at great-est risk of being stolen, for the inner vault is secure enough. The Pinnacle Vault is the pride of place, the seat of honour. Artefacts of historical worth and great power, those most deserving of respect, are kept there. We speak of it little, again, out of respect.'

Van Horstmann nodded. 'It is as I believed,' he said. 'My thanks, Magister Pendorf. I will take confidence from the cer-tainty of such knowledge. Let us return.'

THE CITIZENS OF Altdorf, if they ever heard of the tradition of wizardly combat, would not be particularly concerned with the morality of the practice or of the waste a dead wizard represented. Instead, they would have been horrified to know that such a destructive event might take place in their city, near their homes and businesses. And so the earliest Grand Magisters had in their wisdom selected a site outside the city, a short way down the river where an island breached a wide length of the River Reik. Rapids broke around its upstream banks, and deep pools sunken around the downstream shore. In ages past the place had been sacred, as evidenced by the standing stones that ringed the island and, beyond the dense black trees that grew between them, in the ancient amphitheatre in the island's centre.

Those ancients had dragged huge blocks of stone from quarries the other side of the Empire to build the arena. An age later the Colleges of Magic had redressed the stones and rebuilt the parts that had fallen. The colours of the eight colleges hung, proofed by spells against the elements, flying bright from the lintels raised thousands of years ago.

Wizards from every college took their seats as dusk approached, the sky streaked with pink and the shadows long. Amber wizards sat beside the bears and big cats they often took as their companions, communicating with them through the Lore of Beasts the Amber Order taught. They sat awkwardly beside the elegant Celestial wizards, whose blue and silver robes and delicate stargazing lenses did not mix well with wildlife. The air above the Bright wizards shimmered with heat. The Amethyst Order was represented by Supreme Patriarch van der Kalibos and a flock of ravens that inhabited every available perch. The Gold and the Light Orders were there in the greatest numbers, acting as seconds for the men who prepared for the setting of the sun in chambers beneath the arena floor.

Once, those chambers had held gladiators or arena beasts, who were herded onto the arena floor to fight and die before the sight of gods long forgotten by the time of Sigmar. Now Elrisse and Zhaal emerged from them, at opposite ends of the arena. Elrisse wore pure white robes, looking as much like a body wrapped in a white funeral shroud as anything else. Zhaal's robes were deep bronze, and around his neck and shoulders he wore a metallic collar as broad as a piece of armour, inscribed with enchantments of protection and strength. He carried a two-handed hammer, dwarfen perhaps in origin, with the twin-tailed comet of Sigmar gilded on the head. Elrisse carried his staff in one hand and the Scimitar of the Thirteenth Dynasty in the other.

It was a solemn business. Quite possibly, one of the combatants would die. All present had to be prepared to witness a death. It was traditional for the Amethyst wizards to attend to the dead if neither combatant was from their order, and in the upper rows sat a pair of Amethyst wizards in black, ready to administer the due solemnities. Similarly, two Jade wizards were set aside to act as healers in the event the duel was concluded with one party incapacitated but not dead, or the victor himself sustained threatening wounds. Grass and moss crept along the stones where they sat, the magic of life escaping them even at rest.

'When the Supreme Patriarch told me we would fight,' said Zhaal, 'I felt joy. I had not countenanced it before, but the chance to meet you face to face in combat is one I then realised I craved. Did you feel the same, Elrisse? Or was it some other emotion that found a purchase in you?'

'I felt only sorrow,' said Elrisse, 'that one of our number should die.'

'If you had admitted you were afraid,' said Zhaal, a mocking note unmistakeable in his voice, 'at least I could have respected your honesty. But now there is nothing in you that I admire.' He swung the hammer, and it made a deep thrumming sound as it passed through the air. 'No obstacle to doing you ill. No barrier to our anger. And the anger of the Gold is legendary. Fear the Fire, and flinch at Death, but there is no anger shines as bright as Gold!'

Four Gold wizards had died at the Temple of Shallya. One had been Daegal, of course. Two more had fallen in the nave, and another of his injuries before he could be delivered to the gates of the Jade College. And when such blood was shed, was there any way of washing it away save with more blood?

The two Grand Magisters circled, the whole breadth of the arena floor between them. The sand turned to gold dust beneath Zhaal's feet. Slivers of light fluttered down around Elrisse like blossom falling from a tree. Such was the power built up in each man that it bled out into the physical world.

The first move was Zhaal's. He reversed his grip on his hammer and slammed its head into the floor. Torrents of gold shot up from the ground like water spraying from a geyser, arcing over the arena floor in rippling fingers towards Elrisse. Elrisse's response was to swing his sword around him, inscribing a circle of protection into the air. Sigils of white flame flashed into existence, describing a dome around

Elrisse, and the gobbets of molten metal that rained down burst against the shield.

Elrisse gathered the power in the circle of protection and channelled it through his staff, unleashing it in a furious gout of white flame aimed straight at Zhaal. The hammer in Zhaal's hands was suddenly a shield of bronze and silver, held in front of him as he charged right into the flame. The flame was divided into two tongues by the shield's protective magic, coursing around Zhaal and leaving him unharmed, as he sprinted at Elrisse.

Zhaal was in striking range of Elrisse. The shield shifted in a blur and reformed as the hammer swung at waist height towards Elrisse. Elrisse brought up the Scimitar to parry and the weapons clashed in a shower of white sparks. Zhaal stumbled, thrown aside by the force of the scimitar's magic, but his balance was regained and he backhanded Elrisse across the side of the head.

The Grand Magister of the Light Order fell back a couple of steps and almost fell. Zhaal was bigger than him, both taller and much broader, with muscles that now showed shifting beneath his robe. Elrisse was in good health for his age but that was all that could be said about him physically. He was an old man, and he looked it as Zhaal hefted the hammer back up to strike a killing blow.

Elrisse fired darts of silver power from his staff. They shattered against Zhaal, most of them turned aside by the enchantments of his magical armoured collar but enough finding their way through to his flesh. They dug deep into his chest and leading arm and Zhaal gasped in pain, falling to one knee.

'I am not a conjurer,' said Elrisse, his breathing heavy. 'I play no tricks of smoke. Our power is pure. Ours is the magic of creation and its ending. Yours is the magic of mud and stone and dull, dead things. Teclis knew the Light would one day rule supreme. Our reign begins with your death, Zhaal of the Gold.'

Zhaal bellowed like a bull. His hands were encased in gold now, the sheen of it running up his arms.

Elrisse brought the Scimitar of the Thirteenth Dynasty over his head and brought it down sharply – not into Zhaal, but into the stone surround of the arena, a shoulder-height wall that stood to protect the front rows from errant blades and spears.

The blade shattered. Shards of it flew into the air like silver birds, riding up towards the darkened sky.

For a moment there was silence, heavy and pregnant with the power that every magister there knew had been released.

That power first took form in a distant rumble. Many were not sure what it could be – an earthquake, perhaps, the sound of some great swell in the nearby waters of the Reik. But the battle magisters knew, as did every wizard who had stood on the battlefield. It was the sound of distant hooves hammering the ground.

A spectral mass of cavalry rode through the walls of the arena, onto the arena floor. They seemed without number, a torrent of them, their steeds rushing with such speed and fury that they blurred into a single surging mass. They wore scaled armour and turbaned helmets of an ancient type last seen on the battlefields of what was now called

Araby, in an age that now consisted of a handful of ruins and inscriptions half-buried in the desert. Banners with runes of fire and destruction flowed over them. Mighty djinns, muscular red-skinned beings of glowing magic, surged among them, bellowing and seething through boiling clouds of flame.

The charge of the Thirteenth Dynasty hit Grand Magister Zhaal with all its force. Ghostly lances splintered. Horses reared. Blades hacked down and as the charge surged past, through the opposite side of the arena, it seemed every ghost of that fallen civilisation swung his blade at the place in the scrum where Zhaal was kneeling.

The sound was terrible, like a storm of fiery winds shrieking down from the barren mountains. Waves of desert heat pounded against the arena seats and magisters sitting nearby scattered for cover. The whole island shuddered with the thunder of horses' hooves and war cries in ancient tongues.

The charge passed. The last of the ghosts galloped through the arena wall.

Elrisse stood holding the hilt of the scimitar. Its blade was gone, shattered completely when its magic was released. He dropped it and leaned against his staff, seeming to sag suddenly as if all the energy had drained out of him with the effort of unleashing the Thirteenth Dynasty.

In front of Elrisse was Grand Magister Zhaal.

In any other situation, he might have been mistaken for a statue, a fanciful work of art. He was made entirely of gold, still in the kneeling pose he had been in when the ghostly cavalry charged. His beard looked like a mass of golden thread and his face, perfectly rendered, had its mouth locked open in a yell of defiance.

He was completely undamaged.

The gold surface receded away from Zhaal's hands, turning them back to flesh. His robes followed, then his neck and face. He gasped and slumped forwards, one hand supporting him, the other keeping a grip on his hammer.

'Is that it?' he growled. 'Is that all you bring? By the comet's twin tails, I had thought at least you would give me some sport!'

Elrisse whispered words of power and a silver lance appeared in his free hand. He hurled it and it burst into a dozen screaming bolts of white fire. Zhaal thrust out a hand and a circular golden shield appeared in front of him, hovering there long enough to deflect each missile as it streaked home.

Elrisse ran back towards the arena's centre. Each time he tapped his staff on the ground, a snake with silver scales rose from the sand, tongue flickering and eyes burning bright blue-white with intelligence. They coiled towards Zhaal but he threw both hands to the sky, hammer held over his head, and bellowed powerful syllables of his own. Golden swords fell from the sky, each one impaling one of Elrisse's snakes, and where they died they boiled away into wisps of silvery flame and smoke.

Transparent domes of protective magic sprung up around Elrisse, who was gesturing with his staff as fast as he could while still making the ritual signs legible to the aethyr's power. Zhaal walked up to the first and swung his hammer into it, shattering it into shards of light. He broke through the second, and the third, this one needing two swings of the weapon.

The hammer looked like a cousin to Ghal-maraz, the Hammer of Sigmar itself, gifted by the dwarfen lords to Sigmar as a symbol of friendship between dwarfs and men. It was covered with dwarf-struck runes and though it was sized for a man to swing, it had its origin in some dwarfen runesmith's forge, below one of the Worlds Edge holds, fuelled by volcanic fire. When Zhaal swung it chanting could be heard, deep and distant, as if the spirits of dwarfen ancestors were singing a funeral dirge.

Elrisse was chanting rapidly, and with every word white fire flared around him, coils of it like burning serpents writhing through the air. The gemstones on his staff shone like caged stars as he drove it into the ground. Ripples of earth were forced up as magic bubbled up from below, forming ramparts and parapets around Elrisse, almost hiding him from the sight of the spectators.

Zhaal cast a golden comet into the air. It split into a dozen shards and rained down, piercing the protective shells and impacting against the battlements. They fell, crumbling into sand, as if collapsing before the onslaught of an army and its siege engines. Zhaal strode forwards another pace and shattered another dome of magic.

The two magisters were almost face to face now. When Zhaal reached Elrisse, Elrisse would die. There was nothing in all of magic so stark and pure as that. The Amethyst magisters watching, those master of Death magic, would perhaps admire how all the equations of life and death were brought down to such a simple matter.

Elrisse dropped his staff and held his hands apart. Between them grew a ball of white flame, growing with every moment. Its harsh light flared out from the Grand Magister and cast long, stark shadows among the magisters seated in the arena. It seemed even to reach the night sky overhead, which flashed as if the stars were drawing closer hungrily.

Zhaal hammered through the last dome of magic. Elrisse squared his footing and thrust out his hands, hurling the ball of flame at the Gold magister.

For a moment Zhaal was gone, rendered invisible by the strength of the glare that erupted from the detonation of magic. The arena shuddered. The very earth seemed to recoil.

The magisters' eyes struggled to adjust. They peered through the afterglare, trying to make out something in the centre of the arena floor.

Zhaal stood, hammer dropped at his feet. One hand was pressed to the side of his face, the back of the hand scorched and smouldering, as were the parts of his face he had not been able to shield. The armoured collar he wore glowed dull red with the heat it had absorbed to protect him.

Elrisse was down on one knee. Smoke rolled off him. The force of channelling such a pure blast of Light magic had drained him.

Zhaal took a faltering, painful step forwards. His less-wounded hand closed around Elrisse's throat.

Everyone present had known it would come to this. They had all hoped it would end differently, of course. None of them gained anything from the loss of a powerful wizard – all the orders of magic would be weakened by it. But as soon as van der Kalibos had made his pronouncement that the matter would be settled by duel, it had been clear he was invoking the right of death to end all debates. Van der Kalibos was an Amethyst magister, and he understood death, he respected it and held it above all things in its authority. Of course one of them had to die. Of course.

Zhaal was a strong man. His hands, leathered by hours at the forge, were strong. He squeezed and Elrisse's life flickered for barely a minute before he was gone.

Zhaal dropped the Grand Magister of the Light Order to the ground. Elrisse was dead. Even an unconscious man could not adopt that leadenness of limbs. There was no Elrisse now, just a corpse.

Zhaal stumbled away from the body. His breathing was laboured. The burns on his face and hands were livid and red. He bent to pick up his fallen hammer, and headed back towards the door through which he had entered the arena floor.

A couple of Gold wizards were running towards him. The duel was over and their duties as seconds took over. One of them took the hammer from Zhaal and the other supported him as he walked.

The spectators watched in silence as the Light wizards walked towards their dead Grand Magister. Magisters Kant and Kardiggian reached him and Kant closed Elrisse's eyes, turning the corpse's head gentle away from the spectators. One of the Amethyst wizards joined them, kneeling beside the body and reading prayers to Morr.

No one spoke. Order by order the magisters filed out of the arena, until only the Light wizards were left.

At the top of the stands, van Horstmann had watched the entire duel play out. There was not one move he had not anticipated, not one spell he had not expected to be cast. The Lore of Gold was not a subtle way of doing magic but it was powerful, especially when wielded in anger face to face. The least surprising aspect of the whole affair had been its outcome.

CHAPTER NINE

DRUFENHAAG

'I HAVE SEEN the way!' cried a voice. It was thin and hoarse, for it did little other than scream. 'His eyes! His eyes look on you! He sees you!'

From the next cell came a low rhythmic moaning which, when listened to closely enough, resembled words in a cruel dark language that had not been created for the human tongue.

The inmate of the cell immediately opposite appeared to be dead. He – at least, Kant assumed it was a he, it could have just as easily been a woman – resembled a pile of rags in the centre of the cell. But the body would not be removed for a long time, until it was absolutely certain that it was indeed dead. The curators of this place had been fooled before by one of their charges playing dead, but only once.

Heiden Kant supposed there was a reason that to get to

the shrine, one had to pass through this dank stone corridor lined with cells. He guessed this had once been a wine cellar, situated as it was beneath one of the finer houses in this district. Though the house was outwardly handsome it had seen no refurbishment or new furnishings for decades, because its real purpose was not to act as the seat of some rich burgher family but as a place for similarly driven people to gather.

'One day you will wake up to blackness!' cried the man in the first cell. The glimpse Kant had got of him suggested the kinds of sores and buboes that accompanied a concoction of diseases. He would be dead soon, like his fellow inmate across the corridor, unless he was animated by some force other than wholesome human life.

It was a strange combination of rooms that lay beyond the door at the end of the cell corridor. On the one hand it was lavish, with a deep rug taken from elsewhere in the house, wood-panelled walls and a chandelier that cast the equivalent of daylight into the windowless underground room. Fine cabinets and bookshelves stood against the walls, along with a fanciful circular map of the world hung on one wall. Its imaginary continents butted up against the known states of the Old World.

But it was also a grimly practical place. Where a feasting table or study desk might have been, there was a stone slab on four sturdy legs, its surface scored with knife marks and darkened by layers of bloodstains, still visible as dim ghosts across the pale surface in spite of diligent scrubbing. One of the glass-fronted cabinets held not curios or a set of finest tableware, but dozens of medical implements, scalpels and forceps, and other strange devices of metal with uncertain purpose. Among them was a trepanning drill with leather straps to keep it fixed to the skull of the subject. Beside the map on the wall was a medical chart, not Imperial in origin but florid and colourful with annotations in an unfamiliar language, its charting of the body's innards as fanciful as the made-up lands on the map. Another cabinet held dozens of skulls, their craniums marked up with precise measurements as if they served as a library of criminal types and the corresponding dimensions of their heads. It was a favourite subject of doctors in the Empire, Kant knew – the way a man's criminal or lunatic tendencies could be judged by examination of some physical characteristic.

Such beliefs would not be beyond the man who stood reading beside the dissection slab. He was a tall and broad-shouldered man whose heavy dark-brown robes did not quite conceal a layer of chainmail. A golden pendant of Sigmar's twin-tailed comet hung around his neck. His head was shaven and his eyes bright blue, set in a face that could have been cut from a block of stone. Strips of parchment, with prayers written in a cramped and obsessive hand, were pinned to his robes, and wrapped around the haft of the hammer that hung from a loop on his belt. It was a warhammer, and though it was as brightly polished as a family heirloom, Kant knew that it had seen more use than most.

'Witch hunter,' said Kant with a bow of his head. 'I am expected, I believe.'

The man held up a silencing finger, not taking his eyes off his book. 'Tell me,' he said. 'If you were to walk back up the stairs and out through the front door of this house, and into the streets of Altdorf, what would you see?'

Kant swallowed. He had met this man before, though on a few occasions and never on his own, and he knew of the strange ways in which he conducted himself. He was as likely to bury the head of that warhammer in Kant's chest as to break a smile at him. And he had heard how much the witch hunter liked to test people.

'The people of the Empire,' replied Kant, 'whom we are sworn to protect.'

'Sworn?' replied the Witch Hunter. 'I made no such oath. Oh, I have sworn many. So have you. But not one made specific mention of protecting the people of this land from... from what? From harm?'

'From corruption.'

The witch hunter closed the book and placed it on the slab. 'Corruption,' he said, 'is the answer. On any street. In any home. In the bunks of any poor house and debtor's gaol, in the pinnacles of palaces. Corruption. That is the answer, Heiden Kant. My apologies – Magister Heiden Kant, is that not so?'

'It is so, Lord Argenos,' said Kant.

'The last time we spoke you were an acolyte of the Light Order,' said Argenos. 'How the time passes. It marches on towards the End Times, and at every step we bleed to claw back a little of the pure from the darkness.'

'I know,' said Kant. 'I have seen it. Beneath the Imperial Palace I saw it manifest. That was when I knew I had to join the Silver Hammer.'

'No, Kant, you have not seen it. You do not see what I do. What you saw was the ultimate distillation of evil. One of the rare occasions when its symptoms wax foul enough to be seen with an ignorant eye. No, when I speak of corruption, I speak of what ignorant men call normality. Do you understand, Magister Kant? If you do not strive for purity, if you do not fight for it with every breath, then you are not an innocent or a citizen or anything else that we should be protecting. You are the enemy. Those people you think to protect are nothing more than beds of ordure in which the seeds of heresy can take root. Were you to protect them then you would be aiding the enemy and you would deserve to meet your end on this slab, just like the sorcerers who conjured the thing you saw beneath the palace. Not a comforting thought, is it, magister?'

Kant said nothing.

'But you are on the right path.' Witch Hunter Argenos crossed the room and laid a heavy mailed hand on Kant's shoulder. 'So few are. That is why we band together as the order of the Silver Hammer. And you will reach the end of that path, and see the world for what it is. And I imagine congratulations are in order for the advancement of your rank.'

'Not at all,' said Kant. 'It was some time ago now.'

'A wizard of the Light is a valuable ally,' said Argenos. 'We have counted many among our ranks before. The banishment of the unrighteous and the casting of protective magic are boons that no hunter of witches would ever undervalue. I test you sternly, Heiden Kant, precisely because you may become so valuable to us. I will not let a resource such as you fall by the wayside and be lost to the corruption of the ignorant world. Sit.'

Argenos indicated a chair uncomfortably close to the cabinet with the skulls. Kant took it anyway. Argenos himself sat and let his hammer rest against the stone floor. Kant guessed the chamber had once been a servant's quarters, repurposed along with the rest of the house. The Order of the Silver Hammer, though Kant had met very few of its members, had resources to command. This was just one of many places throughout the Empire the order owned for the use of its members, and Argenos, though a senior figure in the order, was not the highest and was but one of many. Kant understood him to be the order's member in charge of affairs in Altdorf. Perhaps there was a shadowy circle of pure masters above him, meeting somewhere in deepest secret to plan the salvation of mankind. Perhaps one day Kant himself would join them, though he banished that conceited thought from his mind.

'You know that Grand Magister Elrisse is dead,' said Kant.

'I do,' said Argenos.

'It bodes us ill.'

'No doubt.'

'Not just for the Light Order,' continued Kant. 'For all the Colleges of Magic. He died in a duel with Grand Master Zhaal of the Gold Order.'

'Then the troubles between the two orders are ended?' said Argenos.

'We hope,' said Kant.

'We must have the Light. I have performed many exorcisms

and witnessed many more, and the Lore of Light is one of the most powerful instruments we can bring to bear against the daemon. Shame on us all if these children's rivalries deny us that instrument.'

'That is why I came to see you, Lord Argenos.' Kant leaned forward, ignoring the stares from the skulls on the shelves beside him. 'It may not have been a rivalry as petty as it seems.'

Argenos nodded, as if this was no surprise to him. 'You smell corruption,' he said.

'The hand of the enemy,' agreed Kant. 'What do you know of the incident at the Temple of Shallya?'

'That the church of that noble goddess denies all sugges-tions of violence in her temple and that Mother Heloise is suddenly no longer the Matron of Altdorf,' said Argenos. 'And that blood was shed, and that magic was the means of blood-letting. And that this and the doom of Grand Magister Elrisse are not entirely unconnected.'

'It was a summit, supposed to quell the feud between the Light and the Gold. Instead it became bloodshed. A great shame for both orders, and one in which magisters of both lost their lives.'

Argenos thought about this for a long moment. 'The arro-gance of wizards?' he said at length. 'Or the hand of another?'

'That is why I am here. There was another hand stirring that pot. I have contacted through the Silver Hammer's means the lodgings of Mother Heloise, and ascertained that she and I both agree to what we felt there, the moment before the first spells flew.'

'What?' said Argenos.

'The daemon.'

Argenos breathed out a long, considered breath, and nodded his head as if he had expected to hear those words from the moment Kant walked into his sanctum. 'What do you know of it?'

'That before I joined the Light Order I served as an apprentice to the exorcist Helmut Vanhagel of Nuln, and that I felt the touch of the daemon as a clammy hand at the back of my mind whenever we were called to a victim who was genuinely possessed. That I felt it again under the Imperial Palace, at the exorcism of Princess Astrid. And that I felt it once more in the Temple of Shallya. Mother Heloise has also seen many cases of possession and corruption caused by contact with the agents of the enemy. She felt it, too. To her it is a stench, the stink of the otherworld. It was disguised, but it was there, in her temple.'

'What evidence do you have that the daemonic was present?'

'Aside from the testimony of two who have encountered it before? None, Lord Argenos. Unless you count the fact that one of the magisters present did murder against his fellow wizards, and in doing so precipitated a slaughter on holy ground.'

'Then what would you have the Silver Hammer do, Magister Kant?' said Argenos. 'It is no small matter to interrogate a member of the colleges of Altdorf. It is not so mean a matter as entering the house of a private citizen and dragging him off to the cells. There will be consequences. Emperor Eckhardt is mostly ignorant of our activities but storming into the Pyramid of Light would bring us to his attention, and not for praise.'

'Watch them,' said Kant. 'It may not be within the Order of Light that the corruption lies. The Gold Order, perhaps. Maybe even the Church of Shallya, though I can vouch for the purity of Mother Heloise herself. Watch them, and countenance moving against the Light Order if it is necessary.'

'You think it will be necessary, magister?'

Kant did not answer right away. He turned to the cabinet with the skulls, and saw now the lower shelves had other bones: femurs, clavicles, pelvises. 'You said the enemy are everywhere,' he said.

'Everywhere,' said Argenos.

'These are the bones of some of them?'

'From the gallows of Talabheim and Nuln,' said Argenos. 'One of our number collected them and bequeathed them to the Silver Hammer. He wanted to understand what physical characteristics were most common to those in thrall to the daemon.'

'What did he find?'

'That there are none,' said Argenos. 'That the enemy will use the comely and symmetrical vessel just as readily as the lumpen brow and the murderer's thumb. But he kept collecting them, to serve as instruction that the enemy will use anyone, anyone at all, who is not protected by the shield of purity and suspicion.'

'If I were of the enemy,' said Kant, 'and I wished to engage in a grand conspiracy, a work to do great malice to the people of the Empire, I would seek to find a place where many brilliant and powerful people could make common cause away from outsiders' eyes. Where knowledge and items of power could be found and acquired. Where anything at all could be hidden, any outsider could be blinded to all that happens inside, a place which was itself invisible to all but those I permitted within. And do you know what place I would choose?'

'Enlighten me, magister,' said Argenos.

'I would choose one of the colleges of Altdorf. And among them, I would choose the Order of Light.'

'And you believe,' said Witch Hunter Argenos, 'that such a conspiracy exists?'

'I believe nothing yet,' said Kant. 'But the slaughter at the Temple was sparked by something, and within the Light Order is the most likely source for its origin. I will do what I can to watch from within, and I will seek others to help in my vigilance, but no matter what I find I cannot fight it on my own.'

'You will not be on your own,' said Argenos. 'We are many. More than you realise, for our numbers must be hidden. And you can trust in our order. We will be watching.'

Kant bowed his head. 'My thanks, Lord Argenos.'

'No thanks is needed, Magister Kant. We are at war.'

'And we will win.'

'Yes, magister,' agreed Argenos. 'Though it take till the end of time. Though all of us will be long be dead when the final trumpet is blown. We will win.'

* * *

THEY WERE JUST beastmen.

They had lived in the forests and forgotten valleys of the Empire since before history. Along with the greenskins, there had always been beastmen. They roamed in packs, founded filthy warrens in the densest woods, killed and pillaged at random when they were moved to pause in battling for supremacy among themselves. Walking like men but with goatish, bestial features, a beastman was a symbol of everything that opposed civilisation. Children were terrified by tales of how beastmen would snatch them away at night if they didn't say their prayers. Pilgrims swapped tales of red eyes winking in the forested night, waiting for a dawdling traveller to lag behind his fellows.

Sometimes, a leader emerged among the beastmen, or a population of them was driven out of their stomping grounds. Then an army of them might march, a giant herd moving as one to raze and murder as they went. In those times the aristocrats of the Empire raised their troops and took to the field, to drive the hordes of beastmen back into whatever holes they had crawled out of.

Such it was in that season, where inhuman creatures swarmed in the darkness and left whole towns devoid of inhabitants. A host of beastmen was abroad, and it was heading for Reikland. Armies marched out to engage them but these beastmen were cunning in the extreme, not content to simply charge forwards and meet whatever enemy stood in their way, but instead to stalk and vanish, outflank and refuse battle, as if they were led by some instinct not of a savage beast but a feral survivor, something that knew the ways of men and had no intention of dying to them. They were still just beastmen, just animals, but of a strange and cunning demeanour.

It was clear what they were not. They were not rats that walked like men, as some dangerous rumours held it. The learned men and the leaders of the Empire were very stern in that respect, and quashed all such talk where they could. There were no ratmen, much less an organised and intelligent species that laired in their thousands beneath the streets of Imperial cities. That was the kind of talk that sparked panic and chaos. No, they were nothing more than beastmen.

IT WAS AMONG the hills of eastern Reikland that the army of the Emperor Eckhardt III finally brought the invaders to battle. In the wake of Sigmar's conquests the area had been cleared for farmland and was dotted with villages and farmhouses. The open countryside and plentiful pillaging made it a prime invasion route for an army hoping to reach the walls of Reikland's capital. The beastmen seemed to be playing their hand now, gathering in thousands to drive on to Reikland and win whatever victory their gods had promised. It would be the only chance to face them in the field before they struck Altdorf, and perhaps there would never be another chance to pin their army down.

The wizards joined the Imperial army as it gathered in the three towns of Pfiefendorff, Holn and Drufenhaag. Battle magisters from the Colleges of Magic had joined the call from the Imperial Court that had brought knights from the Order of the Blazing Sun to march side by side with the Emperor's own Reiksguard, and drawn militia and state units from across the Imperial heartland. The beastmen had moved swiftly, as they were wont to do, using every hidden and underground path to seep their way from whatever pits they inhabited to the large and prosperous town of Dunkelsteiff. It was unlikely that anyone had escaped Dunkelsteiff alive, for not even tales of swift death and glinting red eyes had escaped the place. From a distance, scouts had reported the town and the fields around it smouldering and barren.

The beastmen had needed time to gather their force together. Quite probably they were coming from across the Empire and maybe beyond, welded into a single force by the will of some prophet among them. The men of the Empire had needed time, too, for gathering an army was no small undertaking. It had needed the presence of the Emperor himself to get it done, and thousands of troops had choked the country lanes as they slogged their way towards the mustering points.

Sorteliger Maarten Scarfinkrae of the Celestial Order had led the magisters who joined the Emperor's army at Holn. Scarfinkrae was a battle magister, a wartime diviner who sought out portents of victory or defeat in the stars, or in the daytime by any one of a dozen means of divination with which he was proficient. He had selected the magisters who were to join him, bringing the battle magisters the colleges of Altdorf could spare in the short time permitted. Kardiggian of the Order of Light. Grunhelder of the Order of Amber, a master of the Lore of Beasts who, it was said, spent more time in the form of a monstrous black bear than as a man. Rootwarder Wseric of the Jade Order. Scarfinkrae had also suggested that a magister be given the task of gathering what understanding could be gleaned about the beastmen, to ascertain what about them had made them so difficult to bring to battle on the Empire's terms.

For this task Kardiggian had suggested his order's pre-eminent mind in the area of research – Comprehender Egrimm van Horstmann, whose work on the hidden writings of Vries had gained him no small acclaim across the colleges of Altdorf.

And so it was that van Horstmann was in Holn the night the beastmen made their move.

THE STINK OF the decaying was familiar. Already men were dying. The men stationed at Pfiefendorff had been struck almost as one by a virulent and debilitating disease that left them lying in moaning heaps in the houses they had taken as billets, unable to be roused to battle even when the scouts galloped back in panic and the regimental trumpets began to sound. The smell of disease wafted through the night to Holn, and van Horstmann knew that the battle was near. It smelled like Kriegsmutter Field. Soon it would look like Kriegsmutter Field too.

Van Horstmann left the simple farmhouse on the town's outskirts. Outside already, the men of a Reiklander militia, who had slept in the rooms above him, were gathering in the yard. Chickens ran around clucking as the militia leader, apparently self-appointed, read a prayer to Shallaya for preservation and to Taal for the swiftness and aim of the huntsman.

These were simple men who carried bows their fathers had probably shot before them, with the well-built shoulders and tough hands of those who had practised with their weapons since they were old enough to hold a bow. For a uniform they wore a red scarf around one arm. Otherwise they were dressed much as they might be if they were working the fields of whatever town they had come from.

It was a patchwork army, thought van Horstmann as he made his way towards the town square. Everywhere they were emerging from their billets and forming up. The wealthier or better trained, those who served as standing state troops or were drawn from the sons of the nobility, were helping one another strap on their armour. Others were swapping dark tales of what these beastmen did when they captured you. Many glanced nervously at van Horstmann as he passed. Few men, even natives of Altdorf, were used to seeing a wizard among them who openly wore the robes of a college of Alt-dorf and carried a staff with which to do unpredictable things to the fabric of reality. Perhaps they were afraid of him, per-haps they were glad to have him on their side, regarding him with the respect one might reserve for a particularly sharp blade. Perhaps the two balanced themselves out.

Ahead, the sky flashed. The stars seemed to be pulsing down at the centre of Holn like signal lanterns. Van Horst-mann could see Sorteliger Scarfinkrae standing on the plinth that held the statue of Holn's mayor, examining the stars with a hand-held lensed device of great complexity. He muttered his findings to a trio of scribes who wrote down what he saw there. Scarfinkrae wore the deep-blue robes of the Celestial

Order, embroidered with stars and planets, and a pair of spectacles with multiple lenses that could be folded into place. He had a long and mournful face with a turned-down mouth and long, straggly grey beard.

'What news from tomorrow?' called van Horstmann.

'Clouds and smoke,' replied Scarfinkrae. 'The future is clouded. I cannot see. There is bloodshed, yes, but beyond that I see nothing. The portents turn their faces away. But that in itself is an omen. They are afraid, Comprehender van Horstmann. They shy away from this time and this place.'

Scarfinkrae stepped down from the statue's podium. 'I saw you,' he said. 'Fates converge on you. I can say no more than that.'

The sound of hooves approached. A trio of scouts were trotting along the town's main road, as fast as the wagon ruts would allow them.

'They're moving on the town!' cried the lead scout. He was probably a huntsman, pressed into service because of his horsemanship and knowledge of the area. 'The hillside's bloody thick with them!'

The buzz of alarm that already ran through the town rose to a panicked babble. Soldiers were running from their billets and taking up position at the barricades they had hastily set up between the buildings on Holn's eastern edge. Into the square rode a dozen or so knights in the yellow and black livery of the Blazing Suns, their horses armoured and caparisoned with the heraldry of some of the Empire's finest families. Handgunners in the yellow and blue of Reikland's state troops were sharing out ammunition and powder for their firearms, the latest matchlocks from the armouries of Nuln. Hundreds of men, thousands, had garrisoned Holn through the night, arriving in columns marching the country lanes, and now before they had forced a decent night's sleep out of the town's paltry bunks and farmhouse floors they had to make ready for war.

Van Horstmann entered one of the buildings, a three-storey inn with guest rooms on the upper floors. He found a window on the top floor and leaned against the sill, looking out onto the darkness.

By Sigmar, he could see them. The hillside was dark against a moonlit sky, but against that blackness he could just make out a deeper darkness. It seethed, as if alive. Because it *was* alive.

Thousands of creatures, indistinct but moving as if scurrying rapidly down the hillside towards the town, a black tide of them.

'To the barricades!' a sergeant was yelling, accompanied by perhaps fifty men as they massed at the crossroads at the end of the street. One of them set up a standard with the crest of some Reikland noble family and the others formed up with bows ready to shoot, sticking handfuls of arrows in the dirt beside them so they could nock and fire them more quickly.

Van Horstmann could hear the chittering of the horde now. The smell of them was mingling with the miasma from the plague billets. Raised voices echoed across Holn as the men stationed there took up their positions.

It would have been better, perhaps, if the Imperial army could have waited until dawn and gone on the offensive, marching on the beastmen positions before they could launch their own assault. But the enemy had played their hand first, and the Imperial force had no choice but to dig in and let the tide of the enemy hit them.

Some of these soldiers were nothing more than boys. Among them were fathers and sons, brothers, bands of old friends from tiny villages along the Reik. Van Horstmann could tell the ones who had fought in the Empire's plentiful wars before – they wore dented and blood-tarnished armour, the greying remnants of their campaign uniforms, the scars of the battles they had survived.

Skarfinkrae was in the street below, on the front line. He was casting handfuls of bones on the ground, and from the glowing patterns they scribbled in the dirt he was reading the tides of battle. He sketched symbols in the air with a finger and they hung there in front of him. Van Horstmann recognised runes of fate, fire and destruction. The Celestial Order specialised in reading the future, but when it came to war, they called down anger from the heavens above. Skarfinkrae was asking the stars for their aid, and some of them seemed to grow in brightness as if they were leaning down towards the earth to watch.

'Here they come!' someone yelled. The chittering became a scream, closer and closer, and now van Horstmann could make out what they were.

Rats. A swarm of them, thousands upon thousands. Each one was the size of a dog, a filthy thing of matted fur, yellow teeth and pink wormlike tails.

So, thought van Horstmann, not beastmen after all. Something else. Perhaps something worse.

'Volley fire!' cried the sergeant in the street below. Fifty arrows thrummed into the air, falling in an arc towards the approaching rats. It would have been difficult for any arrow to miss if the archers had tried, but there was no dent visible in the approaching swarm where they fell. There were too many rats to see if any had been skewered – surely they had, but they would have been few among the swarm. All along the Imperial line volleys of arrows were arcing across the darkness into the mass of the enemy, wave after wave of them.

A preacher was praying loudly, recalling the strength of Sigmar when he cast the greenskins out of Reikland and imploring the Empire's god to lend that strength to the soldiers who fought in his name. A banner with the initials of Emperor Eckhardt III unfurled on the top of Holn's mayoral residence, the grandest building in town, and archers were setting up on the roof around it.

The rats swarmed into the opening to the street ahead, surging down it towards the knot of archers. Another volley streaked almost horizontally into the swarm, and this time van Horstmann could see their bodies thrown down, the rats behind surging around them. Fifty arrows must have found fifty black-furred bodies, but there were hundreds more.

'Down your bows!' cried the sergant. 'Take up your blades! Here they come!'

Van Horstmann ran down the stairs and into the street. The soldiers were terrified. The sergeant was doing well to keep his own voice steady. He was a veteran, van Horstmann guessed, a deeply lined and scarred face with a grizzled beard and a grimy uniform of black and grey with slashed sleeves. He turned to look at van Horstmann as he approached, and van Horstmann knew what he must be thinking.

Here was a wizard. A worker of wonders. Perhaps he and his men would be saved by some grand miracle called down from the aethyr.

'Give me room,' said van Horstmann. The men before him scrambled away, leaving a gap behind the barricade into which van Horstmann stepped.

The eyes of the vermin were red, and they winked brightly in the starlight. Van Horstmann leaned on his staff.

'It will not end here,' he whispered to the golden mask at the top of his staff. 'Not here and not now, Lizbeta. I promise.'

The rats were halfway down the street, pouring through the windows and doors of the houses that lined it. In a moment they would be on van Horstmann, dragging him down with a thousand tiny, sharp teeth, stripping his body of its flesh and leaving him a gory pile of gnawed bones in their wake.

Time slowed, and as well as the vermin-choked street in front of him, van Horstmann stood before the fortress. It was glowering and ornate now, the sky overhead red and shot through with lightning. The ground was torn and barren, broken by clusters of bleached bones. The doors ground open, revealing a host of gargoyles and grotesques carved into the walls and ceiling of the chamber inside. In their mouths and eyesockets were the gemstones of crystallised power.

Snakes slithered along the floor. Van Horstmann forced his lurching stomach down and they receded. He turned his thoughts to three motes of power: protection, fire and the purity of the Light.

The fortress did not like it. The fortress wanted the black jewels of Dark magic to rain down, the magic of ruin and corruption. But van Horstmann denied its wish. The aethyr was conducive to Dark magic here, perhaps because the enemy shamans used it with such abandon. But there were witnesses here. He could only use the Dark away from the eyes of those who might recognise it for what it was.

The fortress was gone. Foul yellow teeth filled a hundred squealing mouths. Van Horstmann drove his staff into the ground and let the power he had dredged up from his soul flow through him, earthing into the dirt of the street, radiating out of him.

The tide of rats broke against the barricades. They surged up like a wave, leaping towards him.

They were met by the wall of white flame that rushed out from van Horstmann. As they passed through it they were incinerated, their bodies stripped of fur and muscle. Charred bones rained against him – tiny curved ribs, malformed skulls, pattering onto the ground.

The force of the rats' charge meant they could not turn away. They surged into the zone of flame around van Horstmann, burning in their scores. Van Horstmann gritted his teeth as he felt the force of raw magic pulsing through his veins and organs, burning as if his blood had been replaced with boiling water. He yelled, forcing the pain down, and the wall of flame flared outwards and died.

He dropped to one knee. He willed himself not to relent

and magic rippled down the skin of his free hand, gathering at his fingertips. More vermin leapt at him and he sprayed a gout of white flame at them. They were incinerated so thoroughly that not even bones remained.

Silence fell. The soldiers crouched by the barricade, shuddering with shock at the conflagration that had just filled the street, blinking its glare out of their eyes. The white flame had not harmed them though it had raged around them, and the street was now full of smouldering bones.

Van Horstmann stood in a clearing in the remains, where there had fallen only ash.

'Take… Take up your posts!' ordered the sergeant. 'There will be more!'

A yellow ball of flame rushed overhead, impacting against the hillside – a chained comet, conjured and thrown by Scarfinkrae. In its fire was illuminated the approaching army. The giant rats had been their vanguard and now the beastmen themselves were marching, ill-disciplined mobs of ragged slave-creatures alongside regiments of armoured beastmen carrying halberds and standards. Their exact details were impossible to make out in their hoods and helms, their bodies hidden by patchwork armour and swathes of rags.

Were there goat's legs under there? Or vermin covered in matted fur?

They were only beastmen. That was what every regular soldier had to think as he stood there waiting for the order to attack. A wizard had more freedom of thought, and a wizard had read more of the Empire's history, of the battles that were not fairy tales but attested events, where the ratmen had been not imaginary but a direct threat to every man and woman in the Empire. When their generations-long plans came to fruition they emerged to claim the surface world for themselves, and when they were put down a pall of unbelief came down to obscure the truth from the collective memory of men. It took a man like van Horstmann to put the pieces together and see the truth for what it was. And it took a man like him to realise that the truth had to stay hidden, or the knowledge of the ratmen – the skaven, as scholars had once called them, when they were free to write about them – would destabilise every city in every province.

And there, among the throng, was a single skaven with pale grey fur. It was carried on a platform of lashed bones by a horde of skaven slaves. It carried a staff topped with a metal sphere, off which electricity was arcing, earthing into the bodies of the slaves. It had one eye, the other replaced with a chunk of glowing green rock, and a twisted pair of horns grew from its brow.

Overhead, Skarfinkrae flew over the inn and alighted on its roof. 'Comprehender!' he called down. 'The enemy approaches! Can we hold?'

'I think not,' replied van Horstmann. 'But then, you are the one who can read the future.'

'And I agree,' said Scarfinkrae. 'We are many, but our lines were unprepared. Already they bend and break. The Emperor's standard has risen and the Reiksguard are massing in Drufenhaag. They will sally forth and bring the fight to the enemy.'

'Then we must join them!' replied van Horstmann.

'Sergeant! Can you send out the word? The Emperor advances and so shall we. We will not wait in these streets to die. We will bring death to the beastmen.'

'I can,' said the sergeant. 'Bugler! Sound the advance! Send the word down the line!'

And so the deciding move of the battle was made, the Imperial army advancing in the wake of its Emperor.

ECKHARDT III WAS not the most martial of emperors. Some before him had belonged on the battlefield, eschewing statesmanship and the responsibilities of rule to charge across the Old World leading campaign after conquest. In this they echoed Sigmar, the first of them, who had won the Empire by war. Eckhardt was an administrator and a diplomat, a stabilising influence chosen because he was unlikely to make too many enemies among the nobility. His role was to help the stability the Empire still craved after the Great War of Magnus the Pious, not to put enemies to the sword in person.

And yet, at what would later be called the Battle of Drufenhaag, the Emperor rode at the head of his Reiksguard Knights. They were the strongest sons of Reikland, and their mightiest and best-bred war steed was reserved for the Emperor. The jet-black charger, the size of a shire horse and armoured in black and gold, led the thunderous charge. The Emperor's lance was tipped with a starmetal blade gifted by an ambassador from the elves of Ulthuan and his red plume was cut from the tail of a cockatrice.

More than a hundred knights rode with him. Along with

them were double that number of mounted militia, armed with whatever armour their fathers had handed down to them and riding horses trained for hunting. Many horses shied or bolted in the wrong direction, others threw their riders or fell. But the charge did not wait for them, and the Emperor was the first man to hit the host of ratmen in the skaven army's centre.

Thousands of beastmen had advanced in a great mob. Those leading them had probably expected to fight in the towns, storming the Imperial defences. Instead they were not ready for the Imperial counter-attack that slammed into them. Eckhardt vanished in a mass of squirming, panicking bodies and shattered spears as the Reiksguard hammered home beside him. It looked like nothing so much as a meteor hitting the enemy army or a volcanic eruption beneath it. Bodies were thrown into the air by the impact. Beastmen turned to run and were trampled by those around them. Hundreds fled at the first impact, the enemy rear lines emptying in seconds, their leaders shrieking in disgust as their clanmates dropped their spears and scampered away on all fours.

Those knights must have seen the ratmen's faces and their squirming tails. They must have realised they were facing the shadowy antagonists of those childhood tales, the ones their parents forbade them to tell, of rats that walked like men and wanted to rule the world. But they were not children any more. They were men, who had sworn to defend the Empire and their Emperor, and they showed no sign of that realisation as they fought on and ground the enemy beneath the hooves of their warhorses.

And suddenly, everywhere was death. Militia marauded forwards into the fire of enemy war machines, chunks of evilly glowing rock falling among them and the bullets from crude iron rifles sniping them down. A horrifying creation, like a great rolling wheel that fired bolts of green-blue lightning in every direction, was loosed from the beastmen lines and carved a bloody, charred path through several scores of men from a state regiment from Averland.

The Celestial wizard Scarfinkrae flew over the battlefield and rained down bolts of orange flame. He cast runes into the sky which shattered and sent shards of starfire down among the clanrats. As the Empire infantry and the enemy hordes met, the front line disappeared in a mass of bodies. There Rootwarder Wseric stood, waves of deep-green Jade magic pulsing off him, the grass growing thick and deep as he knitted the wounds of fallen soldiers together. Magister Kardiggian of the Light Order was there too, and around him blazed circles of protection that beastman spears and war machines could not penetrate.

Somewhere in the bedlam, the Amber wizard Grunhelder died. He had shifted into his bestial form and charged at a towering horror of flesh, like a hundred giant rats melded into one foul monster, and when he lost his battle against the thing his death-scream sent waves of raw magic surging across the battlefield.

Bursts of white flame flashed as the Imperial infantry charge arrowed deep into the hordes of slave-warriors the enemy sent forwards. The slaves were wretched and frenzied creatures, frothing at their boil-encrusted lips, dressed in rags and armed with nothing more than sticks. claws and teeth. But there were thousands of them and with every step the Imperial advance slowed, bogged down by the enemy, whose commanders were content to weigh the human attackers down with a sheer mass of bodies.

The white fire was coming from the hands of a Light magister who strode forwards blasting bodies apart. He left the soldiers around him behind as he pushed on, even as he stumbled with fatigue from the excess of magic coursing through him.

THEY HAD WIZARDS, these ratmen.

The ratman that van Horstmann had spotted in the flashing of its lightning was one of the skaven wizards. He had read a treatise on the skaven from a period of Imperial history in which it had been acceptable to believe in them, and it speculated that the role of wizard, priest, and king might be contained within one such skaven, born albino and horned, the marks of whatever thing the ratmen worshipped. This was what van Horstmann had seen. This was what he fought his way towards, throwing skaven out of his path with blasts of purifying flame that seared his muscles and veins to force out into reality.

On its bone platform, held aloft by a gaggle of scarred and tail-docked slaves, the grey skaven wizard screeched. Its incisors were long and yellow, drooling with pallid slime, and the stone in its eye socket flared bright green as if with anger. It pointed its staff right at van Horstmann. It recognised in the Light wizard an enemy, an adversary beyond a normal man, no doubt because van Horstmann had carved a smouldering path already through dozens of lesser skaven.

The slaves chittered and fled, sensing that their master would think nothing of immolating them with a spell aimed at van Horstmann. The platform sank to the ground and the grey skaven did not even bother to admonish the slaves who abandoned him. Perhaps when the battle was done and van Horstmann was dead it would string them up, or quarter them, or sacrifice them on an altar, or whatever these creatures did to sate their anger.

It spat a string of high-pitched noises at van Horstmann. Though van Horstmann did not understand the skaven tongue – no man ever had as far as he knew – the challenge was clear.

'Men see you in their nightmares,' replied van Horstmann, knowing the skaven would know the sense behind his words, too. 'But your kind have nightmares too, and when I am done with you, skaven nightmares will be about me.'

The skaven laughed to see this hairless, tailless creature who wanted to match magic with a grey seer. Black lightning flickered around its staff and it drew a chunk of stone from a pouch on the belt of its filthy once-purple robes – the same stone with which it had replaced one of its eyes. It crumbled the stone and inhaled the dust, its eye growing wide.

The lightning flared black and red. With a gesture of its whole body the skaven hurled the black lightning bolt at van Horstmann.

The aethyr was not the real world. Lightning did not travel in an instant if it was aimed at one who could manipulate the energies of the aethyr like the caster could. The lightning slowed and coiled like a snake as the skaven tried to force it through van Horstmann's magical defences. He had meditated for days at a time on the rituals that cast permanent enchantments of counter-spelling and mystical defences around him. It bought him the time to cast a circle in the air in front of him against which the lightning crashed.

It kept hammering against the magical shield. Van Horstmann felt himself pushed back, his own efforts matched by the skaven.

The albino ratman was strong. This was Dark magic, dredged up from a place in the aethyr that a preacher or a poet might equate to one of the hells of the Empire's faith. The skaven's mastery of it had been enough to win him lordship over a mighty army, and to make it follow him to win conquests among the lands of men.

Van Horstmann responded with a torrent of white flame that fell down from above, bathing him in it and shattering the magical link along which the lightning was flying. The grey skaven stumbled back, dazed for a moment by the force of van Horstmann's mastery of Light magic.

The two were separated again. They circled for a couple of seconds, having tested each other out and not found one another wanting.

The grey skaven made the next move, but van Horstmann did not know it right away. He felt pain in his joints first, the wrenching in his belly. It was indistinguishable from the fatigue of battle magic until it grew, flaring up and down his limbs.

His hands were crusted suddenly with boils that welled up from beneath his skin. He could feel them on his torso too, and his throat. His mouth was suddenly dry, his tongue feeling like it was big enough to fill his whole mouth and his fingers now bent into claws.

The staff dropped from his hand. Van Horstmann coughed and black phlegm spattered his sleeve.

Dark magic. Plague magic, the lores of death and decay. Such things were written of only by madmen, and a Light wizard would not know anything more than that they existed and that to know them would be to invite corruption and death. A Light wizard would have no defence at all.

Van Horstmann was not just a Light wizard. By day he was, and he had absorbed as much knowledge from the order's library as anyone ever had in its history, But by night, he studied what Tzeentch had willed him to know – the ways of Dark magic and the daemon, of things forbidden, and he was all the more powerful for it.

Van Horstmann caught the strand of magic that the grey skaven was working. He reeled it up with his mind like a fisherman drawing in a net. He could grasp the slippery, deceitful weavings of Dark magic because he knew them too. Perhaps he knew them, in an academic sense at least, as well as the grey skaven. Certainly the ratman did not expect van Horstmann to grasp that working of magic, turn it around and cast that net back at the skaven.

It did not take to the grey skaven's body as it had to van Horstmann's. He had not expected it to. Probably the thing was host to enough diseases to wipe out an Imperial town anyway, and the skaven repelled the plague before it could erode its joints or blister its flesh. It did not matter for the time being.

Light magic was the magic of, among other things, purity. Van Horstmann opened his mind to the aethyr and let the magic flow through him unfocused and unworked. It flushed out his veins of the plague and the boils vanished. Light bled from his mouth and eyes, and all his senses were filled for the moment by the force of it. It was a risk – he was blind and deaf, and the skaven could have just scampered up to him and stabbed him if it had been quick enough. But the plague could not survive the force of such purity, and in another few seconds it would have killed him. He imagined it as black smoke blowing away on a white gale, dispersed and destroyed.

The next thing he saw was the grey skaven's horned form silhouetted against a purple fire. It had rammed its staff into the ground and was clutching onto it as if to keep itself from being blown away. The fire raged up higher, tinting the whole battlefield with its darkness. The eyes of cowering skaven-slaves glinted purple in it and they shivered with dread, mesmerised. They had seen it before. They feared it.

Bolts of purple flame shot into the sky and arced back down at van Horstmann, a shower of black comets aimed down at him. He thrust his hands into the air and felt the Light magic still burning through him spray out, describing a dome above his head. The purple-black fire slammed into the impromptu magical shield and battered him down to his knees, but it held, just.

A swarm of rats composed of chittering shadow flooded across the torn earth towards van Horstmann's feet. He dropped the shield and let it erupt outwards, bursting the rat-shapes as the swarmed forwards.

The grey skaven was shrieking now and van Horstmann thought it was at itself, admonishing itself for not finishing off this creature, for being matched in magical strength in front of the slaves in whose eyes it should have been invincible.

Van Horstmann trawled through the sump of his mind where all the dark things were, all the sour memories and foetid emotions he had banished there for just such a time as this.

This part of his mind was infested with snakes.

Snakes of Light magic sprayed from his fingertips. They wound across the soil and snared around the ratman's ankles, lashing up at its hands and throat. They tore the staff from its hands and one got a purchase around its neck. The skaven tore one hand free to grab the snake around its throat but it could not dislodge it.

The skaven was burning. The opposing forces of magic, the Light of van Horstmann's spell and the Dark within the skaven, could not exist together and their instability ruptured everything around them.

Van Horstmann took his staff in both hands. A glowing point emerged from the end of the staff, a shard of Light magic concentrated and honed by a force of concentration that whitened van Horstmann's knuckles. Ripples of power rolled up and down the staff as van Horstmann took deliberate steps towards the struggling skaven.

Its one natural eye rolled up at van Horstmann. Flecks of blood were in the foam around its limps. Its robes and fur were scorched away in patches showing red, burned skin beneath. Its tail was coiling and uncoiling in spasm. The magical snakes were dissipating, but the skaven only had to stay stricken for a few seconds more.

Van Horstmann was in striking distance. A wizard was not a fighting man. Not even the battle magisters could say that. It was magic they killed with, not blades or bows. But van Horstmann was not yet old, or obese, or crippled, as many magisters were. He could fight, if he had to.

He raised the staff, like a spear, with the point aiming down at the grey skaven. He drove it down, impaling the creature through the gut. He leaned on the staff, forcing the point deeper through its innards.

It screamed and squirmed, limbs thrashing. It looked nothing like a lord of its species any more, but like an animal killed by an incompetent slaughterman who had missed the killing blow. It was messy and loud. Blackish blood sprayed and the skaven convulsed now, eye rolled back, as van Horstmann twisted the staff and felt the point pass through the creature's back and into the bloodsoaked earth.

Van Horstmann put a foot on the skaven's throat and pinned it down. It was still drawing ragged, bloody breaths, but it could not move. Perhaps he had severed its spine, or perhaps the pain and shock had paralysed it.

The blade that van Horstmann drew from his robes had been cleaned dozens of time since he had used it last, but somehow it still kept the sheen of Magister Vek's blood on its wavy sacrificial blade.

'Your nightmares,' said van Horstmann.

The point of the blade reached the place where the skaven's one eye met the socket.

Again, van Horstmann went to work.

BY DAWN, THE battle was already being called the Battle of Drufenhaag, and the Imperial scribes had begun writing down the story of the battle and the rolls of its notable dead. Van Horstmann had seen the aftermath of battle before at Kriegsmutter Field and had no wish to watch it unfold again, especially when the too-familiar smell began to waft down from the corpse-strewn hillside.

The beastmen – that was what they were to be called, by an unspoken agreement by everyone who had fought there – had fled as the Reiksguard shattered the heart of their line, the Imperial lines held fast and their leader had died somewhere in the heart of the slaughter. The battle had been won. Thousands of Imperial souls lay dead though, and so the celebration of victory would have to wait until the human bodies were safely out of sight in their mass graves.

Such was the scale of the ruination, the shock of the battle that still rang around the Imperial army after the break of dawn, that no one noticed the lone Light wizard making his way back towards the walls of Altdorf.

Chapter Ten
Pestilentius

The Emperor Eckhardt III, being a Stirlander, was as common and coarse a man as might ever be found among the Imperial nobility. He wore the garb of an Emperor and carried, in a scabbard embroidered in red and gold, the runefang which was his badge of rank as the Elector Count of Stirland. His robe was lined with purple and trimmed with ermine and his armour was lacquered black and gold, custom-made for his frame in the armouries of Nuln. But he seemed to want to shrug it all off at the first opportunity, as if it were a skin for him to shed and reveal the rough, windburned Stirland son he had been born.

'So,' he said in the provincial accent that Altdorfers mocked behind his back, 'there is no one in charge?'

'That is true, your majesty,' said Master Chanter Alric. He and the Emperor were walking up the main staircase that led from the Chanter's Hall to the level of the pyramid on which the library was found. 'In a sense.'

'What sense is that?' asked the Emperor. He was shorter than Alric, with a square jowly face that made him look like a much taller man who had been compressed. 'The sense where there is a Grand Magister's position but no one in it, or some other sense? Tell me, Master Chanter. You're a man of learning.'

The palace staff who accompanied the Emperor had got used to him by now. One of them was Huygens, the minister who had met Alric and the late Grand Magister during the unfortunate incident with the previous Emperor's daughter. Alric, however, had not acknowledged any recognition of the man. Another was a scribe whose task was to note down anything noteworthy to be discussed later – he was a young man, thin and grey of skin and eyes, in a simple brown robe. The last was a knight of the Reiksguard, the knightly brotherhood native to Reikland and traditional household troops of the Emperor. His armour was brightly polished and his visor was down, as if he anticipated some assassin to leap from the nonexistent shadows of the pyramid at any second.

'The Light Order is not an army,' said Alric. 'It does not need a general to function.'

'I care nothing about a general,' said the Emperor grumpily, as if Alric was a functionary who had failed to lay out the appropriate garments of state in the morning. 'I care about who I will call to account if there is another Great Fire, or some other catastrophe you bloody wizards call down. What if one of you burns down the whole Buchbinder

District? What then? Am I supposed to haul the whole lot of you before my ministers at the palace? No, it must be one man to take responsibility. You're not politicians. You don't understand.'

The party reached the doorway to the Diviner's Hall. There the senior magisters of the Light Order had gathered to receive the guest. The Diviner's Hall was one of the most magnificent in a wholly magnificent building. When it was built the students of Teclis had sought out the finest fresco artists in the Old World to decorate it, and the walls and ceiling glowed blue with a sky filled with clouds on which sat sacred figures of Imperial history. Sigmar himself was one of them though only those who understood the symbolism would recognise the shirtless, wild-haired man with the scar in the shape of the double comet on his chest.

It was the first time van Horstmann had lain eyes on Emperor Eckhardt III since he had seen him sworn in. The Emperor wore the look of someone who was not necessarily particularly intelligent and could be manipulated by cunning people, and whose personal motivations did not run much beyond those of the domestic dog. But van Horstmann suspected that at least some of this was a cover, and that Eckhardt III was a more shrewd man than those around him gave him credit for. Most men of his station would have at least tried to affect a demeanour other than the provincial coarseness of a Stirlander. They would have employed people specifically to have them speaking and moving like a man born to the Imperial throne. But it suited Eckhardt III to have those surrounding him think him something of an idiot. That suggested that while he might be many disagreeable things, an idiot was not among them.

And, of course, he had got himself elected Emperor. Van Horstmann suspected that such a feat, as much as a cynic might put it down to luck, required a certain agility of mind.

The Emperor did not take one of the seats offered to him, which were arranged in a circle around an image of a complicated divinatory diagram rendered in mosaic on the chamber floor. He stood instead, one hand on the pommel of his runefang in the attitude of a habitual soldier. The Light Order's magisters were compelled to stand as well, since one did not sit in the presence of a standing Emperor.

'I am not a man given to a surfeit of words,' began the Emperor. 'It is the wish of the Imperial Court that the Light Order select a Grand Magister without delay.'

Facing the Emperor, along with van Horstmann, were Master Chanter Alric, Magisters Kardiggian, Vranas and Arcinhal, and even Magister Pendorf of the Fourth Circle who had been dredged up from the vaults for the occasion. Kardiggian was the Light Order's most pre-eminent battle magister, a battlefield veteran. Vranas was one of its most powerful practitioners of exorcism while Arcinhal had perfected the protective rituals recently discovered in the works of Vries.

'This is not so simple a matter, your Imperial majesty,' said Vranas, who was probably the most diplomatically able of the senior magisters. 'Each order has its own traditions for the selection of a Grand Magister, many of which were laid down under the auspices of Loremaster Teclis himself.'

'I do not care, magister,' replied the Emperor, 'what that

wretched elf decreed. Teclis isn't here. He's back in his fairy-tale land with all the other pointed-ears. I rule this empire, and that includes the orders of magic, whether you like to admit it or not.'

'There are reasons for this other than the weight of tradition, your majesty,' said Vranas. Van Horstmann was impressed at how unflustered Vranas was by the presence of the Emperor. 'The position is one of great responsibility. There are only a few examples of the wrong choice being made in the appointment of a Grand Magister, but it has been disastrous in all cases. The matter is further complicated when the change is necessitated by the death of the previous Grand Magister. Most choose their own successors, ensure the choice is agreed upon by the rest of their order, and retire from the post before ill health or other circumstance determines it. If, as here, a Grand Magister dies in office without an agreed-upon successor, he must be properly mourned and his own wishes researched before the order can seek to replace him.'

'I see,' said Emperor Eckhardt III. 'Do any of these order traditions outweigh the force of Imperial authority?'

Vranas glanced from side to side, almost imperceptibly, as if hoping for a signal from his fellow magisters. Van Horstmann gave him none and neither did anyone else.

'They do not,' said Vranas.

'Then if there is no Grand Magister before the turning of the winter solstice,' said Eckhardt, 'I will appoint one from within your ranks. I will sign it into law if such is necessary.'

'It will not be,' said Vranas hurriedly.

'If I may,' said van Horstmann.

'To whom am I speaking?' said Eckhardt. 'I know Alric and Vranas here, but I don't know you.'

'Comprehender van Horstmann,' came the reply. 'The Light Order's own methods are arcane and time-consuming. They involve a combination of divinatory sessions, philosophical and practical debates and a ballot weighted by seniority among the magisters. It has been known to take the better part of a year and a half. And as Magister Vranas says, these are not merely traditional matters. If divination is ignored, the responsibilities of a Grand Magister will fall upon one whom the aethyr rejects. Our ritual magic will thus be disrupted and weakened. Moreover the Grand Magister's own philosophies on magic colour the outlook of the whole order. He is a spiritual leader, not merely a temporal one. The whole order must understand them if they are not to have their work jarred into inconsequence by an unexpected shift in the theory of magic. These are questions of the greatest import, your majesty.'

Eckhardt regarded van Horstmann with a slight squint, as if he was sighting at him down a hunting rifle. 'Do you know what is of great import to me, van... Hartmann?'

Van Horstmann, who did not think it politic to correct the Emperor, inclined his head in acknowledgement.

'Blame!' The Emperor banged a fist on the back of the chair beside him. 'I see in this place great power, and men who wield that power without anyone outside having so much as a clue about what they are doing. What if one of you burns down a chunk of the city, like what happened in Wilhelm's reign?'

'The Bright Order's magic is volatile in such a way,' said Kardiggian hurriedly. 'We have no such–'

'That's not the point!' snapped the Emperor. 'Whatever it is you do, what if it goes wrong and Altdorf wakes up to find a few dozen buildings gone? Or you exorcise something and it gets loose? Or whatever it is that you do that is dangerous, I'll wager there's something. What am I to tell the people? That you huddle in your pyramid without anyone being responsible to the outside world? What if there's another duel, and innocents suffer because of it? Yes, I know about your duel. Sigmar's rump, we saw the light show above the island, Altdorfers aren't all blind and stupid. Am I to tell the people of the Empire that it is no one's fault? That responsibility is shared across a whole secret order of mumbling wizards none of whom will be punished? No, there must be someone to blame. One man. A man in charge, like I am, on whom all the sins committed under his rule will fall. By the winter solstice, magisters. That gives you five months. You might never have done it faster than eighteen but with the right motivation I imagine you can do wonders. If I and my Reiksguard marching in and installing a Grand Magister myself doesn't count as such a motivation then there really is no hope for you.'

VAN HORSTMANN WAS not a political creature. He preferred to have things unravel around him while he watched, rather than being the one unpicking the stitches. Eckhard III, he had decided, was not a good man to treat as an adversary because he knew more about the workings of an empire than van Horstmann ever could. That was how and why Eckhardt conducted himself like such an irascible oaf – he knew what he could get away with, and got away with everything he could. Nevertheless, van Horstmann thought he had done quite well. He had made his plea to the traditions and sensitivities of the Light Order sound just feeble and complaining enough, enough like the wheedling of an intellectually privileged elite, that the Emperor had been subtly enraged by it. If Eckhardt III had ever contemplated leaving the Light Order to sort out their own affairs, van Horstmann had probably seen to it that he would not.

It was an uncomfortable time. The order was uncertain. Divinations all gave results of obscurity and confusion. The daily rituals to conceal the pyramid and aid the Light Order's magic were faltering – the uncertainty infected the acolytes in the Chanter's Hall in subtle ways, leaving their ceremonies ragged and substandard. The senior magisters formed an ad hoc ruling council, but without any rules for their decision-making, without any clear responsibility, they would be unable to respond very effectively to a crisis.

Before he had joined the Light Order, van Horstmann would have been surprised to learn a college of Altdorf was so ill-prepared to cope with the death of a Grand Magister. He would have assumed they had volumes of procedure and precedent to deal with just such an eventuality. But he had come to understand that the orders were too slow to move, too obsessive and introverted, to adopt such a sensible practice. There was not one man in the whole order, excepting perhaps Elrisse himself while he lived, who could administer such an organisation. They were scholars and philosophers. Some of them were warriors, and more than a few were wild-eyed madmen. None of them were men who, like Minister Huygens of the Imperial Court, cared only that everything around them ran smoothly.

Van Horstmann thought on this as he reached his quarters. Since the Battle of Drufenhaag he had been here rarely, more frequently attending the gatherings of senior magisters who attempted to steer the order through the mire of collegiate politics. Skaven agents had sewn disorder and disease both before and after the invasion from below, and the mages of Altdorf were battling – metaphorically this time – over how best to deal with this new threat. Even worse than the ratmen themselves was the fear of them and the paranoia that had seen supposed traitors lynched and strung up in the streets of Altdorf. It was not a good time to be in charge of anything, much less to have no one in charge at all.

The Skull of Katam lay on its side on van Horstmann's writing desk. Van Horstmann took from beneath his robes a large book, bound apparently in soiled bandages and kept closed with a tied length of leather. He placed it on the desk beside the skull, untied it, and opened it on a random page. The page was badly stained and all but ruined by damp. Only the crudeness of the symbols scrawled there rendered them legible at all.

'What do you know of this?' asked van Horstmann.

The Skull of Katam rocked and set itself upright again. 'Where did this come from?'

Van Horstmann examined the sacrificial knife he kept on a

shelf beside a few of Magister Vek's knick-knacks. Blood still crusted the place where the blade met the hilt. He had given up trying to clean it – the blood always remained. 'From the dead claws of the skaven warlord at Drufenhaag,' he said.

'And what else did you take from it?' asked the skull.

'Just the book,' said van Horstmann.

'Liar,' replied the skull. 'It is a version of the *Liber Pestilentius*. Dictated to the monks of La Misercordias abbey. This is a severely debased version, in the tongue of the ratmen. I can scarcely read a word of it, but this much I can tell you.'

'You have come across this book before?'

'I have heard of it. There are not many such things I have not heard of. It is for this reason that you sought me out, is it not?'

Van Horstmann closed the book again. 'What does it contain?'

'Diseases,' said the skull. 'A thousand of them in the original, though no complete copy of it now exists to my knowledge. This version will no doubt have hundreds. Perhaps the ratmen added their own, I do not know. I doubt anyone can read it.'

'Do they need to?'

'There is magic in its words,' said the skull. 'Old and deadly magic. Plague magic, much coveted by the skaven. To understand the manner in which each plague kills, how it spreads? Then, you would have to read it. But as a focus for the working of such magic, no. It is enough to possess it.'

'Good,' said van Horstmann.

He walked to one of the huge bull-bodied statues that

Vek had, for reasons best known to himself, had transported up to decorate his chambers. It must have been a daemon's own job to get them in here. Van Horstmann had wondered from time to time just where they had come from, and why Vek had wanted such ugly things glowering down over him whenever he sat down to work on his alchemical formulae. Van Horstmann was glad, now, that he had.

Van Horstmann ran a hand along the flank of the statue, and whispered a many-syllabled word he had concocted for the purpose. Sigils glowed as the hand passed over them and the side of the statue ground open, hinging out and then sliding aside.

Inside was not the hollow interior of the statue, as might have been expected. Instead the opening led to another room, as large as the chamber's main room. It would have to project into the adjoining room for its whole size to be contained within the pyramid, but that space was taken up with the chambers of another magister and a small reading room tucked within the unusual architecture of the pyramid. There was no room for this new chamber, which meant that it did not exist here at all, but somewhere else.

This new room was flooded with light, as was the rest of the pyramid. Panes of polished crystal hung on the walls, splitting the light into shafts of colour. Cushions of crimson and dark-blue fabric were piled on the floor to permit meditation, and several glass-fronted cases held implements of van Horstmann's study of Dark magic.

Here he kept the horned skull, taken not from a bull or a ram but a human mutant executed in an Imperial backwater village. Three shelves of forbidden books were chained shut. A wand of twisted black wood and a tablet of ivory inscribed with images of human sacrifice took pride of place. If anyone were to find this room, which existed in its own pocket of space much like the Light Order's pyramid itself, then van Horstmann's pursuit of Dark magic would be revealed. That was why it had to be secret. That was why he had diverted much of his intellect to building it since ascending to the rank of comprehender, researching and modifying the space-folding rituals of the order to make a place that existed and yet did not.

Van Horstmann added the *Liber Pestilentius* to the book-shelf. The volume next to it, a transcription of possession victims' rantings bound in the scaly skin of some dark-blue reptilian creature, growled darkly at the newcomer. Van Horstmann cast the book a stern glance and it quietened down.

'They will find it,' said the Skull of Katam. 'They can hardly fail to do so. This path will lead you to ruin, van Horstmann.'

'I know,' said van Horstmann. 'And if you continue to bother me with what I already know, I will seal you in here and leave you to stare at the walls, just as you did in the vaults.' Van Horstmann left his sanctum and closed the statue again, the join rendered seamless by subtle magics. 'The book,' he said, 'will make things easier. But nothing will be simple. It is time to move on, Katam. To take another step on the road you think leads to ruin.'

'Then it is time once again to wake up Hiskernaath,' said the skull.

'Yes,' said van Horstmann. 'It is.'

CHAPTER ELEVEN
THE HAND CERULEAN

ON THE FIFTEENTH day of the ninth month, the stars converged such that the Bale Orb that hung hidden among the constellations shone down on the Old World. Power, visible only to the enlightened, poured down from that blinded eye and the Hand Cerulean gathered to bask in the light that only they could see.

They did this in a rotting bank of warehouses, damp and sagging, poised to topple into the sluggish water of the Reik. Here, in a half-abandoned wharf district, the river's water backed up against a quay caked in filth and detritus washed from upriver. The only boats that docked here were those captained by men whose reputations were so dire in the legitimate ports of Altdorf that they could moor nowhere else. Most of the other visitors were the corpses dumped in the river by accident, murder or suicide, who could often be seen bobbing amongst the weeds and trash before some hidden current or predator dragged them from view. The corpses, and the Hand Cerulean.

Van Horstmann saw this sorry place for the first time as the sun went down. From across the rickety Pauper's Bridge it seemed a precarious collection of buildings, only the mould on the walls keeping it from collapsing entirely.

'Not much of a place for planning the apocalypse,' he said.

Beside him stood the witch hunter, introduced to him as Lord Argenos. Alongside them were Heiden Kant, the magister who had recently made such promising strides in the arts of exorcism, and half a dozen grim-faced men armoured like a ragtag militia. Van Horstmann could tell from their scars and their musculature that they were more than thugs – they were killers, and they killed in the employ of the Emperor's witch hunters. Each carried a selection of butcher's knives, wooden stakes and torches, along with whatever signature weapon they had learned to love. All their swords and cudgels had tally marks cut into the handles.

'The enemy waxes great not in our sight,' replied Argenos. 'He is everywhere. It should surprise us not to find him in the unlikeliest of places.'

'Can you tell us more about them?' asked Kant. He had matured greatly ever since van Horstmann had last encountered him before the affair of Elrisse's death, but even so he saw in the magister the pale youth who had shivered beneath the Imperial Palace at the exorcism of Princess Astrid. 'The word was only that the Light Order must attend, and that the enemy calls themselves the Hand Cerulean. We had no time to look into them further.'

'You would have found nothing,' replied Argenos. 'The Silver Hammer does not let just anyone peruse the intelligence it gathers. The Hand Cerulean are living proof of the corruptibility of the human condition. They seek enlightenment, which is the excuse so commonly used by the followers of the Dark Gods. In their case, they seek it by giving their souls to the daemon.'

'You mean possession?' asked Kant.

'Indeed. That fate which all sane men abhor, these cultists crave. It is a sign of the greatest favour for them to be possessed by the daemon. What we have heard of them suggests that only those who have been so violated are permitted to recieve their mysteries. You see why the attendance of the Light Order, and of their expertise in exorcism, was much desired.'

'More and more of them crop up in this city,' mused van Horstmann as he watched the red sky darkening behind the ragged skyline of Altdorf. 'Ever since we threw back the ratmen. Fear and madness have been sewn among its people, and cults like this are the result.'

'No,' said Argenos. 'We are the result. Retribution and redemption. The story ends not with the Hand Cerulean, but with their destruction.'

The sun dipped below the horizon, and the district was swathed in shadow.

'Then let's get to it,' said van Horstmann.

The witch hunting party moved with grim swiftness across the bridge and into the stinking alleyways of the wharf. It had been hurriedly assembled, Lord Argenos recieving intelligence of the cult's whereabouts and gathering his muscle even as a message was sent to the Light Order indicating the need for exorcists. It was the first time van Horstmann had crossed paths with the Silver Hammer, which he knew to be an order of witch hunters, priests of Sigmar and other pious men devoted to rooting out evil among the Empire's people. In their zeal they had been responsible for countless false accusations and mass executions. Quite possibly, for every true devotee of Chaos they executed, more than one innocent man or woman was tried and killed. Van Horstmann also knew that the Silver Hammer themselves would not have a problem with such a statistic at all.

'It is the stars that bring them out,' said Argenos as the thugs lined up beside a doorway, recently rebuilt and sturdy in contrast to the rest of the area. 'These ones watch the skies. A dangerous field of study. Only madness lies there.'

'What is your plan?' asked Kant.

'Fire,' said Argenos. 'Then the sword. Then, for what remains, the ministrations of the exorcist.'

'How many know we are here?' asked van Horstmann. The speed with which the operation had been mounted had left him too many unanswered questions. Van Horstmann did not like those.

'As many as need to know,' said Argenos. 'The enemy has spies everywhere, even among our most trusted. The fewer know of our deeds, the fewer traitorous tongues can take news of it to our quarry.'

Two of Argenos's men had crowbars at the hinges of the door. Two more knelt to light their torches with flints, and the last two took glass vessels from their packs. Each vessel was spherical, stoppered with a rag in a plug of wax.

'Magister Kant,' said van Horstmann. 'It is rare that wizards of the colleges and the witch hunters work so closely together. There are some hunters who would rather see us all burned at the stake than fight alongside us.'

'These are desperate times,' replied Kant, once out of Argenos's earshot. 'The enemy we faced at Drufenhaag has resorted to other means to get at us. And while some of us are battle magisters and others are exorcists, I have perhaps walked furthest of all on the path of the diplomat. It is true, though, that a man like Argenos would not leap to let us in on the Silver Hammer's operations. He needs us, I think, and he knows it.'

The doors were levered open a crack. Witch Hunter Argenos drew his weapons. In one hand he had a warhammer, its bright silver head shining in the starlight, and in the other was a flintlock pistol. Van Horstmann had rarely seen such a weapon, for they were crafted only by the best gunsmiths of Nuln. Argenos kissed the pistol and whispered a prayer, and the ball loaded into its muzzle shone with a blue-white light that bled from the end of the barrel.

The witch hunter nodded. The two men swung the door open. In the same moment the other four lit the rags stuffed into the glass vessels, and hurled them into the open doorway.

In that moment, van Horstmann got his first look at the Hand Cerulean. He had no idea how the Silver Hammer had learned of them, but it had done so with no time to spare. Twelve figures knelt in a circle, wearing nothing more than loincloths, their skin painted blue and covered in silver stars. Three more stood in the centre of the circle and while they had started out dressed and marked the same as the other worshippers, they were something else entirely now. One had, in place of a head, a mass of flesh roughly the shape of a flattened worm fringed with wriggling limbs like those of a centipede. The mass pulsed and flapped, pink veins writhing beneath its taut, shiny surface. The mouth of the second had grown wider and wider until it formed a maw reaching from its chest to the middle of its face, and in that black pit seethed a mass of worms or perhaps stubby, slimy feelers. The left side of the third figure's body had blistered up into an enormous membranous sac that sloshed as if filled with water, its left arm and leg lost in the folds of heaving flesh.

One of the kneeling worshippers turned at the sound of the splintering door. In the light of the flame that tumbled past it, van Horstmann saw its eye sockets, empty and black, as if drilled through to a place of utter darkness.

The two firebombs landed and shattered. One smashed against the side of a worshipper's face, not giving him time to even turn around. The other hit a joist holding up the warehouse's upper level and broke there. Flame billowed and a rush of superheated air slammed into van Horstmann, almost knocking him back from the doorway.

Instantly, the worshippers' reverie was broken. They screamed. Van Horstmann could just see two of them running through the fire, aflame from head to toe, careening senselessly at random. Others were running into the further reaches of the warehouse to find the relative safety of its furthest corners.

The three deformed creatures – possessed, van Horstmann had no doubt – did not run. They turned to one another as if in silent conference, even as the flame caught on the straw and detritus of the floor and wreathed around their feet. It caught on their clothes and skin, and began to consume them even as they turned calmly towards the intruders.

Argenos was first in. 'By my proclamation, be execution upon thee!' he cried. He levelled his pistol and shot the nearest one, the flesh sac, through the head. The blessed bullet tore a channel through its face and sent showers of blue sparks exploding from the ruin of its skull. A pulse of power spread from the impact and the other possessed darted away, lost in the flame and smoke. The body that hauled the flesh sac toppled over and the sac burst, a cloud of foul orange steam sizzling from the corpse.

'Surround it!' shouted Argenos. 'Let none escape! Wizards, you are with me!'

Van Horstmann followed Argenos in. He whispered the syllables of a protective spell, one he had mastered and memorised so it was cast with barely a thought. A shimmering dome of energy sprung into life over him, encompassing himself, Kant and Argenos. Flame rushed towards them and swarmed over the dome. The heat was appalling, barely breathable, but the fire did not reach them.

A worshipper stumbled into their path. Her teeth were bared – van Horstmann saw it was a woman, her long hair cut into a single lock at the back of her neck. Her teeth were filed and pointed, and blood ran down her chin. Argenos knocked her down with a boot to the chest, and shattered her forehead with a downward swing of his hammer. The woman hissed out her last breath and lolled over, dead.

'Thus are your wages,' shouted Argenos over the rush and thunder of the fire. 'Thus does Sigmar repay your service!'

Van Horstmann saw silvery bolts of light springing from Kant's fingertips, scoring deep furrows along the warehouse walls where more worshippers scurried for cover. One fell, but van Horstmann could not tell if Kant had struck him. Van Horstmann himself concentrated on the spell that was keeping them alive, calling down a column of Light magic from the sky to pour over them and douse the infernal heat that threatened to scorch his throat with every breath.

The creature with the worm-like head came charging through the fire. It was aflame itself, the skin of the lower half of its body black and charred. It headed straight for Argenos who was a split second too late with the swing of his hammer. He was bowled to the ground and the possessee rolled over him, thrown off-balance by its momentum.

The thing rolled to its feet in front of van Horstmann. Van Horstmann's mind raced and time seemed to slow down. In front of him was the monster, mutated beyond any semblance of humanity by the daemon that he could almost taste writhing inside the once-human soul. But in front of him also hung a thousand jewels, each a spell he had researched, reconstructed and committed to memory, filed away in the fastidious library of his mind. He chose one that gleamed with deadliness and purity, plucked it from its shelf and let it dissolve through his mind until it hummed with power at the ends of his fingers.

Darts of it shot out and punctured the flesh of the possessed cultist's chest. Silver strands whipped around the supports that held up the roof. The darts held fast and the cultist was pinned in place, straining against the silver bonds that suddenly held it. One arm was twisted almost behind its back and the mass of its head was constrained, even as it tried to strike forward like a scorpion's tail.

It had eyes, van Horstmann saw now, tiny and faceted like those of an insect, and between each pair of centipede limbs a set of mandibles surrounded by bristly black hair.

He knew this daemon. He had read of it in the forbidden books first described to him by the Skull of Katam. It was an offshoot of the Plague God, the one debased men called Nurgle. He had read of what it did to those it possessed – they first turned into a wormlike creature of which this mutation was the first stage, then pupated, and emerged as a gigantic fly with a distended belly full of plague agents. Such knowledge, of course, would mark van Horstmann out as one who delved into the works of the enemy, so he would have to feign ignorance.

Argenos was on his feet. His hammer came down against the cultist's knee, still a human and vulnerable limb. Van Horstmann heard the bone crack and the leg folded the wrong away. The cultist hung in the silver threads, arms flailing uselessly towards van Horstmann.

Kant drove his staff, a long, slender shaft of gold tipped with a shard of crystal, into the chest of the ensnared cultist. Light crackled around the crystal as it punched out through the cultist's back and earthed through its convulsing body.

From the flames leapt the third mutant cultist, whose body had warped into a portal into another extra-real space crammed with writhing worms. It barrelled into van Horstmann, who lost his footing and fell under its weight.

His staff flew from his fingers, and Lizbeta's golden death mask was lost in the fire that crackled along the filthy straw that covered the floor.

The mass of the cultist seemed to grow, its body filling more with the seething mass that pressed forwards through its mouth. The cultist's eyes were pale and dry, like those of a day-old fish at market – the cultist had long gone, his body given over entirely to the daemon that possessed it. That daemon took the form of a mass of worms, and it was reaching out now with its hundreds of limbs to grasp at van Horstmann's hands and face.

The stench of it was awful. Even the smoke and heat took second place to the breath that reeked from its mouth. Each worm had a tubular mouth of its own, tiny teeth gnashing, ringed with black bead-like eyes.

Bile rose in van Horstmann's throat. His heart thudded. He felt himself detached from his body suddenly, as if he was fleeing from the horror of it, and with a lurch of shame and nausea realised that he was losing control.

Some of him recognised it. That relentless, organised, unfeeling part of him, on which he relied so much, could see what was happening. But the rest of him would not obey.

The fortress did not stand before him, anchoring him in the winds of the aethyr.

Instead, there was only the pit.

THOUGH VAN HORSTMANN knew, with every rational faculty he had, that this was not a real place, it seemed as completely real as the burning warehouse and the possessed cultist that pinned him to the floor. That world now seemed far away and only the pit registered on his most immediate senses.

The clammy, cold scales of the snakes writhed against his skin. The press of them crushed his chest and made every breath a fight. The stench of them was worse, somehow, than the otherworldly stink of the worm daemon.

Only Lizbeta's hand in his told him there was any good in this world. He held on as tight as he could and she held on too, and the pain of her grip around his fingers was something he could cherish. He kicked out to force himself upwards towards the open air and bring her with him, pull her from the coils of the snakes and deliver her to safety. But the snakes would not let go and Lizbeta did not budge.

He could hear her. She was sobbing, or perhaps screaming, her voice smothered. He fought all the harder and wrenched his joints with the effort, but he was little more than a boy and he had never been strong. Not in body, at least. For all his intelligence and cunning, he could not think or talk his way out of this.

'Lizbeta!' he cried. 'Don't let go! Don't... don't be afraid. I'll save you. I promise!'

Even as he said it, he knew it was a lie.

Lizbeta's hand was gone. Van Horstmann's stomach turned over as he felt for her slender fingers again, sure that if he found her he would grab her with renewed strength and pull her up from the pit. But she was nowhere. Van Horstmann risked sinking too low to escape as he groped among the slithering coils for his sister. She was gone. He couldn't hear her any more.

Van Horstmann fought to drag himself up. He would clamber from the pit and… do what? Empty it? Wrestle every snake, break its spine, and cast it aside until the pit was empty save for Lizbeta? Would she somehow be alive down there, waiting patiently for him to rescue her?

It didn't matter. He could not organise those thoughts into anything coherent. He kicked and fought, thrashing out a few inches of space at a time. A hand broke the surface into air and he could draw breath now, thick and foul as the air was.

The pit was dug into the floor of a cave, lit by a few smoky torches on the walls. It was a cold and wet place, silty water dripping from the stalactites overhead. Van Horstmann could see the entrance to the cave, the slick rock walls edged in the light that crept down from the surface above.

There stood the woman, watching. From a distance she was achingly beautiful. Up close, she had the look of something that waited for its prey beneath the mud. She dressed well but practically as if for riding, wrapped in a black travelling cloak lined with crimson against the cold. Her skin was very pale and her hair a blonde as light as buttermilk. She had green eyes and thin red lips that, when she smiled to see van Horstmann struggling to reach the edge of the pit, curled up like a wound cut with a curved knife.

Van Horstmann had seen her fleetingly before. He and his sister had needed help – a ride in the woman's coach, for the night before had been stormy and dangerous. Beastmen were abroad and he feared for Lizbeta's safety. He had to protect her, after all. All they had was each other.

He had woken in this pit, and as the serpents tried to drag them down he had told his sister that she was safe, that he would get her out of this just like he had every dangerous place they had wandered. She had promised the same. She would save him. But she was younger, and weaker, and had always relied on her brother Egrimm's quick mind to keep her safe.

'You do not understand this now,' the woman said in a cutglass accent that spoke of the finest city breeding. 'But your gift to us is the knowledge we glean from your death. Thank you, young man. You and your companion have given your Empire in death more than you ever could in life.'

Van Horstmann tried to pull himself onto the surface of the snake pit and drag himself for the edge, to reach the cave floor and run for the way out. But he was tired, and every part of him hurt.

And Lizbeta was gone. She was all he had. What did anything mean now? What did living mean?

The woman vanished from his memory, leaving the echo of her smile behind. Darkness fell.

* * *

'LORD COMPREHENDER!' SHOUTED a voice in his ear. 'We must get out! The whole place is going to come down!'

The voice belonged to Magister Kant, who was bent over van Horstmann shouting at the top of his voice. The roar of the fire almost drowned out his words.

Beside him, Witch Hunter Argenos aimed his pistol again at a cultist who had clambered to an upper level of the warehouse for shelter. The pistol barked and the cultist's head disappeared in a mist of silver and crimson.

Van Horstmann forced himself back into the moment. His protective spell had faltered and the flames rushed closer. He got to his feet, unable to stifle the sense of disdain as he realised Kant had helped him up.

Kant handed van Horstmann his staff. It was hot to the touch, having lain down in the flames, but Lizbeta's face was undamaged. He gasped out the syllables of the spell again, this time tingeing it with a thread of chill magic that fended off the worst of the scalding air. He could breathe again now and he followed Kant towards the nearest way out – a set of double doors, probably for livestock, that the cultists must have thrown open to escape.

He reached the open air to see two of the cultists lying in a broken heap being beaten by three of Argenos's thugs. The cultists looked dead, but the Silver Hammer's men were making sure. Argenos ran out, reloading his pistol with a shot that glowed in his fingers. A wayward part of van Horstmann's mind wondered how many hours a priest must have prayed over the sacred bullets to imbue them with such power.

'What news?' yelled Argenos. 'How many have fled us?'

'But none, Lord Argenos,' replied one of the thugs. 'We caught them all, the few that survived.'

'And alive?'

The thug smiled. From around the side of the warehouse came the remainder of the thugs, dragging the senseless bodies of two of the possessed cultists. One was the flesh-sac creature that Argenos had shot. Though its head was gone, presumably whatever animated it did not need the host body's brain to survive, because its mass still heaved with uneven breaths. The other was the one that had so nearly done for van Horstmann, its enormous maw now a half-closed drooling slit, the worm-daemon retreated deep inside it.

Argenos indicated a building a couple of streets away. 'The fire will spread,' he said, 'but we cannot move them far and so our work must be done here, and quickly. Take them to that building. Magister Kant, prepare a circle. Comprehender van Horstmann, we will need your new rituals now.'

'Not new,' said van Horstmann. His throat was raw and smoky as he spoke. 'Very old.'

'Even better,' said Argenos. 'Let us begin.'

THEY MOVED QUICKLY. Twenty acolytes waited on the other side of the river and Magister Kant sent up a magical flare, in the shape of a white-plumed bird soaring from his hand into the sky, to summon them. They were untrained and without reliable offensive or protective magic of their own, and so had not been trusted to fend for themselves in the assault on the cult's hideout, but now Argenos and the Light wizards needed obedient and reliable ritualists to complete the destruction of the Hand Cerulean.

It was a second warehouse they used, this one untouched for what looked like years. Crates of abandoned cargo – bolts of cheap cloth, furniture, heaps of uncured leather – mouldered in the damp. The Silver Hammer thugs kept watch, peering into the corners with torches in hand as they sought out the enemies the Silver Hammer was convinced lay everywhere.

The acolytes stood in a circle and chanted the passages they had memorised, a new set of ritual exultations that van Horstmann had handed to Master Chanter Alric just a couple of weeks before. Van Horstmann formed a link in the circle and Lord Argenos looked on, his hand never far from the grip of his ensorcelled pistol.

He was watching for any sign of danger from the subjects of this ritual. The two possessed cultists lay tied up in the middle of the circle. The one with the enormous worm-filled mouth lay on its side, heaving with ragged breaths in a puddle of drool. The one with the fleshy sac seemed to have replaced the fluid inside somewhat, the mass of oily flesh hanging from its left side now deformed with shifting, bulbous shapes, as if whatever it was incubating was fighting to be born. This cultist, of course, had no head, and its human portions had bled white from the ragged stump of its neck.

Magister Kant, who specialised in the arts of exorcism, led the ritual. He had brought with him his own implements – a selection of knives, tongs and searing irons – in case the daemons inside the cultists required a physical effort as well as a spiritual one to be extracted from their hosts.

With possessees this far gone, this far corrupted by the daemons inside them, the survival of the host could never be considered a priority.

'Light that bathes the aethyr, accept the sacrifice of our devotion!' called out Kant. He, too, had memorised his part in the ritual. 'Heralds of the enemy, out! From this flesh, we cast thee out!'

The language the acolytes chanted had no equal in the tongues of human lands. It existed only in one place, in the writings that van Horstmann had presented to the Light Order's exorcists as the greatest work of Egelbert Vries. Time and space seemed to warp as the acolytes spoke it. The shadows bowed in, as if the warehouse structure had become malleable and was deforming under the force of the Light magic coursing around the circle. The light of the torches crept up and down the walls in smouldering fingers. Straight lines curved and angles did not add up, and the rules of reality slowly ceased to apply.

The rules of the will would supersede them. And even the daemon would be subject to those rules.

The possessed cultists were changing, too. The flesh-sac became evermore agitated, exposing more of the dead cultist's original form as it tried to pull away. The shape of a hunched figure appeared against the walls of the sac, a broken and monstrous face with one eye and one horn, gnarled hands, a distended belly that itself writhed with life. The mouth of the other cultist yawed wide and the wormy mass was forced out, inch by inch, as if retched up, the tiny ring-shaped mouth of each worm leeching wide as if trying to scream.

'Your gods have no authority here!' shouted Kant. The chanting grew louder and the daemons mewled and growled, like animals cornered and in pain. 'I am in command, and I command you to depart these vessels of flesh!'

The worm-daemon was the first out, vomited from the cultist's enlarged mouth. It was a heaving pile the size of a horse, far larger than should have been able to fit inside the cultist. Its hundreds of worms were rooted in heavy glistening lumps of whitish muscle, like knots of broken and skinless limbs. They unfolded revealing asymmetrical, atrophied fingers that tried to drag the daemon's bulk along the warehouse floor. Large wet eyes blinked in the folds of muscle and a pair of mandibles chattered. It shed dead worms as it did so, and they curled up and shrivelled when shorn of their master and exposed to the reality that abhorred the daemon.

A hand tore from the flesh-sac of the second cultist. The thing that emerged dripped with pale-red birthing fluid but its flesh was a dank, warty green. It was roughly humanoid in shape but its head was thrust forwards on a neck that emerged from its chest. Its face was thuggish and slack-jawed. It had one yellow eye and a single horn in its forehead. Its arms were overlong and its hands dragged on the floor as it forced its way upright, and its belly sagged down, full of its own young of seething insects that spilled from rents in the flesh.

'Back!' shouted van Horstmann. He thrust out his staff, not leaving his place in the circle, and cast a wall of shimmering light around the emerging daemon. The daemon battered its fists against the wall of its magical prison but it held fast. 'A lesser daemon,' said van Horstmann to Kant. 'A bearer of the plague. I can hold it. The other, I am not so sure. It must not leave the circle. Banish them now.'

'I have a destination of my own,' said Lord Argenos, drawing his pistol. 'And I will banish them both there if you cannot.'

'No!' snapped van Horstmann. 'The daemon does not die. It will return. Properly exorcised, it will not escape its bonds in the aethyr for a thousand years. They must be banished by the Light.'

'Begone!' yelled Kant, as the chanting rose in volume. 'Wither and burn in the Light!'

The daemons mewled and moaned. A blue-white glow shone down from above and their skin blistered in it.

Van Horstmann turned his head to look at one of Argenos's thugs. 'Bring him in,' he said. 'Quickly.'

The thug nodded and went to one corner of the warehouse. From among the trash he brought a cultist – the last surviving member of the Hand Cerulean, mouth gagged and hands and ankles tied. He had painted himself to resemble the night sky but much of the paint had rubbed off, revealing the bruises and cuts administered by the Silver Hammer during his capture.

The thug threw the cultist into the circle. The cultist, unable to keep his balance, fell face-first to the floor and fresh blood flowed from his nose. The cultist was trying to speak, to yell, but the gag thankfully muffled his words.

Van Horstmann took the familiar wavy-bladed knife from his robes. He stepped into the centre, the acolytes swiftly taking his place to keep the circle intact. He knelt beside the cultist and pulled the man's head back. The air was thick with power and van Horstmann could feel crackles of it earthing from his fingers and toes into the floor. His mouth was suddenly dry, a metallic taste in his mouth.

The cultist's eyes were wide. The religious ecstasy that had fuelled the Hand Cerulean was gone, and now there was little more than fear there. There wasn't even much hatred. In spite of the oaths he had sworn to his god – the Plague God, van Horstmann guessed, the one they called Nurgle – this man had never truly examined the fact that one day he would die. The day had come, and he was not ready.

'This life,' called Magister Kant, 'in exchange for the strength to cast you from this realm! This life, for your eternal banishment! As the blood flows, so shall you begone!'

Van Horstmann thrust the knife through the cultist's neck. The blade might have been ornamental but it was also sharp. It passed clean through. Van Horstmann twisted it and tore it out through the cultist's throat, the edge cutting clean through the windpipe and voice box. The blood sprayed almost up to the ceiling, the cultist's hammering, terrified heart propelling an arc of it high into the air.

Van Horstmann let the cultist flop back onto his face. The blood pooled in a spreading red-black pool.

Flitting sparks of white fire flew, like insects. They spiralled and looped around the circle, and where they struck the foreheads of the chanting acolytes the young wizards' eyes lit up with pulses of magical power. Their chanting was echoed by cascading notes, like a great but distant choir singing. Fragments of skin lifted off the cultist's body, turning to ash and lifted towards the ceiling on an unfelt current of energy.

The daemons were suffering a similar fate. The plague-bearer's skin was a crackled black carapace, as if it had been charred in a fire, and was lifting away to reveal pale white-veined muscle underneath. It lifted its head and brayed. The worm-daemon was shedding the creatures of which it was composed, each one wriggling as it was carried aloft.

Van Horstmann hurried back to his place in the circle of acolytes, wiping the bloody blade on the sleeve of his robe.

Even Lord Argenos looked impressed by the sight, as the dead cultist and the daemons were all, morsel by morsel, picked apart and winnowed to ash. The plaguebearer was reduced to a skeleton, its mouth locked open as its yellow eye rotted away leaving a filth-caked open socket staring at the ceiling. Its ribs were exposed, and the purple-black masses of maggoty viscera spilled from where its stomach had been.

The worm-daemon was reduced to a quivering lump of muscle. It tried to grow new limbs to drag itself out of the circle but they, too, were reduced to corroded bone by the force of the purity that Light magic forced onto everything in the circle.

The last remnants of them were handfuls of bone. A broken pelvis, a pair of snickering mandibles. A spine. And then they, too, were gone.

Magister Kant held up a hand and the chanting ceased. The acolytes bowed their heads.

'It is done?' asked Lord Argenos.

'It is done,' said van Horstmann. 'Vries's ritual is everything we hoped. They were stripped down to their component magics and cast to the winds of the aethyr.'

'Good,' said Argenos. 'And if what you say is true, they will be the first of many.' He looked at Magister Kant, who still held his place in the circle. 'Kant,' he said. 'You do not agree with the means.'

'With the sacrifice?' said Kant. 'No, I do not. I would have preferred another way.'

'There is none so quick,' replied van Horstmann. 'Or so strong.'

'I know,' said Kant. 'But I would have preferred another way.'

'Then you, Magister Kant, will never understand what it means to take up the hammer and the stake, the thumbscrew and the holy book, in the name of Sigmar.' Lord Argenos addressed his men. 'Leave this place. The flames will consume what little we have left.'

The acolytes and the thugs hurried out, pausing to collect what little they had brought with them. In the alleyway outside were piled the bodies of the Hand Cerulean's cultists, and they would soon be turned to ash by the fire that was threatening to leap across the alley from one rooftop to the other.

'Vries hid these rituals of exorcism for a reason,' said Kant. 'Is that not so? That was how he thought.'

'It was,' said van Horstmann, as the two followed the Silver Hammer's men towards the nearest bridge across the Reik.

'Then he hid them so that they would be found when they were needed,' continued Kant.

'Indeed. And whatever he saw coming, it will be upon us soon.'

'Dark days.'

'Darker even than these, Magister Kant.'

HISKERNAATH WAS WAITING when van Horstmann returned to his sanctum. The daemon, though released from his puzzle box, had been shut up in the extra-spatial room van Horstmann had created within the statue. It was crouching on one wall, drooling ropes of thick green-black spittle when van Horstmann opened the statue's flank again.

'A shame,' hissed the daemon. 'I was just starting to enjoy your taste in cushions.'

Van Horstmann knew better than to answer the daemon. He took the puzzle box from his robe and sat cross-legged on the cushions piled on the floor, avoiding what he hoped were patches of Hiskernaath's drool.

'And now I'm going back in,' it said. 'I look forward to it, you know. I have a hundred maidens in there, trussed up ready for rumplefyking. It's like the Cloisters of Saint Ludmilla on a feast day. You should see it.'

'Quiet,' said van Horstmann. With a well-practiced motion he operated the complex panels of the puzzle box. It sprang open in his hand.

The stench was terrible. The creature that emerged carried with it a stink so foul it was visible as a faint greasy haze. It materialised in the middle of the sanctum – the plaguebearer, the humanoid, one-eyed, one-horned servant of the Plague God.

'So, the ritual did not banish them,' said Hiskernaath. 'It captured them. It worked.'

Van Horstmann shot the daemon a look. 'Of course,' he said. 'I created it.'

'But this is a plaguebearer, van Horstmann,' said Hiskernaath. It reached a limb towards the plaguebearer, which snapped back at it like a cornered dog. 'One of the lowest of its kind. A foot soldier in Grandfather Nurgle's army. Surely you know this?'

'It is the first of many,' said van Horstmann. 'And it is not alone.'

Now, from the puzzle box issued a tide of worms, overflowing onto the floor. The torrent did not stop until a great heap of them lay there. From the centre of the pile emerged the mandibles and eyes of the daemon's core, swelling impossibly until it was even bigger than the creature that had forced its way from the deformed cultist's mouth.

'This is Morkulae,' said van Horstmann. 'The Key to the Nineteenth Gate. The Beautiful and the Pure. The patron saint of torturers and grave robbers. Nurgle's Cup-Bearer.'

The plaguebearer was on its front, grovelling and moaning, as if pleading.

'You will void your bowels with fear when I hold you over Nurgle's cauldron,' growled Morkulae, its mandibles making for a strange, many-voiced sound as if each worm was lending its own voice. 'And from your own leavings I shall concoct the plague that will devour you. Your own guts will eat their way out of you. Your eyes will crawl from their sockets. Your spine will slither from your back and you shall be alive, and aware, for every moment. Do you know how long such a disease can take to claim you? I infected souls at the beginning of the time who have not yet perished, and they cry out still from pustuled throats. Grandfather Nurgle keeps them at his side, for he loves the music they make.'

Van Horstmann pulled open the front of his robe, revealing a fresh tattoo just below his collarbone. There had only been just enough room to cram in the many lines of arcane wording, and seal it with the three-globed symbol of Nurgle.

'You will do no such thing,' said van Horstmann. 'Your Grandfather commands it.'

Morkulae recoiled and hissed, the worms standing up like the hairs on an angry cat's back. 'You dare cage Nurgle's Cup-Bearer with words?'

'I was tutored by the best,' said van Horstmann. 'Before the throne of Lord Tzeentch.'

'He isn't lying,' said Hiskernaath from his perch on the wall.

Morkulae could not reply for a long while. It was by now at its full size, significantly larger than the height of a man, shedding worms as it constantly grew new ones. 'Then,' it said. 'Then...'

'"Master" is an acceptable term of address,' said van Horstmann.

'Then what is your wish... master?'

Van Horstmann turned to one of the sanctum's shelves and took from it the *Liber Pestilentius*. He handed it to Morkulae, who took it in a pair of mandibles it extruded for the purpose.

'Inflict this on the city,' said van Horstmann. 'There will be others of your kind sent to aid you, for all who are banished by the Light Order's exorcisms are in truth sent here, to this prison, and in doing so are bound to contracts I have made with their gods. These are my commands, Morkulae of Nurgle: infect Altdorf. Let the plague spread as quickly as fear.'

Perhaps, if it had possessed the features of a human, Morkulae would have smiled.

CHAPTER TWELVE
THE GARDEN OF MORR

THROUGH THE NIGHT, the fear spread.

These beastmen were cowards. They had been defeated in open battle but instead of being slaughtered in the rout, they had vanished into the countryside of Reikland and seeded Altdorf with hundreds of spies and assassins to take the city by subterfuge.

Such was the gist of the rumours speeding through the city, and there were few who had any interest in quelling them. Enterprising Altdorfers had long sent out criers to street corners armed with scribbled notes of the latest news, to bark them to passers-by and be paid for their trouble in spare coins. The more shocking the news, the more grave the peril it implied, the more Altdorfers would reward it, as if they wanted to be afraid. And so rumours of the beastmen filled the streets.

If the barkers were to be believed, every murder and vanishing in Altdorf was the work of cloven-hoofed assassins rendered invisible by their mastery of strange stealth techniques. Every mutant child and two-headed animal was created by one of the beastman shamans, or was the detritus of some dark experiment they conducted beneath the streets. Even as learned men shook their heads at the ridiculousness of it all, some new horror was speculated to exist on the streets, and Altdorf's masses found such tales only too easy to believe.

One fearsome matron from the city's mercantile district, citing the safety of the city's children from monstrous baby-snatchers, raised a rabble of concerned city folk. They went into the catacombs, old fortifications and sewers beneath the city, hunting for the enemy they were certain lurked there. Although they found many strange things, skulking beastmen were not among them, but of course that was just proof of how good they were at hiding.

It was a curious feature of Altdorf, this quickness to panic. When Magnus the Pious had agreed with Teclis to the founding of the Colleges of Magic, the people had rioted and seen portents of destruction in everything. The wizards, they were certain, would be the doom of them all. They had evacuated the city en masse as the high elves and the students of Teclis created the magical defences that concealed the eight colleges, and when they returned to find their city subtly stranger they never lost their suspicions of the wizards in their midst. A child born fifty years before with the body of a snake was the catalyst for a rash of witch-burnings and lynching, in which hundreds of innocents lost their lives, along with, perhaps, a few genuine witches who should have learned to lay low. Grand Theogonist Thoss had taken advantage of Altdorfer paranoia to launch his crusade against all faiths bar that of Sigmar. It was how Altdorfers functioned. They were boisterous and outspoken, they were bold and cunning, and when they decided to fear something they feared it with a passion that tore out the foundations of their city.

It therefore came as no surprise when the first plague victims emerged. Coughing blood and moaning in pain, they stumbled from the hovels around the Bright College's location and the grim districts adjoining the wharves, begging for cure or release. And the people of Altdorf dug mass graves outside the walls, hoarded wood for funeral pyres, and proclaimed impending destruction as only they could.

THE CHANTER'S HALL was never quiet, but it was not the voices of acolytes that broke the calm now. The hammers of a crew of workmen echoed among the pillars as they scrabbled across the scaffolding stretched across one end of the chamber. Behind the podium that Master Chanter Alric used to address the acolytes was growing a structure of brass and wood, with a bank of great pipes visible through the planking holding it all in place. The brass was inscribed with elegant scrollwork and the hardwood, brought to the Empire in ships from distant lands, was a deep brown-black and lacquered in designs of gold.

Master Chanter Alric watched the men working. The crews had been sworn to secrecy, with a little help from some subtle magics of the mind, to protect the location of the Light College, and they had needed time to adjust from the extraordinary architecture and unbroken light of the pyramid. But now they were working quickly. Within the month, they would be finished.

'Master Chanter!' said van Horstmann brightly as he approached. 'I see our latest project has not stood idle.'

'It is beautiful,' said Alric. He had become an old man in the time van Horstmann had known him, the wrinkles around his eyes seeming deeper than ever. There were tears brimming behind those eyes, though Alric would never let himself show them before the acolytes. 'For decades I have wished for an organ to lend music to the voices of our order. I petitioned Elrisse for it more times than I can remember.' He looked at van Horstmann now, and the emotion on his face was clear even though he tried to keep it down. 'I could never say so to the acolytes, for they must believe the magisters above them are all of one mind. But he and I were opposed. I thought the organ would make our rituals stronger and improve the morale of the acolytes, but he thought it was a needless expense. Morr cherish his soul, our Grand Magister's death granted us this, at least.'

'I believed this project would raise our spirits in these grim times.'

'You spoke for it?' asked Alric.

'I did,' replied van Horstmann. 'Though we have no one leader, yet still one voice can accomplish something. I and the other senior magisters debated the matter and I swayed them.'

'Then this is your doing,' said Alric. 'I do not know what I thought of you when you were an acolyte, comprehender. There was such promise in you, such an organised mind, but I did not see the passion that a magister needs. I know now that you kept it hidden. I should have known better, I should have seen it. I underestimated you then, but now, we all see that you can take our order through this and out into a better future.'

One of the workers hauled a canvas cover away, revealing a triple tier of keyboards with keys cut from ivory. It might take three organists working in concert to use the organ's entire range.

'You flatter me, Master Chanter,' said van Horstmann. 'I am a researcher, that is where my passions lie. No wonder you did not see them.'

'The Emperor was right,' said Alric. His voice dropped, as if he was worried someone might be listening in. 'He said we need a leader. We do. Without it, we cannot react quickly enough to threats. The conflict with the Gold Order showed us those threats can come from anywhere. The other colleges might sense weakness and try to bring us down. It is a dark thing to countenance but plots have existed in the past, between other orders. And you hear what they say about the skaven. If they strike at us, they will try to strike at the colleges first. We must defend ourselves.'

'You are right,' said van Horstmann. 'But there is none who has emerged from among us to take control. Choosing a leader is not a simple business. Without a clear front runner, the process of selection will drag on and on.'

'There is you,' said Alric.

'Me?'

'Grand Magister van Horstmann. You think it strange? I think it is the perfect solution. You have respect among us. Some say you were conspicuous in your actions at Drufenhaag, the Emperor will admire that. And Elrisse trusted you.'

Van Horstmann took a sighing breath. 'I see,' he said. 'How many others have voiced this?'

'Few in the open,' said Alric. 'But I know I am not the only one who thinks it.'

'The Light Order fears a leader who is chosen quickly and for the moment,' said van Horstmann. 'It fears a tyrant. The orders always have.'

'That is a risk many are willing to take.'

'And how would I go about becoming the Grand Magister?' said Alric. 'What if Kardiggian stands against me and demands a wizard's duel to settle the matter? I am not a battle magister, as he is. He would incinerate me. And Vranas has made allies outside the Light Order, no doubt hoping to become Grand Magister himself. He could outmanoeuvre me, for he is a politician and I am not.'

'And if the magisters want you, they will get you. That is what matters.'

'Perhaps,' said van Horstmann. 'But aside from you, I hear no great clamour for me to become Grand Magister. Certainly nothing to shout down another candidate should he make himself known. And it is not as if this is a great ambition of mine. For other senior magisters it is. Vranas, to name only the obvious. Perhaps Kardiggian.'

'Nevertheless, comprehender,' said Alric, 'do not discount yourself.' He waved a hand at the grand pipe organ, now definitely taking shape behind the scaffolding. 'This need not be the only mark you leave on your order.'

'This is your legacy, Master Chanter,' said van Horstmann. 'Not mine. The pipe organ will play when we are all gone. You have left your mark here. Do not deny yourself that.'

'My thanks,' said Alric. 'And do not deny yourself leadership of our order. We need a leader. Altdorf needs us to have one, too. The whole Empire does. Think of it, comprehender.'

'I shall,' said van Horstmann.

Amid the hammering, footsteps on the marble floor caught van Horstmann's attention. An acolyte was hurrying towards them, flustered and sweating.

'Acolyte?' demanded Alric. His demeanour had changed back to the stern, unflappable face a Master Chanter presented to his acolytes.

'News from the Imperial Palace,' said the acolyte. 'Representatives of every order have been summoned at the behest of the Emperor. It is the plague, magisters. The priestesses of Shallya have proclaimed it the work of Dark magic. The city is quarantined.'

THE PLAGUE DOCTORS of Altdorf were a strange breed, in their own way as arcane and secretive as the orders of magic. They trained by apprenticeship, each one picking a successor to train, and parcelling out their secrets one cure at a time. They guarded those secrets carefully, refusing to reveal the laboratories and hidden wards where they perfected their arts, and

were paid collectively by the Imperial Court to watch over
the health of the city. The priestesses of Shallya hated them,
for they used bleedings, humours and strange concoctions
to do what Shallya taught should be done with faith and
prayer, but when disease ravaged the city no one could say
to whom the citizens turned the fastest.

One plague doctor led van Horstmann through the narrow
passageways towards the hospital. It was a makeshift place,
hardly fit for taking care of the sick. It looked like a length
of sewer that had been half-completed and then abandoned,
leaving a section of dressed stone tunnels and junctions
beneath the ground connected to nothing. Masons had
decorated the place with grotesque gargoyles and scratched
their names into the stone blocks, their etchings still visible
beneath the mould and damp.

'Every day, perhaps three dozen more cases are found
in this district alone,' the doctor was saying. His voice was
muffled by the conical mask he wore, the beak of it stuffed
with herbs to keep infectious fumes out of his lungs. Van
Horstmann was reminded of the doctor he had encountered
beneath the Imperial Palace, the one who had tended to the
possessed Princess Astrid. For all he knew it was the same
man. 'If the relatives permit, we bring them down here, where
they cannot infect anyone save us and each other. But many
refuse. They fear us, it seems, though I cannot fathom why.'

Van Horstmann could fathom perfectly well, given that the
plague doctors hid their faces behind goggles and masks, and
were only seen in the streets of Altdorf when disease stalked
the city. 'How many survive?' he asked.

'It is difficult to say,' said the doctor, 'given that the outbreak began only recently and has moved with impressive swiftness. We do not know if we have seen the disease run its full course in any one victim yet. Some seem to be recovering, but it might be that this is just the space between two stages of the plague, as with Wharf Rot or the Fingerbone Ague.'

'And can you tell how it moves from one person to another?'

'I believe it is a miasma of the air,' said the doctor. 'But some insist it is transmitted by vermin, others body fluids. With so many theories it is impossible to mobilise our resources to test any one. We are all fools, magister. Such ignorance is the means by which all disease is propagated.'

'Then ignorance is what we will fight,' said van Horstmann. He had brought with him a leather case, similar in size to the case of implements the plague doctor himself carried. He held it up. 'A device of my own design. Like everything in this world, a disease can be seen as a problem of logic. With this, I will discover the root principles of logic that lie behind it and thereby solve the problem.'

'A novel approach,' said the doctor. 'Personally, I fear the maladies of the human body are immune to logic. A place like this I cite as evidence.'

The two reached the ward itself, a junction of two sewers with a great vault overhead and deep channels lined with decorative stone. Sigmar knew how much money and man-hours had been sunk into these unfinished sewers, which had never seen a drop of excrement until now. Dozens of wooden beds had been set up and on almost all of them

were what resembled heaps of rags. From time to time one of
the piles would moan or turn over, or was spoken to by one
of the men and women who had evidently volunteered to
tend the suffering. Some were washing the sores and boils of
the victims, others were reapplying bandages to their limbs.
The smell was awful, and the volunteers wore scarves around
their noses and mouths.

'Most of our volunteers have relatives down here,' said
the plague doctor. 'They have already been exposed in their
homes so they assume there is no harm in further exposure.'

'I need to see a victim in the advanced stages,' said van
Horstmann, 'but not on his last legs. A strong one. One who
is fighting.'

'I see,' said the plague doctor. 'Here. I have just the man.'

At the end of one sewer section was a large man lying on
a bed, his shirt removed revealing the spiralling red-black
marks typical of the disease on his barrel chest. Van Horstmann saw right away the broken nose and cauliflower ears
of a man who fought for a living. His hands were big and
gnarled, and his skin was covered in old scars.

'Helmut,' said the doctor. 'Someone is here to see you.'

'I wish,' said Helmut, 'it would hurry up and bloody kill me.
Stuff this for living. If I wasn't so bloody-minded I'd have given
it up but damn me every way there is, I just can't let it all go.'

'Do not fear, Helmut,' said the doctor. 'You will be dead
very soon. I can promise you that.'

'Not often you can make us promises, eh?' replied Helmut
with a smile. There was blood on his teeth. He forced his
head up to look at van Horstmann. 'Who's the ghost?'

'A magister,' said the doctor.

'Gonna magic me better?'

'No,' said van Horstmann. 'But perhaps if I learn enough from those such as you, I can do so in the future.'

Helmut made a low gurgling sound that might have been a laugh.

Van Horstmann placed his case on the floor beside the bed. He unfolded it, revealing several pockets in which were held brass fittings and several lenses. He assembled the device swiftly, and a tripod holding up a contraption of half a dozen lenses and mirrors held in sequence took shape.

'This is my speculum,' he said. 'Designed to focus the wind of Light magic and allow examination of the hidden knowledge revealed thereby.'

'Van Horstmann's Speculum,' said the doctor. 'Most interesting.'

The device was adjusted so it stood beside the bed and aimed at Helmut's chest. 'The symptoms, if you will,' said van Horstmann. 'Rumours name everything from blindness to swelling of the extremities as indicators of this plague.'

'Well, the first signs share much in common with any number of maladies,' replied the doctor. 'This makes it difficult to distinguish if it is this new plague or one of the other diseases that we have been quite happy to die from throughout all human history. Nausea, pain in the joints and belly, difficulties in digestive matters. Various others; it differs. Then the marks appear.'

'It's the worms,' said Helmut. 'Hungry little devils. Got plenty of meat on me so they must have thought they were in maggot-heaven.'

Ben Counter

'Indeed' said the doctor. 'The worms are either the cause of the disease or one of its other symptoms. Perhaps they are introduced in a larval form to the body and thereby give rise to the plague, or the plague creates conditions within the body conducive to their development. I personally believe they rise from the flesh as creatures of the river are birthed from the mud, but again, opinions differ.'

'And then?' asked van Horstmann, continuing to tinker with the speculum.

'The organs are stressed to the point they overheat. They burn, often. They cook within the body. The skin might itself be burned from the inside. There is great pain. Sometimes several non-essential organs can fail in such a manner before the victim dies. If they are lucky, it starts with the heart. If they are unlucky, it can begin with the entrails and not stop for several days.'

'And this is not a natural disease,' said van Horstmann.

'No,' replied the doctor. 'It is not. Whether from a beast-man's cauldron or some wayward alchemy, it is not on the natural world we can lay the blame.'

Van Horstmann made the final adjustment, and the lenses clicked into place. The mirrors and lenses took what dim light there was in the hospital and focused it in a patch of yellow in the centre of Helmut's chest. 'And what do they call it?'

'Many things,' said the doctor.

'It needs a name,' said van Horstmann. 'The first part of any solution is to label all the parts.'

'It's the Gods' Rot,' said Helmut. 'We pissed them off, the gods, and this is what we get. Can't remember who I heard it from. But I crossed them often enough so I suppose I deserve it.'

'Do not speak,' said the doctor.

'Gods' Rot,' said van Horstmann. 'That will do. Helmut, what did you do before you were stricken?'

Helmut ignored the doctor's admonition for silence. 'Fought. For money. For gamblers.'

'I see,' said van Horstmann. 'Then you are strong?'

'Very.'

'Good.'

Van Horstmann whispered the ritual phrase and made the required gesture. As was the way of the Light Order, the spell that infused the speculum with magic was made up of rote words and motions. They were the mechanism through which the Light wind could be tapped, brought from the aethyr into the real world. The gears and levers of the speculum clicked and whirred and the lenses shifted, focusing the light and tinting it different colours as it played across Helmut's chest.

It found a point and focused. Helmut arched his back and gritted his teeth as a hot beam of yellow-white light burned against him. The skin was translucent now and the shapes of his ribs could be seen ghosted underneath, the shifting slabs of muscle in his pectorals and abdomen, the squirming shapes of his organs.

In the yellow glare, shapes were appearing in the air above him. Snakes coiled. Jaws clamped home. In the swirls of light were shapes half-glimpsed, tantalisingly vanishing just as they seemed to take on a definite form. One lens folded out from the device and cast a shaft of yellow light up to the ceiling, and the shifting forms were forced to become more distinct.

Snakes. They formed symmetrical patterns, as if following an infinitely complex dance. Faces – no, masks, death masks perhaps, features echoing the idealised art of long-dead civilisations with high cheekbones, stern eyes, elongated jaw pieces, all golden. Hands with long fingers, that spun and coiled in on themselves in endless swirling patterns.

Helmut gasped out in pain. His upper body was almost completely transparent now. His ribs were clear, lifting and closing as he drew painful breaths that filled the quivering bags of his lungs. Several of the organs crammed into his torso were like shrivelled fruit, withered away by the heat. His guts were a mass of pale tubes like dead snakes. The fat bulge of his tongue was just visible as the transparency crept up his throat towards his jaw.

The volunteers had all stopped their work and were watching the spectacle. Several of the plague victims sat up in their beds, their red-rimmed eyes wide to see such strangeness. Perhaps they thought it was a hallucination, one more cruel symptom of the Gods' Rot. Perhaps they thought that this was how it killed – it lit you up and projected its final mocking message into the air above you.

A new shape was emerging in the show of lights. This one was darkness, a void in the light. It was the shape of a great head, like that of a bull or a horse, on muscular shoulders. Four eyes burned in its face and its jaw opened to show that it was, in shape, nothing that resembled anything that had ever lived in the natural world. Horns appeared, twisting together above its head, spreading behind its cranium like the spires of a crown. A long forked tongue lolled from its mouth, bright red.

The eyes turned to van Horstmann. The speculum shuddered and emitted sparks.

The mouth was wide now, and it roared. The sound reached all the way from the aethyr. The stones of the unfinished sewer shook. Chunks of mortar fell on the patients and the volunteers.

'It sees us!' cried the plague doctor. Someone in the hospital screamed. Another voice was raised in wordless panic.

Van Horstmann stood and yelled a word of power. The speculum shut down and folded up. The light show diminished just as the daemon's head rushed forwards to fill it. The device clattered to the floor, spilling brass gears.

The transparency of Helmut's body faded. His ribs disappeared, replaced with skin, newly scorched and blemished. The man's eyes were closed and his mouth hung open. Smoke coiled from his chest and mouth.

The doctor bent over Helmut, feeling his wrist and throat. He put his ear to Helmut's chest. Van Horstmann could feel the heat coming off the man.

'He is dead,' said the doctor. 'His heart has stopped.'

'Then he got what he wanted,' said van Horstmann.

'And did you?' asked the doctor.

'Perhaps. I know now more than I did when I arrived.'

'Where is this disease from?' said the doctor. 'Magister, if you know, if there is hope, then you must tell us.'

'A cure I cannot give you,' replied van Horstmann. He began to scoop up the components of the speculum and dismantle the device, patiently placing each piece back in its assigned compartment in the case. 'But as to what caused it? I can make some suggestions about that.'

'Such as?'

'You saw it as well as I did, doctor. The daemon. The plague is the work of the daemon. The leader of some cult hidden in our city, or a lone daemonologist possessing great learning and malice, has concocted it and unleashed it on us. Perhaps they are in league with the beastmen, but it is not shamanic magic itself that we are facing.'

'And that makes it easier to fight?' asked the doctor.

'Perhaps,' said van Horstmann. 'It makes it easier for me to understand. And if we are ever to find a cure, that is the first stage.'

IN THE LIGHT Order's pyramid, the exorcisms were continuing.

'Fear breeds them,' said Magister Kant. He was watching another ritual. A man, in his later middle age he guessed, was lying on his back in the middle of the exorcism chamber surrounded by chanting acolytes.

'How many have there been?' asked van Horstmann. He rarely came by this chamber, its proportions and materials carefully chosen to create greater magical resonance. The Light Order's exorcists had gone one way, the battle magisters another, pure researchers like himself yet another.

'Today?' said Kant. 'Three. This week, a dozen.'

'I see. Strange times.'

'Strange indeed. Some of them are just hysterical. Nothing daemonic at all. But most are real enough.'

The man in the circle howled and convulsed. Van Horstmann could hear his bones cracking. Hands were pushing up against the skin of his belly from the inside, forcing his abdomen out of shape.

'No!' yelled Kant. 'The seventh declaration! Make the seventh declaration or you will lose that thing! It will run to the aethyr and we will never see it banished!'

The lead acolyte scrabbled in the pile of parchment and implements beside him. He found a scroll, unrolled it and began a new chant, gabbling through the syllables as the man's screaming grew louder.

'Vries's declaration,' said van Horstmann. 'It is of use, then?'

'Just like everything you brought in,' said Kant. 'That isn't the problem. There aren't enough of us. There are few enough priestesses of Shallya in the city now, so the burden lies on us.'

'What of the Silver Hammer and their warrior priests?' asked van Horstmann.

Kant looked at him. 'I wouldn't know, comprehender,' he said. 'Who does? It's the Silver Hammer.'

'Of course.'

Van Horstmann left the chamber behind. Fear bred the possessed. Minds became obsessive, or inflamed with a passion of madness. They became desperate. They begged for someone, for something, to make sense of the chaos in their minds. Sometimes, something answered. And the result was a man like the one lying in that chamber, probably about to die, a daemon being dragged out of him.

It was a short walk through the glare of the pyramid's incessant light, through the many corridors and sub-chambers towards van Horstmann's quarters. Many of the walls were translucent, allowing light sources to shine through, or were plated with polished gold or mirrors to send the light cascading in an infinity of reflections. Perhaps someone who was not a wizard would have been driven mad by the strangeness of the place, and ended up himself a gateway for daemons. Van Horstmann had accepted the place as he had accepted the warping of reality that occurred within himself every time he focused the winds of magic.

The Skull of Katam was quiet when he entered. Several books and heaps of parchment lay on the floor where he had been researching notes from various expeditions sponsored by the order. Men had ventured across the Sea of Claws, to the Southlands, into places thought to be cursed, or not to exist at all, and had written down what they saw. It was fascinating – not what they had actually encountered, but the strange things their minds conjured out of nothing. They saw sea monsters in the wave-tops and vast flying beasts in the clouds. Sometimes they were real, but it was the illusion of them that van Horstmann found more interesting. When a mind was not organised and aware of its own workings, it filled in those gaps of ignorance with whatever it feared or desired the most.

Van Horstmann opened up the side of the statue, revealing the extra-spatial sanctum. It was quiet there, too, which was good. If any of his guests learned to escape the puzzle box it would be a severe problem. He would deal with it, but not without compromising much of the rest of what he had to do. As it was the puzzle box sat undisturbed on its shelf beside the *Liber Pestilentius*.

Van Horstmann turned to one of the panes of crystal that hung on the walls. They were finely polished and without flaws, and had cost as much as van Horstmann could appropriate from the coffers of the order without creating suspicion. The same craftsmen who had made the lenses of the speculum had also, after overcoming their bafflement at such strange instructions, cut and polished these panes to van Horstmann's specifications.

He raised a hand and let the winds of the aethyr flow through him, just a breath of it. The pane illuminated in a jumble of colours, and through the light a shape coagulated.

It was a familiar one. Ugly as a violent death, part insect, part lizard, and just enough human to make it capable of an expression of annoyance. The face of Hiskernaath.

'What do you want?' hissed the daemon. 'You're too good now to speak face to face? You're finally afraid of what I'll do to you when I get the chance?'

'Our contract will never be broken, Hiskernaath,' said van Horstmann. 'And I keep the box closed for now because it will be a swine of a task to cram you all back in.'

'How much longer must I endure?' demanded the daemon. 'A hundred are in here. The stench! The lies! Hatred such as men will never know exists a thousand times over, and it is the hatred one daemon feels for another.' It was an exaggeration. There were a couple of dozen in the puzzle box with Hiskernaath, at most.

'You were created to serve,' said van Horstmann. 'Not to be friends.'

'Not to serve you!'

'And yet,' said van Horstmann, 'I have further instructions, and they will be obeyed. Is that not right?'

Hiskernaath spat and grumbled in some arcane tongue.

'Is that not right, daemon? I am your master. You will answer.'

'Yes,' said Hiskernaath. 'Your will is my will.'

'Master.'

'Master.'

'Good. The plague is well-advanced. The daemons captured by the new rituals have done their job well. It is rampant throughout the city. Morkulae and his cohorts probably enjoy their task rather too much.'

'Good for them.'

'There is another stage to this plan. That is where you come in. I need someone possessed.'

'Then I will…'

'You will be free, yes. For a time. I know that is what you crave, Hiskernaath. But this is not another case of making one angry soul lash out at the right time. This requires more complexity and subtlety. And a lot more power.'

'Meaning?'

'Meaning I need all of you,' said van Horstmann.

Other panes were swimming with light and shapes now, more faces forming. Some were knots of broken fingers, or bunches of angry muscle. Some were all fangs and horn, or drooping handfuls of sagging, flabby flesh. None of them looked remotely human. Dozens of them crammed into the panes, like faces trying to look in through a window.

'What?' asked Hiskernaath, now drooling with anticipation. 'What do you desire?'

Van Horstmann explained what he was going to do, and what he needed the daemons to do to make it possible. He explained how they were all bound to him by the same contracts inked and burned onto his skin, and how their few moments outside the confines of his puzzle-box prison would only be earned through performing this task for van Horstmann.

Halfway through, Hiskernaath began to laugh.

THE PROCESSION WOUND its way from Königplatz to the river, and had already gathered more than three thousand Altdorfers. Drummers at its head beat out a slow gait and behind them were the widows, dressed in what had once been their finest dresses, now torn and smeared with mud and ashes. They tore at their hair and sang long, old funeral dirges.

Then came the main mass of the procession. They were from every segment of Altdorf's society. Nobles in fine purples. Skinny urchins, as filthy as the widows. Burghers holding pomades against their noses to ward off the stink of the masses. Bakers, smiths, paupers, the rough-handed men who punted boats across the river, wan maidens apprenticed to the city's temples, builders, gamblers, fighters and farmers who had only come into the city to visit the markets and found themselves trapped by the quarantine.

'What do they want?' asked Kardiggian. He was a large

man for a Light wizard – the order did not much value physical strength or presence, and Kardiggian's height and broad shoulders made him stand apart. If any of the Light Order looked the part of a battle magister, it was Kardiggian, whose full, black beard and equally black eyes gave him the look of a warrior taken from an ancient battlefield and wrapped in the robes of a wizard.

'I don't think they want anything,' said van Horstmann. 'They have to do something. For many the worst part of the Gods' Rot is that it leaves them helpless. They can't do anything to help those who have it, and there is precious little they can do to avoid it now they are forbidden to leave the city. So all they have left is to take to the streets.'

Altdorfers loved protesting and rioting if the object of their anger was egregious enough. But this wasn't a protest. It was more like a funeral march, where every member was marking the death of someone they cared for – someone who had died, or was going to die, or was at great risk of dying. Judging from the obvious weakness and sickliness of many, some of them marched to mark their own deaths.

'It is pitiable,' said Kardiggian.

'You surprise me,' said van Horstmann.

'How so? You do not feel pity?'

'To see so many people, moved to action not because there is any practical purpose but because there is a compulsion built deep into them, all the same? I find it fascinating. When I am afforded the opportunity to witness such an example of the mind's frailties, there is never much room left for pity.'

'Will it be a problem?'

Van Horstmann shook his head. 'They will be gone from the Garden's vicinity soon. I do not think we need pay it any more mind.'

Kardiggian was there as, for want of a better word, muscle. His skills lay with destruction, and he might be called upon to use them. Van Horstmann's role was to operate the speculum – van Horstmann's Speculum – and because it was right that he be there. He had, after all, been the one to set the Light Order's investigations on this path. Vranas was an expert exorcist and also had the political savvy to cope with any fallout from their mission. Arcinhal, meanwhile, was an expert at protective magics, which would most definitely prove useful. Vranas was, by unspoken consent, their leader.

The four magisters had gathered in a side street, looking onto the road choked with the marchers. Arcinhal had cast a protective circle around them – one that, as long as the magisters did not leave it, turned onlookers' eyes away. It was not true invisibility, for that was much more difficult to achieve and was a specialism of the Grey Order. Instead it simply implied to any potential witnesses that this group of men was not worth looking at, so ordinary must they appear. It was impossible for the wizards to look like normal Altdorfers without magical aid. Even if they had not worn their Light Order robes or carried their staffs and wands, they would have looked like trouble of some kind. Arcinhal's spell was the only way they could go about their business without attracting a crowd of onlookers.

'I would rather we had requested the assistance of the priests of Morr,' Vranas was saying.

'They would not countenance us doing what we must,' said van Horstmann. 'They would call it grave robbing. They are protective of their patch, are they not?'

'The Amethyst Order, then,' continued Vranas. 'This is more their–'

'The less people know, the better,' said van Horstmann.

'I agree,' said Kardiggian. 'There are many… perhaps you might say, exalted guests in the Garden. One of them might be involved. I can trust us to be discreet, but I do not extend that trust very far.'

Vranas raised an eyebrow. He was a tall and pale man with a shaven head and a long, sharp nose. He had a cultured accent and a slickness of speech that made him the ideal magister to step forward when the order had to converse with people on the outside. Van Horstmann had developed an instant dislike of Vranas that had no logical base, save perhaps that he represented a breach in the isolation of the Light Order. Van Horstmann appreciated that isolation. Vranas, if he tried to make the Light Order more open to the scrutiny of outsiders, would have to be discouraged.

'Night will fall soon,' said Arcinhal. 'That is when it must happen. I can't keep us hidden if I need to protect us from harm, too.'

Van Horstmann had no quarrel with Arcinhal. Arcinhal was a brilliant man, quiet and organised, one who drove the acolytes beneath him to distraction with his exacting routines. His acolytes copied out reams of protective enchantments, over and over again, or pored over fragments of old magics recovered by adventurers and explorers. Van Horstmann conducted his research in isolation, but most other magisters worked in some way with Arcinhal as they delved into the Light Order's collection of magical texts.

'This will not be as neat and organised as you are used to, comprehender,' said Vranas. 'It may well tend towards the ugly.'

'You forget, exorcist,' replied van Horstmann, 'I was there at the banishment of the creature that had taken Princess Astrid.'

'You were there?' asked Arcinhal. 'At the Imperial Palace? I did not know that.'

'I understand van Horstmann here likes his secrets,' said Vranas with a smirk. 'The wharf district fires destroyed evidence of some such secrets, is that not right, van Horstmann?'

'You would have to ask the Silver Hammer,' said van Horstmann. 'Best of luck with that.'

Van Horstmann regarded Vranas again, this time from the point of view of an enemy. Vranas had no way of knowing the worst of what van Horstmann had done, that was certain, but no doubt the magister kept tabs on every prominent member of the Light Order. Even the Half-Circle's stewards and cooks would not be beneath his notice. There was nothing unusual about the fact Vranas had collected rumours and secrets about van Horstmann too. The only difference was, of course, that there was a lot more to find about van Horstmann than any other magister in the Light Order.

And as an enemy, Vranas had his weaknesses. Vranas considered himself an inviolable, indispensable part of the Light Order, as essential to its existence as the foundations of the pyramid. Elrisse's death had, though Vranas would never articulate it as such, been a great boon to the exorcist. He no doubt imagined himself the natural choice as the next Grand Magister, and assumed – rightly, van Horstmann thought – that if the Emperor was compelled to appoint a new Grand Magister he would choose Vranas. But the assumption of indestructibility did not make for a position of strength. It meant that Vranas was ignorant of the threats that might be gathering beneath him – the opposite of the Silver Hammer's paranoia, an inability to jump at shadows. If someone moved against him, Vranas would – perhaps literally – never see it coming.

'If you are wrong, van Horstmann,' said Arcinhal. 'If this… this device of yours–'

'The speculum,' said van Horstmann.

'Yes, this speculum, if it is wrong–'

'It is not.'

'If it is wrong and we dig up some… I don't know, some saint, some ancestor of who knows what family, then we might never hear the end of it.'

'I am not wrong,' said van Horstmann with gravity. 'I have seen what this plague does. I have seen where it comes from and what it leaves of those it infects. And I am not wrong.'

Kardiggian looked up at the sky, squinting at the horizon still aglow with the dying sun. 'Sun goes down in seven minutes,' the battle magister said. 'Let us begin.'

The four magisters, still cloaked in Arcinhal's mantle of disinterest, headed across the street, down which the last few stragglers of the funeral march were hobbling. They were the old and sick without family to help them along, and a couple of young urchins who trotted along to keep up. No one looked at the magisters as they moved towards the gates.

The side street that ended with the gate was, uniquely for Altdorf, scrupulously clean. No ordure ran down the channels cut into the middle of the street, and no wheel ruts had been worn into the stones. Trash did not gather in the corners, to be picked over by the vagrants who haunted the dusk and pre-dawn streets of the city. At the end of the street rose the intricate wrought iron gates of the Garden of Morr.

'For a place that serves as this city's symbol of death,' said Kardiggian, 'have you imagined how many of Altdorf's people are actually buried here? One in ten, perhaps?'

'Less than that,' said Arcinhal. 'Perhaps once it was more, but not now. A grave in the garden is beyond almost everyone. Even money isn't enough any more. Most burghers won't get in, no matter how much they might pour into Morr's coffers. You need power and status. Good breeding, too.'

A figure emerged from the shadows that, until then, had not seemed deep enough to hide him. He wore a long black habit and his head was tonsured, the exposed scalp white and newly-stubbled. His habit was held closed by a rope belt fastened through the eyes of a large bird's skull and around his neck hung a small book on a length of twine.

'Father,' said Vranas. 'We seek passage to the Garden.'

'I have been told to expect you,' said the priest of Morr. 'Do no dishonour to the interred. Mark the nobility of those within. And, good sirs, pray be careful where you tread.'

'We will,' said Vranas.

'I shall be without. Though you may not see us, none of us will be very far away.' The priest unhooked the chain that held the gates closed. The gates themselves were of black-painted iron and depicted two skeletons holding up a slab on which lay a body as if in state. The gates squealed as they opened, and the magisters moved into the garden.

Arcinhal let the concealing spell fade. There was no one in here that would be alarmed at the sight of them, and he had to be ready to put up any other form of protection they needed. Everywhere there were grave monuments – statues, full tombs like miniature mansions, grave slabs with the images of the interred carved onto their lids. Some were new, with the metal fittings of statues untarnished and the mottling of mould yet to gather on the stone. Others had been worn smooth by the ages – they had been here since before Altdorf itself, when the lords of the keep on the Reik had buried the dead from wars with the greenskins.

'What might a Light wizard have to do to be buried here?' asked van Horstmann.

'Save the city,' said Arcinhal. 'Or become Emperor.'

'They would never let one of us in here,' said Kardiggian. 'Altdorf hates the wizards. No matter how many times we might save them all, they will never trust us. It is part of what it means to be a wizard.'

'Focus,' said Vranas. 'Remember why we are here. Van Horstmann?'

Van Horstmann placed the case for his speculum on the ground and began to assemble it. The other magisters watched with some interest, for none of them had ever used such a device. Van Horstmann had designed it himself and had the pieces crafted by the Altdorfer craftsmen who usually made stargazing implements for the Celestial Order or navigational devices for sailors. It was not the kind of thing that was ever seen among Light wizards, who relied on the magical labour of their acolytes rather than complex tools.

'Quite the contraption,' said Vranas.

'We must have more than one way of looking at the world,' said van Horstmann as he worked. 'That is the weakness of the colleges. Each order only sees through one eye. Through the concept of the world created by the way of their own wind of magic. The Bright Order sees everything as creation and destruction, always in violence. The Amethyst wizards as decay and dissolution. We see it in terms of purity and corruption, everything in those terms. It is how a wizard becomes blind to the reality of the world, for he rejects whatever does not fit into his view of it. I see through the eyes both of a Light wizard and of a man curious about the world. That is how I stave off stagnation.'

Van Horstmann's Speculum was assembled, a waist-high collection of lenses and mirrors. The sun was down now and night had fallen, yet still the speculum gathered enough light from the stars to send fractured reflections glimmering across the headstones and monuments.

The light formed into a single beam, playing across the garden. This place was not just a graveyard – it was a monument to the most exalted dead of Altdorf. The Emperors had their own burial places in the crypts of the Imperial Palace but other leaders of the city, the noble-born and rich, had their resting places here. The priests of Morr kept the place flawlessly tended, including the elegant beds of flowers they planted between the monuments. The light caught the names of famous families from Altdorf's past, some of them still among the leading households of the city, a few others forgotten save for the graves.

'There,' said van Horstmann. The beam had settled on one part of the Garden of Morr, a side-plot centred on a grand tomb with three wings. SALZENHAAR, read the name inscribed on the lintel.

'Damnation on high,' hissed Arcinhal. 'It's the Salzenhaars. They built half this city. One of them's the Burgomeister.'

'Opening the tomb may be difficult to explain,' added Vranas.

'I am not wrong,' said van Horstmann. He stood up and walked towards the tomb. He had his staff held across his chest, as if ready to fend off an attacker with it.

'You say you can find the source of the plague,' said Kardiggian, 'but what does that mean? An infected body buried here? The ratmen?'

'No,' said van Horstmann. 'Not the skaven.' He reached the door. It was of greenish bronze, with no apparent means of opening it. He pushed at it, then put his shoulder against it and shoved. It did not move.

'If this device of yours works,' Vranas said, 'then it should at least–'

The rest of the sentence never got out. The door boomed open, throwing van Horstmann back across the flowers planted outside the Salzenhaar tomb. A foul, hot gale blew from the tomb, with the sound of a hundred voices howling.

'Arcinhal!' yelled Kardiggian.

Arcinhal swept his staff in a circle and the circle sprang up around himself, Vranas and Kardiggian. It took the form of the images of several hooded acolytes, blue-white, translucent and ghostly, standing heads bowed at guard around the wizards.

A hand gripped the door frame from the inside. The fingers were long and bony, held together by greyish, ropy muscles. The hand of a corpse.

Kardiggian yelled the words of a spell and bars of white light sprung up in front of the open door. Van Horstmann rolled away from the doorway and got back to his feet, pushing himself up with his staff. He held up a hand and conjured a circular shield of white fire around it.

'Black heart and unwelcome stranger!' yelled Vranas. 'By the light of the aethyr be blinded! By its fires be constrained! Slaves to darkness, there is no darkness here!'

Above Vranas swelled a globe of light, a miniature sun that cast its harsh light against the statues and tombs of Morr's Garden. Beams of light seared the moss encrusting the oldest headstones and withered the flowers to dust.

The skeleton of a son of the Salzenhaar family reached through the bars of light. The light burned the scraps of muscle and skin from his arms and set fire to the stained remnants of his funeral vestments. He had been wrapped in dark purple and gold-threaded ivory silk, and buried in the red-lacquered armour he had been wearing when struck down on the battlefield.

A bony hand grabbed van Horstmann's ankle. Van Horstmann rammed the butt-end of his spear into the leering skull's eye socket, forcing it into the mulch that filled the cranium. He let the wind of Light magic flow through him, from the core of his body through his arms to his fingers. White heat filled the staff and the skeleton's skull burst, sending hot bone shrapnel flying.

More bodies were clambering over each other to get out. Some were fresher than the first, still with half-recognisable faces clinging to their skulls. Others were just bones.

Van Horstmann rolled onto his front and ran to Arcinhal's circle. Behind him the bars of light shattered and the dead spilled out.

Darts of light impaled one, a woman, going by the long burgundy dress she had been buried in. The darts had spat from Kardiggian's hand and the battle magister's eyes were glowing now, the Light magic forced through his body in such quantities that it threatened to immolate him from the inside. Kardiggian had to condition his body to keep it intact when he wielded the raw force of battle magic.

Another corpse lurched through the edge of the protective circle. The parchment skin was scorched off it as it fell through the ring of glowing images. Vranas's sphere of light descended and bathed the undead creature in fire. Smouldering bones fell off its frame until its spine and pelvis came apart.

'Vranas! Banish them!' cried Arcinhal.

Vranas knelt on the grass and aimed his staff at the tomb. Half a dozen more were struggling out, burning in the fire raining down. A spray of silver blades sheared from the staff and broke like glass against the undead.

'This is fell magic,' gasped Vranas. 'Dark things animate them.'

Another stumbled close. Its fingers were like nails of bone, raking at van Horstmann's face. Van Horstmann swiped his staff at its skull and a burst of yellow-white flame erupted from the impact, the charge held in the staff released in violence.

'Hold them!' yelled Vranas. Arcinhal was sweating now, shoulders drooping. The circle was flickering, the images of the acolytes close to fading out.

The tower drifted from the back of van Horstmann's mind. It took form against the backdrop of the burning graveyard and time slowed down, the old channels of discipline giving shape to his thoughts.

This time the fortress was black stone and pitted iron, lashed by acidic winds and bounded by a moat of stagnant, corpse-choked water. Heads and hands were nailed to the battlements. Bodies were splayed across spiked barricades. A flaming beacon on the roof flickered against the dense, dark clouds.

The gates opened. Van Horstmann imagined himself drifting across the foetid moat and into the tower.

Chains hung from the rafters overhead. From each chain hung a dozen bodies, stripped and bloody, swinging bloated with decay like grapes left on the vine to rot. The eye sockets of each one had been hollowed out and in every socket was a gemstone.

Every time van Horstmann had meditated on magic, he had crystallised a single instance of it into one of these gemstones. There were hundreds of them here – some of them purely mundane, enabling him to conjure a light or a flame quickly. But many were more powerful, the result of months of hunting down the most dangerous and complicated spells and committing them, syllable by syllable, symbol by symbol, to memory.

Devonion's Seventh Circle, a spell that, when cast around a bound and subdued subject, compelled the subject to answer any question truthfully. The Conjunction of Martyrs, which caused the energy channels of the target's body to align and tear his organs apart with a burst of unfettered power. And the Argent Storm.

Van Horstmann had placed the Argent Storm in the tower years before. He had known he would need it one day. As time had gone on, as the pattern of events had unfurled, he had known exactly when he would have to call on such spells. Each one had taken months of study before van Horstmann had been able to hide them away here. But when the time came, he knew he would have to let them shatter and be destroyed.

Van Horstmann plucked the Argent Storm from an eye socket. It was deep blue and glistening with silver sparks. In his hand – though it was not really his hand, just a part of the mental image he had made of himself – it vibrated coldly, as if angry and impatient to be released.

Outside, in the real world, the dead had broken through Arcinhal's circle. Van Horstmann had known they would.

There were not just the walking dead, such as might be summoned by any petty necromancer. Vranas had been right – there was something darker animating them.

Van Horstmann let the tower recede. He felt the coils of snakes around his feet, their clammy flesh pressing against him, but he banished the sensation and forced himself to ignore them.

Not now. He would not fall apart now, as he almost had when facing the Hand Cerulean.

The Garden of Morr shifted back into place. The nearest skeleton emitted a loud hiss as it dragged itself on its sternum towards van Horstmann. Its legs had been blasted away by a volley of darts from Kardiggian's hands, and as he watched another was impaled by a spear of light that fell from above and transfixed it through a shoulder blade. The other magisters had bought van Horstmann the few seconds he needed.

The gemstone shattered in his mind. The patterns of the Argent Storm burned against his skin, spiralling through his mind like tunnels of light. Van Horstmann dropped to his knees, the force of the power bearing down on him almost enough to knock him unconscious.

Bolts of silver lightning hammered down, each accompanied by a crack of thunder that shook the ground. The bolts earthed in searing light, separated by curtains of darkness.

Where it struck, the lightning shattered animated bone. The long-dead sons and daughters of the Salzenhaar family were destroyed in rapid succession, fragments of burning bone falling like hail. One bolt struck the family's tomb and shattered the pediment, a deep crack splitting the miniature mansion in two. Another blew a crater in the middle of the magisters, throwing them off their feet.

The sound left van Horstmann's ears ringing, and fingers of glowing light were burned against his retina. He tried to blink them away and clear his head from the cacophony.

The Garden of Morr drifted back into focus. The starlight had returned as the storm clouds dissipated, and it illuminated the shattered stones of the Salzenhaar tomb, the smouldering tears in the grass and flowerbeds, and chunks of smoking pelvis and skull littering the Garden. A haze of metallic-tasting smoke hung in the air.

Vranas coughed and got to his feet. Van Horstmann was still kneeling, leaning on his staff.

'Holy stars,' said Vranas. 'Comprehender, what was that?'

Arcinhal was in the worst way, almost exhausted. Kardiggian had to help him to his feet – there was ice on Arcinhal's breath and crystals of it clinging to his eyes.

'Are they gone?' said Kardiggian.

'Van Horstmann?' asked Vranas.

'Maybe,' said van Horstmann. 'The Argent Storm leaves little in its wake.'

'Powerful magic,' said Kardiggian. 'Battle magic. I tried to master it.'

'You were working from a transcript that was flawed,' said van Horstmann. 'It took me months to find a complete example.'

'Arcinhal?' asked Vranas.

'I can walk,' said Arcinhal. 'But no more. They were almost on us. I am sorry, magisters. We could all have died here.'

'The tomb,' said Vranas. 'Some might remain.'

Van Horstmann followed Vranas to the shattered tomb. The crack down the middle of it looked like it ran right down to the foundations. Vranas held up a hand and a light appeared in his palm, illuminating the inside of the tomb like a torch. Van Horstmann could see the stone slabs with their coffins, each one with its lid torn off. This place had been more lavish than the houses of most living Altdorfers, gilded sculpture running across the walls depicting the generosity or prowess in war of the Salzenhaar family.

'There,' said Vranas, pointing to a flight of stairs that led beneath the upper chamber. Van Horstmann followed him to the staircase and saw that here, too, the coffins had been ripped open from the inside. This was where the older dead were buried, the matriarchs and patriarchs who had founded the bloodline.

In one corner was the stone sarcophagus of a knight. Its lid had been forced aside. It was filled now with nothing more than dust, the remains of whatever this body had been buried with. HEINRICH GRUNHALD-SALZENHAAR, read the name inscribed on the side.

The place smelt of mould and great age. A few loose bones were scattered around the floor along with the leavings of rats and insects.

'If this is the source of the plague,' said Vranas, 'perhaps the evidence of it was lost with the bodies of the dead.' He stood now beside the sarcophagus of Heinrich Grunhald-Salzenhaar and bent over it.

He ran a hand through the fine dust in the sarcophagus.

He paused and reached in further. When he stood again he had a book in his hand.

The book was bound with bloody bandages that van Horstmann knew, from experience, never dried out. Vranas was holding the *Liber Pestilentius*.

PART THREE

Chapter Thirteen
Tyrant

Rumours grew stale. Even the tales of the newest district to fall to the Gods' Rot, of the red crosses daubed on the doors of yet another street, grew old. The criers on the corners, whose lists of newly-infected streets had been a staple of every Altdorfer's morning just a week before, had to pad the daily news of the plague with accounts of hapless souls cut down by the Imperial Palace guards who were stationed at the gates to prevent anyone breaking the city's quarantine.

Spouses, parents, children and friends wailed at the gates for their loved ones to be allowed out, or for themselves to be allowed in to wait out the horror of the plague with their families. The usual crowd of self-appointed oracles described the juicy categories of sin for which the plague was a punishment, or described ever more bizarre cures dictated to them by an angel of Shallya, or the spirit of a long-dead king.

It was as if there existed a script to be followed. The well-worn ruts of Altdorf's superstition were brimming with the word that immersion in chicken hearts would cure the plague, or that archers on the rooftops were shooting anyone who made a rush for the walls. They still invented stories about beastmen in the city, only now they were brewing cauldrons of infectious bile and pouring it into the Reik.

And then, that morning, there was a new word on the criers' lips. A name.

Salzenhaar.

ONE OF THE Salzenhaars lay there now, tied down with a stick clenched in his teeth. He had been taken in the night and he still wore his nightshirt, now wet with perspiration though the house's cellars were cold.

Witch Hunter Argenos stood over the man and looked at his prisoner. Salzenhaar looked like any other man. Perhaps mid-thirties in age, a little weighty around the middle, as was fashionable for those wealthy enough to eat more than they had to. In good shape otherwise. Thick dark-brown hair. The heavy lower lip that was typical of the Salzenhaars and the various branches of their family tree.

Mikhael Salzenhaar didn't need to speak to express a mix of fear and anger. Argenos was intimately familiar with that particular mix. Salzenhaar's eyes stared, lids pared back as if he was trying to bore twin holes on Argenos's face with a look. He wasn't quite panicking yet. He did not despair. Sometimes they did, sometimes they didn't. You could never tell before they were dragged down here and introduced to the way the Silver Hammer conducted its affairs.

Argenos took the stick from between Salzenhaar's teeth. Salzenhaar spat out the taste in his mouth, spittle clinging to his goatee beard. 'I know what you're going to do,' said the nobleman. 'I've heard of it. I have friends who know about this sort of thing.' He spat the words out, trying make them sarcastic, but his throat was dry and there was a crack in his voice.

'Then you also know that everything you fear will not come to pass,' said Argenos, 'if you just tell me what I want to know.'

Salzenhaar closed his eyes and seemed to deflate. Argenos had seen the look on men hundreds of times before. Either Mikhael Salzenhaar did not know anything in which Argenos might have an interest, or he was exceptionally good at pretending he didn't, which in Argenos's experience was not a skill men like Salzenhaar had.

'I don't know anything,' he said. It was the first time he had said it, but already it sounded like a weary refrain he had trotted out more times than he could remember. Argenos knew he would say it again, many times more.

'I see,' said Argenos. 'Then we are going to perform that dance, are we? I know the steps well. I know them a lot better than you, Salzenhaar, and believe me, you will tell me something.' The witch hunter turned from the table on which Salzenhaar was restrained and took a large metal jug from the bench behind him. 'Just what you tell me is not important to you, though it might be to me. What matters is that you will tell me, sooner or later. Sooner.' Argenos lifted the jug so Salzenhaar could see it. 'Or later.'

Salzenhaar swallowed, with obvious difficulty. 'I have money,' he said.

'Ah, yes. That particular step. Done with haste but very little grace. I know that one, too. But do you know this one?' He nodded at the jug. 'Holy water, Herr Salzenhaar. Blessed by priests of every pious faith in Altdorf. Good, sacred stuff. And drawn from the purest well in the city. Pure enough even for one of your high birth to drink. But can you drink it all? At once, and without a single drop escaping your lips? If you tell me lies, the holy water will recoil and you will gag. If not, you will imbibe it cleanly and you will be proven innocent and honest. Will you drink, Herr Salzenhaal?'

Salzenhaal looked more confused than afraid. 'That's insane,' he said. 'That's... that's the most ludicrous thing I've ever heard.'

'I have burned witches that were exposed by the trial of water,' said Argenos. 'And they were most definitely witches.'

'And who else? How many who weren't?'

'Few enough that the trial has proven its worth,' replied Argenos without a pause. 'So, will you drink?'

'Of course I won't drink! I can't down that whole thing without bringing it back up! No one could!'

'Then you will talk?'

'And say what?'

Argenos bent low over Salzenhaar. He could smell the sweat on the man, stale already. 'Tell me the secrets you have sworn never to tell a man like me,' he said. 'Tell me where you got the book.'

Salzenhaar's expression now hovered between disbelief and resolve. He made a decision, somewhere down there among the dread.

'I bought it,' he said.

'From whom?'

'From an Estalian,' said Salzenhaar, his words rapid. 'I heard tell he was in the city with something to sell. I learned it from a monk of Taal who spreads such news in the guise of advising our households. I met him one night and bought it.'

'For how much?'

'For a chest of… silver. A bottle of innocents' tears. A statue that I bought five years ago from a wandering pedlar, who told me it was an idol of the beastmen who lived in the Forest of Chalons. It had amber for eyes. And he gave me the book in return. I did not learn his name, nor he mine, so far as I know.'

'Good,' said Argenos. 'Good. That saves us a great deal of time and anguish. Good. Now tell me.' Argenos stood at the end of the table behind Salzenhaar's head, so the man could not see him, and leaned down close to speak in his ear. 'Now, what is the book called?'

Salzenhaar took two or three rapid breaths. '*The Forbidden Codex*,' he said.

'Wrong.'

Salzenhaar gave a strangled noise, like cry of anger forced down into the back of his throat. 'What do you want me to say?' he shouted.

'Tell me what I want to hear.'

'I tried! You know more about it than me! I know nothing! Shallya's teats, you should be asking yourself!' Salzenhaar was hyperventilating now, his face red.

Argenos leaned down over his prisoner. 'You know nothing?'

'Nothing,' gasped Salzenhaar, his breathing shallower and shallower.

'What a shame,' said Argenos. 'Then what follows will be wasted effort.'

Salzenhaar's eyes rolled back in his head. He strained against his bonds in spasm, and fell still. Argenos turned his head one way then the other, and opened the man's eye. He was unconscious.

The door to the chamber opened. Argenos could not quite hide his annoyance at the intrusion.

Magister Heiden Kant stood in the doorway. He had a handful of loose parchment in his hand. 'Lord Argenos,' he said. 'A moment.'

Argenos indicated Mikhael Salzenhaar, contorted around in his restraints. 'I have all my moments spoken for, magister. There are none to spare. Once my guest wakes again I must go to work.'

'The Salzenhaars won't know anything, no matter how many of them you put against the grindstone.'

'I shall ascertain that for myself.'

'There's no need. It's not them.'

'The book was found in their tomb.'

'And I know who put it there.'

Argenos cocked his head to one side. 'You do, Magister Kant?'

'I suspect.'

'Ah, you suspect. I suspect things, too. I suspect them about Mikhael here.'

'Just listen, Argenos! Just for once, listen!' Kant had never spoken to Argenos with such bluntness before. Very few ever had. Even people who did not know what the Silver Hammer did had instincts enough to know that Argenos was a man who assumed he would be respected and had the capacity to create unpleasantness when he was not. Kant threw his papers onto the table, beside Salzenhaar. 'The memoirs of Mholik.'

'And who, pray, is Mholik?' Argenos's voice had a note of danger in it that Kant did not seem to notice.

'A one-time Grand Magister of the Celestial Order,' replied Kant. 'That is why the connection was not made. The colleges do not speak to one another, witch hunter. We keep what we know to ourselves, as if there never was a Teclis and we all sprang into existence of our own accord. Mholik was a scholar above all and everything he wrote survives, but no one outside the Celestial College ever set eyes on it before now. It was only the form of the ritual that gave me the connection. I had heard of something similar among Mholik's ceremonies for observing the conjunctions of the stars.'

Argenos looked through the papers. They were covered in diagrams and cramped writing that had faded to light-brown on the ivory-coloured parchment. 'I fail to…'

'You fail to see any relevance. Yes, Argenos, I know. The

relevance is that these are the root ceremonies on which the protective rituals attributed to Vries are based. But Egelbert Vries is supposed to have invented them. That was the whole reason the Light Order put such effort into rediscovering them in his writings. The writings that van Horstmann earned his spurs deciphering.'

Van Horstmann?' said Argenos. 'You have ever had an evil eye for Magister van Horstmann, Kant.'

'And now I understand why,' continued Kant. If he recognised the impatience in Argenos's manner, in the dangerous way his eyes narrowed and his voice dropped, it did not dissuade him. 'Vries did not invent what he hid in his works. He copied them from Mholik, who broke the same ground a generation earlier. Vries was a plagiarist. He took advantage of the fact that the evidence was hidden away in the library of the Celestial Order to leave a legacy that wasn't even his. It was lies. All of it. He was a barely competent wizard at best. Nothing he wrote was ever worth a damn.'

'And you went to the Celestial College to find this out?'

'And I will never be owed another favour by a wizard in this city because of it,' said Kant. 'I didn't think I'd get through the gates. But I did, and when I told them I could prove one of the Light Order's favourites was a fraud they gave me free run of their library. But that isn't the point.'

'Indeed not,' said Argenos, 'otherwise I would have to dig up Egelbert Vries and tie him to this table.'

Kant looked down again at Salzenhaar, almost seeming to see the prisoner for the first time. 'What is more important to you, witch hunter,' he said, his tone now more measured. 'Finding the truth, or being the object of fear?'

'The truth, of course,' said Argenos.

'Then let Salzenhaar go. I know the truth. The absolute reality of it, this I swear. But it only means anything if you will act on it. Otherwise you might as well believe in whatever this poor idiot makes up to keep you from cutting his fingers off. Will you believe the truth, Argenos? Will you show that much faith?'

Argenos folded his arms. 'Go on,' he said.

'Egrimm van Horstmann researched a new cycle of exorcism rituals. You saw them used against the Hand Cerulean. He said they were more works he had deciphered from Vries's books. But I know that cannot be the case. Vries couldn't write a limerick, let alone a ritual that could do what you witnessed. So it came from somewhere else.'

'Where?'

'Van Horstmann himself. He created it. Using this.' Kant picked up one of the parchment sheets. This one had on it a single shape, a twisted figure that might have been a letter or a numeral but in no alphabet that either man had seen before that day. 'The key sigil of van Horstmann's exorcism. It is supposed to represent destruction. The component that severs the daemon's presence in the real world and sends it back to the aethyr. But it doesn't mean destruction at all, witch hunter. I found this in the Temple of Sigmar, and I had a daemon's own job getting them to let me into the section where they held it.'

'I have been to the Temple many times,' said Argenos.

'Then you know what I mean. It was transcribed from a

menhir in Norsca, a place heaped with corpses and skulls.'

Argenos looked at the sigil. It was easy to imagine it cut into the weathered stone on a chill Norscan mountain, glowering down over a heap of sacrificial victims rotting away as a feast for the birds. 'And it does not mean destruction?'

'No,' said Kant. 'It means enslavement.'

Argenos looked up at the magister. 'Then the daemons were not destroyed, they were enslaved?'

'All of them,' said Kant. 'Every possession since the Battle of Drufenhaag. Enslaved and bound to Egrimm van Horstmann.'

'The same van Horstmann,' said Argenos, 'who brought in the *Liber Pestilentius* and claimed it to be the source of the plague. Meaning–'

'Meaning,' interjected Kant, 'that there is every chance that he was lying, that the *Liber Pestilentius* was planted by him and that he has an interest in the plague continuing. Perhaps even that he is its source. Given the magnitude of the damage he has done with his corruption of our rituals, that would certainly not be beyond him.'

Lord Argenos thought about this for a long moment. 'And I take it you bring me this revelation because I am the one who must bring Comprehender van Horstmann to justice?'

Kant held up his hands. 'I am here because I am a member of the Order of the Silver Hammer, and the Silver Hammer must know. If it is you who acts upon it, if it is another, if it is I alone, my duty must be done.'

'And you would attempt to bring down van Horstmann alone, Magister Kant? If there was none other?'

'I would.'

Argenos nodded, as if he had just heard an elegant solution to a complicated problem. 'Yes, I think you would. The Silver Hammer has before countenanced moving against a target within the Colleges of Magic. There is no little suspicion of wizards among my kind, and Sigmar knows it has been proven justified. I have seen many chill evenings made bearable by a rogue magister burning at the stake. But we have never staged an assault on one of the colleges. The Pyramid of Light is as secure a location as exists in the Empire. The Imperial Palace would be easier to storm. The entire strength of Altdorf's Silver Hammer could descend upon it and even with our own wizard in the shape of yourself, Magister Kant, we would stand little chance of getting through the gates.'

'Van Horstmann must be stopped,' said Kant. 'If I die in the attempt then it is not a bad death.'

'For you, perhaps,' said Argenos. 'For those who are lost in the attempt. A fine epitaph that would make. But for those of us left behind, such an attempt would leave a crippled Silver Hammer. Our enemies would wax great in the wake of such a catastrophe. As we are, there is no way the Order of the Silver Hammer will attack the Pyramid of Light directly.'

'I can get you more magisters,' said Kant earnestly. 'I am not alone in my suspicion of van Horstmann. We can get inside, perhaps even bring a sizeable force to van Horstmann's location. It will be us against him then.'

'What if van Horstmann has been as busy as you, though? If he has won his own faction to his side, primed to believe that the Silver Hammer wants him ousted on trumped-up charges for some reason of our own? Make no mistake,

Magister Kant, I want van Horstmann brought down. If what you say is true he is a daemonologist doing his work at the very heart of what should be our most stalwart institution for the destruction of the daemon. But I cannot make war. Not with Altdorf's gates closed, not with what we have.'

'You have us,' said a third voice.

Kant and Argenos looked down at the slab as if they had both forgotten Mikhael Salzenhaar was there. Salzenhaar had woken up, though he still looked worse for wear.

'Why be so surprised?' said Salzenhaar, his voice weak. 'Is this van Horstmann the swine-dog who planted that damn book?'

'Quite probably,' said Argenos.

'More than probably,' added Kant.

'Then he despoiled the tomb of my father,' said Salzenhaar. 'I saw it torn and broken. I saw the bones scattered around the Garden of Morr. The bones of generations of my families. My father... and my cousin, dead at nineteen. I swore I would look after her when she was alive but thanks to this wretched witch I couldn't even keep her body safe in her coffin. And my family's name has become a thing of hate in the mouth of every Altdorfer. Isn't that why I'm here? Because everyone across the city thinks they know the Salzenhaars are black magicians who brought down the plague? If this man is half of what you say he is then everything the Salzenhaars have in this city is yours to kill him with. We have men. Our own troops, and those of a dozen other houses bound to us by patronage. Probably the greatest armed force that could be summoned from the population of Altdorf. I will carry a blade myself, witch hunter, if you will have it.'

Argenos bent down over the table and removed the pin that held the restraints around Salzenhaar's wrists. The prisoner tried to sit up, winced and lay down again, gingerly testing his shoulders and arms for twisted joints and pulled muscles.

'You can get me more wizards?' asked the witch hunter.

'I can,' said Kant.

'Men are not enough. An army is not enough. We must have allies in the pyramid.'

'And I swear we will have them.' Kant turned to Salzenhaar. 'I need your men by next sundown, armed and ready to march.'

'Why such haste?' asked Argenos. 'We will strike the harder the more we can gather our strength.'

Kant swallowed, took a breath, and explained in as calm a manner as he could what he believed van Horstmann was about to do.

THIS TIME, HE went in stripped to the waist, displaying the cramped writing of the contracts etched into his skin. It had been a tedious and painful job having them all tattooed onto him – he had probably gone to every needle artist in Altdorf, having a line here, a paragraph there, to make sure none of them ever read enough to recognise the nature of what they were creating. The words of contracts sealing the services of a daemon to Egrimm van Horstmann for eternity. Woven among them were the older tattoos, the spiralling wards that concealed the Dark magic clinging to him from the aethyr-sight of his fellow magisters.

The crystal panes of the sanctum looked again onto the interior of the puzzle box in which van Horstmann had trapped the daemons. Obscene, inhuman faces of every description, of appearances beyond the capacity for the most deranged artist to draw, loomed from each window onto the world inside the puzzle box. Behind them, dark and indistinct, was a landscape that hinted at barren wastes, dense leafless forests, the churning blackness of an endless ocean. Van Horstmann had never given any thought to what that world must feel like to Hiskernaath and the other daemons he had trapped there. He had not cared. He still didn't. He cared only that they listened.

Hiskernaath was there, not exactly a leader among them but perhaps an ambassador to van Horstmann, a spokesman for his kind. Others, more powerful, were less inclined to engage in diplomacy with their captor. Morkulae, Cup-Bearer of Nurgle, never spoke save to curse. The plaguebearer who accompanied it was probably incapable of speaking at all, just staring out with its single filmy yellow eye. A thing like a serpent of bone, another like a mountain of seething vermin, humanoid foot soldiers and endlessly changing creatures of glowing flesh, all were gathered there to see what van Horstmann would command of them next.

They had done much for him already. They had spread the plague, those that were creatures of the Plague God Nurgle. Others had possessed the corpses of the Salzenhaar family, and been thrown back into their prison when those corpses had been shattered by van Horstmann's magic. It had been a painful experience for them, and they barked and slavered with anger.

Van Horstmann had brought with him into his magical sanctum a brazier, normally used for burning ingredients for alchemical experiments, and an iron brand. He did not speak as he heated the brand until its tip glowed a dull orange in the coals. Sitting cross-legged, he brought the tip to a point on his chest were his signature was inked at the end of one of the contracts.

The sizzle of flesh was pleasing to the daemons, who for all their anger at being imprisoned still took delight in violence done to mortal bodies. Van Horstmann did not cry out, but his eyes were screwed up, his jaw clenched, and he shivered and sweated as the brand scorched his skin. The smell of burned meat filled the small room.

Van Horstmann took the brand away, gasping out the breath he had been holding. Where his signature had been was now a bubbling red scar on his chest.

He placed the brand against his skin again, this time to his abdomen. He growled out the pain and flesh sizzled.

Next, his shoulder blade, using his reflection in one of the panes of crystal to guide his hand.

One by one, he erased his signature from the contracts on his skin, until there was just one left – in the centre of his torso, just below his sternum.

'You will be free,' he said. His voice was hoarse and sweat ran down his face. 'The contracts that bind you to me are void. Your allegiance lies with your gods, and with me no more.'

'Then open the box,' said Hiskernaath. 'Let us run free.'

'I will,' said van Horstmann. 'But there is one contract still in force.' he pointed to the passage written in the centre of his chest. 'A condition of your freedom. A single task to be completed before you have the run of this world.'

Hiskernaath spat and slavered. 'Then this is no freedom at all! What is your plan, van Horstmann? To set us a task that can never end? A task that, were it ever completed, would lead to our destruction? Others have tried such ploys before and the will of the gods always puts paid to their little games in the end.'

'Not this task,' said van Horstmann. 'This one, I think you will like.'

Van Horstmann stood and, taking a length of cloth he had brought with him, wiped away the worst of the blood from his burns. He opened the doorway to the sanctum and walked into his chambers in the Pyramid of Light, leaving the daemons behind to contemplate the final task he had set them.

'You are insane,' said the Skull of Katam from its place on Vek's alchemy table. 'You do know that, van Horstmann.'

'There was a man once named Katam,' replied van Horstmann as he went into the bedchamber and opened one of the trunks there, 'who thought he knew everything. He can surely appreciate the power that revenge has. Mere sanity is nothing compared to revenge. Men have built empires for it, and ended them. Men have killed, died and come back from the dead for it.'

'This is more than revenge,' said the skull. 'I don't think there is a word for what this is. Can you honestly say that all you have done is just to get at the one you hate?'

'You sound awfully concerned for me, Katam,' said van Horstmann. 'I didn't know you have such kindness in you.'

'I care only that I don't spend another century in the vault!' snapped the skull. 'Which is exactly what will happen when you are ended by whichever magister gets the killing spell on you. And you know full well, comprehender, that they will be falling over themselves to say they cast it.'

'You will not be cast into the vault again, Katam.'

'You are insane.'

'So are you.'

Van Horstmann had the feeling that if the skull could smile wryly, it would have done. 'I was insane,' it said. 'I have had a lot of time to reflect.'

Van Horstmann did not reply to that. Instead, from the trunk he took a robe he had not worn before – it was Magister Vek's full dress robe, so lavish there was more gold than ivory. It weighed easily twice as much as the magister's robe he normally wore. It had been packed with bundles of fragrant spices to keep it from going musty and had been made, perhaps decades ago, by one of Altdorf's finest outfitters. It was a garment fit for the occasion.

Van Horstmann pulled on the robe. He checked to see if the blood from his burns would seep through, but the fabric was dense enough to hide any sign of the injuries. He picked up his staff, and glanced for a moment into its diamond eye.

'Come,' he said, and picked up the skull. He had previously fixed a loop to the back of the skull so he could hang it from a belt and he did so now, so the skull dangled from his waist as he walked out of the chambers of Magister Vek.

It would be for the last time he left these chambers. He would not miss them.

The corridor outside was lined with acolytes, and they cast their eyes down in deference to him as he passed. The floor ahead of him was scattered with leaves and petals. Banners bearing the heraldry of great magisters of the past had been hung up on the walls, their rich colours brought out by the relentless light that poured down through the pyramid.

Van Horstmann had requested that this occasion be held in the pyramid's library. It had been the place where he had spent the most time, and it was the most closely associated with his position of comprehender and his reputation for eking out the secrets of the order's long-dead geniuses. When he reached the doors to the library, a pair of wardens of the Half-Circle, their armour polished mirror-bright, held them open for him.

The senior magisters of the order applauded as he entered. He saw among them Kardiggian, the battle magister, Vranas and Arcinhal, and Master Chanter Alric. Towards the back hovered Magister Pendorf, again given leave to cease haunting the vaults for an hour.

In the centre stood the Emperor Eckhardt III, flanked by the pair of palace guards who went everywhere with him. The Emperor wore the Imperial robes of state, rich and purple, that van Horstmann had last seen at Eckhardt's investiture. He wore the Stirland Runefang and the Silver Seal, marks of his rank as elector count and honorary commander of the Reiksguard respectively. As ever there was little emotion to read on his wide, rough face, but perhaps there was some approval to be found there.

'Magisters. Wizards all, it is a glorious occasion that we here observe.' It was Vranas who spoke, the natural master of ceremonies. Van Horstmann recalled him exhausted, propping up the almost insensible Arcinhal at the Garden of Morr. He looked as grand as possible now, like everyone else in his finest robes and carrying the many golden implements of magic with which a Light wizard liked to adorn himself. 'Let our sorrow at the passing of Elrisse turn to joy that we now heal the wound his loss left in our order. That we have found among us one with the wisdom and prowess to take upon his shoulders the responsibility for the College of Light. That we are gathered to acknowledge a new Grand Magister.'

Vranas extended a hand towards van Horstmann, indicating the new Grand Magister. The magisters applauded, and even the Emperor clapped along. Someone patted van Horstmann on the back as he walked up to Vranas and shook his hand, and then found himself doing the same with the Emperor.

'It is good that the order has done what it must,' said the Emperor. 'The Colleges of Magic will all be the stronger for this. It benefits us all.'

'I agree, your majesty,' said van Horstmann. 'In these times above all others, we must be strong.'

The applause was dying down, replaced with expectancy. Van Horstmann turned to the assembled wizards. These were the men who, if they knew what he really was, what he had done and what he was going to do, would kill him. Not arrest and imprison him, not challenge him to a duel. They would kill him.

He smiled, and bowed in deference to their applause. 'Brothers of the Order of Light,' he said. 'I need not say how honoured I am to be taking on this role. But there is more to this occasion than honour. The gravity of the situation in which Altdorf finds itself, and with which our order must deal, has curtailed the traditional ceremony and procedure of the selection of a new Grand Magister. So it is that I will be brief, too.

'Altdorf needs us now. Above all others, it is the wizards of the Light that will guide her through these long nights and sorrowful days. We are beset on all sides by the deadliest of threats. The plague rages, the beastmen lurk, the witches and heretics plot to take advantage of the chaos. It is my hope that by serving as your figurehead and guide, I can lead us with decisiveness to do what must be done. We must assume a position of leadership among the other colleges. I will bring us there. Not because I want to, or because it is the stepping stone to something greater, but because I have a duty to the people of the Empire and the orders of magic and it is as Grand Magister that I can best discharge it. My thanks, brother wizards. Let this be the beginning of a new age of the Light.'

More hands shook van Horstmann's. Voices were raised in oaths of praise. Van Horstmann was officially invested with the authority that had belonged to Elrisse before him, which only a handful of men had borne since Teclis and Magnus had decreed the establishment of the eight colleges.

'A fine speech,' said the Emperor. 'Strength in dire times. Most appropriate.'

'And on that subject, your majesty, I would speak with you,' said van Horstmann. 'In private, if possible.'

'Taking to your duties right away, then?'

'There is no time, as I have heard it said, like the present.'

The Emperor indicated that his guards were to follow him and van Horstmann, and the two of them left the library. Van Horstmann led them to a small reading room, its ceiling painted with a star map of the summer sky over the Empire. The guards stood at the door, their halberds crossed to indicate that Emperor Eckhardt III was not to be interrupted.

'I have received an envoy of House Salzenhaar,' said the Emperor, pulling up a chair. 'My ministers suggest hanging every last son of them, lest the people riot for lack of justice. I have friends among that family and I gave assurances that if the plague was to be curtailed, there would still be a House Salzenhaar. Could that happen?'

'I can only speculate how the *Liber Pestilentius* came into their possession,' said van Horstmann. 'Perhaps its owner merely used their tomb as a lair, although he could scarcely have chosen a less ostentatious place to hide. But you raise the exact point I intend to address head on. The end of the plague.'

'It can be done?'

'I believe that it can.' Van Horstmann sat down opposite the Emperor, the reading table between them. 'As Grand Magister I have the authority to access our most precious relics. They are held in a place I should not speak of, a place that few know exists, that I should not name, even to your Imperial Majesty. There have been Emperors since Magnus who have not been informed that the vault is there, but it does exist, and there are held the artefacts of the Light Order that not only must be protected, but from which Altdorf must be protected.'

Eckhardt III absorbed this, nodding slowly. 'I see. And there is something in this vault, this secret hidden vault that I am privileged to have heard of, which can cure the plague? If that is so then I can save my city and can forgo the destruction of House Salzenhaar.'

'There are other issues,' said van Horstmann. 'Its use could create complications for your reign. That is why I would speak to you on the matter before opening this vault.'

'How so?'

'The artefact in question is the Mantle of Thoss.'

Eckhardt III was not a man given to wearing his emotions on his face, but he could not hide his alarm. 'It exists?' he said. Leaning forwards on the table.

'It does,' replied van Horstmann levelly. 'And we have it.'

'Gods above,' hissed Eckhardt III. 'When you said it would create complications, you did not speak in jest. Your kind exist in isolation, Grand Magister. Do you truly understand what the Mantle of Thoss could do to this city? To the whole Empire?'

'I am not so ignorant, your majesty. Grand Theogonist Thoss is the most divisive figure in the Empire's history since the Great War. Even before him, there are few who could claim to split opinion so fervently. I am well aware of what Thoss did and the scale of emotions that still flare up whenever his name is mentioned. But the Mantle of Thoss is the only answer if Altdorf is to be spared the Gods' Rot.'

The Emperor shook his head, as if reliving a bad memory. 'Thoss waged open war against the old faiths. All priests save those of Sigmar were clubbed to death in the streets. There were execution pyres all along the road from here to Talabheim. There are adherents to those faiths who treat his crusade as if it were within living memory, as if the man did them a personal injury. And there are Sigmarites who secretly wish there would come another just like him. If the Mantle of Thoss was to be used, if it became known that the Imperial Court permitted the use of such a relic... it could be civil war, Grand Magister. Worse, a religious war. Brother against brother, father against son, and fought under my reign.'

'The alternative, your majesty, is to see Altdorf made a ghost town under your reign.'

'Can you even be certain it will work?'

Van Horstmann nodded. 'Thoss himself swore it on his deathbed. It was the Grand Theogonist's final miracle. Take his Mantle, cast it into the Reik upstream of the river, and the waters will cure any malady. Whatever else might be thought of Thoss, when he promised a miracle it came to pass, and his final miracle was sworn on the altar in the Temple of Sigmar itself. I am as certain as a man can be of anything. The Mantle of Thoss will cure Altdorf.'

The Emperor seemed to study the surface of the table for a while. 'Can you do it in secret?' he said.

'Every day there is a new cure announced on the streets,' replied van Horstmann. 'It will be no great task to make a draught of the Reik's waters another one of them. When it works, everyone in the city will be drinking it. Not one mention need be made of Grand Theogonist Thoss at all. Thus far, you and I are the only ones who know the Mantle would be involved at all. If needs be, one of us could throw the Mantle into the river. Aside from a magister of the Fourth Circle, who administer the vaults and are most adept at keeping secrets, no one need ever know.'

'Do it,' said the Emperor. 'But on your head fall the consequences if word gets out. That is the price of power.'

'It is a price I know well,' said van Horstmann. 'And I will pay it, if I fail.'

The Emperor stood. The guards at the door lowered their halberds. 'Congratulations, Grand Magister van Horstmann,' he said, and left the chamber with his guards in tow.

Van Horstmann waited in the chamber for a moment, thinking. The sequence of events that would follow had its complexities, its vulnerabilities even, but van Horstmann had gone through every permutation and filed them and their solutions way in the labyrinthine library of his mind. It was a lot to think of at once. He had meditated on it for hours, and still he found himself checking and rechecking every eventuality.

No. It was perfect. He had thought of everything.

Outside the reading room, waiting for him, was Master Chanter Alric. Van Horstmann was used to seeing Alric in a position of authority, for much of the time he had spent in the presence of the man had been when van Horstmann was an acolyte and Alric had been the lord of his domain. Now

Alric looked like a subject, his eyes looking down and only for a moment flickering up to meet van Horstmann's.

'Grand Magister, I must speak with you,' he said.

'Of course, Master Chanter,' replied van Horstmann. 'Though I have yet to adjust to answering to that title.'

'I spoke with Elrisse on this matter before you,' said Alric. 'It is… sensitive. I am reluctant to speak of it to anyone at all, but… well, the Grand Magister must know these things. It is personal, and perhaps not worth your time, but it is a duty of every magister to speak up on any matter that might compromise his duty to the order.'

'This manner does not become you, Alric,' said van Horstmann. 'The man I see here is not the same one I feared and obeyed as an acolyte. Speak, Master Chanter, and do not fear it.'

Alric nodded. 'I shall keep it short. I have a wife.'

'I see,' said van Horstmann.

It was not unknown at all for wizards to have families outside their order. There was no prohibition against it, not in Teclis's decrees and not in the present. In some Orders of magic, however, it was more common than others, and the Order of Light was not among them. The isolation it forced on its acolytes, who were not permitted to leave the pyramid save with the word of the Master Chanter, meant they rarely formed outside bonds. Wives and children were rarer still. But, again, not unknown.

'There is no law against it,' continued van Horstmann. 'But it is good that you told me. The Grand Magister must know these things. Does she live here in Altdorf?'

'She does,' replied Alric. 'Near the Königplatz.'

'Then the plague must concern you greatly.'

'Yes, most certainly. Every time I hear of another district falling, I imagine the white cross painted on her door and her in her sickbed. I have received word in this past week that she is well, but one can never know what the next day might bring.'

'What is her name?'

'Albreda,' said Alric.

'Then fear not for Albreda, even on account of the plague.' Van Horstmann placed a hand on Alric's shoulder, and it seemed for all the world like Alric had been reduced in age to that of a child who needed comforting and reassurance, and that van Horstmann was his elder. 'Master Chanter, I swear that it will be over soon.'

Chapter Fourteen

Battle

Upon the border of the Buchbinder District, where the homes of Altdorf's middle-class burghers adjoined the cramped, teetering tenements that surrounded Midday's Mirror, Witch Hunter Lord Argenos drew together his army.

He had a hundred and fifty men. Most of them were of House Salzenhaar. Among them were the younger sons of client families, youths who, without the likelihood of inheritance and the accompanying responsibility, fell to brawling in the streets. They were useful men to have in a tight spot, such as was sure to occur at the Pyramid of Light. Even now they spat, swore and gambled, as if looking for excuses to start a fight already.

Others were household troops, men armed and armoured by House Salzenhaar to guard their estates, chaperone their ladies and accompany the family's patriarchs to lend them the gravity of presence that came with an armed escort. They wore yellow and blue plumes, their mark of family allegiance, and were led by Mikhael Salzenhaar himself. Mikhael had recovered sufficiently from his interrogation by Argenos to carry a sword, but he was pale and shivering in the moonlight, sweating in spite of the chill.

The rest of Argenos's men were the thugs who occasionally lent their weight to the Silver Hammer, such as the ones he had taken into the wharves to destroy the Hand Cerulean. And then there was Argenos himself. Argenos could handle himself in a fight. It was a necessity of his role as a hunter of witches. He always kept himself prepared for the possibility that the witch would fight back, and he had a plentiful supply of blessed shot for his pistol.

Two figures were approaching the gardens where Argenos had gathered his strength. These gardens had been the pride of the burgher family who had built it, but the flowers were now trampled beneath the feet of Argenos's thugs. No doubt the family in the adjoining house were watching from the windows, but they knew better than to confront Argenos. The two men approaching wore hooded travelling cloaks but Argenos knew well who they were.

Magister Heiden Kant threw back his hood. 'Lord Argenos. Are we ready?'

'It is never a question of being ready,' said the witch hunter. 'Are you?'

The second figure pulled down his hood. Argenos peered at the man's features, trying to read them in the moonlight.

'I take it,' said Argenos, 'that Magister Kant has explained to you our purpose?'

'He has,' replied the man who wore the robes of a Light wizard under his cloak.

'I am Witch Hunter Lord Argenos.'

'Magister Kardiggian.'

'Ah, the battle magister. A man who wields magic as a weapon of war. Kant, you have done well.'

'Well enough?' asked Kant.

'To storm the Pyramid of Light?' asked Argenos. 'That remains to be seen.'

'Magister Kant told me of his suspicions,' said Kardiggian. 'More than suspicions. He had pieced together a compelling argument. And I have had suspicions myself of late about our new Grand Magister.'

'So, van Horstmann is wearing dead Elrisse's boots?' said Argenos. 'I had imagined it was only a matter of time. On what did you base your own suspicions, battle magister?'

'At the Gardens of Morr,' said Kardiggian, 'I fought along-side van Horstmann. It seemed to me that he knew full well what he would have to fight, and had prepared for it very specifically. He had mastered the Argent Storm, I believe, because he knew that he would need it to defeat what came out of the Salzenhaar tomb. That suggests he had foreknowl-edge of what lay there, and that can only mean his hand in the events of the plague. I can prove nothing, of course, but then I believe the Order of the Silver Hammer rarely holds out for the luxury of proof.'

'Can you get us into the pyramid?' asked Argenos.

Ben Counter

'I can,' said Kardiggian. 'I hold great seniority among the magisters. Once we are inside, some will side with me. More than that, I cannot promise.'

'Then that will be enough,' said Argenos. He turned to his men. 'Brothers! Men of House Salzenhaar and of the Silver Hammer! The time has come to move out. Our destination is Midday's Mirror. Move swiftly and quietly. Pray that Morr casts on you a kindly eye, for some of you will meet him soon. Come, place your souls under the guardianship of Sigmar and your bodies under the protection of your blades.'

Argenos led the force out. Above them Morrslieb, the ill-omened witch moon, glimmered near the horizon, as if peering over the edge of the night to see what bloodshed might unfold.

THE PYRAMID OF Light was reflected beneath the grounds in the basement levels that made up the vaults. The outer vault was haunted by the magisters of the Fourth Circle, who catalogued and guarded dozens of relics relating to the Order of Light and the deeds of its wizards. Below that, as van Horstmann had learned, was the inner vault, where alone in the pyramid shadows were permitted to gather and artefacts with wills of their own roamed in a constant, bloodless struggle with one another, a microcosm of some world where the sole inhabitants were items of power forged an aeon ago and infused with the most potent of magics.

Beneath that, corresponding to the middle levels of the pyramid above, was nothing. A great endless light, like an ocean of it, without substance or, to the naked eye, an end. The shore of this ocean was reached through a doorway in the inner vault that looked like an empty pedestal where some relic had once stood, only to have fled or perhaps been consumed by a magic artefact turned predator. The pedestal lifted up to reveal a short flight of steps down, onto a shore of crumbled masonry.

Overhead was a ceiling of stone, the floor of the inner vaults stretching off into a distance made hazy by the glare. In front and below was nothing but light.

Van Horstmann knelt on the shore and dipped a hand into the light. It was not liquid, but a tingling warmth. His eyes, well used to the constant glare in the pyramid, still smarted at the brightness.

'A reservoir of magic,' explained Magister Pendorf. Pendorf, when told to allow the Grand Magister into the Pinnacle Vault, had not seemed perplexed or concerned by the demand. Perhaps he had always known that van Horstmann would reach the lowest point of the Light College, just as he had reached the top. 'It bleeds down here from above. In their wisdom, Teclis and the founding wizards made sure there was a place for it to gather, or the tide of it might have destroyed the pyramid.'

'They were wise men,' said van Horstmann. 'And a wise elf. How do I get across it?'

'Elrisse never sought the Pinnacle Vault,' said Pendorf. 'We were blessed, perhaps, that events were never so dire that he needed to.'

'And today, Altdorf's future depends on what lies down

there. Yes, we were blessed, Magister Pendorf. But now we are cursed, unless we make use of the vault's secrets.'

'I must ask, Grand Magister,' said Pendorf, 'how you came to learn of what lies there. I have never been within, nor have any of the current Fourth Circle so far as I know.'

'A Grand Magister must know everything about his order,' replied van Horstmann. 'A body of knowledge is passed on from one to the next. Among that knowledge was the contents of the vault. Now, Magister Pendorf, if you please?'

'Of course.' Pendorf pointed down into the light ocean. 'You are a worker of wonders. You are a master of Light magic. Master it.'

Van Horstmann nodded. 'And so none but a magister can cross it.'

'But of course.'

Van Horstmann felt the channels in his body open up, just as they had done when he had first sought to marshal the winds of magic. His veins and arteries, the invisible lines of power that connected every point to every other, opened wide and the wind of light blew through them. They connected into the spider's web of power that lay as potential within every human body, but was realised only by the few with the capacity to feel it.

He felt it now. He directed everything through his mind, focusing the wind that blew with the lens of his will and imagination. Like light through the lenses of the speculum, the wind of magic took on new shapes as it passed through his mind.

Van Horstmann imagined great blocks of matter coalescing

from raw magic, rising up like islands. His will was echoed in the ocean below, and glowing slabs like rock with veins of light rose up to meet him. He stepped off the shore onto the first and imagined now a whole spiral of them, winding down towards the lowest point that corresponded to the pinnacle of the pyramid above.

Pendorf followed as the steps rose up to meet them. Below the surface, van Horstmann's whole body felt suffused with the light. He felt it leaching in through his pores, pouring in through his eyes, and it became easier to create the staircase down.

He could see the far shore now, still some distance below. A rocky island, where a portion of the pyramid's ornate masonry held a wall with a single doorway. On the door was raised in silver the image of an elven woman over a crescent moon – Lileath, the high elf goddess, and a seal of Loremaster Teclis himself.

Van Horstmann continued down until he reached the shore, conjuring the last block of solid ground with a thought. He placed a hand against the door, and felt that it was warm.

The door slid open at his touch, and beyond, too, there was light. It shone through stained glass windows high overhead, which ringed the domed ceiling of a chamber that could not exist beyond the door. Here the space-folding magic of the pyramid was in effect, creating the bubble of existence in which was held the Pinnacle Vault.

The walls were not walls at all, but cascades of glittering silver light that poured down over the windows and over the edge. The light through the windows was in every colour, a choir of light that almost dazzled even a Light wizard like van Horstmann. White flame rippled without heat along channels cut into the floor, as if this place were so suffused with magic that it could not stay pent up in the aethyr and was compelled to flow free.

In the centre was a cylindrical structure of polished marble, veined with grey and pink. Around this structure were built a dozen shrine-like enclosures, each with a pedestal like an altar on which stood a single artefact.

Van Horstmann had spent years, and a goodly portion of his soul, to learn of what treasures the Order of Light had stored in the vaults beneath the pyramid. Even he, however, knew that he would be ignorant of most of the relics down here. The knowledge of their existence had simply never escaped. No doubt they were vastly powerful and even more dangerous. The sword he looked at now might be enough to slay an army on its own – the mask he glanced at next might grant him some mind-expanding magical sense or let him see into men's souls. It did not matter. There was only one thing here that van Horstmann needed.

Well, two. But the second could wait.

Pendorf hobbled across the spectacular chamber, the thrum of contained energy the only sound save for his shuffling footsteps on marble. He led the way to one of the shrines where the pedestal held a wooden mannequin, on which was hung a splendid cape of grey fur. The cloak was trimmed with ermine and lined with crimson silk, and the clasp was a heavy golden brooch in the shape of Sigmar's twin-tailed comet.

'The Mantle of Thoss,' said Pendorf.

Van Horstmann saw the hem of the cloak was stained pink with blood. It looked fresh. Perhaps it was – the Pinnacle Vault might have strange magics about it that trapped the artefacts inside in time so they did not decay or tarnish. 'He wore this at the scourging of the Taalite monks,' he said as he walked up to the cloak. He reached out a hand and touched the ermine, felt its power fizz and hum through his fingers. 'And the burning of Huntsmistress Evraya.'

Pendorf swallowed. 'I saw the book,' he said. There was a reluctance in his voice, as if he had forced the words out unwillingly.

'The book?'

'The *Codex Aethyrica.*'

'I see.' Van Horstmann let his hand drop from the Mantle of Thoss.

'It was gutted,' said Pendorf. 'Its pages scattered to the fates, replaced with trash and scraps. Oh, it was a beautiful book. I wept just to look on its cover when I thought of the sacred things written inside. The learning therein. I had opened it once, when I was young, newly descended to the vaults. That memory came back when you took it out and when it was returned, I felt the need to open it again. It was so beautiful. It was everything I studied with the Fourth Circle to be near. And so one night I was weak. I opened it again. And I saw.'

Van Horstmann did not answer. He just looked at the wizard, the way the old man's skin had sunk into his face and his shoulders hunched, the way he looked less like a man and more like a mannequin, much like that which held the

Mantle, on which someone had haphazardly draped a wrinkled and faded wizard's robe.

'Why did you do it, van Horstmann?' asked Pendorf. His eyes were wet. 'I do not know why you are truly here and I do not expect to learn. And my life has been a long one, and I have no complaints. I just want to know why you had to destroy something so beautiful.'

'I cannot tell you, Magister Pendorf,' said van Horstmann levelly.

'I am not going to leave this place. Not now there is nothing else you could possibly want, not that you could need my help with, at least. Please, tell me. It was so beautiful. I just want to know why.'

Van Horstmann held up a hand, palm towards Pendorf as if to silence him. Black flame flickered around his fingers, their chill running down his arm. The flame leapt up around his hand, forming hypnotic shapes as it flared higher.

It had been a long time since van Horstmann had been able to wield Dark magic to its full potential. There had never been a time when he could not be certain he was unobserved. Even when he had fought the ratman general, he had taken a huge risk. Another magister might have seen him, even in the thick of the battle. It had been a necessity, and there had been no time to enjoy it. Now, there was no one who could witness it. And even if there was, at this point it did not matter.

'I see,' said Pendorf sadly.

Van Horstmann imagined the beam of black energy leaping from his palm, and it did. The beam lanced through the centre of Pendorf's face, boring right through to hiss against the falling light behind him.

Van Horstmann let the beam play around, burning a path through the old man's scalp, until it sliced up through the top of his skull. Pendorf's head flopped into two scorched halves and he toppled over into one of the flame channels on the floor. The fire flowed over his body like water, not burning him but suffusing him, his flesh glowing as it began to slowly disintegrate.

Van Horstmann watched Pendorf's corpse for a few moments. He marvelled that anyone had ever thought killing another man was difficult. He had accomplished far more troublesome tasks on that day alone.

He looked again at the Mantle of Thoss. Perhaps it really could have cured the plague – perhaps old butcher Thoss's bloodstained garment would have somehow, against every turn of history and fate, released something other than raw hatred into the waters of the Reik. Stranger things had happened, although not very many.

Van Horstmann turned away from the Mantle of Thoss. It did not interest him now. He was inside the Pinnacle Vault, and the mantle could burn like Pendorf's body for all he cared.

What he sought was in another of the shrines. He passed by the magical sword, and for a moment his eye was drawn, unwillingly, to the glow on the edge of its blade where it was so finely honed that the metal was transparent. He looked away. A standard stitched of red cord bore the image of a golden boar and, from the look of it, was of antique enough design to have flown over Sigmar's own battlefields. A hunting horn was held up by an ornate stand carved from animal skulls. A mirror-polished shield reflected not only van Horstmann's face but Elrisse's, Vek's, even the ratman sorcerer's, with Pendorf's looking confused in one corner. Van Horstmann passed them all by.

Finally he reached the relic he was looking for. It was perhaps the least assuming object in the innermost vault. He had first read of it when he was little more than a child, his limbs still recovering from the broken bones and torn muscles inflicted by the coils of a hundred snakes. His plan for it had been confirmed in the communion with Tzeentch, where all the possible paths of fate were laid out before him like the veins through the marble of the vault.

At last, van Horstmann had found the key.

THE HALF-CIRCLE STEWARDS did not stand in Kardiggian's way, even though he was not alone. A battle magister had both the authority and the raw strength to go where he pleased. The guards stood aside as Kant, then Argenos and the men of House Salzenhaar, filed through the doorway into the pyramid.

Salzenhaar's men were afraid. They had been afraid even before they had plunged through the waters of Midday's Mirror into the folded space around the pyramid. They knew Argenos to be a hunter of witches by the implements of burning and torture he carried, as much as badges of office as for practical use, and many an eye fell on the ornate pistol with its glowing barrel he had tucked into his belt. And they knew that anything involving not one wizard, but two, must be serious business indeed.

'Kardiggian!' demanded Master Chanter Alric, running across the Chanter's Hall as the Silver Hammer force walked blinking into his domain. 'What is the meaning of this?' He pointed at Argenos. 'Who have you brought into our midst?'

Acolytes watched as Kardiggian threw back his hood and stood up to Alric. Though the acolytes had obeyed Alric as if he were a god, they had also heard of the battle magister and the way he could incinerate whole regiments of men from afar.

'We are here for van Horstmann,' said Kardiggian.

'And you expect me to give him to you, Kardiggian?'

'We will go through you to get to him, if you compel us to.'

'And I ask again, who are these men?'

'We are the Order of the Silver Hammer,' said Lord Argenos, striding forwards with his hand on the hilt of his ensorcelled pistol. 'Grand Magister van Horstmann is accused of foul and degenerate crimes, for which he will be tried. You can try to stop us, or you can stand aside, or you can join us. It matters not to me, for Sigmar's will shall be done regardless. But it matters to you, because as Magister Kardiggian says, it troubles me not to lay waste to anyone who stands in my way.'

'What has the Grand Magister done?' demanded Alric.

'Decide,' said Argenos. 'Stand before us or with us. What do you choose?'

'Master Chanter!' cried one of the acolytes. All eyes turned to follow the acolyte's finger as he pointed towards the ceiling of the Chanter's Hall.

Something scuttled there, between the tops of the pillars. It was something like a spider, but enormous and asymmetrical, shimmering as if only half-real.

From near the Master Chanter's dais lumbered another intruder, this one a bent and shambling shape, taller than a man even though its head hung low between its shoulders. It had a sagging belly and a single eye, and behind it shambled many more. Alongside them was a greater horror still, a mass of writhing worms belching out a trail of slime that hissed as it dissolved a furrow in the marble behind it.

The smell hit the acolytes and the men of the Silver Hammer. It was beyond foul, something that defied description, a stench beyond the worst of the charnel pits or the dankest of Altdorf's sewers. Acolytes retched and fell to their knees. Several of the House Salzenhaar soldiers tore their helmets off so their visors would not hinder them from vomiting up their disgust on the floor of the Chanter's Hall. Others pulled off a gauntlet to wipe their eyes, which were suddenly streaming.

'Daemons,' growled Witch Hunter Argenos. He drew his hammer with one hand and his pistol with the other, and the weapon's harnessed magic glowed bright as if hungry for the fight. 'This is what he has done, Master Chanter! He had communed with daemons and brought them forth! He has opened the doors of this very place to their foulness! And to the heart of your order, he has brought war!'

Between the plaguebearers swarmed tinier versions of the daemons, scurrying, pudgy things, little more than mobile bags of filth with wide grins full of needle teeth and glowing yellow eyes. Clouds of flies burst from bulging cysts in the plaguebearers' sagging bellies and rose up, so dense they cast the first shadows the Chanter's Hall had ever seen.

The first plaguebearer bellowed, a sound halfway between a roar and a thunderous belch. It raised a weapon shaped more like an enormous rusting butcher's knife than a sword. It was a signal for the charge, and the mass of daemons loped forwards to kill.

'Form up!' yelled Mikhael Salzenhaar, his throat raw and his eyes and nose streaming. 'Form up! Hold! Hold!'

The daemons charged across the Chanter's Hall and slammed into the men of House Salzenhaar. The men had been thrown into disarray by the appearance of the daemons and in those first few seconds men died, hacked down by the swinging blades of the plaguebearers. Mikhael leaped into the front row, thrusting with his thin, basket-hilted blade with the family crest on the pommel, turning aside a sword that scythed down at him with all the strength he had.

'To me, acolytes!' cried Alric. He brought up his hands in a rapid sequence of gestures, conjuring a circle on the ground from which sprung a wall of rippling white flame. Acolytes dived into it as the worm-daemon slithered towards them and the spider-daemon scuttled down and leaped into their midst.

'You!' yelled Alric as he saw the spider-daemon up close. 'I know you! You were at the Imperial Palace! You took Princess Astrid!'

'Took her I did,' hissed the spider. It looked less and less like a spider the closer it got, and more and more like nothing that should ever be permitted to exist in the mortal world. Eyeballs rolled in the central mass of its body and every moment a new clawed limb unfolded from beneath it. 'I taught her what pleasure there is in pain.'

Magister Kardiggian rose over the battlefield on wings of gold and silver light. He aimed an outstretched hand towards the daemons butchering Mikhael's men and three bolts of white fire punched into the daemons, incinerating two down to their misshapen skeletons. The third bolt blew the arm off another – Mikhael darted forwards and thrust his blade through the wounded daemon's eye. The creature howled, a noise cut short as its body discorporated and its flesh fell away.

The worm-daemon slithered towards Witch Hunter Argenos. Argenos took aim and fired, the pistol barking out a shot as bright as a falling star. It speared right through the daemon, scattering charred worms as it left a black smoking hole right through it.

The daemon reared up, revealing the mouthparts on its underside. It seemed to grow as it unfolded. Limbs uncoiled and claws bit into the marble underfoot. Its shape shifted with every half-second – what had been a pulsing mound of worms was now a bipedal creature with a muscular body, a low-held head like that of an insect or a crab, and from each shoulder a fan of bladed limbs. The worms whipped and coiled on its back and the daemon screeched, the whole Chanter's Hall shuddering with the sound.

'Morkulae,' said Argenos. 'Herald of rot. Cup-bearer of the Plaguelord. I have read of you. I hoped I would kill you one day. Thus does Sigmar reward His servant.'

Morkulae, its transformation complete, screeched again and darted forwards, unnaturally light on its feet. Argenos ducked and slammed his hammer into one of Morkulae's arms, splintering the chitin that encased it and sending shreds of torn muscle spattering to the floor.

'Battle is joined!' cried Argenos, as more bolts of light sliced down from Kardiggian overhead and Magister Kant was surrounded by a halo of silver flame. 'Give thanks! Cry joy! Battle with the daemon is joined!'

Chapter Fifteen
The Key of Isha

ONE DAY, THE elves of Ulthuan knew, there would rise an enemy who could not be killed. They knew this even before the Sundering, when the elven nation split in two through treachery and the meddling of its aristocrats in Dark magic. Their sages foresaw a foe who could not be slain by blade or bow or spell, only incarcerated. So they prepared a means to create a prison that would serve to house this enemy.

The tears of the goddess Isha were collected where they had fallen and crystallised into flawless gemstones the colour of the sky. The early scholars of High magic took them to the workshop of Vaul, the smith god of the elven pantheon, and it was said that the god himself cut the shape from those infinitely precious stones. He carved from them a single key, inlaid with gold melted down from glittering dragons' scales and hung from a chain of silver links.

For an age, the enemy did not appear. The Key of Isha remained in the temple of the goddess on the island nation of Ulthuan, guarded by the goddess's templars. But in the turmoil of the Sundering, when the temple and much of Ulthuan was ravaged by civil war and plundered, the Key of Isha was lost. The high elves, as was their wont, thought the dwarfs were responsible.

Whoever was responsible, the Key of Isha vanished and reappeared centuries later in the hoard of the dragon Ashenspine, slain by an expedition of dwarfs and men into the peaks of Norsca. It was handed down as an heirloom among the early nobles of Sigmar, until once again it was lost – or stolen, or bargained away – and disappeared.

During the Great War against Chaos, when Magnus led the Empire's armies against the Dark-worshipping hordes marching down from the north, the Key was found hanging around the neck of a Chaos champion slain by the Warrior Priest Lothar Sunderhelm. He gave it to the Colleges of Magic, who, uncertain of its purpose and origin, placed it in the most secure place they had – the Pinnacle Vault of the Pyramid of Light.

Van Horstmann did know what it was for. He had been told during his communions with Tzeentch, in return for which he had sacrificed several artefacts looted from the outer vaults of the Order of Light. It had been surprising that the Fourth Circle had taken so long to notice any of the artefacts were missing or despoiled. They treated the artefacts in the vaults with such deference that to open a book or examine a magic chalice was an operation on a par with a major religious observance. Had they been more thorough, Pendorf and his fellow magisters would have found several other books gutted and replaced with offcuts from the Buchbinder District's workshops, enchanted blades replaced with mundane, if finely-wrought, replicas and other artefacts simply missing. The originals had been consumed as offerings to Tzeentch, just like the *Codex Aethyrica*, and van Horstmann had been furnished with the knowledge that had led him here.

He took the Key of Isha from its velvet cushion. In spite of its long history, it was still flawless and gleamed like a shard of lightning in his hand, reflecting in its hundreds of facets the light that made up the walls of the Pinnacle Vault.

Van Horstmann now took from a pocket of his Grand Magister's robes a pane of crystal, similar to those he had mounted on the walls of his sanctum but much smaller. It reflected a view of the sanctum, with its own crystal panes blank.

He could hear the ripples of magic shuddering down from above, where the battle was being fought. Van Horstmann could trust Morkulae to put up a decent fight, and Hiskernaath to sow confusion among whatever ranks his opponents had brought to capture him. There would be no doubt now that van Horstmann had practiced the arts of daemonology. The Order of the Silver Hammer would be certain they had their man.

WITCH HUNTER ARGENOS wrenched his hammer from the body of the plaguebearer, wiping his gauntlets across his face to get the worst of its foetid blood out of his eyes.

The Chanter's Hall was awash with the blood of daemons and of men. Mikhael Salzenhaar still stood, but he was wounded. He had a deep cut in one thigh and Argenos knew that it would be infected by the fatal diseases that dribbled from Nurgle's cauldron. The nobleman would die. Many of his men, and many of the Light Order's acolytes, already had.

The plaguebearers were gone, destroyed or driven away by the cascades of light that spilled from the hands of Magister Kardiggian. One such barrage had immolated Morkulae, which Argenos had finished off with a swing of his hammer. Kardiggian drifted back down to the floor beside Argenos.

'We are free of them for the time being,' said the battle magister. 'We must press on.'

'Where is van Horstmann quartered?' asked Magister Kant. Kant had fought too, and well. He leaned on his staff as he walked up to Argenos. He had surrounded himself with a halo of flame that had driven off the disgusting little daemons swarming around him, but it had taken a grave toll.

'In Magister Vek's old chambers, above us,' said Kardiggian.

Argenos was in the process of reloading his pistol as he spoke. 'I would be surprised if he is there,' he said. 'At the first sign of our ingress he would seek to hide. Perhaps there is somewhere in this pyramid he has prepared in case his perfidy was discovered. A bolthole or a way out.'

'Unlikely,' said Kant, wiping the sweat from his eyes with a sleeve. 'The whole pyramid is held in a fold of space. A significant alteration to it would have been felt here, in the rituals to keep it hidden.'

'The cunning of the daemon-led is infinite,' replied

Argenos. 'We must be swift and hunt him down before he is…' Argenos's words trailed off as he looked up to the ceiling, following a movement he had caught in the corner of his eye.

Before any of the battle's survivors had picked out what he had seen among the columns, Argenos had taken aim with his pistol and fired. The flailing shape of the daemon Hiskernaath hit the floor before the chanter's dais with a wet thump.

'There is no hiding from the eyes of the righteous!' shouted Argenos as he advanced on the stricken daemon. His bullet had ripped through its body and thick purple-black blood was oozing from it. The smell of it was awful enough to be distinct among the appalling stench left behind by the plague daemons.

Hiskernaath tried to flip over onto its front, but darts of light spat from Kardiggian's fingers and impaled it through the limbs, pinning it to the floor. Argenos took from the inside of his cloak a small vial of clear liquid – holy water – with a blessed silver icon of the twin-tailed comet immersed in it.

'Where is Egrimm van Horstmann?' demanded Argenos of the daemon.

'Ask your sister,' spat the daemon.

Argenos removed the stopper of the vial and poured a few drops onto the daemon. Hiskernaath screamed, flinging gobbets of gore and drool as it convulsed.

'I lack time and patience. Where is Egrimm van Horstmann?'

'You will beg like Astrid did,' hissed Hiskernaath. 'When I have taken you over you will watch everything I make you do… I will find everyone you love and with your own hands I will…'

Argenos poured a trickle of the holy water onto the open, smoking wound he had blasted into the daemon's body. Hiskernaath screamed again, and chitin cracked as it thrashed against the magical darts that transfixed it.

'When this is used up,' said Argenos, 'I can always bless more.'

'The Pinnacle Vault!' gasped Hiskernaath. 'I hope your life pours out through your bowels! That infested become your nethers! He has gone to the Pinnacle Vault to seek the Mantle of Thoss!'

'Sigmar on high,' said Kardiggian. 'He's going for the Mantle.'

'You have it here?' demanded Argenos.

'We have,' said Kardiggian. 'None save for the senior magisters know of it. He could start a religious war with it. He must have learned it was here when he became Grand Magister.'

'And lost no time in getting his hands on it,' said Kant.

'There we must go,' said Argenos. 'And also to his chambers. There may be the means by which these daemons infiltrated the pyramid. It must be sealed.'

'I will go,' said Kant.

'Not on your own,' said Argenos. 'You are all but spent, Magister Kant.'

'Then I will, too,' said Master Chanter Alric. Alric was kneeling beside one of his wounded acolytes, trying to stem the blood pouring from a deep tear in the youth's abdomen. 'I know the magic that keeps the pyramid hidden. If van

Horstmann has altered its form, I am best placed to discover it.'

'Then take Magister Kant to Vek's chambers, and be quick,' said Argenos. 'Kardiggian, can you get to the Pinnacle Vault?'

'If the Fourth Circle magisters are still alive, and if they know there is a crisis, then yes,' said Kardiggian.

'Then you and Master Salzenhaar are with me,' said Argenos. 'We will confront the heretic before he can steal the Mantle and be gone.'

'What do we do about that?' asked Alric, pointing towards the stricken Hiskernaath.

'Something quick,' replied Argenos.

Kardiggian aimed his staff at the daemon. A spear of fire leapt from it, bathing the daemon in flame. It shrivelled up, its limbs curling around it like those of a dead spider, and its last scream was a pathetic withered sound that ended in the crackling of its burning flesh.

'Sigmar be with you, magisters,' said Argenos as he followed Kardiggian towards the entrance to the outer vaults.

'And with you, witch hunter,' said Alric, as he hurried past the bodies towards the stairs that lead up to van Horstmann's chambers.

Their feet left prints in the swathes of blood starting to congeal on the floor of the Chanter's Hall.

KANT AND ALRIC approached their destination first. Magisters were everywhere, demanding answers and swapping rumours about the stench and sounds of battle reaching them from the floors below. Kant drew looks for his exhaustion and the smoke that still coiled off him – Alric drew looks for the blood soaking the hem of his robes.

The two of them reached Magister Vek's old chambers. Alric tried the door , which was bolted, as he had expected. Alric put his hands against the door and shuddered as heat flooded out of them, white flame licking around the door. The bolt came away as the wood charred and crumbled, and the door swung open.

'Stay alert,' said Alric to Kant. 'He could have prepared this place for us. Left a trap, perhaps.'

'Let us hope,' said Kant, 'he is in too great a hurry.'

The chamber was largely as Vek had kept it. The two statues, with their bull-like bodies and muscular human fore-parts, were still there, along with Vek's alchemy desk and the shelves full of items he had collected from the magical tradi-tions of a dozen different cultures.

'I can smell sulphur,' said Kant. 'Crushed mandrake. No trappings of Light magic.'

Alric moved warily through the chamber, stepping care-fully. 'There,' he said, pointing towards the various alchemical devices and implements on the table. 'Vek's puzzle box.' The small wooden box indeed stood on the table.

'I thought it was lost?' said Kant.

'Van Horstmann found it,' said Alric.

'Van Horstmann was able to join the order partly because we had just lost Vek,' said Kant. 'Did van Horstmann kill him, and take the box?'

Alric ran his hands over the walls, kneeling down and lay-ing them against the floor. 'The space here is altered,' he said.

'Folded again. There is more in these chambers than can be seen at first glance.' Alric touched the side of one of the huge statues and held them there, as if some hidden knowledge were being transmitted through his palms.

'Here,' he said.

'Take care, Master Chanter,' said Kant.

Alric breathed a few syllables of a spell and the statue shuddered, dust spilling from its ancient stone. The side of the taurian flank split apart and swung open, revealing a space beyond it.

It was not just the inside of the statue. That would have been substantial enough, easily large enough to fit a hiding man. But the door hidden in the statue revealed a whole room beyond.

'This is false space,' said Alric. 'Van Horstmann has created a room where none can fit. I had not thought him capable of such magic.' He looked around at Kant. 'I could not do this.'

Alric walked into the room, the light reflected from the crystal panels on the walls illuminating his face. The floor was covered in cushions, as if set out for meditation. More than a dozen crystal panes of various sizes were mounted on the walls and there stood a bookcase loaded with volumes. Alric examined the bookcase, pulling out one book after another.

'The *Worms of Saakinhand*,' read Alric. 'Lost for more than seventy years. And the *Second Moon of Lamentations*. I remember when this was banned, back when I was an acolyte. All the copies were burned. Well, not all.'

Alric put the book back on the shelf. Something had caught his notice on top of the bookcase.

Kant, standing by the doorway in the statue, strained to see it. It was small, and glinted wetly in the glittering light.

It was an eyeball. It looked fresh and bloody, sitting watching Alric as he peered at it in puzzlement.

VAN HORSTMANN LOOKED back, through the pane of crystal in his hand. It was linked magically to the eyeball in the sanctum. On the pane was the image of Master Chanter Alric, confusion on his face.

A noise caused van Horstmann to look away from the sight. It was the sound of a door opening. The door to the Pinnacle Vault.

'Egrimm van Horstmann!' called a voice well-used to laying down accusations at a witch's trial. The man who walked into the vault wore the battered leather cloak and wealth of weapons and torture implements that marked him out as a witch hunter. Behind him, shielding their eyes from the glare of the light, was a gaggle of noble household troops carrying swords and halberds, who looked as afraid of the man who led them as of anything they might find in the vault. The battle magister, Kardiggian, was with them. Kardiggian must have led them down through the sea of light to the vault's door, and the expression on his face made it clear he looked on van Horstmann as an enemy and not a fellow magister.

'You stand accused of daemoncraft and the practice of forbidden magic,' continued the witch hunter. 'The vows I have made compel me to demand of you a plea to these charges, lest I be moved to believe you innocent. I must inform you that I have never been moved so.'

'You would be Lord Argenos,' replied van Horstmann. From across the floor of the Pinnacle Vault, he could read nothing from Argenos's face. The witch hunter wore a mask, a face he had crafted through the years to show nothing but sternness and disdain. 'I knew one of you would come to take me in. Either you, or a magister from one of the other colleges. Mother Heloise was a possibility. But no, you were always the most likely.'

'That you have prepared yourself for this moment displays only a further depth to your guilt,' said Argenos. 'I know that you seek to do violence to the Empire by the use of the Mantle of Thoss. Clearly you intend no contrition with the revelation of your crimes. I hereby pronounce you guilty of all charges. In the name of Sigmar, kneel and receive your punishment.'

'There is no action you have taken,' said van Horstmann, 'or that you will take from now on, that I have not foreseen. Think on the path that led you here. What manner of daemonologist would I be to show my hand so early, by casting a host of daemons at you the moment you walked in through the door? And what manner of a witch hunter would you be, if you did not storm down here yourself, to lay down Sigmar's law in person? Every step of that path, I have set out for you. You are here because I have brought you here.'

'Then you have prepared the battlefield for us to fight,' said Argenos. 'So be it. I have faced a dozen champions of the Dark Gods, and bested them all. I have broken their bodies and torn out their souls. I have—'

'Do you think,' snapped van Horstmann, 'that any of this

is about you?' He held up the Key of Isha in one hand. 'Or about the Mantle of Thoss? Do you honestly believe, hunter of witches, that you understand but a fraction of what I have wrought?' Van Horstmann's hand was wreathed now in black flame, the same flame he had used to kill Magister Pendorf minutes before.

Argenos drew his pistol. Even as he aimed it at van Horstmann, the flame flared up around the Grand Magister's hand, and a terrible chill radiated from it so profound it snatched the breath from the throats of House Salzenhaar's men.

With a sound like a distant scream, the crying out of the goddess herself, the Key of Isha shattered in van Horstmann's hand.

THE DOOR TO the sanctum slammed shut. Master Chanter Alric whirled around at the sound of it banging shut behind him. He ran up to the door, which from this side was a slab of stone, and pushed against it. It did not yield.

'Master Chanter!' cried Magister Kant from outside. 'Master Chanter, can you hear me?' Kant, exhausted as he was, tried frenetically to find a means of opening the door, or a crack into which a lever might be inserted to pry the door away. But there was none, not even the slightest mark to show a doorway had ever been there.

Kant could not hear Alric as he pounded against the door, nor could Alric hear Kant's voice. It was as if the sanctum had always been sealed, always formed its own tiny world separate from the rest of reality.

Magisters from outside van Horstmann's chambers were

rushing to heed Kant's cries. They joined him trying to find a way into the statue, but none of them succeeded.

'Back!' cried one of them and Kant realised it was Magister Vranas. Vranas stood with both hands against the side of the statue as the other wizards backed away from him. The chamber rumbled as sparks of white power, like fragments of lightning, flickered around Vranas's hands and over the surface of the statue.

The statue shifted. Vranas stepped back a pace and the statue went with him, the effort of moving it making the veins stand out on Vranas's face. As the statue came away from the wall the magisters saw, not an opened passageway into the room that Kant had seen, but just the blank wall of the chamber.

'There is nothing there,' said someone. 'Magister Kant, where is Alric?'

'Kant, did you him enter the statue?' demanded Vranas.

'I did. There was a room in there, with windows of crystal. Alric went inside and now…'

'Then where is he?' asked Vranas.

Kant could not look at his fellow magister. 'I don't know,' he said.

CHAPTER SIXTEEN
BLACK MIRROR BROKEN

THE PINNACLE VAULT echoed with the shattering force of the shot. The cascade of light shuddered and the troops of House Salzenhaar scattered at the sound.

Argenos's shot was well-aimed. Anyone else would have been drilled between the eyes. Even as the bullet was in flight, van Horstmann conjured up a shield of light that deflected the blessed shot.

'Forward!' cried the leader of the household troops. 'For the kill!'

Van Horstmann recognised them now as the men of House Salzenhaar, their leader a son of that family. Mikhael Salzenhaar ran past Argenos with his blade out, his men running with him.

Van Horstmann had his staff to hand before Mikhael reached him. He struck it against the ground and silvery

ripples went out across the floor, and in the zone they encompassed time seemed to run thick as treacle. Salzenhaar's
movements were laboured and painful, each step seeming to
stretch out forever.

Van Horstmann batted away Salzenhaar's sword with his
staff and stepped aside, letting the nobleman's momentum
carry him past. He drove the head of the staff, with its death
mask, into Mikhael's back and sent him sprawling to the
floor.

Time snapped back into reality. Van Horstmann turned
to the men now bearing down on him, ready to chop him
up with their halberd blades or run him through with their
swords. He swept a hand, hissed words of power, and threw
them away from him on a pulse of white flame. They were
thrown from him, their livery catching light. They screamed
as they burned.

Van Horstmann put a foot on Mikhael Salzenhaar's neck.

'It is amusing to me,' he said, 'that having spent so many
hours elbow-deep in Salzenhaar dead, I am about to be surrounded by dozens more.'

Mikhael tried to cry out, either in despair or defiance.
Before any sound could escape him, the white fire had turned
black, now moulded by van Horstmann's will into a spike
that projected from his palm. He drove it through the back
of Mikhael Salzenhaar's head, and Mikhael's head became a
vessel for the black flame. It rushed from his eye sockets and
between his teeth as the flesh was stripped away, leaving a
blackened skull that rolled away as van Horstmann took his
foot off the corpse's neck.

Witch Hunter Argenos slid into the cover of the pedestal that held the Mantle of Thoss. 'This way there are no answers, van Horstmann!' he yelled. 'Only in the extirpation of your corruption can you ever find peace.'

Van Horstmann let the black flame turn in on itself, surrounding his fist like a bouquet of black roses. He stalked across the vault, backing up against the structure in its centre. 'I do not want peace,' said van Horstmann. 'I could have found peace decades ago.'

'Then what do you want?' demanded Argenos. With a well-practiced motion he filled the chamber of his pistol with powder from the horn that hung from his jerkin, and rammed home another bullet into the barrel.

'It benefits me nothing for you to know,' replied van Horstmann. 'So you will die in ignorance. Rather, I think, as you lived.'

This time, the tower in van Horstmann's mind, the anchor that kept him connected to the realm of the aethyr, was a bizarre creation of lapis and gold. Shimmering blue walls supported arches and battlements of gold, glimmering in the strangest of colours under a sky so loaded with stars that it seemed a smeared mass of mottled light. In the real world Witch Hunter Argenos was rolling out from behind the pedestal with the agility of a far younger man, gambling everything on one magical shot that would end everything. But in the aethyr – realer, perhaps than the 'real' world – van Horstmann was walking under the tower's raised portcullis, a moat of blue and pink fire roiling beneath his feet in which gambolled daemons with iridescent flesh. Inside everything was bulbous and asymmetrical, columns of twisted, blue stone running up the height of the tower festooned with chains of silver and gold. The floor was studded with swirls of diamonds and amethyst. The deep-blue light fizzed and shuddered with pent-up power.

Van Horstmann had been saving one gemstone for this occasion. He had known it would come, and he had studied and meditated accordingly to inscribe this spell in his mind. He had found it when still an acolyte, split up and hidden in the appendices and footnotes of a dozen books of otherwise tedious lore. Maybe the Changer of Ways had whispered to an early sage of the Light Order to plant it where van Horstmann would one day find it. More likely it was another example of a wizard's pride, to share his teachings only with those willing to piece them together. Van Horstmann didn't care, as long as he had it ready.

He took the gemstone from its place in the tower wall, where it had formed one of the many eyes of a bestial face seemingly frozen in the blue stone. The gemstone was jet-black, the size of van Horstmann's fist, with flashes of light in its heart as if a bolt of lightning had been imprisoned there.

Outside van Horstmann's body, Argenos was bringing his pistol up to shoot. Van Horstmann was not familiar with the latest contraptions emerging from the workshops of Nuln, but he knew that a well-placed shot could blow a man's head clean off even without the blessed ammunition Argenos doubtless used. The eventualities of the next couple of seconds spiralled out in van Horstmann's mind, each possibility forking the path of fate. Some of the paths ended in van

Horstmann's death. Others did not. Van Horstmann aimed himself towards the latter.

A spell learned by rote, unleashed by instinct, flashed blackly in van Horstmann's palm. It formed a vortex, an ice-cold hole in space which sought to draw all energy into itself. The cold flooded through van Horstmann as the heat was leached out of him but he held his shaking arm up even as the flint sparked and Argenos's pistol roared.

The speed of van Horstmann's thoughts outstripped the bullet. The vortex caught the bullet and drew it in, robbing it of heat and speed. The lead ball orbited the vortex in van Horstmann's palm, slowing until it fell and plinked harmlessly to the floor.

Argenos did not break stride. He drew his hammer, which glowed an angry orange. Van Horstmann dropped to one knee as Argenos charged, and the hammer blow passed an inch over his head.

The heat seared van Horstmann's face.

'We have magic of our own,' growled Argenos, drawing the hammer back for a killing blow.

A lance of glass speared down from the ceiling and impaled Argenos through the thigh. Van Horstmann whispered, made a chopping gesture with one hand and another followed it, piercing Argenos's shoulder and pinning him in place.

Argenos fought and shattered the two spikes that held him. Broken shards still sticking from his chest and leg, he loped another step closer to van Horstmann. The head of his hammer was aflame now, trailing twin fiery tails like the comet of Sigmar.

Van Horstmann slammed his staff into the ground. A hundred spikes erupted now, from every direction, criss-crossing the vault with Argenos at their nexus. The spell was the Chain of Purity, an early and powerful working of Light magic which was used to pin a violent and physically strong daemon or possessee in place while rituals of banishment were enacted. Now Argenos was caught in it, blood trickling down the glass shafts as he struggled to break out.

He was speared through the body and all limbs. One punched through from his collarbone to the middle of his back, another went through the back of his hand.

The witch hunter roared. Glass shattered. Argenos fell forward to one knee, some lances breaking while others slid further through his body.

'Now!' cried Argenos. 'Now, by Sigmar!'

The roar of heat behind van Horstmann was just enough warning for him to throw himself to one side as the gout of white fire roared past him. His robes caught fire and he rolled on the floor to put them out, scrambling behind the nearest pedestal.

Magister Kardiggian shot past, flying high enough to brush the vault ceiling. He scattered a hail of white bolts from his hands, and they seared through the floor where they hit. Most thudded into the pedestal, but one raked across van Horstmann's back and he felt the heat of its purity blistering his skin. He gasped and yelled out, not in pain but in anger.

'You know full well I am better than you, Kardiggian!' he shouted. 'You saw it at the Garden of Morr! You were never anything more than a conjurer of tricks!'

'And I have tricks enough to kill you, van Horstmann,' replied Kardiggian. He halted, hovering in the air, and gathered a great ball of white flame between his outstretched arms. 'What you sought in Dark magic, I found in the purity of my soul! Let us see which is the stronger!'

Van Horstmann had taken shelter behind the same pedestal Argenos had used moments earlier – the one on which stood the mannequin wearing the Mantle of Thoss. Van Horstmann tore the grey fur cloak down and threw it over himself as the fireball erupted from Kardiggian's hands and the storm of flame broke against him.

The Mantle of Thoss was described, by those who knew it had ever existed, with all manner of miraculous powers. It could be lain on the floor, said some, and when removed would reveal a portal to one of the hells of the Sigmarite faith into which the Grand Theogonist had hurled those he judged guilty. Others maintained that it was the fur of the greatest wolf ever killed in the Empire, and that while wearing it a man took on an aspect so terrible that all who saw him fell down in awe and terror. It was rumoured to heal, of course, a belief that van Horstmann had exploited to gain entrance to the innermost vault. But most commonly, the Mantle of Thoss was said to protect the wearer from harm.

Thoss had been shot with an arrow, stabbed twice, thrown off the balcony of the Temple of Sigmar and set alight. None of the attempts on his life had succeeded. He had died of old age, and many blamed the Mantle of Thoss for keeping the hateful old man alive for so long.

As van Horstmann learned in that moment, the Mantle of

Thoss did indeed possess that particular property. The fireball battered against him like a gang of men with clubs, and the heat snatched the air from his lungs, but the flames did not burn him. The air rushed back in, van Horstmann gasped down a scalding breath, and threw the Mantle back off.

In the aethyr, the black gemstone shattered in van Horstmann's hand.

The ceiling of the vault seemed suddenly gone, replaced by a sky heavy with lead-coloured clouds. The light that drenched the vault dimmed as during an eclipse, and freezing rain drove against van Horstmann's face.

Black lightning crashed down from the sky, earthing through the hovering form of Magister Kardiggian. Kardiggian was bent almost double backwards as his muscles spasmed and the raw Dark magic tore through him. It burst from his eyes and mouth, it forked off his fingers. His staff shattered into shards of gold.

When Kardiggian hit the ground, his white robes were scorched black and tattered. His skin was the same. He coughed out a mouthful of blood and ash, broken teeth spilling from his lips.

Another bolt hit him in the back and slammed him to the floor. Another cut through his shoulder and sheared his arm off. There was no blood, for the flesh was seared closed. Kardiggian dragged himself a pace or two as van Horstmann stepped out from behind the pedestal, leaving the Mantle of Thoss on the floor.

He watched Kardiggian die. It took only a few seconds, during which the clouds dissolved away and the light returned, illuminating now the burned and broken mass of ashes and scorched meat that had been Magister Kardiggian.

Van Horstmann turned to Argenos. He had made a little progress in escaping the glass spikes that impaled him, but not much. His blood was now a sizeable pool on the floor beneath him.

'I had been saving that for you,' said van Horstmann. He drew from his robes the sacrificial dagger with the wavy blade, the one which was never clean of the blood no matter how many times it was washed. 'But as it is, your death will have to be much more prosaic. I apologise.'

Van Horstmann grabbed the back of Argenos's head with one hand and yanked it back. Argenos tried to speak, blood flecking his lips. Van Horstmann had no interest in what the witch hunter had to say. He stabbed the blade into Argenos's chest, twisted it, and withdrew it when he felt Argenos go limp.

Van Horstmann let go of the witch hunter's head. Argenos's head flopped down so his chin touched his chest and the blood spread more rapidly now as what remained of Argenos's life pumped out of him. His hand, which had still been clutching his hammer, finally fell lifeless and the hammer hit the floor with a ringing like a bell. It was as good a sign as any that Argenos was dead.

Van Horstmann was suddenly aware of how exhausted he was. The Black Mirror Broken, the Dark magic spell with which he had killed Kardiggian, was one of the most powerful he had ever encountered. It had pushed back the limit of what he was capable of. The flowing of Dark magic through him had robbed him of his energy and his legs were heavy. Even picking up his staff from the floor was an effort. He wiped a sleeve across his brow and when he removed it the light was not as bright and the smouldering corpse of Kardiggian seemed to lie very distant.

He could hear scales on scales, the coils of them.

The tower in the aethyr was half-buried in a sea of snakes. That third place, where van Horstmann's mind fled when it was under mortal strain, was vivid and close now. This was the place where his memory dwelt, the one he had not been able to master. So much of himself had been sliced into manageable pieces and filed away, like volumes on the shelves of the Light Order's library, but that one memory had never been tamed. It had a life of its own, making itself remembered when it chose, sinking away into obscurity when it suited.

It was the memory of his sister's death, of the pit of snakes. Van Horstmann saw himself, felt and smelt it, as he dragged himself to the pit's edge.

The woman had watched him. That same woman had watched his sister sink below the surface and die – Lizbeta, who had never so much as let a cruel thought enter her head. That woman had thrown both the youths in, and stood by the pit to watch them die.

Van Horstmann saw her now with the smirk on her face. It amused her to see van Horstmann, little more than a boy, still struggling for life. That smile was the ugliest thing he had ever seen. A painter would have made the woman beautiful, but that smile was a red slash in her face like the mouth of a fish, the amusement in her eyes as disfiguring as a facial scar.

Behind her was another figure. A man. He put his arm around her shoulders and kissed her hair.

'Do you see, dearest?' he said. 'The serpent is the icon of purity. It separates the corrupt from the pure. You were right.'

'Of course I was,' replied the woman in a smooth, dark voice. 'They must let me in. No one understands the principles better than I.'

'They would never permit a woman to join,' said the man. He had no beard and his was many years younger, but nevertheless it was unmistakeably the same face. Van Horstmann had never been more certain of anything than that. 'Not the Light Order. They take a mountain's age to change. We will not see a woman magister of the Light in our lifetimes.'

The woman turned to her lover. She touched her hand to his cheek. 'Then it will have to be you,' she said.

'It will be your learning that takes me to their ranks,' said the man. 'Your brilliance that causes me to shine.'

'I love you,' said Albreda.

'I love you too,' said Alric.

CHAPTER SEVENTEEN
COMMANDMENT

VAN HORSTMANN WAS on his knees, coughing and gasping down breaths. He composed himself and stood again. From his robe he took the small pane of crystal that looked on to his sanctum.

Master Chanter Alric was pounding on the sanctum door. Van Horstmann's face was reflected in every pane in the sanctum.

'Alric,' said van Horstmann. Alric heard the voice and turned to see dozens of reflections of van Horstmann's face looking at him. 'Tell me. Did you ever recognise me?'

Alric looked around, confused. 'Grand Magister, whatever you have done, there are men who will kill you for it. Whoever you have bargained with, whatever contracts you have–'

'I asked you a question,' said van Horstmann, keeping his voice level. 'Did you ever recognise me? When I was an acolyte, when I first walked in through Midday's Mirror, did you recognise me?'

'Of course not,' said Alric. 'I had never met you before. What are you saying?'

'You forget so easily the ones who had to suffer,' said van Horstmann. 'How many were there? How many experiments did she conduct before the snake pit?'

Alric seemed to deflate. He sank to the floor of the sanctum. 'The pit? How did you–'

'Because I went in,' snapped van Horstmann. 'My sister and I. But only I came out. What did you two hope to achieve, Alric? What did she think it would tell you?'

'That the serpent would sort the corrupt from the pure,' said Alric. His face had blanched and his eyes were wide. Sweat was starting to sheen on his forehead. 'She was brilliant…'

'Your wife.'

'My wife.'

There was a part of van Horstmann, tiny and all but silent, that had never truly believed he would ever make it here. He had shut it away with all the rest of his doubts, all the fears that might have stood in his way. He could feel that memory flaming up and burning away now. The warmth of it flowed through him, a tingling that started at the back of his head and wound its way down his neck, down his chest, around his limbs. 'I joined the Light Order. I studied the magic of Light and Dark. I sacrificed wonders to the God of Lies, and I contracted with daemons. All for revenge. All to make you both pay for what you did to Lizbeta, and to me. Have you heard of the Key of Isha? The key to forge a prison. The key that when it was broken, would seal any door, forever, never to be opened. To create a prison for all time.'

Van Horstmann held up a hand to the crystal pane, so Alric could see it. In his hand were the broken shards of the Key of Isha.

Alric realised what van Horstmann had done. His eyes welled up and he began to cry. 'It was her!' he cried out. 'All her idea! I would never have even studied the Light at all, were it not for her! She did all this!'

'You mean her?' said van Horstmann.

One of the panes in the sanctum changed. It was now showing the image of a room in a well-furnished Altdorfer town house, with curtains of burgundy velvet and a four-poster bed. Standing in front of a mirror was a woman, middle-aged but, from a distance at least, still beautiful. She was peering worriedly at a buboe growing on her neck, examining it as if she was seeing it for the first time.

'I gouged out the eye of Magister Vek at Kriegsmutter Field,' said van Horstmann. 'I placed on it the enchantment that causes everything it sees to appear here, in your cell. And then I placed it on the wardrobe in your wife's chamber, so you can watch her. She has just discovered the first symptoms of Gods' Rot. But it is not the strain that kills quickly. Morkulae the Cup-Bearer of Nurgle created a strain for me that kills very, very slowly, and with great suffering. She will live even beyond her natural lifespan, as bit by bit she decays. She will soon be bedridden. After that she will never leave that room. And you will watch it all.'

Another pane changed. This one showed the Chanter's

Hall, looking towards the Master Chanter's dais and the huge musical organ. 'I cut out the eye of the ratman seer at the battle of Drufenhaag, and put the same enchantment on it. Without you there, no one will take on the responsibility for maintaining the organ you worked so hard to have built. It will tarnish and fall apart until it is forgotten, like the legacy you wanted to build with your wife's knowledge in the Light Order. And you will watch it all.'

Van Horstmann cast a third subtle spell, and another pane changed. This time it showed a view of Altdorf, from the very topmost tower of the Imperial Palace. Through the haze of smoke from a thousand chimney stacks, it was possible to make out the charred area beyond the fork of the Reik, all the way to the outskirts of the city where the walls gave way to the fields and forests of Reikland.

'And I plucked out the eye of Heinrich Grunhald-Salzenhaar, from his tomb in the Garden of Morr. It was remarkably well-preserved, for in life he was a patron of the priests of Morr and they rewarded him with an incorruptible corpse. Through it you can watch the fate of Altdorf. At first it will trouble you not. But time will seem to speed up. The hours will flit by. Your wife's body will decay, your legacy will become dust, but then the worst will come. Altdorf will change. It will wax and wane. It will burn and be rebuilt. All without you. And you will understand just how little your life meant. Watching it, you will go mad. And you will stay mad, tormented, in my sanctum forever. Time does not flow there. You will not want for thirst or hunger. You will watch forever as the world leaves you far, far behind. And mine is the last voice you will hear, ever, until the end of time.'

'Van Horstmann!' yelled Alric. 'It was not me! It was her!'

'She was insane,' said van Horstmann. 'She was compelled. But you went along because you wanted her. You made a choice.'

'Damn your eyes, van Horstmann!' screamed Alric. 'Rot you in hell, you mad–'

Van Horstmann snapped the pane of crystal in his hands. Alric's face vanished and his voice cut off.

In all of this, in all the intricate planning, the consideration of every possible thread of fate, he had not given any thought to this moment – to how he should feel. He had done it. He had his revenge. Alric would watch everything he loved die, then the world he knew change, and he would watch it trapped forever in a room created to drive him mad.

He did not know how he was supposed to feel. Triumphant? Elated?

He could give it some proper thought later. Van Horstmann turned now to the structure in the centre of the innermost vault, letting the broken pieces of the key fall to the vault floor. He took up his staff again and let the spiral of Dark magic begin working its way through him, opening the energy channels of body and soul up to the darkest impulses of the aethyr.

He had finished what he had come to the Light Order to do. Now all that remained was to escape.

BROKEN AND MUTILATED, every muscle and chitin section torn, Hiskernaath the daemon dragged its form down the last few steps. Surrounded there by the pulses of raw Light magic, it was agony. But Hiskernaath was sustained by a force more fundamental even than the magical flesh of the daemon. The very hand of its god was moving it on.

Morkulae and the plaguebearers were things of Nurgle, budded off from the Plague God's unholy flesh. They were despicable things deserving of no more respect than the lowest of animals. No imagination. Hiskernaath was a creature of Tzeentch, and it took pride as, in those final moments of its existence, it was moved directly by the will of the Changing Lord.

Hiskernaath reached the shore and the doorway. It had rendered itself invisible, but even so a glistening smear of blood and torn flesh was left behind it like the trail left by a slug. It crawled through the doorway and into the innermost vault.

It saw van Horstmann standing at the lock which was concealed among the scrollwork in the central structure. Hiskernaath did not care – it was not there for van Horstmann. The daemon's destruction had signalled the end of its contractual obligations to van Horstmann, but Tzeentch had saved it from annihilation and restored it anew, free to follow its god's will instead of the wizard's.

Hiskernaath headed instead for the blood-soaked form of Witch Hunter Argenos. Argenos was also still alive, but not because his god had intervened on his behalf. Sigmar rarely played his hand so directly. Unlike the gods of Chaos, Sigmar did not answer prayers to him in person. No, it was bloody-mindedness that kept the witch hunter alive, as if each stuttering beat of his heart was compelled by another hateful thought of revenge.

Hiskernaath reached Argenos. Even if Argenos had been fully conscious, he would not have seen the daemon there. He would not have known it was a daemon that spoke to him then. Perhaps, with the last few trickles of his blood oozing from his chest wound, he thought it was Sigmar speaking to him.

'Splinterwing,' whispered the daemon Hiskernaath into the witch hunter's ear.

Then, his final task completed, Tzeentch permitted Hiskernaath to dissolve away, his substance rejoining the winds of the aethyr in blessed oblivion.

VAN HORSTMANN HAD learned that the key to unlocking the Light was using the Dark. A shard of black lightning formed in his hand, and he had to fight to keep it from breaking out and streaking across the vault. But he held it firm, aimed it at the swirl of dense sculpture that was the vault's hidden lock, and hurled the lightning with all his force of will.

The marble shattered, leaving a smouldering hole through the wall. In the darkness beyond, something stirred. Something huge.

There was no way van Horstmann could get out of the Pinnacle Vault the way he had entered. All the magisters in the Order of Light would be gathering at that moment around the entrance to the vaults, descending through the sea of light ready to ambush van Horstmann with every destructive spell they knew. If they had to, the magisters could seal the pyramid's space-folding magic, cutting off the way out via the Midday's Mirror and trapping van Horstmann as surely as he had trapped Alric. But van Horstmann had never intended to get out on foot.

Two great shapes loomed through the darkness, crowned with spines and set with bright burning eyes. One shape was as brutal as a slab of stone, fangs gleaming in an undershot jaw. The other was slim and wicked, an emaciated snout topped with narrow eyes as cunning and sharp as steel.

'Baudros!' called van Horstmann. 'I offer you freedom from your prison. In return, I ask only passage to the lands of Norsca, far away from here. After that you will be free to do as you will. How do you answer? Will you accept my offer?'

The reply was a terrible twin roar. For the first time in its existence the Pinnacle Vault turned dark as the cascades of light were blasted away. The structure at the heart of the vault shattered, chunks of marble falling away. An icy gale blew, catching the Mantle of Thoss and throwing it away into oblivion. Magical swords and chalices clattered on the floor. A tapestry followed the Mantle into nothingness. Flying debris smashed an urn full of goddess's tears.

Baudros emerged from its prison. Its scales were grey-black, its horns and fangs white bone. Its tattered wings spread out above it as its two necks stretched out to their full extent, each head opening its jaws wide and howling out a gale. Its imprisonment had caused its flabby bulk to waste away and now it was slender and powerful, nothing but muscle and scale coiled up to strike.

It was like standing before a natural disaster incarnate. As if every earthquake and storm had coalesced into one form and was now standing before van Horstmann roaring its anger at being imprisoned for so long.

'Teclis imprisoned you, but Teclis failed,' shouted van Horstmann over the din. 'Take me to safety and you will be free to avenge yourself on him!'

Four burning eyes fixed on van Horstmann. The wizard did not take a backwards step, even as the dragon's claws dug into the marble as it stepped towards him.

One of its heads, the cunning one, lowered to the floor. Van Horstmann found a foothold in the gnarled scales behind its head and vaulted up onto its neck, like a rider mounting a horse. The scales were as sharp as broken flint but he held on tight, his hands cut deep.

'Fly, Baudros!' yelled van Horstmann. 'For Tzeentch! For vengeance! Fly!'

WITCH HUNTER ARGENOS knew that the dragon was the last thing he would ever see. His vision wavered and he could not be sure if the monster had one head but two. It did not matter. He knew only one thing now – that he had a single task to complete. Because Sigmar had told him to. His whole life he had longed to hear the voice of his god in person. He had followed every scripture, abandoned everything in his life, given everything he had ever earned to Sigmar. He had sacrificed his body and done things that had made him abandon even the simple morality of every man. And he had not heard his god reply.

Until now.

Argenos forced his head up, to look the dragon in the eye. This head was brutal and animalistic, and its eyes fell on the witch hunter.

'Splinterwing,' said Argenos, with the last gasp of his last breath.

The dragon inhaled, and breathed out a fatal black wind. Witch Hunter Argenos was stripped to the bone, his skin and flesh sloughing away as a handful of ash. The glass spears holding him in place shattered and his very bones were carried away, leaving nothing to suggest Witch Hunter Argenos had ever existed.

But it did not matter.

Because his final commandment had been fulfilled.

Chapter Eighteen
Splinterwing

BAUDROS, THE TWO-HEADED dragon of Chaos, flapped his wings once and took flight. Another beat of his wings and he hurtled upwards, and from his twin throats roared a blast of black fire that tore through the vault ceiling. The dragon burst through into the ocean of light and kept going, streaking up towards the floor of the vault above.

Again its fire bored through the floors of the pyramid. Generations of artefacts were shattered and thrown aside as the dragon crashed through the vaults. It burst up into the Chanter's Hall, throwing aside the bodies of acolytes still carrying away their dead from the battle against van Horstmann's daemons. Pillars toppled as its enormous serpentine body tore through the chamber.

Its path took it through the exorcists' chambers, ripping apart protective circles and obliterating the frescoed ceiling beneath which the senior magisters had met Emperor Eckhardt III. It blasted through Magister Vek's old chambers, and many of the magisters gathered there were ground to pulp by the dragon's scales as it rushed by.

The top of the pyramid erupted as the dragon's flame punched out through its pinnacle. Great blocks of stone tumbled down the pyramid's side, smashing into the square below. Beyond the fold in space, the whole Buchbinder district shuddered, and ever after the inhabitants would speak of the earthquake that had struck without warning, toppling buildings and setting fires that claimed dozens of houses before the flames were doused with the waters of the Reik.

The force of the dragon's escape ripped through the folded space and it emerged high above Altdorf, its shadow passing over the Reik, the burned district around the Bright College and the city walls. Then it was past the city, soaring over the hills of Reikland, every beat of its mighty wings taking it further from Altdorf. The Empire rushed by, forests and farmlands, province by province, towards the north of Sigmar's land.

THE COLD AND speed almost robbed van Horstmann's throat of breath and he had to fight to stay conscious, such was the din and the battering of the freezing air.

He crawled, handhold by handhold, towards the dragon's ear. He could not be certain where he was, but with the incredible speed of the dragon he must have left Reikland far behind.

'To Norsca,' he yelled as loudly as he could, although he

could not hear his own words. 'To Norsca, and you will have your freedom!'

The dragon's other head, the bestial one, turned to face van Horstmann.

With a fury and speed impossible for its size, Baudros's bestial head darted forwards, jaws bared. Van Horstmann let go of his handhold and slid down the dragon's neck, finally grabbing another scale before he was thrown completely clear of the dragon.

Where he had clung a moment before, the bestial head's fangs sank into the neck of its second head. Baudros yawed to one side and the dragon began to tumble, wings flailing, as it plummeted from the sky towards the lands of the northern Empire.

Van Horstmann was in the pit of snakes again. This time he was not a child, and Lizbeta was not with him – he was a man, and she had died long ago.

He knew that this was not real. He was not really in that pit. The snakes were not snakes at all, but what his mind made of the unconsciousness that had fallen on him. He could fight it if he chose to. That was what he had done all his life – he had chosen to fight what other men would accept as inevitable. He had not accepted that revenge against a wizard, against a magister of the Light College, was impossible, nor that he could not master the magic of Light and Dark as was needed for his vengeance to come to pass. He would not accept that he should fall insensible now, not when he was so close to escaping and starting his life anew.

He fought. He kicked and struggled. And finally he dragged himself over the edge of that pit, left the snakes behind, and returned to the real world.

He was lying in a barren stretch of the Empire, sparsely scattered with clumps of trees. Perhaps he was in Troll Country, where the Empire's people had struggled to forge their northern frontier. It depended on how fast Baudros had flown. Certainly van Horstmann had not yet reached the Sea of Claws or the lands of Norsca beyond, a place far removed from the eyes of the Silver Hammer or the orders of magic.

The sound of crashing and flesh against flesh was coming from beyond a low, forested hill. As van Horstmann watched, Baudros crashed through the trees, rolling down the hill and coming to rest in the scrub nearby. The two heads were battling, thick purple-red blood spattering down from the wounds down both its necks.

The bestial head gained the upper hand for a moment, battering the skinnier head down to the ground. It looked up at van Horstmann, and again its eyes focused on the wizard.

'We had a deal!' yelled van Horstmann.

The dragon's lips peeled back, revealing its rows of titanic fangs. When it spoke, it was an earthquake, channelled and turned into sound that rumbled up through the ground into van Horstmann's soul.

'You made a deal with Baudros,' snarled the dragon. 'But I am Splinterwing. I am that which Baudros once was. I walked in darkness, but I heard my name again and now I remember. Your gods made me into this abomination. I will make them pay. I will begin with you.'

Van Horstmann yelled out, a wordless sound of desperation and abandonment. It was drowned out by the gale of black fire that erupted over him.

The flames charred van Horstmann's skin. His hands blackened before his eyes. He toppled over into the layer of ash that remained of the ground beneath him.

Somehow, his heart still beat. Somehow his mind still thought. But that was all he had. The black flame seared his skin, then his muscles and organs, then his bones, leaving him a blackened husk to which life could barely cling. One eye socket was scooped clean by the fire – the other remained open, watching.

The cunning head took the moment's distraction as an opening. It struck as fast as a snake, sinking its fangs into the back of the other head. The other head bellowed and was driven down into the ground, shuddering as the cunning head bit down deeper.

The cunning head now looked at van Horstmann. Its voice was a slithering whisper, like a sharp, cold wind knifing through the mountains.

'Tzeentch is my master,' it said. 'And has been since I was pledged to it. What remained of Splinterwing is dead. And so will you be. In a few moments your heart will stop and there will be nothing more. But there is hope. Tzeentch brings hope even to you.'

Van Horstmann wanted to answer, but he could not. It was not just that he could not speak. He did not know what to say. Somewhere, beneath the panic and the pain, there sparked the feeling that he had not been the only one planning, manoeuvring in the shadows, making sure all things were to rights.

'Serve Tzeentch, give yourself to him, and you will live. Or, you will die, and only oblivion waits for you.'

Van Horstmann tried to raise a hand, but the bone cracked and the flesh flaked away.

'I will take you to a forge in the mountains of Norsca, where the forge masters of our god will create a suit of armour to sustain you,' continued Baudros. Van Horstmann knew by some instinct that it was not the dragon itself that spoke, but a power far more distant and powerful, one that rarely moved its hand directly, preferring always to move through proxies and pawns. Pawns like Egrimm van Horstmann. 'In return Tzeentch will have your soul. You will not refuse, for you will not suffer your genius to be snuffed out. And you always knew, van Horstmann, that one day you would pay Tzeentch his due.'

Van Horstmann's neck and tongue firmed up, the flesh restored just enough to let him speak. He croaked out the only two words that his mind could form in that moment.

'I obey,' he gasped.

For the tenth day, or the hundredth, or the millionth, Master Chanter Alric stared at the wall.

He could see his wife, decaying. Sometimes it was slow and cruel. Sometimes it was so rapid the horror barely had time to develop in her eyes before she was gone. Maybe he had only seen it once, and it echoed again and again in his mind, rattling around like a pebble in a bucket until it became all mixed up into one terrible vision of her, in pain.

He could see the organ in the Chanter's Hall. It was broken and crumbling after the destruction wrought by the dragon that thundered through the hall. Then it was patched up half-heartedly, hardly a priority. Some cared for it and tried to have it restored, others neglected it. Everyone forgot why it was there. Eras of history hurtled by, and days seemed to last forever, each speck of dust settling on the pipes another hammer blow. Those pipes were Alric's own guts, rotting away, and he kept forgetting who he was each time the organ was torn down or put back up again, unfinished.

He saw Altdorf. The city was alive. And it hated him, for why else would it mock him by growing, changing, suffering sieges and hosting triumphs, without him? Had he never existed? Had there never been a man named... named what?

In the sanctum, which by now he was certain was the only world he had ever known, the man without a name continued to weep.

FROM THE FAR north, at the head of an army, came a champion of Chaos who wielded magic as deftly as a duellist wielded a sword. Whose armour was impervious to harm, and who rode to battle on a mighty two-headed dragon that could devour whole armies in its maws. Of all the warlords who had taken the Chaos Gods as their patron, it was said that he was perhaps the greatest. He ruled the Silver Cabal of corrupted wizards who had promised their souls to Tzeentch in return for forbidden knowledge. His was the God of Change, the Liar Prince, and he was that god's hand in the world when trickery and deceit were not enough.

Some said he could not die, for Tzeentch owned his soul and would not give it up to anything so mundane as death. Others said he had already died, many times, and was not permitted to rest. No one knew the whole truth, for wherever Tzeentch's shadow was cast, there could be no such thing as the truth.

And so this champion embarked on a dozen wars, a hundred battles, untiring in the name of his god.

So began the story of Egrimm van Horstmann.